Towers Destiny

For Carolyn!

[signature]

BOOK 3 ~
The Towers Trilogy

BUCK BRANNON

outskirts
press

D1378102

Outskirts Press, Inc.
http://www.outskirtspress.com

ISBN: 978-1-9772-4556-4

Library of Congress Control Number: 2021919024

Cover Photo © 2022 www.gettyimages.com. All rights reserved - used with permission.

Outskirts Press and the "OP" logo are trademarks belonging to Outskirts Press, Inc.

PRINTED IN THE UNITED STATES OF AMERICA

DEDICATIONS

*There were 100,000 drug overdoses from May, 2020-April 2021.
The majority involved opioids.* *

*That's 100,000 families torn asunder and
grieving each and every day - since!*

*TOWERS DESTINY is DEDICATED to thousands
of our youngest generation that overdosed and died
needlessly during the last quarter century!*

But more specifically for the following individuals:

*SEAN HERMAN - OHIO
MARCH 8, 1988 - SEPTEMBER 21, 2015*

*ASHLEY VIVIAN PARKS - KENTUCKY
OCTOBER 17, 1996 - FEBRUARY 23, 2019*

*KELLY JAMES O'BRIEN
JUNE 22, 1980 - SEPTEMBER 29, 2021*

*"May their lives and my words - not have
been in vain!" - Buck Brannon.*

Prologue

I couldn't erase the image of Mark's grotesquely tilted head, dangling to his left side like a rag doll. My brain was busy manufacturing thoughts intended to exonerate myself from any blame in his death. And yet in that moment there were a couple of gnawing, persistent memories that weren't going away. After all, Mark was indirectly responsible for me beginning my quest to become a dentist. In my sophomore undergrad year, Mark walked into our Ecology class, carrying an application for the Dental Aptitude Test. Up to that point, being a dentist was the last professional option occupying my mind. Indeed, it also ended up being just that for Mark, as he eventually gravitated toward studies in molecular genetics. Next was an image of Mark standing next to me, whispering nonsense and trying to distract me as Marty walked up the church's aisle—to join me at the altar for our marriage vows. Both flashbacks were as clear as if she and I were repeating them all over again.

Marty's cell phone call jarred me back to reality. I fumbled the phone and swerved across the double yellow line in the road.

"Marty, Mark is dead...murdered, most probably—according to Tommy!"

"What!"

"Someone shot him in the head, Marty!"

"What do you..."

"I want you to grab some luggage and start packing. Pack a little bit of everything. I'll be home in a few minutes."

Like the old-fashioned slide carousel, my brain produced in

quick succession photos of all the past places that I'd visited—coaxing me to choose a location that would qualify as the best spot to hide out for a while—or forever!

The phone jumped to life a second time. It was Tommy.

"Where the hell you'd go, Rob? One minute you're gawking at Mark, and when I turn around—you're gone."

"Tommy, there's no way I'm sticking around here. I just talked to Marty and she's packing our suitcases right now. If I'd stayed in that track's bathroom earlier with Mark—there'd have been two murders. Hell, I'm not certain I wasn't the primary target!"

"Jesus, Rob, calm down! Don't leave yet! I'll be out to your house by sunset. Let's figure this out together." And then he hung up.

He was right. My panic was real, but my reasoning was suspect. Other than Marty, there was only one individual that I totally trusted. I arrived home and parked in the driveway and waited for Tommy to arrive.

Our lives—mine and Marty's—were about to drastically change... "for better or worse," if my memory was correct.

# HAPTER 1

I mentally began to compose a list of items we would need to establish new identities. At the top of the list, a new Social Security number was an obvious must-have. I stifled a laugh while wondering what long-deceased individual's former numbers would soon be mine. The same applied for Marty.

Then there was our physical appearance. For Marty, perhaps it would be shorter hair, and a change in color and style. She'd been through LASIK surgery, but I pictured her with tinted non-prescription eyeglasses. Then my imagination took a U-turn toward other possibilities.

"How about a nose piercing or lip ring ... anything to take someone's gaze off the entirety of her face," I mumbled.

For myself, I needed glasses just to see—period! I'd always admired Jack Nicholson's look and wondered if I could wear the orange-colored lens that Jack had made famous. Then there'd be a mustache-goatee combo, or maybe even a full beard. Topping it all off, I'd have an ear piercing or perhaps even two!

Both of us would need new credit histories and credit cards—and our automobiles couldn't be ostentatious. Chevy models would replace the Audi and Toyota Supra that we currently drove.

No matter how hard I tried to focus, my mind kept going back and forth to specific groups and individuals who would want me dead. The most recent conflict with Antifa's anarchists certainly put those folks at the top of my list. Any revolutionary leaders who had escaped capture would surely love to see me dead. Whether one of them had the balls to do it themselves or hire a contract assassin probably didn't make a difference.

On more than one occasion, Tommy had referred to America's intelligence agencies as dysfunctional. He and I had thwarted and embarrassed a number of their clandestine activities. According to Tommy, the Director of National Intelligence supposedly lorded his "power" over the various intelligence groups to make certain they were all on the same page. However, the current POTUS had exposed just how independent each agency had been, during the 2016 election and his first term in office. Perhaps these agencies would continue their harassment if POTUS were elected for a second term in office. While Tommy had earned a level of respect over several years, eliminating him would violate an unwritten code among the various agencies. Since I was not a member of their fraternity, that made me a liability.

I was less certain about a couple other threats, so I tagged them as "wild cards." One was Mark's "assignment" to work with Saudi thoroughbred officials to restore their magnificent horse to health, subsequently resulting in a functional Nidalas, easily capable of performing at stud. I wondered if Mark had fully confided in the Saudi Royal Family about the genetic alterations he'd engineered. I was also fairly certain that Mark had a hand in selecting their champion thoroughbred's name. It confused me though, that the Saudi Royal's hadn't made a big deal that the name Nidalas, when spelled backwards, became Saladin—one of ancient history's significant warriors who'd led the Muslim military campaign against the Christians and their Crusades. Following his victory, Saladin established a Caliphate encompassing the modern-day countries of Palestine, Syria, Yemen, Jordan, and Egypt. Perhaps the fact that Saladin had been a Sunni Kurd became the influencing factor with current modern-day geopolitical alliances, thus quashing any hoopla. However, I was the one who had played an indirect role in preventing a fanatical Sunni ISIS terrorist attack on Ohio Stadium.

The least of my threats not to be ignored or discarded out of hand were the ramifications of Mark's genetic breakthroughs in equine genetic science. Within the last month, Donnie had tipped me off about some angry rumblings regarding ancestry circulating in the thoroughbred community. For decades, a thoroughbred's bloodstock agent's domain was ancestry research. Combining a horse's ancestry and history with the experience and keen eye of a seasoned horseman more often than not led to the investment in a worthy yearling. Unfortunately, what Mark accomplished as a government employee had made equine breeding almost foolproof. He'd refined the process of producing the precise amounts of specific cellular proteins—and this in turn dictated which genes were "turned on" versus those that were "turned off." This genetic engineering was essential to the precise moment of fertilization of a mare's egg following mating. The results were foals that had better than a 75 percent chance of being almost perfect thoroughbreds. Due to this genetic advance, an entire segment of the thoroughbred industry was no longer needed and effectively became unemployed—and these were folks who were accustomed to healthy paychecks. Rumors about disgruntled Bloodstock Agents were plentiful, and Mark and I were to blame for their anger. Since Tommy was now back at the racetrack, I made a mental note to add this latest information to my "hit list" for his consideration.

The ringing of my cellphone interrupted my train of thought.

It was probably a good thing, because I was about to start down the dark path of exactly how I would meet my demise.

"Where are you?" Marty screeched into my ear.

"I'm in the driveway waiting for Tommy to arrive."

"Rob ... please come inside—now! We do have a doorbell."

Marty was right, as usual! The last thing either of us needed at the moment was to be alone. My paranoia was peaking, and some last dark thoughts hastened that pace.

What if there were multiple assassins, all working independently of each other?

It's truly amazing how secure one feels inside their own castle!

# HAPTER 2

I punched the garage door button on the remote, got out, and slowly opened the entry door into our home. Marty was nowhere in sight, and I headed toward the family room. My only concern was whether Marty would confront me while standing or sitting down. My intuition leaned toward a running confrontation.

I wasn't disappointed!

Her incessant questions spewed out in pairs, and I swore there was even a triple expletive thrown at me. Finally, I made a "zip it" motion with my index finger and thumb before sitting down in my leather recliner.

"Hear me out, Marty—please," I begged. I began to rehash all the events of the day from the time I arrived at the racetrack, ending with an explanation of why I bolted from the murder scene. I included most of my thoughts about what we needed to do but chose not to share my thoughts about those individuals and entities who might cheer my demise.

"You're not thinking Hawaii?" Marty blurted out. "I won't go," she quickly declared.

I wasn't surprised. About ten days on any of the Hawaiian Islands was all she could tolerate. Just the thought of being permanently confined to an island would only feed her major life's anxiety: claustrophobia.

"Marty, stop! Give me a chance to finish. No, I didn't even

consider Hawaii. But I was thinking that we could go out West. We've been all over Colorado. To me, places like Nederland and Allenspark would be ideal hideouts." I watched Marty's face for any hint of approval and saw a smile briefly forming at the corners of her lips—just as the doorbell rang.

"Shit ... I don't have my gun!" I motioned for Marty to stay put as I ran to the bedroom to get my weapon. Again, the doorbell rang, but was now followed by the sound of a fist banging hard on the oak panels of the door. As I loaded the filled clip into the gun, my cellphone began to ring.

I answered and immediately heard, "Hey, Marshal Dillon— open the damn door and holster your gun! I'm not in the mood for a shootout!"

I hurriedly ran to the door, burying my gun in the rear waistband of my pants. I slowly opened the door and much to my surprise, it wasn't just Tommy standing there. His son Steven was by his side and both men were grinning like Cheshire cats.

"Rob—where's Marty?'"

I pointed to the family room, watching as Tommy and Steven headed in that direction. I began to follow, but Tommy turned and put up his right hand to halt any further advancement on my part.

"I need to talk with her one-on-one, Rob," Tommy stated.

Tommy knew that Marty would balk at leaving Kentucky— and also knew that any success at concealing Dr. Rob Becker from recognition depended on her approval. Besides, she also would have to go through a major metamorphosis. Having been kidnapped in Portland made her easily identifiable, strengthening the necessity for her disappearance as well.

"Marty, I don't know how much Rob has told you already.

He vanished before we began scouring the death scene for clues. I know you don't want to leave your home, but it's the best move for both of you at this moment. You and Rob have earned my respect, and I want to help.

"I'm going to share some classified information with you. There are seventeen US intelligence agencies—and the CIA has assets buried deep within every one of them. I'm also certain each agency has attempted to infiltrate the CIA. Do you remember the cartoon strip 'Spy vs. Spy' that was made popular by *MAD Magazine*?"

Marty shook her head.

"I've got to tell you, Marty ... that cartoon is a classic example of how our intelligence agencies operate, and all of them have been doing such for years. Look up some of the cartoons on Google!

"One hour after Mark's murder, my Director received an encrypted message from one of our assets working at the DIA. The message basically stated that several DIA senior officials were exchanging high-fives and Mark's name was being bandied around while they celebrated. And that was before there was even a press announcement about Mark's death. Does that mean that the DIA had someone kill Mark? Maybe—or maybe not. They could have had an agent at the track keeping an eye on their former asset.

"I don't think you'll have to stay out of circulation for more than six months. My boss has already assembled a task force to find out who murdered Mark. But it is his assumption that Rob was also a target and supposed to die today.

"I'd like to finish this discussion with Rob present, but first I need to know if you're going to be all in or not?"

Marty walked over to the dining room window, staring out at

the acreage fronting a creek five hundred yards away.

Tommy patiently waited for an answer, but that didn't stop him from speculating about her thoughts.

I don't believe him. Six months could easily become six years. I'm totally at the mercy of the government. If I refuse and Rob leaves, who's to say I won't face another kidnapping? were just two of Tommy's guesses.

"Okay, Tommy—but Rob and I need 24/7 protection, and the same goes for our children and grandchildren!"

Tommy turned and walked back to the great room where he'd left Rob a few minutes earlier.

"First things first: have either of you ever been in South Dakota?"

Marty and I both nodded.

"I have a spot picked out that would be a perfect place for both of you. Now Rob, I'm not yanking your chain, but the town is named Oral and it's in South Dakota! It's west of the Badlands and just a bit south of Custer. About three hundred people live in Oral and they're included among the county's total population of about 7,500. Steven's mother lives there."

"Come again," I said.

"...You heard me—Steven's mother, and her name is Tika."

I glanced at Steven and his face was glowing.

"Steven will be accompanying us?"

"Actually, I will, Rob," Tommy replied. "Ted appreciates all that you've done for the horse-racing industry, and he gave me another extended leave of absence. You can thank Steven for negotiating my return to that region of the country where my first and only love lives. Steven is actually now on board with the agency and knows how to reach me and vice versa—plus I still have access to the Director. There are only three people alive who know about Tika and our past history, and that's why South Dakota is perfect for laying low for a while."

Tommy paused and looked at both of us, trying to gauge our responses. We were both somewhat taken aback, and I was certain that our facial expressions were giving our emotions away.

"So Rob, I know you've thought about disguising yourself. Go ahead and start growing that mustache and goatee, but you'll need to color it. There's not much you can do with that wiry hair, so you're going to have to shave it off. We've got a guy in Indianapolis who makes wigs for us. Next week you, Marty and I will travel up there and get fitted for some custom hairpieces. Marty, I know you don't wear glasses, but I'm betting you're going to now! I'm not certain what color your hair will be, but Stan is running your photo through a computer program at Langley to determine the color that works best as a disguise. Rob, I need your optometrist to fax you the prescription for both eyes and I'll forward it to our opticians up in Indy where they'll probably grind lenses for new eyewear."

"Can I have the same type of glasses as Jack Nicholson?"

"Uh ... no! Good God, Rob, the reason Jack wears those glasses is because he wants people to look at him and recognize him. Those glasses are his calling card!

"Listen to me, Rob. We've got an entire week to close up shop here in Kentucky—we'll travel late next week. Now, if it's not too much of an imposition, would someone show me where Steven and I will be bunking? Steven has the first watch tonight, and I'll spell him just before dawn. I'd appreciate you giving the rest of your family a call and telling them to expect company.

"I hope you realize that Stan went high up the ladder to get this protection for you guys. POTUS personally approved it! Y'all are 'impotent' people." Tommy broke out in laughter following his purposeful mispronunciation as Marty escorted both men to their respective sleeping quarters.

I sat down and began making calls to my daughters—fully expecting an earful of grief from each one of them.

 **HAPTER 3**

I was up and about before sunrise the following morning. As I walked into the kitchen, Tommy was making a cup of coffee from the Keurig.

"Morning, Rob. What's on tap for you today?"

"Well, which one of you is going to be my traveling partner today? Marty and I talked with all three of our daughters and their husbands late last night, and they're pretty disgusted with me. Marty managed to calm them down, but that was literally after I hung up on them during the conference call. Marty went to bed mad—most probably at me. Not more than a half hour after that, my middle daughter calls me back on my cell phone … in tears! She's beside herself because she thinks her son Harry, the youngest of her two children, is vaping. I told her I'd drive up today and see if I can help."

"Oh Jesus, Rob, that's terrible news! Let me guess—he's Juuling!"

"That's my guess, Tommy. Vaping has been around for years and hardly anyone knew about it. Along comes some West Coast techies who invent a new tool for folks to get their nicotine fix. They've developed the perfect vape product and named it 'Juul.' I've seen the Juul—even held it in my hand. A user can palm it, and nobody knows they're even using it. The company that manufactures it has even obtained FDA approval for the Juul—they met all the FDA requirements for a non-combustible smoking cessation product.

"Every generation has to have something that's cool, and this is an example of that. Once a teen gets over nearly passing out from the first drag on a Juul—after inhaling the menthol- flavored nicotine that's in the vape pod—sadly, some will become hooked and addicted."

"You nailed it, Rob, but you're missing an even more troubling fact," Tommy replied.

"What?"

"Drug dealers have now become chemists. They've managed to come up with the wherewithal to incorporate mood-altering ingredients such as marijuana's THC and the lethal opium derivatives, heroin and fentanyl, into the liquid portion of the Juul pod!"

I looked down at my cup of coffee, nervously laughed and thought, *I'm here drinking a liquid that contains caffeine—a stimulant that can also be lethal if consumed in too great a quantity! And yes, it works on the same brain centers that nicotine and opioids do!*

"Your car or mine, Tommy?" I said.

"Let me move cars around. There's not enough room in your Supra to hide out in the back seat, so we'll take Marty's car. Once I'm certain we're not being tailed, I'll stop and you can get up front," Tommy replied.

I said goodbye to Marty and we were on our way, heading north on I-75 toward Lexington.

The first half of our trip north was made in silence. Tommy knew I was mentally occupied, and he was also concerned. We were about a half hour away from my daughter Kathy's home when Tommy posed a question.

"Rob, have you ever been addicted to anything?"

The sudden shattering of silence took me back to a time I wasn't proud of and frankly detested.

"Yeah … yeah I was and still am! Even though the last cigarette I smoked was in 1992, I still consider myself an addict. I never really wanted to quit and really enjoyed smoking my Salem Light 100's. They acted as a stimulant yet had a calming effect on me. Cigarettes were my stress reliever. To date, quitting combustible cigarettes was the most difficult thing I've ever done in my life. Still—even today, I swear if a physician ever tells me that I have terminal cancer—with the tiniest five-year survival chance, I'll start smoking again.

"Ya know, Tommy, in every quit smoking program I tried—and I tried them all—every facilitator stated emphatically that breaking the smoking habit was harder than kicking a heroin habit. Now I haven't done heroin, but I took opioids for seven-plus years because of chronic pain. I had surgery on my left shoulder every other year during a six-year period. The first surgery was botched and the other two surgeries were clean-ups from the first hack job. I was even told I needed an artificial shoulder replacement after the last surgery! The strange thing was, I never liked the feeling Vicodin gave me. Yes, Vicodin took my pain away, but when the pill wore off and I was coming down from the high, the pain came back. My brain hated how the opioid dropped me into an emotional funk … and mental misery. I refused to chase the drug high because I knew it would result in a mental and physical addiction, so it was no problem quitting pain pills—at least in my case."

Tommy continued driving, stone-faced. Either I was boring him or he was agreeing with what I was sharing with him—at least about my adolescent years.

"For me, the teen years were all about dealing with hormones, zits, fending off bullies, getting good grades, making the basketball team and trying to score a date!

"Adolescence was perhaps the best and worst times of my life! The years were consumed with some of my highest highs and lowest lows. My teen years were the perfect storm of emotions and rage! And I have to assume a whole lot of Boomers have felt the same as I do!

"When you throw in the temptation of experimenting with drugs that can make someone feel like they're on top of the world, one can easily throw caution to the wind and an addiction can be created!"

Tommy turned and stared at me for a quick couple of seconds. I had hit on a memory, not knowing if it was a good or bad one for him. I continued my story.

"Both of my parents were nicotine addicts. I was constantly lectured about not smoking, but watched them put out ash trays for their bridge party friends who for the most part smoked directly or got their nicotine fix via second-hand smoke. At night, my father would leave his pack of Kent cigarettes on the fireplace mantle in the living room. When I thought both my parents were sound asleep, I would sneak out of my bedroom and go steal a few cigarettes. A bad night was finding a pack that only had a couple smokes left—and I would then fall asleep angry. I had become addicted at the age of sixteen and didn't even recognize that as a fact. So how about you, Tommy?"

I never got an answer, because we had arrived at my daughter's house.

Kathy was outside, awaiting my arrival. I introduced her to

Tommy and asked if Harry was home.

"He's over at a friend's house playing basketball—at least that's what he told me," she said with a touch of disgust.

"So what tipped you off that he was vaping?" I asked, as we all sat down in the kitchen.

"He was sleeping in so I started doing his laundry and found a Juul pod tangled up in a handkerchief in a pocket. All of a sudden, he comes sprinting into the laundry room and grabs his jeans, giving me a lame excuse that they're not dirty. I know a lie, and I also recognize a guilty look when I see one!

"Do you have the pod?"

"No, I put it back in the pocket."

"And …?" I asked.

"I called his school and talked with the Resource Officer. I figured if anyone knew who Harry was hanging out with, he would! He asked for my phone number and said he'd call me back. Ten minutes later, he called from his cruiser. He'd left the school property and told me he could now talk freely. At that point I just blurted out and asked if Harry was vaping. The officer went into this long explanation about how difficult it is to catch teens actively vaping. It's hard to get the drop on someone they think is vaping, he said … often the teen will double clutch and inhale deeper, and the vape moisture dissipates in the deepest part of their lungs.

"The officer went on to say that the school staff had compiled a list of students who were thought to be vaping, and teachers update the list on a weekly basis. So now, for example, when a student asks for a hall pass for a restroom break, the teacher or an aide will follow the student and attempt to catch them vaping in the bathroom. Hell, Dad, they've even taken the doors off the stalls in the bathrooms to try and discourage vaping!"

"Did the cop give you a time frame for how long they believed Harry had been vaping?"

Tears started to form in Kathy's eyes—I tried to stay composed and not break down with her. Harry was named after me—my middle name is Harold—and he was physically the mirror image of what I looked like as a teenager.

"For … over … a … frigging year," was my daughter's answer in between sobs. I slowly got up and walked to Kathy, holding her in my arms for a good five minutes until the tears subsided. I glanced at Tommy, but his head was bowed down and his hands clasped together—tightly squeezing the blood out of them.

"What do I do, Daddy?" barely escaped from my daughter's lips.

I was just about to respond when Tommy stood and came a bit closer, wanting to add his thoughts to the discussion.

"Kathy, I want you to read this article if you would, please. It's here on my cell phone, but don't dwell on the photos."

I scooted closer to Kathy's chair to read along with her. It was an internal FBI document about vape products and how they are being modified to deliver dangerous narcotics. It was complete with photos of dead teens who had become statistics in America's ongoing battle against the drug cartels south of the American border.

And Kathy's tears began streaming again.

I looked at Tommy again and I knew my eyes were sending a pleading message—*Good God, help, dammit … no more documents, please!*

"Kathy … Kathy … I'm sorry. I know that article is horrifying—and I'm not your father, but I've gotten to know Rob over the past few years, and I truly love him like a brother. What I'm going to tell you is my opinion—and it's not based on facts. If Harry was my son, I would take him out of school now … no ifs, ands, or buts! I would put him in a drug rehab program that has strong security. And I would leave him there for six months at a minimum. The first thing they'll probably do is slap some nicotine patches on him. They'll start with the 21mg patch and administer that dose for two months. Then they'll do the 14mg for two months, and they'll finish with the 7mg patches.

"After this regimen, Harry will be weaned off his nicotine habit. Along with this medical therapy will be mental rehab. They'll begin rebuilding your son's self-esteem. They'll institute a workout program that will make him physically healthy again. There will also be nutritional rehab. You know the old saying, you are what you eat. Again, if he was my son, when he's done, I'd put him in the Culver Academy up in northern Indiana. If you put him back in his current school, the temptation for a relapse is high."

I was now staring at Tommy. Where the hell did all this information come from? Had he placed Steven in Culver when he was younger? Or perhaps Tommy was referencing his own past experience.

It didn't matter. The substance of what Tommy said just sounded right. And I could tell that Kathy had taken his advice to heart.

I looked Kathy in her eyes and said, "You know your mother and I will help!"

All three of us were emotionally tapped out. Kathy kindly offered to make us a late lunch, but we both declined. It was time to leave—nothing more would be gained by lingering. The decision was up to Kathy and her husband Mike to make—and they needed to do it now! I stood, holding her in my arms again, and gently kissed her forehead before saying goodbye.

Tommy got in the driver's seat, and we headed back to my home in southern Kentucky.

I couldn't resist. "…Like a brother, huh?"

# HAPTER 4

Upon arriving back home, Tommy immediately huddled with Steven, but I was not included in the conversation. Marty flashed me a look I'd seen numerous times in my life, causing me to retire to the bedroom for a second huddle in our home—and this was our personal huddle.

"How did it go, Rob?" Marty asked immediately. For the next half hour, I gave my best effort to summarize what Kathy, Tommy, and I had discussed. Marty didn't interrupt my narrative.

The furrows on her face deepened when I shared the information about how drug dealers were now engineering and introducing a new form of Russian Roulette by providing potentially fatal vaping pods for use in a Juul.

She buried her head in her hands and began weeping at the thought of losing our grandson, and for the second time that day, I did my best to console someone I deeply loved.

"What do you think Kathy and Mike will do?" Marty asked.

"I offered them our help. In case she missed the meaning of that comment—you can reinforce it when we call them tomorrow and make sure that she understands that 'help' includes financial needs.

"But I'm afraid that after the shock of what Tommy said subsides, she and Mike will confront Harry and threaten him with extreme lifestyle consequences if he continues to vape."

"But ..."

"Let me finish ... please! Kathy never smoked when she was younger. I know she tried it but told us she didn't like it. She doesn't get how difficult it will be for him to quit. Harry is an addict now—he's been vaping for over a year! That's the point you have to emphasize when you talk with her.

"Look, Marty, I'm sorry but our plate is more than full right now. We've got to be supportive of whatever decision they make and pray that nothing serious happens to Harry. Hell, Marty, make sure you also suggest that she insists on the school's help. Tell her to talk with the principal and give him the authority to threaten Harry with expulsion for the remainder of the school year! That would mean he'd have to repeat the year—plus he'll be kicked off the soccer team. That might shake him up enough to cause him to stop vaping. Don't forget—they also have government protection now. Have her enlist the agent's help with Harry, during the after-school hours!"

I should have remembered how the todays and tomorrows often blur together and that yesterdays are ever present. Marty reached for her cell phone and called Kathy—right now!

I broke away and took a shower as Marty spoke to our daughter, while subconsciously thinking I could wash away the filth of America's ongoing drug problem.

∩ ∩ ∩

"Steven, get Stan on the phone, please." After about five minutes, Stan was on the line exchanging pleasantries with Steven. In just a few seconds, Steven was able to cut Stan short and hand the cellphone to Tommy.

"Before you say anything, Tommy, please know that you're being recorded. Since you're no longer an active agent, that's the way it has to be. Sorry."

"No problem, Stan. I understand. Listen, I was up in Lexington with Rob Becker today and one of his grandkids is vaping. I don't know if you've been watching the news coming out of the Bluegrass region, but central Kentucky has had a recent spike in fentanyl overdoses, including deaths. In fact, a couple were vaping deaths where someone doctored some used Juul pods. You might want to assign an additional agent to help keep track of this teenager in case Rob's daughter drags her feet about getting her son into a rehab program—and make sure they have plenty of Narcan available just in case there's an overdose."

"On it—anything else, Tommy?"

"Just one question, Stan. Is there anything developing with the murder of Mark Shaw?"

"Hang on ..."

After about thirty seconds, Stan returned to the line. "Sorry about that—I had to turn off the recorder. So far, it looks like the DIA's involvement was only as a cheerleader. I've set up another meet and greet with Bud—and that's set for tomorrow at noon."

"Thanks, Stan. I'll get back with you before we head west, and please encourage the analysts to hurry with the new paperwork for the Beckers—I can tell they're getting antsy." Tommy handed the cell phone back to Steven, knowing that Stan might have some parting words for his son.

After hanging the phone up, Stan leaned back in the chair at his Langley office and sketched out the positioning of agents who would be along the route he intended to walk the next day. The last time he and Bud met, Stan had information that Bud wanted. This time the reverse was true. Stan needed to know if the DIA had put out a contract or had killed Mark Shaw using their own in-house talent. He speculated that the meeting site would be crawling with agents from multiple intelligence agencies and tensions would be high. Finally, he shuffled his papers together and headed for home, satisfied he was ready for the next day.

∩ ∩ ∩

Day Two was a wrap, but sleep didn't come easily for me. My thoughts wandered back to my teen years and the punishments I'd received for inappropriate behavior. Everything that was dished out, I deserved! I thought about what might be happening or was going to happen at my daughter's home.

First Kathy and Mike would strip Harry's bedroom from top to bottom. Most likely he would have hiding places that he thought were undetectable, not taking into account that his parents used to believe the same when they were teens. After perhaps finding a spare Juul or even two, they'd find his stash of Juul pods. Some would be full and some would be empty. Then Kathy and Mike would search other rooms that Harry spent time in. And finally, the search would proceed to Mike's office—a place that was normally off limits for Harry.

Once they were satisfied that they'd scouted all the potential hiding places, Kathy and Mike would drop the hammer on their son. There'd be no escape clauses or quid pro quo options. Once the punishment was administered, it would be followed by a stream of cuss words, "I hate you" comments, and the slamming of doors. Corporal punishment would not be an option. After retreating to his bedroom, Harry would begin searching for his contraband. And when he'd discover that all of it was gone, his rage would heighten even more. He'd begin thinking of ways to hurt his mom and dad. He'd finally conclude that the best way to pay back his parents would be to take his own life.

Harry's rage would begin to subside because there's only so much adrenaline a body can produce. Fatigue would begin to take hold of Harry, and sleep would soon follow.

Been there, done that ...

My stream of thoughts was finished for the day.

 HAPTER 5

After another fitful night of sleep, I decided it was time to visit Donnie and Mike to say my goodbyes. I showered, dressed, and walked into the kitchen, but nobody else was awake. I put a half-caffeine pod in the coffee maker to brew and had my usual raisin bread breakfast. Still no one was stirring. I grabbed Marty's keys, opened the garage door, and started toward the driver's side door.

"Hey! Where do you think you're going?"

"Jesus, Tommy, you scared the crap out of me!" I shouted.

"Rob, did you even bother to knock on my bedroom door to see if I was awake? How about Steven's room? Rob—Mark's death wasn't a chance occurrence! You can't trivialize the possibility that you'll be the next casualty! I'll let you drive off to wherever you're heading, if you insist, but otherwise I need you to promise me that this will be the last time you ever head out alone."

For a few seconds I was speechless. Tommy was right—as usual—but my pride and feelings of invincibility had again tripped me up.

"Agreed!"

"'What did you say?" Tommy replied.

"I agree to never go anywhere by myself! Dammit, Tommy, don't make me grovel."

"Where to, Marshal Dillon?"

Part of me wanted to smack Tommy, and the other half

couldn't resist smiling.

"Listen up, asshole—if that's my nickname, by God, I'll take it!"

I tossed the car keys in Tommy's direction and again assumed the previous day's position in the back of Marty's car. Tommy climbed into the driver's seat and backed out of the garage.

"I will say one thing that's certain—you sure are easy to train now." This was followed by his heavy laughter.

"Okay, Doc—once again, where are we headed?"

I handed Tommy my cell phone with the Waze app already opened. "Here are the directions to Mike's clinic. We'll head there first and then we'll visit with Donnie for a bit."

Thirty minutes later, we arrived at Mike's large animal clinic. Tommy followed me inside and did a walk through first. Finally, he signaled me to proceed while he settled into a reception room chair.

I knocked on Mike's private office door and slowly peeked inside.

"Damn, Rob, it sure is good to see you! What brings you here this early?"

"Thanks, Mike. I wish I was bringing good news, but I'm not. Marty and I are going away for a while, and I can't tell you where or for how long." I watched as Mike's jaw suddenly went slack and his stare became intense. "I won't be at Mark's funeral services. In fact, government sources think I was also supposed to be killed!" Mike started to shake his head, trying to rid himself of more bad news.

"Oh my God, Rob, I'm so sorry! Please tell me how I can help. There has to be something I can do!"

I closed the distance between us, wrapped my arms around Mike, and just hugged him. Nothing was said out loud, but it felt like a ton of words were being exchanged between two long-time friends.

"Jesus—I totally forgot! I was going to call you today," Mike stammered. "Come over here!"

Mike led me toward his rolltop desk and grabbed what appeared to be a diary of some sort.

"This came in the mail this morning. As much as I can figure, it's Mark's journal. I flipped through it. I think it basically documents his government genetic research, and at the end of the journal he details his most recent written work. Check out the date—and it's not just any summary! Through his research, Mark discovered an identifier of sorts for selecting a mare that carries the same genome that Towers Above's mama had. Of course, as you already know, Mark had previously reverse-engineered TA's genome—and that's not all. He even researched all the breeding mares in Kentucky and found the exact mare that TA should breed with! You realize what this means Rob? We could have a chance of witnessing the creation of a second Towers Above."

"What's the mare's name and where is she located?" I asked.

"Her name is Chevytothelevee and she's stabled at a small farm up in Paris. According to Mark, the owner breeds her every other year. Mark talked to her about selling the mare and her response was 'Make me an offer.'"

"You're shitting me, Mike! As in 'American Pie?'" I asked.

"That's my guess," Mike answered. "Do you think Donnie would want some of this action? It sure would be cool to have another Secretariat-type thoroughbred out at the farm!"

"I can't speak for him, Mike, but my next stop was going to be at the farm, so I'll ask him. If he's willing, why don't the two of you set up an escrow account at the bank. I'll forward whatever a third of the price is and have Martin, our lawyer, set up another corporation for our future foal. Damn—this is exciting!"

I asked Tommy to come into Mike's office and I reintroduced him to Mike.

"Tommy, I don't know how my sabbatical is going to work, but I figure Mike and Donnie should have some way of contacting one of us, and I'm thinking it should be you. I'll leave the room and let the two of you work it out ... and I didn't think to tell Mike that he should hire some security folks, because it's pretty much common knowledge about our partnership group."

I extended my hand for a parting handshake, and Mike pulled me close for one last hug. He let go of his grasp and I turned quickly away, not wanting to show the tears welling up in my eyes.

Tommy broke the silence during the car ride to the farm by asking how my friendship with Donnie, Mike, and Mark started when I was an undergraduate in college. It was the right question at the right moment. My mind instantly travelled back to happier times, and I regaled Tommy with the immature exploits of the group's freshman college year and fraternity life. Then I transitioned through the upper-class years when all four of us buckled down and focused on our life's purposes.

"Tell you what, Rob, when we arrive at the farm, I'm going to stay in the car while you visit with Donnie. He and I didn't exactly meet under ideal circumstances."

"God, Tommy, I totally forgot that you and Danny kidnapped Donnie and then interrogated him!"

Donnie's wife Val welcomed me into the kitchen of the farmhouse, and after a quick peck on the cheek, I asked where Donnie was.

"Let me call him, Rob," she said as I sat down on the edge of one of the kitchen table chairs. I caught Val glancing at me a few times, me not realizing my body language was giving my angst away.

"Rob, are you okay—is something going on with Marty?"

"No, Val ... I mean, yes, Val ..." as I shook my head and started laughing at my feeble answer. Donnie came through the kitchen door at just the right time.

"Hey Rob, welcome. How ya doing?"

"I'm good, Donnie, real good. How's TA doing?" Donnie picked up on my heightened stress level even quicker than his wife. "Tell ya what, let's walk to TA's barn—I know he's expecting to play your game 'guess which hand the peppermints are in,'" Donnie replied.

"Thanks for bailing me out, Donnie—and no, I'm not okay!'" I stated. I shared with Donnie everything I'd talked about with Mike earlier that morning, including the information about Mark's journal and research. Donnie immediately said, "I'm all in."

"One thing I didn't tell Mike was that if the mare's owner balks at an all cash offer, then the two of you should come up with a reasonable percentage of Chevytothelevee's foal's winnings when he or she begins their two-year-old racing campaign."

"Look, Donnie, you were the one who made my dream come to fruition. Without your thoroughbred knowledge, Towers Above would never have accomplished all that he did. I'm counting on you to continue the dream. Mark may have had a minor influence on TA, but he didn't screw with his genetics."

I reached in my pocket and pulled out the piece of paper that Tommy handed me as I exited the car a few minutes earlier. I thrust it toward Donnie. He reached for and unfolded it.

"Whose phone number is this?" Donnie asked.

"I suspect it's Tommy's—right now he's sitting in your driveway in Marty's car. I'm certain he feels you would have been uncomfortable if he had joined us. Please, find a spot for his number in the contacts list on your cell phone. He told Mike that the number was the only way he could pass a message on to me. So, swallow your pride and if need be, call or message him about anything. Nothing is too trivial! And re-evaluate your security here at the farm—I doubt that you or Mike would be a target, but it always pays to be safe!"

I started to feel my emotions again begin to take control and I gave Donnie the same tight parting hug that I'd given Mike. About twenty yards down the path to the car, Donnie shouted, "Did you forget about Towers Above?"

I didn't turn around and just kept walking. I just couldn't force myself to say another goodbye.

CHAPTER 6

Stan arrived at DC's Reflecting Pool a half hour early. He began a slow walk and immediately realized that the pathway was draped with agents from numerous government intelligence agencies—agents who would apparently be joining him for some late-morning exercise. As the walkers passed by Stan, he spotted their earpieces.

He chuckled to himself and thought, *There's only so far one can stick those contraptions in the ear before it punctures their eardrum!*

It was more difficult to detect those who were wearing the skin-colored ear sets, but for an accomplished agent like Stan, it was still quite obvious. However, the earpieces that were impossible to detect were those totally customized for fit and skin tone color—and designed to be anatomically perfect!

"Well … the FBI, DIA and CIA are here for sure," Stan said silently. "I wonder which other of the seventeen intel agencies are also here?" He laughed to himself one final time and mumbled, "Good God ... it looks like we're having a track meet here today!"

As usual, Bud arrived five minutes before noon and started walking with his usual quick pace. It was cloudy and he was carrying an umbrella. Within ten minutes, he caught up with Stan.

"Hello, Stan—how's the family?"

Stan answered, "They're fine, Bud, and how about yours?"

"Everyone's good," Bud replied.

Stan started to speak but was immediately cut short by Bud.

"No ... the DIA did not order a hit on Mark Shaw—but I'm not going to say we weren't happy it happened! He was going rogue on us—and yes, we were shadowing him—trying to intimidate him into shutting the fuck up!

It was at this point that Bud opened the umbrella, which was the largest umbrella Stan had ever seen. It was at least a third bigger than a typical golf umbrella and it easily covered both their heads and extended onto their torsos.

"Okay ... now we can talk without some listening device recording our conversation. This umbrella is made from a material that offers a new type of sound blocking. Nobody, no matter how sensitive their listening device is, will be able to hear what we discuss."

Stan began to ask his questions but was again interrupted by Bud.

"You're familiar with President Eisenhower's farewell address, aren't you?"

Not waiting for Stan's answer, Bud continued talking. "He warned about the growing influence, not only economically but also politically, of the Military Industrial Complex. Ike also warned about possible public entities that would be developing technological advancements that would threaten the existence of America's democracy. Just a couple years after his speech, America became entangled in the Vietnam War. Chemicals like Agent Orange made their first appearance on the battlefield, and leaders like Robert McNamara prevailed in convincing President Kennedy and LBJ that America could not afford to be defeated in Vietnam. McNamara brought his corporate policy of systems analysis to the government—after being plucked from his position as president of the Ford Motor Company. Thousands of

American soldiers lost their lives as a result of that conflict ... and the Military Industrial Complex became an even larger and more entrenched segment of our democracy."

"Are you suggesting what I'm thinking?" Stan asked, finally able to sandwich in a question.

"Stan ... it was the Vietnam War that resulted in the creation of the DIA. The CIA's formation was earlier, born immediately following WWII. Your man Tommy—who's watching over Rob Becker right now—may be correct. Certainly, if Becker had been present in that restroom, he'd also have been taken out.

"Stan, I'm telling you that today and for more than the last half century, there's been an organization that none of our official seventeen intelligence agencies knows about. The individuals who are a part of this group are totally anonymous, but their tentacles are long. These next words I'm about to say are sheer speculation on my part—but I believe this organization may not be exclusive to America. Its members are globalist folks, and they are the ones ultimately controlling the most critical worldwide decisions. I believe this group ordered the murder of Mark Shaw."

"What the hell are ..." Stan tried to ask before being throttled again.

"Look, Stan ... Rob Becker has made a lot of enemies. He's pissed off the thoroughbred industry—and he's probably got a bounty posted on his head by ISIS. They're still going strong, even though POTUS says they've been destroyed. But the wildcard is this globalist group which the DIA knows nothing about. And frankly, Stan, Becker is not our problem! He's your problem. We're too busy putting out fires created by this secret group that is so determined to thwart POTUS from potentially exposing their organization. He calls it a swamp—I call it quicksand and there's no escape from it."

Bud finally stopped talking and Stan just stared at him. He knew that Bud was spot-on about those enemies he'd just described, but the existence of such a globalist group was a huge stretch for Stan. He searched Bud's eyes for any glimmer of doubt, but he saw no indication of even one. It was obvious to Stan that Bud was deadly serious.

The meeting was over. Stan extended his right hand and Bud grabbed it with his right hand.

"If you recorded this conversation, Stan, I'd destroy it if I were you. Nothing good can come from it. And good luck in hiding Rob Becker and his wife. Mark Shaw unfortunately will not be the last death!"

Bud turned away while collapsing the oversized umbrella.

Stan remained standing in the same spot for another couple of minutes. It was almost as if his feet had been buried in cement— or in this instance, quicksand.

CHAPTER 7

Most illegal immigrants entering the United States from Mexico generally believe that it's far better to cross the border anywhere but at a port of entry checkpoint. Crossing at a bridge and checking in with American immigration agents—the legal way to claim asylum—is often assumed by immigrants to lead to detention.

However, crossing illegally and getting caught by a border agent will lead to an appearance before a judge and then being released, as soon as one claims they're seeking asylum. Skipping out on a court date seldom leads to adverse consequences.

Welcome to America!

Muhammad had no intention of crossing at an international bridge and declaring his desire for asylum in the US.

His hired smuggler, Edgar, who suspected his clients were from the Middle East, had no factual information about Muhammad's country of origin—and he didn't care! He'd smuggled several Middle Easterners into the USA previously, and as far as he was concerned, this journey was just another business deal. The $6,000 American dollars per person cash transaction was more than enough to guarantee safe passage. Another six grand for Muhammad's female companion, Alia, was icing on the cake.

Muhammad and his faux wife had just completed their safe passage on an Iranian merchant ship which was transporting medical devices to Nicaragua. As they disembarked at the Port of

Bluefields, Edgar approached the pair and introduced himself to his new travelers.

The first leg of their trip was due west to the Port of Corinto on the Pacific Ocean. There everyone boarded a thirty-foot cruiser and headed north toward Cabo San Lucas, Mexico. Once at Cabo, Edgar intended to transport his contraband to the American border, just west of El Paso in Southeastern New Mexico—where they would make the illegal crossing into America.

As Edgar, Muhammad, and Alia thanked the captain and disembarked from the cruiser, Alia suddenly stopped, telling Muhammad that she'd forgotten some documents. She sprinted the eighth of a mile back to the boat just in time to catch the captain in the beginning stages of casting off. In fluid Spanglish, she told the captain what she forgot and brushed past him, heading below deck. Alia was in her early twenties—quite attractive and appeared to be slightly pregnant. Wearing a sheer halter top had caught the captain's attention earlier in the morning ... and she knew it!

The captain should have immediately followed her down the steps, but he hesitated thirty seconds too long. Sexual arousal can often mess up one's thought process at times.

As he reached the bottom of the stairs and turned his head to the left, an arm pulled his head backwards and a razor-sharp knife blade quickly sliced through the outer skin of his neck just below the Adam's Apple. Blood immediately filled his trachea and esophagus, and for the next four seconds, only gurgling noises could be heard. Finally, he mercifully became unconscious and was dead.

Alia swept through the cruiser searching for onboard cameras while also methodically wiping down everything Muhammad and she had touched during their time on the boat. Two security cameras were found and removed, and she deposited both in her backpack. In thirty minutes, her tasks were finished.

Two new ISIS terrorists had unofficially arrived in Mexico!

Alia rejoined Muhammad and Edgar, and they proceeded afoot for another thirty minutes. As they rounded a bend in the trail, Edgar spotted the expected all-terrain vehicle parked some four hundred yards ahead.

After loading their belongings onto the vehicle, everyone climbed in and on. Edgar started the ATV, and their trip north-east toward the border began.

ᴖ ᴖ ᴖ

The CIA had a fleet of speed boats registered in Mexican wa-ters. José and Diego had been shadowing the now-docked cruiser for more than an hour. After waiting a couple of hours longer, they cruised closer to shore. With a high-powered sniper rifle, José scoped out the cruiser from bow to stern.

"Diego, I don't see any signs of life on board. Let's tie up a few yards north of the cruiser and I'll take a walk."

José put his earpiece in and ran a sound check with Diego. He placed his gun in his rear waistband and jumped ashore. Carrying a metal detector and looking every bit the part of a scavenger, he slowly approached the cruiser. Once abreast of the bow, José called out to the captain of the boat. There was no response, and he continued calling out in a low voice, advising that he was boarding the cruiser.

Moving from the top deck to below, José descended the stairs and spied the body.

"Hello ... are you okay?" he asked first in Spanish and then in English.

"Either he's passed out or …" José whispered to Diego through the microphone.

As José knelt down, he saw the pool of drying blood. After slowly turning the body over on its back, he immediately saw the captain's slashed throat. He and Diego had seen their share of people murdered during their careers—but a throat-slashing was a unique form of murder and an immediate "tell" characteristic of Middle Eastern terrorists.

Reaching into his pocket, he pulled out his cellphone and began taking forensic photos. He checked the body for identification—but found none!

He then searched the rest of the ship. The sleeping quarters gave away the fact that more than just the captain had been aboard.

"Diego, bring the property bag and Rusty. There's a dead person and no obvious drugs."

Rusty was the DEA's trained drug-sniffing German Shepherd. Once aboard, the dog began frantically searching for cartel contraband, anticipating the treats that would be commensurate with how many drugs were found. This time, Rusty would come away without the usual supply of treats, as only a few grams of marijuana were found.

José concluded that the person or persons who had been aboard—not drugs—were the valuable cargo on this boat's last voyage. After gathering the bedding, José and Diego left the ship and headed back out to sea. About twenty-five miles offshore, the evidence was transferred to a US naval submarine. By the next morning, the bag would be on its way by air to Langley, Virginia for testing.

The photos José took were transmitted electronically to Langley that afternoon and subsequently on Stan's desk the next morning.

Stan had issued orders earlier in the month that anything suspicious concerning Middle Eastern intelligence should be sent directly to him. Mark Shaw's influence, even after his death, just wouldn't go away.

CHAPTER 8

The message from Stan to Steven was brief. "The transport vehicle will land at 0900 hours. You are to stay behind and protect Dr. Becker's home."

Steven finished his coffee and checked to see if his dad was awake. Then he proceeded on to our bedroom, knocking on the door and announcing our departure time for Indianapolis.

I assumed we'd be gone a couple of days and packed accordingly. Marty was less optimistic and packed for four days. We had no clue it could be longer.

Much longer!

We all had breakfast before Marty and I dragged our suitcases out to the garage. I mumbled to myself, "This is going to be interesting—trying to fit all of our luggage and all of us into Marty's car, with Marty and me also slumping down in the back seat trying to hide ourselves."

My earlier experience in the Mt. Hood wilderness prepared me for the next surprise. I thought I recognized the clatter outside that was increasing in intensity.

"What the hell is that noise?" Marty stammered.

Without a second's hesitation, Steven replied. "That's your transport vehicle arriving to take you to Indy."

"What?" Marty replied.

"That noise is coming from a helicopter, Marty. Let me go get some Valium for you," I said. The last time Marty had been aboard a helicopter was years previously in Maui and I remembered her stress then. I got up and retrieved a couple of 5mg pills from the bottle—pills generally taken to help her relax—but would now serve to keep her nerves calm during the chopper ride.

The helicopter, provided courtesy of the Kentucky National Guard, landed in our backyard. Steven greeted the pilot with a question requiring a specific password as the answer for "Operation Blackjack," which was now the code name Stan had obtained for Marty and me, with approval of the White House.

The ride was uneventful and by noon, Tommy, Marty, and I were settled in the Indy makeover facility, each of us waiting for our individualized metamorphoses to commence.

Marty and I were taken to different salons.

My first clue that two days wouldn't nearly be enough time to become "Prince Not So Charming" started with my feet. The nails on my two big toes were about to be removed permanently—nail fungus had sealed their fate. While I was numbed for the procedure, I tried to figure out which people might recognize me from my gross-looking big toes, but arguing was apparently not an option! I quickly thought back to Tommy's description of what occurred when he interrogated an Antifa revolutionary who had tried to blow up the Bonneville Dam on the Columbia River east of Portland, Oregon. Perhaps my pain was payback for the discomfort that I'd inflicted on Mateo in Mt. Hood's wilderness.

From that clinical site, I was taken to what was called their dermatology department. There were no questions asked—just commands given.

"Remove your watch, please!" I was told.

My response of "Why?" was met with a Ninja-like movement and suddenly my left arm was affixed to the arm of the recliner chair with Velcro straps. As I tried to remove the straps, another person who, unbeknownst to me was standing behind, grabbed my right arm and performed the same maneuver.

"Please cooperate with us, sir," the technician advised.

I only had one tattoo and it was on my left wrist, intentionally positioned to be covered by my watch. The University of Kentucky logo tattoo, now almost pale blue, was about to have dermabrasion performed on it. Although somewhat archaic, the process would be the least likely to produce a secondary infection. Besides, the clinician knew about the other imminent procedures that would be even more invasive. The area was sterilized and a dremel-type instrument was turned on. The abrasive wheel began sanding away my skin, one layer at a time. That's when I realized that Marty had been right to pack for four days. There'd have to be at least two or more additional abrasion sessions—days apart—to erase my Wildcat tribute.

As my cosmetic tattoo-removal session ended, my imagination was nervously anticipating what part of my anatomy would be targeted next.

I glanced at my phone to check the time—it was already late in the afternoon. Certainly, there wouldn't be time for anything else on this day.

"Come with me, sir," yet another staff member commanded. I was beginning to feel like the only thing missing on my body was a collar attached to a leash. We got on the elevator and I noticed there were no floor buttons on the panel. However, my escort pushed a small red button and a voice similar to Siri's immediately asked "What department?"

"Ophthalmology, please," my escort responded.

"How about we do this tomorrow?" I blurted out. My request

was met with silence. A half minute later, the elevator doors opened and I was taken to examination room No. 1. It was later that Tommy told me the red elevator button served as a fingerprint I.D. and that the elevator moved only upon voice recognition.

"Please have a seat—the doctor will be in shortly."

My mind again started wandering. "Maybe I'll get contact lens or perhaps just new eyeglasses." Suddenly my mind flashed back to an old Elton John video when he was wearing huge pink heart-shaped glasses.

"Good afternoon, sir ... I'm going to do your pre-surgical exam. This will take about an hour."

"Hold on a second, bud," I said angrily. "All you folks do is push me here and there like I'm a steer on the way to slaughter! I'm walking out of here right now unless you tell me about the surgery I'm supposed to have tomorrow. Start talking, dammit!"

The clock started—my line in the sand had been drawn!

The doctor turned and walked out of the room, closing the door behind him.

After about thirty seconds, I got up and walked to the door, only to discover that it was locked. I scanned the room for video cameras and assumed the room was wired for sound as well.

"I'm giving you five minutes and then I'm going to start messing with your expensive equipment. The countdown starts now!" I began counting to sixty out loud. It took about four counts of sixty when the door lock began to make a whirring noise. The door popped open—and in walked Tommy, with anger written all over his face.

"Tommy ... what the ...?"

"Shut it, Rob! These people have no clue as to who you are and even if they did, they know what the consequences would be if they ever leaked any information about you. That's why they refer to you as 'sir.' Let me explain a few things to you. You have an email address, right?"

I nodded yes.

"Have you ever changed your email address?"

I again nodded up and down in the affirmative.

"So, what happened when it was changed?" Tommy asked next.

"Jesus, Tommy, I don't remember!"

"Well, I'm going to tell you! You probably were getting emails that promised to fix your erectile dysfunction. You also were receiving spam about all the different diet fads and programs. I'm certain you were receiving insurance company solicitations. And guess what ... all of those emails disappeared when you signed up with a new internet provider and email address. And then, as soon as you changed your email address on Facebook or other sites that needed you to update your information, maybe within hours but certainly within a few days, you started to receive new spam email. Your electronic history may have changed, but I'm willing to bet that some of your old email solicitors soon found you once again.

"It's called a footprint. Rob, your electronic nine and a half double 'A' is out in cyberspace for anyone with the Internet skills to dig up. You think your personal information is safe—it's not. Anyone that has a photo of themselves on Facebook, whether it's a head shot or full-body photo, generates a total physical profile for anyone to use. Do you know what happens when you walk into most retail stores?"

"No," I sheepishly replied.

"The stores use high-tech video analytics. They use facial

recognition programs and have pinhole cameras placed everywhere. The minute you walk into the store, their technology
program begins tracking your cell phone signature. Your mobile phone is constantly broadcasting an International Mobile
Subscriber identity number. If you've been in the store previously,
then your pattern of shopping is merged with your past retail
buying habits.

"Rob, the folks here at this identity change facility are trying
to create a new you—someone who has no footprint whatsoever.
The surgery they intend to perform tomorrow is a Lasik-type
procedure. Your current dominant facial identifier is your eye
hardware, and they intend to eliminate that.

"I can't force you to undergo any of these procedures. If you
think you know more about creating a new you, then we'll stop
this process right now. But I'm telling you—you're not POTUS
or a legislator. The security that you and your family enjoy right
now is not forever!

"I know what you're afraid of, Rob! You don't want anything
bad to happen with that eye surgery because you're holding on
to the idea that you can still practice dentistry. You're worried
that there'll be a glitch and your eyesight will be screwed up!
Remember, it was just a few months ago that you said you'd never
be able to practice dentistry on another human being.

"Rob ... you're a horseman now. What's past is past! It's time
to move on—you need to finish your transition both mentally
and physically—now!"

Tommy turned and exited the examining room, and the ophthalmologist immediately returned. For the next three hours, I
was moved from one piece of equipment to another. I assumed
it was the required work-up and analysis needed prior to the

actual surgery.

"Sir, I'll do your operation tomorrow morning, but please, no eating or drinking after midnight. My assistant will take you to your residence now."

After I had left—the surgeon pulled out his cellphone and texted a message that read:

There's a person here that might interest you!
He's not complete as yet!
I'll try to get a finished photo for you, but it's going to cost at least high six figures—cash!

I arrived at my suite, but Marty was not there. On the bathroom counter was an electric hair trimmer, a Gillette razor, a makeup mirror and some Cremo shaving cream. An attached note stated, "Enjoy the new you and thanks for being a fan," and it was signed "from Yul Brynner." Next to the hair products was a "Cubs" ballcap with a note attached. "From this point on, never take this cap off! Do not trust anyone. I intend to be present during your surgery tomorrow!"

Somehow, Tommy could always manage to coax a smile out of me, but somehow, I doubted a bald me would look like the "Broadway King."

# HAPTER 9

I plugged in the hair trimmer and raised it toward my scalp—
but then quickly powered it off. I sat down on the toilet seat
and began thinking about Tommy's warning to always wear the
ball cap.

I mulled his statement over and over in my mind before the
reason finally struck me.

Tommy's warning to me was not to trust anyone and yet here
I am in a CIA-sanctioned facility. He, however, went to Langley
for his makeover, while I'm in Indianapolis. There's no way I'm
going bald until I get home.

The door to the suite opened and Marty strolled in, now
sporting raven-black hair. My mind flashed back in time—forty-
plus years back, when I was casually introduced to her one evening—and she was a blonde.

One week later on our first date, the front door of her home
was opened and she greeted me—but I was now looking at a
woman with jet-black hair!

"What the ..."

I was staring at Marty as she began to whirl around 360 degrees, then suddenly stopping on a dime with a huge grin on her
face.

I started laughing uncontrollably.

"I know exactly what you're thinking! Whoever said that history repeats itself sure had us pegged," Marty exclaimed, laughing.

I walked over to give Marty a hug—and almost immediately, her laughter turned into tears.

The reality of the seriousness of our situation had struck home!

After the tears subsided, I showed her what Tommy had left me. I started to further stress the point when she casually reached to the back of her neck, and slowly removed the most perfect wig I'd ever seen.

For once—Marty and I were totally on the same page!

∩ ∩ ∩

Edgar knew this might be his last border crossing for a while. He knew that just west of El Paso, Texas, his favorite entry point into the US from Mexico, was being cut off! An organization known as "We Build the Wall," with help from the "American Eagle Brick Company," was installing a portion of new border wall.

It was a unique project. A non-profit entity, along with an American business, were utilizing the non-profit's donated funds—and the brick company's equipment and workers. They were moving ahead on the project quickly, working day and night to install new sections of border barrier.

With little to no fanfare from the mainstream media, thousands of dollars donated from all over the US was now helping to pay a private company to install a high-tech border wall, without the federal government's Army Corps of Engineers' oversight.

The owner of the property was a Vietnam War veteran who had granted permission to place the wall on his land, which was situated on a portion of Mt. Cristo Rey. For years, the government had claimed that the mountain itself served as a natural barrier that prohibited illegals and drug traffickers from crossing the border. The exact opposite was the case. The mountain terrain couldn't house enough Border Patrol agents to stop the flow of flesh and fentanyl from entering America.

The existence of this geographic area, which once almost guaranteed a free passage portal across the border, would soon become blocked. Access to this particular route used by illegal immigrants and their trail guides known as coyotes, and drug smugglers—referred to as mules—were transporting approximately one hundred thousand dollars of drugs from Mexico into New Mexico and beyond . . . every day. It would soon be sealed off.

The brick company's social media page was predominantly filled with positive patriotic posts - congratulating American Eagle Brick Company for its work on this project. But interspersed among the praise were posts from people who hated any type of border wall and detested the company for its actions.

For Edgar, this region had been the equivalent of America's "Route 66." He'd lost count of the number of people he'd personally smuggled across the border.

It was nearly Memorial Day in 2019 when Edgar, Muhammad, and Alia were approaching the base of Mt. Cristo Rey, just short of the US and Mexico border. Edgar knew from past crossings where the American border agents would be positioned. He also knew that the usual response and apprehension time—once the border agents spotted illegal traffic—was about thirty minutes.

Now, because of the new construction, the border patrol had a new eagle's nest on high ground, and their reaction time was much quicker.

The new wall stretched almost a mile up the mountainside and all the old trails had now been rendered obsolete. Edgar considered himself the hunter, not the prey!

Leaving Muhammad and Alia at the camp, he intended to spend the entire day scouting out a new trail he'd heard was being carved by the drug cartel's "mules." He purposely let two other groups of illegals pass him in the mid-morning and was now watching from a high perch—as the border patrol reacted swiftly in rounding up those two groups.

As with anything new, the advantage is with the hunter. It will take the animals a while to learn new tricks, Edgar thought.

Edgar remained in the hideout well into the early morning hours. One last group of illegals had passed by him on the trail around midnight. It was now 3:00 a.m. and Edgar had not observed any flashlights shining their beams.

Perhaps because of the unknown terrain, or happening upon a nest of rattlesnakes ... traveling in the pitch-black darkness of night was prohibitive, Edgar mused.

"Whatever ... we're traveling tomorrow night!" he mumbled out loud. He soon fell fast asleep and was awakened by the dawn's first rays of light a few short hours later.

Upon Edgar's return back at camp, Muhammad began peppering him with questions. After hearing at least five questions in rapid succession, Edgar held up his hand with his palm facing Muhammad.

"Dejame hablar," Edgar shouted. Muhammad obeyed, letting his guide talk.

Edgar told Muhammad and Alia about the plan for that evening while suggesting that they find some shade for the remainder of the day—someplace where they could also take some short naps. Crossing the mountain was going to be strenuous.

It was time to leave on their trek, which would take about three hours. There was zero moonlight to show the way, and

Muhammad and Alia were forced to play follow the leader with Edgar. They were amazed at how Edgar did it—hunched over, using the flashlight from his cellphone on the dimmest setting so they wouldn't be detected. From the peak of Mt. Cristo Rey, the group headed due west and reached the railroad tracks west of Sunland Park, in New Mexico. Edgar stopped and crouched down, finally taking a well-deserved seat on the ground.

"Welcome to the United States ... this is as far as I go. Once you cross the railroad tracks, I'm sure your connections will be there to meet up with you," Edgar stated. He knew that was a fact because he'd been watching Muhammad continuously pulling out and looking at what he figured was some kind of GPS hardware buried in his left pants pocket.

And he was right! About three hundred yards due north of their position, a flashlight suddenly turned on and began blinking out Morse code in dots and dashes.

Just as suddenly, a border patrol vehicle's spotlight lit up the entire area, exposing the group of three.

Officer Diaz's voice boomed over a loudspeaker mounted on the truck.

"No te muevas—US Border Patrol!"

The driver's side door on the truck opened and Officer Diaz slowly approached his prey. Officer Dana Jennings, his female partner, also exited the truck as she unholstered her gun and provided cover for her partner.

"Bajar en sus estomagos y poner las manos de la espalda" was Diaz's next command. Edgar understood and complied instantly but Muhammad and Alia were not as quick to respond. They both eventually followed Edgar's example, slumping to the ground and ending up on their stomachs.

Alia suddenly began grabbing her abdomen and what started out as moaning quickly escalated into shrieks, signaling extreme pain.

"My water just broke!" Alia began yelling to no one in particular. Her legs were now spread apart and what appeared to be amniotic fluid was now puddling on the ground between her thighs.

What Officer Diaz hadn't seen was that Alia took out her knife and sliced into her fake pregnancy hump. A concoction of distilled water, saline water, and clear Karo syrup made for a life-like blend of amniotic liquid that even an experienced gynecologist could initially buy into. It was no wonder that Officer Diaz forgot his training for just a few seconds, as he bent down to help a woman supposedly giving birth to her child.

"Dana ... give me a little help here! I have no clue what to do," Diaz shouted.

As Officer Jennings closed the distance to Alia, Muhammad was on his feet instantly, pouncing on Officer Diaz.

The knife's razor-sharp blade sliced through Officer Diaz's neck in a millisecond. Officer Jennings took aim, preparing to shoot Muhammad when Alia quickly silenced her as well in one throat- slashing motion.

It took Edgar less than a second to realize he was facing the same fate. He whirled, retreated backward, and began running up the mountainside to escape.

Alia sprinted for 30 seconds before catching up with Edgar. He never stood a chance. His body crumpled onto the trail with his blood streaming slowly down the hillside.

Muhammad and Alia began to scour the landscape, looking for anything that might implicate either of them. After cleaning out Edgar's wallet and retrieving the down payment money paid to smuggle them across the border, both headed toward their collaborator's hidden position. They exchanged customary Arabic greetings before their courier transported them to a safe house for the remainder of the evening.

The radio in Officer Diaz's truck kept summoning him to reply and give an update on his status. Finally, additional border patrol units began to respond to a possible "Officer Down" situation.

Border Agent Diaz was survived by his wife and three daughters, along with other family members who had legally immigrated to America in the early 2000's. His wife Elena wanted desperately to share her husband's story with the media, but a blackout on the release of any information had been issued by the Office of Homeland Security.

Officer Jennings was single with no living relatives.

Within twelve hours of Officer Diaz's demise, Steven received a text message from Stan. It read:

Border crossing near El Paso ...
Three murdered!
Two were Border Patrol agents!
The other was a smuggler.
All three were murdered—their throats were slit!
Same M/O as previous murder along the Mexican Coast!
ISIS/Al-Qaeda???

What was hidden between the lines of Stan's message was the CIA's intelligence that Muhammad and Alia had escaped capture ... either during or following the defeat of the last ISIS stronghold in Baghouz, Syria! That meant the whereabouts of the father of Ahmad and Jamil was unknown and Stan had to plan for the worst of possibilities, since Dr. Becker and Tommy were indirectly responsible for the deaths of Muhammad's two sons.

Edgar also had a family. But since his wallet was empty, there was no way of identifying him. Photos were taken, and copies printed and placed on the new trails being carved out by the drug "mules" and smugglers. The photos requested help in identifying Edgar and offered a sizable cash reward, but weeks passed, with no information forthcoming. Edgar was laid to rest in an unmarked grave in El Paso alongside other unidentified illegals. Only the Lord knew his identity.

Perhaps a fitting headstone for Edgar might read, BAD KARMA!

Steven immediately forwarded the information to his father.

# CHAPTER 10

Marty and I flinched upon hearing the knock on the door of our suite.

"Now what?" I asked Marty.

I slowly opened the door to Tommy, who entered the room, showing no signs of emotion on his face.

"Is Marty still awake?" he asked. I nodded.

"We need to talk!" Tommy replied.

I went to the bedroom, waving for Marty to come out into the main room. Her scowl was met with a slightly more intense scowl of my own.

Marty and I sat down on the couch and Tommy sat on the edge of a cushioned chair facing both of us. His body language spoke volumes before he even uttered any words.

"Stan sent Steven a message today. CIA information indicates the probability that more than one ISIS terrorist crossed our southern border recently." I started to interrupt Tommy, but he raised his hand, effectively silencing me.

"Rob, there's a possibility that one of the terrorists is Muhammad—Ahmad and Jamil's father. Needless to say, you and I are at the top of the list of folks that he intends to kill. Anyone else around us will also be at risk." Tommy glanced at Marty. A cold shiver climbed my spine as memories flashed back to that day at the track when Towers Above and Nidalas finished in a dead heat.

"C'mon, Tommy, you and I both know there are multiple Al-Qaeda and ISIS collaborators already hunkered down in America. Why all of a sudden has Muhammad become a threat?" Tommy shot me the same frustrated gaze I'd seen many times before.

"We had him, Rob—both he and his female companion were detained in Syria. Then Turkey pulled a military stunt and there was a jailbreak—the two of them vanished. The Agency thinks they escaped to Iran before ending up in Central America. Then they were transported north by boat toward the Baja Peninsula. The boat's captain was slaughtered in that region of Mexico, in a similar manner to a couple of border agents at the Texas-New Mexico border who were also murdered. Rob ... the timing fits all the events. I'd be remiss in not including this worst-case scenario, but yeah, you could also be right. However, I have to anticipate all contingencies."

I turned toward Marty, who had buried her head in her hands. I gently wrapped an arm around my wife, pulling her closer to me. The silence in the room lasted forever, it seemed, before Tommy spoke again.

"Stan is convinced he'll head to Kentucky, but that will take a few days. When he gets to Kentucky, we'll be gone.

"Now for some good news! Your friend Donnie reached out to me. He wants you to know that the owner of Chevytothelevee signed a sale contract today. The price was $50K plus 10 percent of the winnings that any of her foals produce."

I fist pumped the air like LA's Kurt Gibson did in the 1988 World Series against the Oakland A's. Tommy's face broke into a huge smile. "Damn—we've got a chance to do it all over again! Can you imagine if we're blessed to have another protégé that repeats what Towers Above, American Pharoah, Justify, and Secretariat accomplished in their careers?"

"That's not all—Chevytothelevee is in heat right now and Donnie's text indicated that tomorrow she'll be introduced to Towers Above!"

I leaned back on the couch and closed my eyes for a moment. First Donnie would bring a teaser stallion into the breeding barn. The teaser stallion would warm things up and prepare Chevytothelevee for TA's entrance.

Towers Above knew the routine. His sense of smell would be stimulated first. Then as he was led to the breeding barn, the memory of past experiences would kick in. He'd begin to get aroused, and by the time he entered the barn, he'd be fully erect. Padding would be placed on Chevytothelevee's back, shielding her from injury from TA's mounting her. Her vagina would have been cleaned and prepared for intercourse. With the assistance of the breeding tech, Towers Above's penis would be guided into place. In an instant, ejaculation would occur, and the mating ceremony would be over. That old saying, "Wham, bam, thank you ma'am" couldn't be more appropriate than when thoroughbreds mate. With no glitches, a foal would enter the world in eleven months and Donnie and Mike would get their first inkling of whether our group had another potential champion to raise and race.

A smile crossed my face just as Marty elbowed me in the side. "Rob, quit daydreaming ... Tommy is talking to you!"

"Rob, get that head shaved ... I'll see you tomorrow." Tommy stood and headed toward the door.

"Yeah, yeah, I was just getting around to doing it. See you tomorrow, Tommy."

"Why'd you lie to him?" Marty asked.

"I wasn't in the mood to argue, Marty! Let's get some sleep. I'm not looking forward to my eye surgery! Good night."

I set my cellphone's alarm for an early wakeup in the morning and then stared at the ceiling for at least an hour.

Identity change sucks! I silently kept thinking.

CHAPTER 11

I arrived at the Ophthalmology Department fifteen minutes before my appointed time. The same physician was in the procedure room, accompanied by a nurse seated on my left side as I was positioned on the operating table. As she began looking for a vein to put in a needle, I reached over toward her with my right hand, covering my forearm to stop her.

"What are you planning to give me?" I asked.

"A sedative—twilight sleep medicine," she responded.

"Nope—I'm not doing twilight sleep. You want twilight, then give me a 10mg Valium. You want me dry, give me some Atropine. Look, my wife had this surgery and she wasn't knocked out. Go ahead and numb my eyes and get on with it! If that doesn't fit your agenda, then our time together here is over!"

As I was digging in my heels, I was also watching the doctor's reaction. Forty years of dealing with patients more than qualified me to read body language—and it was quite obvious that he was pissed off.

The doctor told his assistant to follow him, and they both disappeared from the operating room theater.

After a few minutes, they reappeared—now with additional surgical assistants.

"Okay, here's your Valium and Atropine. Just a small sip of water, please," the nurse stated.

After swallowing the medication, I turned to the doctor with an additional demand.

"That camera up there," I said, pointing at the video camera above the operating table, "turn that damn thing off or better yet, cover it up."

Again, I casually glanced at the doctor, immediately realizing that I'd thwarted him from taking any photographs or videos of me.

Another five minutes passed before what I'd demanded had been done. I then delivered the final ultimatum.

"Which of you folks is the back-up ophthalmologist for today's procedure?"

A woman to my right raised her hand.

"Your name is?"

"My name is Allison, but my friends call me Allie."

"Well, Allie—you're doing my surgery today and he's not!" I pointed directly at the lead surgeon, whose face was now beet red with anger. "You, sir, can leave the operating room—now!"

Checkmate!

Finally, the surgeon turned away from me and left the operating theater.

Thirty minutes later, the operation began and in another forty-five minutes, my surgery was complete. I was now in a recovery room with both eyes bandaged but I sensed Marty's presence by my side—now adorned with a platinum-blonde wig that I obviously couldn't see. Tommy, who was also in the recovery room, complimented Marty on her color choices.

Whatever that surgeon's agenda was, something told me that his actions would jeopardize both Marty and me. Call it divine intervention or blind intuition—I just knew that he was a threat!

Alone in the surgeon's locker room, the frustrated ophthalmologist retrieved his mobile phone and texted:

Not able to get the required documents that you need ...
Sorry for the failure!
If anything changes, I will let you know.

∩ ∩ ∩

"Marty, could I have a few minutes with Rob, please?" Tommy asked.

Marty hesitantly stood, giving my hand a slight squeeze before leaving the recovery room.

"Okay, Rob, what the hell was all that about in the operating room?"

"Tommy—I'm not really certain! I know you probably think I'm paranoid, but that doctor was giving me the wrong vibes. Look, my bullshit detector is pretty keen after all these years of dealing with people—and there was definitely something about him that just wasn't warm and fuzzy.

"You know me—not just my name and appearance but you know ME. You can tell what I'm thinking. You anticipate what I'm about to do and know when I'm going to lose it! I truly believed that this particular eye doctor had an agenda, and it wasn't in my best interests. You had your makeover at Langley—but this is Indy—not exactly the spy capital of the world.

"I'm telling you, that guy may not have recognized me, but he knew I was someone important undergoing a transformation to change my identity. I'm positive he is connected with some person or some entity that is willing to pay handsomely for information about me. That's it in a nutshell—and if that's the definition of paranoia, then so be it!"

I'd finally done it. I got my fears out of my mind and off my chest, and my body finally relaxed for the first time in over twenty-four hours. Then Tommy dropped the hammer.

"You're right, Rob—110% correct!"

My body stiffened. "What … you agree?" I stammered.

"We intelligence folks can readily identify almost all the bad guys. Russia during the Cold War utilized the KGB, and now it is known as the FSB. The East Germans had the Stasi back in the day. The CIA knows about all the different worldwide state intelligence agencies. We try to infiltrate every one of them!

"Now consider this. What if there's a group of individuals worldwide who have no allegiance to any country or state? This group believes they're above any state or national allegiances, and their opinions and beliefs are the only educated concepts that will universally safeguard man's earthly existence! They can and do act to enforce their beliefs on a global basis. Mind you, these folks are extremely wealthy and are convinced that they are the chosen ones who have been selected to protect our planet's human race.

"Rob, I'm being honest with you—it's these folks who may have you on their radar screen. They're an indiscernible group—untouchable, if you will—with resources and connections that frankly, I have no knowledge about.

"The fact that Stan has identified ISIS as a real threat is great. I know about them and know of their philosophy and how they behave. They're easily profiled. Likewise, Antifa members are predictable as well.

"These globalists, as I like to call them, are totally unpredictable and absolutely dangerous. I believe they became very active in America and globally following World War II. What I'm about to share is total conjecture!

"After the 2016 election, their plans for the world became altered. Our current POTUS is a wild card—he's not influenced by their beliefs and certainly is not under their thumb. Do you remember Ron Brown?"

"Vaguely," I answered.

"He was head of the DNC during the 1992 presidential convention, the year that Bill Clinton was elected president. Brown went on to be Secretary of Commerce for Clinton, and led several entourages of entrepreneurs, businessmen, and financiers on trips to Africa, South America, the Middle East, and some Asian countries. These globalists paid dearly for their seats on these trips. Ron Brown was very successful in introducing these folks to new markets—and the quid pro quo for them were their contributions to the Clinton Foundation.

"Loral Space & Communications, an American satellite communications company, was one key company with Chinese connections. Johnny Chung, purportedly a bundler of Chinese contributions, funneled foundation monies through Loral, and in exchange, Loral was allowed to supply satellites for launch by China. Not amazingly, American rocket technology soon became Chinese technology.

"The DOJ began an investigation into Mr. Brown's finances, and he supposedly threatened to do a tell-all, if necessary. Mr. Brown's last trip was to Croatia on a converted Boeing 737. As the Air Force plane approached the Dubrovnik airport, the airport's ILS signal momentarily disappeared or failed ... or whatever.

"Do you remember the movie *Die Hard 2*? That's the movie

where a paramilitary faction shuts down the airport's instrument landing system and they immediately replace it with a substitute system. In the movie, the glide path is altered, and a plane crashes way short of the runway.

"Well, in Croatia, the ILS broadcast signal that was beamed to the plane instantly shifted to a new signal—far away from the airport. The 737 adjusted its heading and unknown to the plane's crew, they were now flying toward a mountain. News reports stated it was a stormy night, but that information was false.

"With the mountainside ILS beacon now guiding the 737, the plane plowed into the mountain and thirty-four passengers perished! Immediately upon impact, the ILS beacon on the mountainside shut down, and the airport's ILS system resumed its normal operation.

"The Air Force's male agent sent to recover the black box— and by the way, it really is an orange box with black stripes—flew back to the US with it. Before it could be delivered to the proper authorities, he met with an untimely death. The black box was never found.

"Ron Brown's body was flown to our capital. Radiographs were taken because a forensic pathologist had discovered a hole in the top of his head—the hole was about the same size as a 45-caliber slug would have made. The original radiographs demonstrated what was described as a 'snowstorm' of lead particles in his brain.

"Guess what? The original radiographs then disappeared. The official cause of death was reported to be death by blunt force trauma.

"Team members of the forensic group were divided in their thoughts about what was going on—these same staff members were subsequently moved to different duty stations and their careers were ruined. The entire investigation ended and quietly disappeared from the limelight.

"Anyway…Once we get you moved out west, if you get a chance, there's a good book to read about the entire incident. If nothing else, go online to Google and search all the articles about Ron Brown and then read them."

"So you're saying the Clintons ordered his death!"

"Nope! They didn't have to. It's my belief that the group of global elites took care of Ron Brown. I know there's a huge list of people who have met their demise from many different causes - and they all had an association with the Clintons. C'mon Rob! It's my belief the Clintons are innocent!"

I couldn't see Tommy, and it was probably just as well. What he said was totally unexpected.

And I thought I was paranoid, I silently said to myself.

"You said all of this started after World War II—how so?"

"Rob, President Eisenhower put the message out in his farewell speech to America. He warned about the Military Industrial Complex, and the growing power and influence that this specific segment of our society was amassing. The only additional economic group to join that late '50's complex is our modern-day 'technology businesses' group.

"Look, Rob, this all may sound like something made up by Marvel Comics. If I had hard evidence, I'd tell you—and I guarantee that if I'm thinking it, there are a whole lot of others above my pay grade who believe the same thing."

I imagined Tommy could tell he'd just added another layer of stress to my life. He gently wrapped his hand around mine and spoke one final time.

"Now do you understand how important this identity change is?"

Tommy had no idea that the head of the DIA agreed with him. I assumed he certainly had never shared these thoughts with anyone other than his son Steven.

 HAPTER 12

B ecause time was of the essence, both of my eyes had been operated on at the same time—and it was truly amazing how well I could see after the surgery. It even amazed me how well I could read wearing a pair of Marty's slightly magnified over-the-counter reading glasses. I quickly realized that after wearing glasses for forty-plus years, I needed to break the habit of pushing them back up on my nose. I knew it would take some time, especially because my right index finger kept automatically poking at the nonexistent eyeglasses no longer sliding down my nose!

I was tired and tried to take a nap, but in less than half an hour, Tommy was again knocking on our door. There would be no nap for me!

Tommy was holding a packet of documents that he dumped onto the coffee table. Marty and I sat down with Tommy, and we began wading through our new personal documents. Among the items were:

- New social security cards
- New American Express credit cards
- New Medicare Supplement cards
- New birth certificates
- New 401k identification paperwork
- New motor vehicle insurance papers

The only other important documents missing were our new driver licenses, which in my case would require me to shave my head, grow a mustache or even a beard, and perhaps add a hairpiece.

Gone was my dental license and association membership documents.

As far as the American Dental Association was concerned, Dr. Rob Becker had disappeared or died. My memberships in the American College and International College of Dentists had also ended.

Tommy grabbed my arm and looking at my wife, said, "C'mon. Marty, you can come too and watch how it's done."

"Close your eyes, Rob," Tommy said, while turning on the hair clippers. He covered the sink's drain and began to trim my hair. When he stopped, I wiped the hair off my face. As I gazed into the mirror, I now understood what a Marine haircut looked like. I saw Marty covering her mouth with a hand, but her eyes gave away her emotions—she was silently laughing.

After I was left with stubble on my head, I barked out, "Okay, give me the shaving cream." I needed to do the rest myself. I remembered a conversation I'd had years previously with a jeweler friend of mine whose father had cancer and was undergoing chemo treatments that caused him to lose his hair. As a gesture of solidarity, my friend shaved his head to show his love for his father.

Now I was doing this for someone I loved. "Okay, Mark, this is for you, my friend," I quietly mumbled.

Using a Gillette razor with a double safety guard, it took just thirty minutes for my head to look like a cue ball. I quickly realized that my sister, who swore my head was shaped like a football as a result of repeatedly ramming me into a wall when I was an infant, was right all along! I glanced at Marty and all her attempts at hiding her emotions had disappeared. She was doubled over with laughter. I then glanced at Tommy, who quickly turned away—but not before I caught a glimpse of a huge smile on his face!

"Ha ha, go ahead and laugh, you two!"

"Sorry about that, Rob."

"Tomorrow, everything else we need to get done will be done here in this suite. I talked with Steven about your security concerns, and he agrees that all future work should be done away from the limelight. He's having Stan do a thorough review of the ophthalmologist you have concerns about, as well. We're almost done with everything, so get some rest now."

∩ ∩ ∩

Stan got Steven's text about the Indy facility later that same day. Besides Langley and Indianapolis, there was a West Coast facility in Salem, Oregon. Stan asked the IT staff to create a computer report on every individual who had been physically transformed in the past ten years. His rationale for choosing a ten-year period was because that was how long the ophthalmologist at Indy had been employed there. It took the computer about two hours to run the report on every person before Rob who had transitioned into a new appearance and identity.

During those ten years, twenty-eight individuals had undergone transformations at the Indy facility, and of that number, four subsequently died. Autopsy results on three of the four determined that cancer was the cause of death. The other death resulted from an automobile accident, one in which there was no other vehicle involved. Weather was not a factor in the accident;

the road was dry. For Stan, that didn't mean a deer hadn't run in front of the driver, thus causing the fatal accident, but he still needed to get more information from the accident scene. The police had determined that the driver misjudged his need to slow down, even though it was clearly marked to reduce speed, due to the extreme curve ahead in the road. There were no skid marks, but the investigation report indicated that part of the guardrail had penetrated the windshield and decapitated the driver.

Stan almost closed up shop for the night, but for some reason, he decided to call the sheriff in the county where the accident happened. He asked the sheriff about the accident site and was told that accidents occur there all the time—and that in fact, over the past ten years, there had been more than thirty accidents at that curve in the road. Invariably. the guard rail was totally de-stroyed. Stan asked one last question.

"How many drivers or passengers had been injured or killed?"

"We've only had that one fatality. There have been injuries, a broken this or that, along with contusions and cuts, but just the one fatality," the sheriff replied.

"Did that strike you as odd at the time, Sheriff?" Stan asked.

"Well, since it was just last year and now that you've asked that question, I'm going to answer yes. I just never thought about analyzing it in that fashion."

"When I read about the accidents, I noticed that the guardrail was destroyed each and every time. Were there any other incidents where the guardrail broke away and pierced the windshield?" Stan asked.

"I've only been sheriff for three years, but the answer is no. That curve has been there for years. It can't be re-routed because of the terrain and water drainage in the area. The Department of Transportation purposely designed and installed a specific type of guardrail at that site. It's designed to cushion and safely deflect collisions so that the vehicles don't roll over and cause the driver or passengers, who might not be wearing a seatbelt, to suffer broken necks. I hate to admit this, but we're so used to folks crashing at this site that perhaps I should have taken a closer look at this particular accident. I'm truly sorry."

"Sheriff, that's no problem. Don't beat yourself up over this. I've got a few other things to check out, and maybe after that I'll come and visit your county. Thank you, Sheriff."

The next program Stan asked his techs to run was a financial report. He requested a print-out of every employee's personal finances for the past ten years, specifically asking to have the program flag any extreme income variances of more than fifty percent among these individuals. It was now late evening and finally at 2:00 a.m. the next day, Stan got the finished report.

Stan immediately went to the ophthalmologist's name and sure enough, the doctor's name had been highlighted. Stan looked at the date and amount flagged, and quickly realized that his eyes weren't being deceived. The doctor's net wealth increased by a half million dollars exactly one week after the fatal accident occurred.

At 3:00 a.m., Stan messaged Steven.

It read:

Have security at Indy detain Dr. Vance immediately! Transfer him—NOW—to Wright Patterson for future transport to D.C. and then to Langley in the a.m.
Share this information with Tommy and tell him thanks!

Stan next messaged the director of the FBI with the details of the case and asked for an investigation to begin. He left out the ophthalmologist's name. Dr. Vance was in his possession now, and the CIA would handle his interrogation.

# CHAPTER 13

When Tommy awoke early the following morning, he checked his messages.

Well, I'll be damned! Rob's intuition was right. I've created a monster, Tommy thought.

After I woke up, the protective eye patches came off and Marty and I sat down for a quiet breakfast. We made small talk while circling around the question of how many more procedures needed to be done in order to complete our metamorphoses.

Again, a knock on the door interrupted us.

A group of people entered the suite with a cartful of various containers to be used for a purpose that neither Marty nor I had a clue about.

In the kitchen area of our suite, a tarp was unrolled and a chair was placed in the center. I was told to come and sit down on the chair and was quickly wrapped in protective plastic. The only parts of my body exposed were my head, neck, and shoulders. Patches were again put on my eyes.

One of the techs approached with what looked like a face-shaped plastic mold, which she pressed against my face. It was too small, and a few seconds later she tried a larger mold that fit better. In the space around my nostrils were two slits for straws to stick out of the mold, which would allow me to breathe. She nodded to the other two members of the team who began mixing what I quickly thought was alginate, a material I'd used for years when taking impressions of a patient's teeth.

"God, Marty, they're going to make an impression of my face," I said as one tech took the cold material and began smearing it into every nook and cranny on the front of my face and head. Another tech pressed the mold filled with the same material onto my face while shoving the straws up both nostrils. I felt a sense of suffocation before the tech in charge barked out an order!

"Breathe, dammit!"

Thirty seconds passed before the techs began to pry the impression off my head. A tech who appeared to be the supervisor carved away some of the mold before pressing it back in place. The techs then began to fit another mold to the back half of my head—almost instantly, an impression of the back of my head began.

Thank God that's over with, I thought. But they weren't finished.

The two techs left the suite, no doubt going someplace to create plaster models of my head. Shortly following their exit, two new techs came into the suite.

The lead tech directed her staff to begin fitting me with prefabricated neck and upper shoulder molds. After determining which molds fit the best, the plastic covering over the upper portion of my shoulders was cut away.

Good God, are they going to take full body impressions and make a statue of me? I silently wondered.

Fifteen minutes passed and the two techs who left earlier rejoined the group, and all four began furiously mixing alginate to begin the neck/shoulder impressions.

What a waste of good seaweed, I thought to myself while beginning to laugh!

The lead tech shouted, "Stop laughing!" which I knew was intended for me, but Marty also quickly froze in place!

After another half an hour, the whole process was finally completed, and the suite was cleaned. The group of technicians left without uttering a word of thanks. For the next ten minutes, I stuck Q-tips up my nose to remove alginate that was now stuck to the hairs in my nostrils.

"Brother, that was pleasant," I sarcastically said to Marty. "How come I got that treatment, and you didn't?"

"Because she's not the main target—you're the one wearing a bullseye," said Tommy, who had entered the suite as the techs were leaving.

"Do you mind telling me what that was all about?" I asked.

"You'll find out in due time, that is if everything fits properly," Tommy replied.

"C'mon, dammit. Quit screwing around with me!" I shouted.

"Tomorrow, Rob ..."

I'd heard that cryptic type of reply from Tommy before and knew it was useless to pry any further. Instead, I spent the rest of the day reading *Towers' Progeny*, a suspense novel written by an author named Buck Brannon—the man I gave the okay to author a book about Towers Above.

∩ ∩ ∩

Sunrise at the New Mexico/Texas border was brilliant. Muhammad made a cup of coffee, and after determining as close as he could which direction was east, began his morning prayers using a prayer rug borrowed from his host. He was not at peace on this morning, knowing he was about to shave off his beard and mustache. These adornments were his fitrah, part of the natural order of Islam—an order patterned after the prophet Muhammad, who had both forms of facial hair.

A Muslim man's mustache is generally trimmed, but the beard is left in its natural state. As the prophet Muhammad had a beard and mustache, this style naturally becomes a Hadith—and without Hadith(s), there would be no teachings from the prophet and thus no Quran.

Today, he begged Allah for forgiveness for what he was about to do with his facial hair, and asked for strength as he set out on his quest of revenge.

What Muhammad didn't have was intelligence. Not intellect intelligence, but an intelligence network of ISIS compatriots who would have been surveilling Woodlands Park during the beginning of its Spring Meet. Yes, one of his brothers was awaiting Muhammad's arrival, but he had no idea that Dr. Rob Becker wasn't even in the Commonwealth.

Muhammad's host gave him a set of car keys, along with a fake Kentucky driver's license. However, the Kentucky license plate was legitimate, as were the car's registration papers. The car was registered in Kentucky's Fayette County, known as a progressive home to a significant contingent of Middle Easterners.

During the Obama presidency, many Arabic immigrants were welcomed to specific US states—and many of these immigrants maintained their Salafist-jihadi philosophy. Every religion has its zealots, but only the Islamic religion demands that if someone doesn't believe that Allah is their God, then that individual must either be enslaved or killed. That is the Muslim edict.

By noon, he and Alia set off on their journey. Alia was wearing jeans, fashionable athletic shoes, and a University of Kentucky T-shirt. Muhammad was also Westernized. He still looked like someone from the Middle East, but without the facial hair, he was now looking somewhat politically correct—and that was all he wanted.

Muhammad no longer looked like he was a member of the Taliban.

CHAPTER 14

What I assumed was our last night in Indianapolis was anything but comforting. I wasn't certain if Marty and I would return home one final time or if we'd immediately leave for Oral, South Dakota. The thought of not having a chance to say one last goodbye to our home, which held so many memories, was disheartening. There was no sleep for me that night.

At the break of dawn Marty asked, "Are you awake?"

"I haven't slept—even a bit," I answered.

The phone rang and I picked up.

"You awake, Rob?" Tommy asked.

"All night, Tommy ... all damn night!"

"The tech is on her way to your suite ... I'll be there shortly."

Sure enough, a knock on the door followed the phone call almost immediately. For the second day in a row, she pushed a cart into the room, but there was nothing on it like the previous day. Tommy walked into the room and grabbed a seat on the couch—sporting a huge grin on his face. The chief technician again placed a chair in the kitchenette area and summoned me to sit on it. I complied, as she placed a blindfold on my face to protect my eyes.

The next thing I knew, I felt her place some kind of garment or hat on my head. It only took a moment to realize that it was a very precise fit. On the back of my head, toward the mid-level of my neck, I swore I felt something soft just barely touch my neck.

Then I heard the sound of Marty's laughter in the background.

"Okay Tommy. What the hell is going on?" I demanded.

The technician removed the blindfold and handed me a makeup mirror, telling me ... go ahead and take a look."

I first looked at Marty and she was beaming with happiness. I then turned to Tommy and he was shaking his head side to side while also laughing. Finally, I decided to take a peek.

On top of my head was a toupee—or what some folks might have called a wig. It was totally grey in color, and in the back was a pony tail. I must have stared at it for half a minute.

I looked at Marty and I could tell that she knew—that I knew—that she was responsible for the pony tail. She and I had been on a buffalo tour and steak cookout in Custer State Park a few years earlier and our guide was a cowboy in every sense of the word…and the dude was sporting a pony tail!

I remembered calling Marty out because I caught her staring at the cowboy during the entire tour. I recalled saying to her, "You liked that look—that cowboy pony tail look!"

Marty and Tommy had set me up, and darned if after about a half dozen more looks in the mirror, I had to admit that I liked it too.

"Okay sir, one last thing," the technician said. "Please sit up straight, and no slouching."

She began to place the first part of what seemed like a jigsaw puzzle-like contraption on my shoulders, with it rising slightly up my neck around the C-7/C-8 vertebrae. The apparatus design consisted of several pieces held together with powerful tiny magnets.

"Now try to raise your arms above your head," the tech ordered.

I couldn't do it, no matter how hard I tried. Every time I tried to lift my arms up, the exoskeleton prevented me from doing what she asked.

"As you can now see—you're restricted from any activities that require you to raise your arms. You'll get used to it," she advised me in a matter-of-fact manner. Not seeming to care what I thought, she then began fitting the two neck pieces, which again were held together by some very powerful magnets. The two puzzle pieces locked into place at the invisible line separating the dorsal and ventral parts of my upper body. Magnets attached the two neck pieces to the much larger shoulder exoskeleton.

I noticed that at my jawline, the shell-like structure transitioned from an immobile material to a softer, more flexible material which allowed me to move my head slightly forward and backwards, as well as side to side.

After about five minutes of wearing my new cosmetic prosthesis, I realized just how poor my posture had become over the years. My neck muscles were now fatigued from their new stretched positions. I began to feel pain shooting up to the top of my head from both sternocleidomastoid muscles—the matching right and left muscles that basically hold everyone's head steady on their torso. I instantly realized I was clenching my teeth together. I now realized just how miserable my temporomandibular joint disorder patients felt. For me, there was no way to cross-fiber massage my neck muscles to lessen the pain.

"Marty ... would you get me a couple of Tylenols, please!" I pleaded.

When I swallowed the tablets, I quickly realized that I'd also be somewhat restricted in the amount of food I could stuff into my mouth since swallowing was also now slightly restricted. I turned my entire body toward Tommy and began my tirade.

"What is this for and when do I have to wear it ... because I can tell you right now, it's a pain in the ass!"

"Well, Rob, we're pretty certain that there's at least one assassin, if not more, coming for you. These folks are into throat-slashing and they love doing it. That exoskeleton material is cad-cam generated. It's lightweight, and we've developed a process to bake on some pigmented skin-like material to make it look natural."

The technician handed me a hand mirror. I held it up and surveyed myself in more detail while thinking, *Now I know how turtles must feel.*

"Well, I'll be damned!" was all I could say.

"So, Rob ... I'm pretty sure you'll want to wear this anytime you're out and about. You can't count on me being your lifeguard every day. In fact, I'll probably be the first target of the assassin's wrath. Now mind you, that material won't let a knife get anywhere near your actual skin. So, if anyone attempts to slash your throat, they'll quickly realize that something isn't right and then they'll try and stab you to death. When we get out West, we're going to work on your self-defense training. Now, do you have any other questions about your new prosthetics?"

I started to try to shake my head, but quickly again realized that my range of motion was limited.

"Rob, when I'm done with your training, you'll move like a Ninja," Tommy stated while laughing...and knowing he had been less than truthful.

# CHAPTER 15

"Get your belongings packed up—we're out of here tomorrow," Tommy said as he was leaving the suite.

I looked at Marty and her gaze met mine. It was obvious she was thinking the same thing that I was. "What ... we're finished ... really?" I walked into the bathroom and stared at myself in the mirror. My mustache was nowhere near completion, nor was the goatee.

We both began packing our possessions in total silence. The one question still unanswered was: "Were we going back home to Kentucky or to our new home in South Dakota?"

We got our answer at 4:00 the next morning. All of our belongings and Tommy's were collected and quickly moved to the roof of the building. An Indiana National Guard Black Hawk helicopter was loaded with all of us and our possessions, in what seemed to be less than two minutes ... and then we were airborne.

"The element of surprise, Rob, just in case the ophthalmologist wasn't the only one," Tommy said.

What I didn't know was that there were three other Blackhawks in the formation, about twenty miles due south of Indy. All four of them split off from each other, after ten minutes of close contiguous flight. If someone was tracking us, they had a 25 percent chance of guessing which helicopter we were on.

And the answer as to whether we'd be going home soon became apparent.

Steven had been busy during the time we were away. He gathered Marty's and my clothing and shoes that we'd need for South Dakota's four seasons. He also went through some personal items he thought we might cherish and packed them up—but nothing that tied us to our past lives was included. That meant that any pictures of family members remained in Kentucky.

All of the items collected by Steven were already awaiting us in Oral, South Dakota.

The Kentucky home would remain our possession, just unoccupied! If we thought of something that we wanted in the future, then the CIA would send agents to fetch it and approve, before sending it to us.

Marty had an Apple Watch and a compatible Apple cell phone with a compass that told her we were heading north. She leaned toward me and rested her head on my shoulder and began to weep softly. The reality that our true home was now off limits bore in, and the mental anguish that she'd been suppressing was now unleashed. This hurt me, and I was also close to losing my composure. After all, I was to blame for everything.

We landed in Ft. Wayne, Indiana—the city's municipal airport and location for an air wing of the Indiana National Guard. We were immediately shuttled to another Air Force plane, this one an executive-type jet. After about twenty minutes, we again were airborne. Marty checked the phone's compass once the plane reached cruising altitude, and showed me that we were heading west.

I guessed we'd be somewhere in South Dakota in a couple of hours. I'd previously Googled Air Force bases located in that state, and the closest one to Oral was Ellsworth Air Force Base on the outskirts of Rapid City. When we landed, Tommy confirmed my thoughts.

"Rob and Marty, welcome to Ellsworth Air Force Base."

We deplaned and were directed to a transit van. After exiting the Air Force property, a second shell game took place. The van we were in was joined by three identical vans and all proceeded onto Interstate 90, with the vans changing positions and lanes at least thirty times before each splitting off and heading in different directions. Marty tried keeping up with the compass, but after about a dozen changes in direction, she finally gave up.

Finally, ours was the lone van on the road and we were heading to Oral, South Dakota and our new home.

$$\cap \cap \cap$$

Muhammad and Alia passed through the track's security magnetometer tower without incident.

Ted had technologically moved beyond the wand-type magnetometer checks years earlier. His philosophy was "Why not have the best?" and he was not going to make the track liable for his stupidity or stubbornness. Some of the track's trustees and directors disagreed with his decision—and Ted told them they had the option of firing him. Nobody suggested exercising that choice.

Muhammad wasn't about to test the track's electronic technology. This trip was a scouting excursion, and he hoped it would be the only one.

His targets were the men in the caramel-colored sports coats, grey slacks, and name tags with the Woodlands Park "WP" logo. Anyone with those brown coats would be fair game.

He and Alia were dressed in business casual clothing. Their physical Mediterranean features were still obvious, but the

Midwest attire more than balanced out their appearance from the suspicious looks of other track patrons. As long as they stayed together, the thought of the two of them being a threat was somewhat blunted.

Before the first race, they treated themselves to some Kentucky cuisine. Their liquid refreshment was, of course, non-alcoholic. The first station they positioned themselves at was near the tunnel area leading out to the track. Two of the park's men in WP brown coats were making small talk with patrons. Alia waited patiently, finally approaching one of them and pointing to a date in the track's program before asking her question.

"This coming Saturday is Towers Above day—will Dr. Rob Becker and the other owners be here for autographs?" she asked of Louie and Ned.

Louie was quick to answer. "Ma'am, usually TA gallops in front of the grandstand back and forth a couple of times, and will stop for photos near the Winners Circle. I'm not sure if the owners will even be here."

"Thank you," Alia said.

Next, they casually walked over to the Clock Tower portion of the track.

Muhammad noticed that one of the brown coats was more than willing to chit-chat. The name tag on his coat indicated he was William.

"Bill ... one question, if I may. On Saturday will the owners of Towers Above make themselves available for meet and greet or autographs?"

"I'm not certain about that, sir." Bill turned to another brown-coated employee.

"Tom, do you think the owners of Towers Above will be here

on Saturday?"

Tom was pulling the crowd control strap, which was Bill's signal to also pull his strap on the other side of the paddock crossover. He gave Bill a look of irritation, as if to say, "Why are you asking me that question?" A third WP brown coat, named Dwayne, responded. "We really never know who's going to show up! You folks need to come back on Saturday."

Muhammad and Alia strolled along the outside of the saddling paddock until they reached another entrance gate and a brown coat named Len.

Len seemed to have quite a following. He would ask parents if it was okay to take their child out into the paddock to stand near one of the thoroughbreds. After the first race was finished, there was a lull in traffic at the gate. Alia asked the question.

"Excuse me, sir ... Len, is it? I'm a huge fan of Towers Above and I noticed in the program that he'll be here this coming Saturday. Do you think any of the owners will be here? I'd love to get some autographs."

Len gave her the once-over and determined she was sincere.

"I'm not sure if they'll be here. I know Towers Above will be, but whether he's accompanied by Rob, Donnie, or Mike is uncertain. I saw Rob Becker on Opening Saturday, but I haven't seen him since then, which is unusual."

Alia thanked Len and turned away, followed by Muhammad. Muhammad silently said to himself, *He's ours now!*

Alia and Muhammad waited until the tenth race. She began walking toward the employee parking lot while Muhammad went to fetch their car and move it as close as possible to the same parking lot.

Alia intended to casually place a GPS transmitter on Len's

car. If he challenged her about being in the wrong parking lot, she would simply tell him that her sister worked in the clubhouse restaurant and that she had given her a ride to the track.

About half an hour later, Woodlands Park's race card was finished, and in another thirty minutes, Len exited the employee bus and headed for his car. He never bothered to look around, and didn't see Alia keeping pace about twenty yards behind him. She watched as Len punched his key fob to unlock the car and its lights blinked. She quickened her pace to close the distance between them. As he turned left to get in the driver's side, Alia swept in and placed the magnetized GPS transmitter on the underside of his car.

Len had no clue that his life had just become very complicated.

HAPTER 16

Oral, South Dakota was due south and just east of the Black Hills mountains.

The ride from Ellsworth Air Force Base to Oral was pretty much a silent one. Marty was riding in front—her claustrophobia made back seat traveling a definite no! Both Marty and I assumed this would be a homecoming of sorts for Tommy. The question would be just how warm a reception he'd receive. I tried to break the ice once we exited I-90.

"Pretty much just farmland, huh?"

"Yep," was his terse response.

I could tell immediately it was not the time for more questions. When folks answer with a single word, it usually means they're in no mood to talk.

The rolling South Dakota landscape was deceiving, and I had no idea we were almost at three thousand feet in altitude. I sat back and tried to imagine what Tika's place would look like.

It's just like driving west from the Kansas/Colorado border. Every mile traveled slowly takes you higher—until the outline of the Rocky Mountains appears in the distance. When you finally butt up against the mountain range, you're already a mile high, I thought silently to myself.

I'd already searched the internet about the town of Oral and sure enough, the town was named after a postal worker's child whose middle name was Oral. I chuckled to myself while thinking about Marty's relatives who lived in West Chester, Ohio. Similarly, that town was named after a postman, Chester, who lived west of the post office.

We crossed a set of railroad tracks and passed several houses when Tommy suddenly announced we were at our new home. We turned onto a dirt road and traveled about three hundred yards more before stopping in front of a modest ranch house. It appeared to be a two-bedroom house with probably fifteen hundred square feet of livable space. There was construction underway on one side of the house—an obvious attempt to add more living space. The plywood had not as yet been covered with brick, but it was under roof and shingled. I failed to realize that I was looking at our new living quarters.

Tommy pulled into the driveway and got out of the car, heading to where Tika was waiting. She opened the front screen door with a broad smile on her face, as she slowly advanced toward Tommy. They embraced each other, but their only sign of affection was pecks on each other's cheek.

Tika turned toward us and escorted Marty inside, while Tommy and I strolled around the grounds of the home.

"I gotta say … that wasn't a very enthusiastic greeting you got, my friend," I dared to remark.

"Appreciate the analysis, Rob," Tommy sarcastically replied. "I want you and Marty to stay isolated for a couple of weeks. You need to fill out that mustache and goatee while I mosey around town and spread the word that you're my uncle and aunt visiting Oral from Indiana. Hell, just my being back will be the talk of the town for the next few days. The construction area is your new quarters, Rob—and don't thank me. Stan told me that POTUS is personally footing the bill. He really admires what you did out in

Portland ... and I do too."

Tika escorted us to our still-under-construction living quarters. Up against one wall was our king-sized bed, recently shipped to Oral, from Kentucky. The bathroom was totally finished and I could tell from looking at Marty's face that the colors of the tile and paint, along with the walk-in shower and soaking tub, were perfect choices. Tommy had done his HGTV homework well!

"Oh, Tika, your choices are magnificent!" Marty said excitedly. Tika turned toward Tommy, smiling warmly.

"I had a good friend help with the choices," she answered.

I could feel the temperature in the room go from freezing to lukewarm ... and that was a positive sign.

The rest of the day and evening, including during dinner, was spent getting to know Tika. When Marty and I retired for the evening, Tommy was making a bed for himself on the couch.

I guess lukewarm will have to do for the time being, I thought.

In the middle of the night, Marty woke up with indigestion and asked me to get some milk to calm her stomach. As I walked through the family room heading to the kitchen, I couldn't help but notice that Tommy wasn't on the couch. I continued to the kitchen, got the milk, and while returning to the bedroom, paused for a few seconds in the living room. The sounds coming from the master bedroom were unmistakable.

The temperature in the house had moved from lukewarm to sauna hot. A huge smile broke out on my face. All was right in Oral, South Dakota!

# CHAPTER 17

Charles got the call about 8:00 p.m.

"Sir, this is William at the track. I've been reviewing today's videos and there are a couple of patrons I'd like you to view."

"Is it something I can look at tomorrow, or should I come in now?" Charles asked.

"Sir, I'd feel a lot more comfortable if you'd come in now and take a look … please." William quickly replied.

"I'm on my way."

Heading to Woodlands Park, Charles figured it had to be pretty important, since security had been raised to the highest alert level two weeks earlier because of recent ISIS activity at America's southern border. Ted had given him a detailed description of what had taken place a few years earlier, when both the Ohio Stadium and Woodlands Park were targeted.

As Charles wheeled himself into the audio-visual room, he spotted William and Ted.

"I'm sorry, Charles, Will thinks we had a scouting party here today. I'm going to let him do his briefing, then we'll decide on what our options should be. Go ahead, Will," Ted directed.

"Well, as you both know, our system screens for individuals demonstrating Mediterranean/Middle Eastern characteristics. We had ten patrons who fit that description and were present at the track today. Eight of the ten either had reserved seats or were in the clubhouse with a specific group. I'm going to roll through each of these eight individuals and their actions during today's race card."

Will proceeded to run video footage that switched from camera to camera, showing the actions of each patron from the time they entered through the turnstile until they left the track's property.

Every one of the eight patrons acted like normal thoroughbred aficionados in every way. Any interactions with track employees were either with food vendors or betting exchange attendants. There were no extended conversations with any employees.

The review of each individual took about 30 minutes.

"Okay, now I'm going to present video of the other two patrons—and they seemed less interested in the races and more interested in our personnel. It appears that they're also a team that is working together."

Will started with video of Alia and Muhammad entering the turnstiles—the footage then followed them from one venue location to the next. The video showed them pause at the tunnel and then a more extended pause at the side gate. What was notably absent was the placing of any wagers or apparent interest in any of the thoroughbreds by either of them. Also, the track's daily program that they appeared to share was hardly opened. Will next voiced specific concerns.

"I also want you to watch the male and his continuous looking around throughout their time at the track. It's almost as if he was searching for our video cameras. Now I'll admit, nothing they did was extraordinarily clandestine—and they took no photographs. Other than talking with our Brown Coats, they acted normal. What was abnormal, though, was their lack of activity we generally see with traditional patrons in the course of their visit during an active race card."

"Will, do you have any footage of them when they exit through the turnstile?" Charles asked.

"Yes, sir, and that's what really raised the red flag for me. First I'll show the male suspect and his activity outside the track and finish with the female's actions after exiting the track."

All three men watched as Muhammad went to his vehicle and instead of exiting from the visitor parking lot, moved his car to another spot in the same lot.

The next frame of footage showed Alia heading toward the employee parking lot and lollygagging until the employee transport bus arrived at the lot. She started walking again, following one of the Brown Coat employees as he walked to his car. Then, further down the row past where the Brown Coat's car was parked, she stopped and waited until that particular employee drove off. She then left the employee parking lot, hurrying to her companion's car in visitor's parking—and in a spot now conveniently closer to the employee lot.

"Can you run that last segment of the video one more time, Will?" Charles asked.

"Certainly," he answered. Within just a few seconds, the video began to replay.

When the footage was at the point when Alia placed a tracking mechanism on Len's car, Ted urgently shouted, "Stop the video!

"Can you run that at a slower speed and enlarge the video?"

Will complied … several times. Each time he enlarged the picture, stopping finally at the exact moment Alia reached down and placed the GPS device. That particular angle of the camera made it appear that she had stumbled slightly. Charles was the one who shouted next. "Freeze it!

"That's not a stumble! What the hell is she doing?" Charles stammered.

There was total silence in the room for thirty seconds before Charles spoke again. "Damn, she put something on the employee's car!"

Ted immediately responded. "A tracking device—I'd bet on it!"

"Great work, William. Can you blow up the video and give us some frontal views of their faces?"

"Way ahead of you, boss." It took Will just a few seconds before photos of Alia and Muhammad popped up.

Ted pulled out his mobile phone and dialed Steven's number—it was almost 11:00 p.m. —but Steven answered. Ted explained what had happened at the track and asked about the best way to transfer the video images of his two suspects to Langley. Steven told Ted he'd call him back.

It was now after 11:00 p.m. The ringing of his mobile phone woke Stan.

It took only five minutes for the CIA to electronically tap into the track's video system. Will not only shared his photos, but also ran the video one last time for the analysts at Langley. The data transfer was complete. Stan thanked Ted and Charles, adding one last caveat.

"Whoever that employee is … I'd get some security out to his home immediately and bring him in from the cold—permanently!"

Ted looked at Charles, asking, "So, who is that employee?"

Charles looked toward Will for the answer, knowing he wouldn't have to repeat the question.

"That's Len Jansen. He has worked at a paddock side gate for years."

"I'm on it, Ted." Charles wheeled his motorized chair out

of the room, heading to the human resource office to get Len's phone number—and to call the police and get them dispatched to Len's home.

Charles placed calls to both Len's mobile and landline numbers with no success.

The police had no success either. Ted had the officers break into the house, but other than Len's dog, no one was home. It was SEC basketball tournament weekend and Len was elsewhere.

The police relayed the information to Ted, who then shared it with Charles. Ted also texted the information to Steven.

Stan received a text from Steven and sat down on the side of the bed to contemplate what would happen next—and every time, he came to the same conclusion. Another evil act would be committed in the name of Allah, and the majority of Americans would just shrug it off.

# CHAPTER 18

After the race card finished, Len went to the Silver Ladle restaurant and had dinner and drinks with his best friend John while watching basketball. The two televised games that evening were semi-finals, with the league championship game scheduled for Sunday.

If it had been a few years earlier, I would have also been sitting at the bar with Len and his friend.

But alas, 2016 came and went…

…as did our friendship.

Back then for me, the thought of our country's continued divisive intervention in the Middle East for another four years or more was too painful to even contemplate. The previous POTUS had drawn red lines in the sand and continuously redrew them over and over again. The 2016 presidential choice was simple for me. Even though both candidates were severely flawed, my choice to support Trump was not that difficult. I no longer had a party affiliation.

As far as I was concerned, the party system had contributed and would continue contributing to America's demise.

Following the election, no matter how many positive Trump policies I believed in and tried to explain, Len always had an opinion that countered my beliefs. It got to be that no matter how much I argued, our conversations always became politicized. I always sensed the presence of conflict hanging like a storm over our heads. Our get-togethers became fewer and fewer until finally, friendship was no longer an option. What was even sadder was that this same type of fracturing of precious friendships was occurring across every state in our republic.

Only historians henceforth would be able to judge how much divisiveness was created during these times and whether it was worth it or not. My personal belief was that the Portland insurrection was just the opening salvo of civil strife in America.

On this particular evening, Alia and Muhammad waited patiently in their car—in a spot close to where Len had parked his car. Muhammad knew this was likely going to be his only opportunity to get information about me, via the interrogation of Len. He also knew that returning to the racetrack would be fruitless and almost certainly result in his capture. After all, he had watched the track's security cameras follow Alia's movements as well as his own during their day at the track.

It was nearing 11:00 when Len headed back to his car. Alia, sitting behind the steering wheel with the car door open, again began her "having a baby" routine ... complete with shrieking and "my water has broken." Len stopped in his tracks and went to assist her—but in a couple of seconds was on the ground and knocked unconscious. Alia got out and helped Muhammad load Len onto the back seat of their car.

Muhammad put restraints on Len and duct-taped his lips shut. In another five minutes, the couple, with their hostage, were on the way to their secret home in central Kentucky.

The Kentucky State Police issued an all-points bulletin for Len's automobile, and in less than an hour, it was found in the restaurant's parking lot.

Detectives began questioning restaurant employees, who

confirmed that Len had been there.

The police had no choice but to enlist the media's help, because no one knew the name of Len's friend, and Len had picked up the tab for their evening's purchases.

John saw the news report and immediately called the police. Detectives arrived within minutes to interview him.

Hidden from the media was the ultimate reason for the importance of finding Len quickly. Nighttime turned into daylight, and Len was still missing. For Ted and Charles, it was just a matter of when and where Len's body would turn up.

Stan was kept abreast of the activities and immediately released photos of Alia and Muhammad to all his field agents and to police departments throughout the US.

The CIA had photoshopped the photo of Muhammad—now complete with facial hair—creating an ISIS warrior. The photo matched the picture CIA agents had obtained when Muhammad was captured in Mosul. These pictures were also circulated, in case the terrorist decided to un-Westernize his appearance.

Stan texted Tommy about the situation; he had no choice but to inform me of what was now happening. Stan needed to know just how much Len knew about my personal life.

Needless to say, I was shocked and heartbroken. I immediately thought about the members of my family and questioned anew their safety. Tommy was insistent that all of the agents had reported no suspicious activity and reassured me that each agent was more than qualified and understood the gravity of the situation.

Len knew where I lived—we had shared family information on many occasions while playing numerous rounds of golf over the years. He knew about my favorite vacation spots, but not about my most recent trip to the Badlands and Yellowstone Park.

He also knew Marty and I enjoyed cruises in the Caribbean.

It was now Stan's call. He ultimately had to make the decision whether to keep Marty and me in Oral, South Dakota or to move us to a secondary location that had been picked out weeks earlier. Stan also notified Steven to stay where he was while he worked on a ruse to lure Muhammad and his companion to my Kentucky home—hopefully resulting in their capture.

Stan had a late evening discussion with Tommy, and it was decided that the western states were expansive enough to hide me and Marty—besides, Stan knew that Tommy had earned a respite from conflict. Oral, South Dakota was his reward—and it was now my purgatory.

# CHAPTER 19

Muhammad didn't have an elaborate holding area such as a CIA safe house might have in America. It was just a basic animal cage, only man-sized. It was situated in the basement of the home where no one could hear Len's screams. Len was an infidel, a non-believer, and at least for a short period of time, he'd be a slave.

There were no amenities. There were pet training pads for Len's bodily waste—and that was all that the cage contained.

Muhammad knew it would take a while to break Len's spirit, but time was on his side. The owner of the home that they were staying in had crossed the southern border in 2005 and readily assimilated himself into American society. He also had Westernized his appearance and started his own landscape business. He was like many other ISIS brothers throughout America who were hiding and biding their time—while awaiting specific orders for committing a future jihad.

ISIS' enhanced interrogation techniques are not as sophisticated as the CIA's. Their methods are downright mean-spirited and beyond dehumanizing. But then again, poking a needle in someone's nerve canal matched anything that ISIS dished out.

Flogging and branding were just two of Muhammad's sadistic favorites.

It wasn't that Len felt any particular loyalty to me. He knew that even if he told Muhammad anything, any promises of freedom would never happen. He knew he was expendable, but his past Navy training made him stiffen his resolve even more. He would give them nothing—for a while—and pray for salvation.

∩ ∩ ∩

Life as we knew it now was as if Marty and I were essentially under quarantine. I couldn't speak for Marty, but for myself, it brought back memories from my childhood when I was constantly coming down with respiratory infections and was confined to a croup tent.

Tika had satellite television and Marty was pacified somewhat by *The Price Is Right, Let's Make a Deal,* various cooking shows, or HGTV. I was astounded that she could watch these shows, day in and day out, without setting off her claustrophobic syndrome.

The boredom and lack of human contact were invisibly strangling me.

I'd grown a mustache during my active-duty Navy years and kept it for ten years. Back then, I would constantly trim it with my teeth when I had nothing better to do … then I would have to Water-Pik away the stubble that would become trapped between my teeth. Old habits never die—if they're allowed to reestablish themselves.

My thoughts wandered. I found myself wondering what it would be like to live in Alaska during the winter solstice when sunlight was present no more than three hours each day. No wonder newcomers to Alaska would imbibe more alcohol.

Every hour or so, I found myself unconsciously walking into the bathroom to look at myself in the mirror … checking my goatee and mustache to see if they'd become any fuller.

Tommy knew exactly what was happening to my psyche, but

never once let on about the true reason for my confinement. Stan directed Steven to text Tommy, telling him to keep me confined until my transformation was totally complete. Even though I'd explained that I hadn't told Len about my most recent trip to Custer, South Dakota, my protectors wanted to make certain it would be almost impossible to identify me, especially because Len was still missing.

∩ ∩ ∩

Stan knew that Muhammad and his companion wouldn't settle for just hostage-taking.

The fact that Len was missing meant that Muhammad was woefully short on intelligence sources.

Donnie had been warned to heighten his security at the farm and did so in case Muhammad had learned where Towers Above resided. Mike also hired an extra security guard for his facility.

In addition, it was going to be Towers Above day at Woodlands Park on Saturday. Long before this day, officials at Woodlands Park had formulated a plan in case extreme measures were needed.

Donnie and Mike were also prepared for this type of eventuality on Saturday. They spared no expense in finding a stallion that resembled Towers Above as closely as possible.

There was actually one day when TA had been turned out to pasture in the wrong paddock … right next to his carbon copy. The two stallions tried to get at each other and by the time the farmhands arrived, both stallions had broken several boards of fencing that separated each of them.

On Saturday, TA's twin would be the thoroughbred parading at the track.

A special thoroughbred blanket had been made that would

adorn our fake Towers Above. It was constructed of a hybrid material developed at Northwestern University and designed to include Kevlar and carbon nano-tubules.

TA's twin would not parade on the dirt during the tribute, but instead would canter on the grass oval in front of the grandstand … keeping him as far away from the crowd as possible. Donnie would be the rider.

Ted told Donnie that this would be the last time the track would host a Towers Above tribute day. The risk of someone ambushing a famous thoroughbred might not only fail, but such an event could also jeopardize innocent patrons.

Steven arose early on Saturday and said a prayer that this would be the last day of Muhammad's terrorist activities.

CHAPTER 20

Fahim was the odd man out. He'd received his marching orders from a fellow Arab brother three weeks prior to Muhammad and Alia's arrival.

He'd purchased the Freefly Alta 8 Pro drone online with a credit card furnished by his Phoenix contact. His instructions were to modify the surfaces of the drone to make it stealth-like in color. The drone weighed only slightly more than thirteen pounds, but its lift capability topped out at just over twenty pounds. Fahim painted the under-surface a combination of sky blue, grey, and white. When the drone was in the air, people on the ground might see what appeared to be a cloud, if they saw anything at all. The sides and top were painted in traditional camouflage colors designed to blend in with spring foliage.

Fahim knew a little about drones. *This one wasn't meant for speed*, he thought.

The faster the props turned, the closer they'd get to the speed of sound and then the noise generated by the rotating propellers would become high-pitched…thus drawing attention to the drone. Fahim assumed that this drone was going to carry a payload that would be dropped. He further speculated that the droppings would be lethal.

Additionally, the Alta 8's Pixhawk software package would allow the best in waypoint flight planning.

Friday night after dinner, Muhammad began attaching an

array of grenades to a special platform that would be mounted on the belly of the Alta 8.

Alia just watched.

These grenades were relatively new American weaponry that were currently being tested under battlefield conditions.

The crafting of the Enhanced Tactical Multi-Purpose grenade eliminated any fumbling that was characteristic of the older M-67 grenade. The safety pin from the older M-67 grenade had been eliminated from the ET-MP grenade, making it easier for those who were left-handed to handle the weapon.

It was during a tug-of-war battle early in ISIS' creation of its Caliphate State that they launched an attack and reoccupied a Syrian town. The Kurds withdrew hastily and left behind a crate of American-made grenades. Muhammad was present and elated by the good fortune. These fourteen-ounce grenades became a trophy for Muhammad. Along with Alia, they were his most prized possessions.

Now, years later—in fact, in less than 24 hours—he would kill Towers Above and extract at least a portion of revenge against Rob Becker.

∩ ∩ ∩

Just before daybreak, Ted had a half dozen snipers take their positions on top of the grandstand. One would be assigned to each compass point on the roof, while others were assigned at the two primary portals of entry for patrons. Accompanying each sniper was a spotter. All this wasn't an attempt to hide the snipers from Muhammad—Ted knew that he'd assume snipers were present. The early-morning deployment was designed to hide the possibility of potential violence from patrons on that day.

If Tommy had been present, Ted would have relied on him to literally get into the mindset of what a terrorist would attempt. His best alternate option was Charles. It was 6:45 in the morning when he called him into his office.

"I need your help, Charles. I want you to crawl into the mind of Muhammad and give me your best guess as to what he's going to do," Ted asked.

"I couldn't sleep at all last night. Finally, I got up and pulled out a yellow legal pad and started jotting thoughts down." Charles reached down to the side of his motorized wheelchair and removed a yellow pad from a briefcase strapped to its side.

"You have to assume Muhammad knew he was being videotaped the other day. So, if he enters the track today, he'll act quickly. Undoubtedly, he'll be disguised in some fashion to slow our response time. The same would apply to his female companion. Our magnetometers will be calibrated to their highest settings—and I'm also sure Muhammad would assume that would be a certainty. With that in mind, I wouldn't expect him to attempt smuggling in a handgun or knives.

"As to when he or she acts, I'd expect it to be during the Towers Above tribute between the fifth and sixth races. Any other time would not deliver the impact and message he wants to convey. I'm quite certain he hates Rob Becker and the rest of that ownership group.

"That leaves how he intends to inflict whatever form of carnage he can. We literally hold the high ground—and he can't do any physical damage from up on the mountain where the younger folks gather. So that leaves an attack from the air. What I'm not privy to is whether he has any piloting skills—my gut tells me he probably doesn't. He most likely has experience with drones—you know, quadcopter drones! ISIS used them in Iraq. He has to be knowledgeable about their use and technology.

"I took the liberty of texting Stan at the CIA, asking for whatever help he can offer. He's going to get back to me this morning. Until he does, I'd advise our snipers to be aware that there's a high probability of a drone attack. I'd also ask for help from the Kentucky State Police to patrol our property's outer perimeters. If we can spot the drone before it reaches its target, we'll probably be successful in thwarting the attack."

Ted knew Charles was intelligent. He was the brother of Tommy's best friend in the CIA, Danny. But it was at this particular moment that Ted finally comprehended just how valuable an asset Charles was.

"Let's do this. Bear down on Stan one more time, about the urgency of our situation. Tell him that we don't want a repeat of what occurred with Towers Above just a few years ago."

Charles nodded and began maneuvering his wheelchair out of Ted's office.

"Hey, Charles, we'll reconvene no later than 8:45 this morning!"

Charles raised his free hand, affirming the message. Charles drew a deep breath of relief, but words and promises weren't going to win the day!

**HAPTER 21**

Muhammad knew nothing about writing code. He was, however, familiar with Google Earth, and used that app to plot his course of attack. The accuracy of Google's GPS measurements is supposedly correct to within three meters.

Google Earth was kind enough to reveal the longitude and latitude of each waypoint in his attack flight plan.

Muhammad's code writer was Fahim, and computer programming became his first love during his first days attending school in France. He was also influenced by the Islamic religion and left for Lebanon and ultimately Iraq, where he joined ISIS.

The drone's launch point would be in the parking lot of a small Baptist church just beyond the Woodlands Park property line. The first waypoint was a line of trees along a small creek that flowed in a southerly direction. The drone, though, would travel north. At an opening where the creek made a sudden northwest turn was a second waypoint. At this juncture, the drone would head eastward toward a group of barns that housed thoroughbreds whose trainers were not permanently affiliated with any particular horse farm. The thoroughbreds stabled in these barns trained at Woodlands Park's track in the spring and fall during the racing season.

Once the drone reached the southernmost barn, it would hover behind the barn's western side at waypoint number three. Wearing virtual goggles, Muhammad would take a look at the drone's three-hundred-sixty-degree camera views for a few seconds. The drone would then fly up and along a small hillside to reach the fourth waypoint. Just beyond number four, the drone would fly along the far side of the track's dirt surface to reach waypoint number five. There'd be a momentary stop to again allow for another camera scan.

At this point, the drone would skirt over the track's oval boundary and proceed to multiple waypoints in a series of zigzags at varying altitudes. The final waypoint would be just in front of the big video screen and tote board on the track.

At this point, Muhammad would take command of the drone and begin targeting Towers Above - eventually dropping the drone's payload.

Alia would stand at the rail near the finish line during the fifth race and wait patiently for Towers Above to appear. She would serve as a spotter, communicating with Muhammad via cellphone.

As for Fahim, his intention was to be a couple hundred miles away from the track when Muhammad dropped the drone's grenades.

Ո Ո Ո

It was nearly 9:00 p.m. when Stan called Charles to update him with some new information. A Chinook helicopter would be dispatched to Woodlands Park, carrying an experimental radar-directed laser weapon designed to kill drones. The Chinook would leave the Bluegrass Station near Winchester, Kentucky at 1:30 p.m. and would arrive near Woodlands Park no later than 2:00 p.m.

When given the signal, the chopper would go airborne again

and circle the racetrack just before the start of the fifth race. It would move within range of the track during the race and would begin detection operations after the finish of the race, just prior to and during Towers Above's appearance.

Stan wondered specifically about another of Charles' tactical defenses. "Just one more question, Charles. Is Jerry going to be at the track with Icarus?"

"Yes, he is—I'm sorry I didn't mention that," Charles quickly responded. *The day wouldn't be complete unless Woodlands Park's resident bald eagle made an appearance*, Charles quietly thought.

"Make sure you tell Jerry I highly doubt that Icarus will be able to wrestle this drone to the ground. I'm fairly certain this drone won't be as small as the hobby quadcopters he tracked around Mt. Hood and Portland," Stan emphasized.

"Will do, and thank you for your help." Charles said before hanging up.

Ted and Art walked into Charles' office.

Being the boss, Art spoke first. "You know, Charles, we can call off the Towers Above appearance. It would be no different from scratching a favorite horse in a Challenge Cup race. Tell me why we shouldn't do that!"

"Sir, I can't argue with your logic. I truly believe Muhammad is so set on vengeance that killing Towers Above—even though it may not be as satisfying as slitting Rob Becker's throat—would give him some of the satisfaction he craves. I think he'd expect Dr. Becker to show up for the stallion's burial and that would give him another chance to fulfill his jihad. If we scratch TA's appearance, Muhammad might just say 'fuck it' and attack some patrons standing at the rail or up in the grandstand! This guy is a killing machine."

Charles' impassioned reasoning hit the target.

"Well, we don't want that. Okay men, carry on and say a prayer!" Art turned and left the room.

"Do you think we can get this guy, Charles?" Ted asked.

"I give it at least a fifty-fifty chance. We know there are two of them and I expect one of them to be inside the confines of the track. After the attack occurs, we'll immediately shut the track down and all the exits will be closed. Someone is going down, damn it," Charles stated, slamming his fist on the desktop.

"Okay ... let's meet up at 11:30 this morning and finalize everything. I'm going down now to meet with the Brown Coats and fill them in." Ted stood and shook Charles' hand. Charles was well aware that Ted wasn't a glad-hander—and when he shook someone's hand, it meant trust and approval.

Charles had one more call to make, one he hadn't shared with Ted and Art. He punched the numbers on his cell phone and waited for Donnie to answer.

# CHAPTER 22

"Donnie ... are you here yet?" Charles asked.

"I just got here, Charles. The fake Towers Above was just unloaded from the trailer and is settling into his stall. We're still set to go, right?"

"We hopefully just had our final meeting. Art wanted to scratch the event, but the risks from doing so basically overwhelmed him and now he's on board—that discussion was just minutes ago. He can still pull the plug, but I'm pretty certain Ted is all in, and I think Art totally respects his opinion."

"You did tell Ted about the plan, right?" Donnie asked.

"Uh ... not yet."

"What? Why not?" Donnie shouted into the cell phone.

"Calm down, Donnie. I'll tell him after the National Anthem is sung. Look, you know Towers Above is a huge draw—and other than on opening weekend, this day is going to bring a huge crowd to the track. The closer to the start of the race card, the less likely Ted will waver. Now tell me one more time what's going to happen."

Donnie didn't answer right away. He never was one for politics or playing games.

"After the winner of the fifth race exits the track, I'll bring the twin out onto the track. The grounds crew will open a section of the rail next to the turf at the far end of the tote board. Slade will be on my com-link through my ear buds, talking with me. The kid's a whiz at multitasking. He'll tell me where the enemy is. By the way, I doubt Muhammad will come at us at a right angle. I'm guessing it's better than a fifty-fifty chance that I'll be attacked frontally or from behind. Your idea of cantering in front of the tote board is sheer genius.

"The biggest unknown is what Muhammad's going to use in his attack. I'll be covered in SWAT type armor, and Towers' twin will be wearing a special Kevlar blanket for protection. A shot to the head of either one of us is my greatest fear. If Muhammad is going to drop some type of munitions on us, that's when I'll lay the horse down," Donnie stated.

"Come again, Donnie?" Charles asked.

"Rob Becker told me about Tommy using an injectable sedative, etorphine, on Mark when they kidnapped him in Miami. I asked Mike to get me the right amount of the drug so as to bring our horse down, but not kill him. There's a small opening in his blanket just in front of the saddle where I'll inject the sedative—it'll be just like someone being put to sleep before a surgery. If our faux 'Towers' could count backwards from ten, he'd never get to seven. Mike says our horse should go down softly and the chances of his hurting himself are slim.

"Your veterinary ambulance has to be on top of us in a heartbeat. We'll load the horse on a stretcher and put him in the ambulance. Before the end of the final race, Ralph, the track announcer, will state that Towers Above did not survive the attack.

"I figure that between the snipers on the roof and Icarus, the drone will be brought down. The important thing is convincing Muhammad he was successful and that Towers Above is dead. Any other questions?"

Charles paused a few seconds before answering. "No,

Donnie—and good luck!"

The hands on the clock in the office couldn't move quickly enough as far as Charles was concerned. It was in earlier days like this that he'd normally pace back and forth, thinking about what was going to happen. He needed to clear his head, but since he was now wheelchair bound, motorized circles would appear odd to others.

# CHAPTER 23

The crowd was streaming in, and it was a perfect day for horse racing. Miss Kentucky had just finished singing "My Old Kentucky Home" and paused briefly before starting to sing the national anthem.

Once again, Alia was casually dressed, but this time she was a blonde—and she was gorgeous. Her jeans were skin tight and her blouse was unbuttoned just enough to reveal cleavage and half of her breasts. She purposely went to the scanning area where only male Brown Coats were working. She probably didn't need to change her hair color, because neither man ever raised their eyes above her neckline. In less than a minute, Alia was through security and being scanned by a second tier of cameras.

Will was watching the video feed, and he too was focused on the shapely blonde patron entering at the side entrance of Woodlands Park. The central computer generated a short staccato warning in the security office. Alia had triggered just enough facial identification landmarks that were programed to set off an alarm, a result of her previous track visit. The next bank of cameras also locked on her as she passed the clock tower. Thank goodness for computer programs.

Will notified plainclothes security officers in the area, and two of them began shadowing Alia.

Next he called Ted to let him know that Alia was now on track grounds and being followed. Within five minutes, Ted arrived at the security office and began reviewing the earlier videos before clicking on the live feed.

Alia was now seated on a bench near the finish line, just in front of the grandstand. She had no program, so it was obvious that the thoroughbreds that were racing today were of no interest to her. Ted told the two officers to remain in their current position and notify him if she even twitched.

No doubt she's going to be a spotter, Ted thought to himself as he headed to Charles' office.

Ted tapped on Charles' door to announce his presence but didn't pause before entering.

"Alia is here and has parked herself down by the rail close to the finish line. I'm sure she is Muhammad's spotter," he advised Charles, pushing his cell phone across the desk so Charles could watch the live video.

"Interesting … she's a blonde now, huh? Well, that's Part A … now let's see if Part B plays out the way we think it will. Have you alerted your perimeter officers about the situation?"

"Yep … I did that on my way over here. Donnie and Towers Above are here, aren't they?" Ted asked.

"Donnie is, but Towers Above is not."

Ted's eyelids opened wide, and he started to speak, but Charles put his hand up before Ted could utter even one word. Ted was ready to explode with anger and his face had turned beet red. He wasn't used to anyone hushing him up.

Charles began to explain. "With my agreement, Donnie brought a thoroughbred that looks exactly like Towers Above into the park. The stallion can pass as Towers' twin. I've been to Donnie's farm and witnessed the animal for myself. Donnie is willing to take the risk of sacrificing a horse as well as himself,"

Charles stated.

Charles proceeded to fill him in with the full story, watching as Ted's face slowly transitioned to its normal skin color.

"Well, I'll be damned. Was this your idea or Donnie's?"

"It was all Donnie's, but I've got to tell you that he also ran it by Tommy and Steven. Donnie is in contact with Tommy—but don't ask me to share that contact information with you, because Donnie promised Rob Becker that he'd never give the information out to anyone," Charles replied.

"If you want me to submit my resignation, Ted, I will … but I'd like to see this day through to its end!" Charles pleaded.

Ted buried his head in his hands on the desk. The silence seemed like an eternity to Charles before Ted slowly raised his head. The smile on Ted's face told Charles that his job was safe.

"You son of a bitch! This is brilliant," Ted said emphatically, slapping both hands on his thighs. He stood, extending his hand to Charles and shaking it vigorously in a congratulatory motion.

Ted was halfway out of the office before Charles could say "thank you."

∩ ∩ ∩

After dropping Alia off at the side entrance of the track, Muhammad headed for the Baptist church. There was only one car in the parking lot when he got there. Muhammad got out of his car, went to the main entrance, and pulled on both doors of the church. They were locked.

He began banging on the doors non-stop.

It took nearly three minutes before he heard the sound of a lock being unlatched. The church secretary opened the door about three inches and asked, "How can I help you?"

Muhammad, who was holding an empty gallon milk jug in his hand, pleaded for some water. "My car overheated and I stopped in your parking lot. You can help by giving me some water?" he stated.

The secretary responded, "There's a spigot on the side of the building—go ahead and help yourself." She started to close the door, but Muhammad was quicker, wedging his foot into the small opening and giving the door a strong, swift push.

He was in.

...and just ten seconds later, the secretary was lying on the carpet ... bleeding profusely.

"That was for Allah," Muhammad said aloud.

He relocked the church doors, grabbed a chair, and calmly waited for Alia to call. If someone else happened by to interrupt his wait, he would deal with them in the same manner.

It was now just after 1:00 in the afternoon, and the starting gates at Woodlands Park sprang open. The day's races had begun.

∩ ∩ ∩

The fourth race finished a little before 3:00 p.m.

Horses running in race number five were in the paddock and waiting to be saddled.

A Western-style saddle was put on Towers' twin, positioned over the special protective blanket he was already wearing—the horse was also wearing Kevlar blinkers.

The thoroughbreds moved to the second paddock and the jockeys were given a leg up before the horses headed out onto the track. Some cantered around while others were ready to load immediately into their numbered post positions.

Alia twitched!

She reached into her purse, pulled out her cell phone, and

punched in a speed dial number.

"Hello," Muhammad said.

"Okay, it's time for our early dinner!" Alia said back.

"Give me some time to wash up and call me back when it's on the table!" Muhammad responded.

The conversation between the two was in code. They knew that their phones were not secure and that their voices would be detected by NSA Stingray mobile surveillance devices positioned around the track.

Muhammad stepped over the secretary's body and left the church. He ran to the car, unloaded his armed Alta 8 drone, put on the virtual goggles ... and powered on the brushless motors of each propeller.

Back at the track, the horses were rounding the final turn and onto the homestretch—and it was soon announced that URWORSTNIGHTMARE was the winner of the fifth race by three lengths.

Most of the people on the grounds were unaware that the end of this race was a foreshadowing of what was to come.

The horse's owner and all of the shareholders gathered in the winner's circle as the other horses exited the track from an open gate beyond the tote board. Finally, it was time for the winning horse and its entourage to exit the track.

Alia put the phone back to her ear and hit redial.

"Dinner's on the table," she advised.

"On my way," Muhammad answered.

The powered-up drone was now heading to its first waypoint.

Charles spoke calmly into his hand-held walkie-talkie, talking to all the security officers and snipers, as well as to Donnie.

"Ladies and gentlemen ... it's game time!"

CHAPTER 24

The Chinook hovered about 2500 feet directly over the center of the oval racetrack.

Glen was sitting in front of the laser radar screen and firing platform, watching, waiting ... and ready to act. The laser was charged and ready to burst to life from the belly of the helicopter. The energy source was a small nuclear reactor, being used experimentally in a fleet of Chinooks. This wasn't the first use of nuclear reactors on flying platforms, though. In the 1950s and early '60s, General Electric had been tasked with creating nuclear-powered jet engines, but the project was cancelled.

"We've got a bogey ... Southwest quadrant!

"Targeting now ... taking the shot!"

The Chinook shook after the shot, shifting several feet in a northeast direction. "For every action, there's an equal and opposite reaction," Glen mumbled to himself, with a huge smile on his face.

The laser was on target, but instead of hitting the drone, it knocked a huge tree limb to the ground. Muhammad didn't see the laser blast, but he did see the limb fall while looking at his rear-facing camera video.

That's strange, he thought, before realizing that his drone was under attack.

"My dinner is too hot ... it's on fire!" Muhammad shouted into his cellphone.

"Must be God's wish…always look above and behind your-self," Alia told him. She saw the Chinook and assumed some type of weaponry was onboard and shooting at the drone. She hadn't been looking at the helicopter until that moment, and observed a laser burst traveling at the speed of light.

Muhammad arrived at his second waypoint and paused to see what was happening behind him. He saw several tree branches that had been felled.

Glen was pissed off. "Captain, my targeting is spot-on, but the drone's computer program or the pilot himself has chosen a path that's shielding it and preventing me from bringing it down," Glen communicated tersely to the Chinook pilot.

Captain Flannery clicked on the com line. "Do you still have the bogey on radar?"

Muhammad was quickly advancing to the next waypoint when he suddenly realized that the drone's computer guidance system needed to be shut down—and he manually took over the drone's direction, speed, and altitude. He cancelled the next pre-planned waypoint—at the rear of the horse barn—and instead sped to the track's outer boundary, juking left and right … climbing and then dropping … zigging and then zagging—all in an erratic pattern. Glen took several shots at the drone, but every shot missed the target because of Muhammad's evasive maneuvers.

Donnie, who was riding Towers' twin, emerged on the dirt track, approaching the turf where the rail had been opened for the TA lookalike to pass through. The crowd erupted with applause, but the sound was muted because of the hovering Chinook. At least half of the patrons were watching the laser bursts coming from the bottom of the helicopter. Some thought they were watching a new type of fireworks display.

The track's snipers attempted to reacquire the drone, but those that were in a position to bring down the target also couldn't get a clean shot.

Charles was not happy with the way things were going.

He grabbed a walkie-talkie and ordered the two agents who were shadowing Alia to arrest her and shut down her cell phone. There was no longer any point in letting her continue to be Muhammad's trackside spotter.

At about that same time, Muhammad made a shrewd decision, deciding to follow the homestretch rail surrounding the dirt oval. As soon as the drone reached the boundary of the grandstand, he maneuvered it just above the crowd and continued his evasive maneuvers.

"Captain, I don't have a clean shot! He's using the crowd as cover. I can take the shot but there's a fifty percent chance that when I shoot, he'll juke and my laser burst will strike some patrons. Please advise, sir!"

"Stand down, soldier—that's an order," Captain Flannery stated.

The expected had become the unexpected.

Muhammad's drone was now flying perpendicular to the tote board, and he prepared to commence his first attack. Continuing his evasive flying maneuvers, he decided to drop the first rack of grenades at a height equal to the top of the tote board, and then take a sharp right turn and loop around to make his second run at TA's twin from the horse's hind end.

He'd performed this type of drone warfare before, in the Middle East, but hadn't practiced that maneuver with this particular drone. He punched the release button and the inertia of the grenades caused them to bounce off the tote board and careen toward the outer boundary of the oval turf.

It was decision time for Donnie. The syringe in his right hand began a downward descent, penetrating the horse's flesh—and the sedative began to course through the thoroughbred's body. Six grenades exploded just as Towers' twin slowly slumped to the ground. Donnie had practiced his dismount several times, now sliding off the saddle…as if he'd slipped on a banana peel.

However, Donnie didn't know that the drone had completed its ninety-degree turn and was beginning a second attack.

Icarus had been watching the drone from the moment it approached the track's perimeter.

The laser bursts were new for the bald eagle and something he'd not previously experienced. The bird continued to circle, progressively getting lower in altitude. Laser blasts had stopped! Any noise was now coming from the Chinook's propellers and the panicked, screaming patrons, following the explosion of the fallen grenades.

Icarus began his dive, and it was sheer beauty to watch his legs and open talons swing forward in concert with his streaking body, in anticipation of latching onto the drone.

His talons locked onto a supporting strut of the drone, but the drone was too heavy to bring down. Icarus decided instead to move the drone as far away from the crowd as possible.

Muhammad toggled the power up to its maximum, but Icarus managed somehow to flip the drone upside down.

He then decided to release another rack of grenades, hoping the shrapnel would take out the bald eagle.

Responding to the threat from a second release of grenades, Donnie scrambled to the downed horse, draping his own body over the animal's head.

Muhammad was not familiar with the concussion grenades or the damage they could cause, but the majority of the grenades fell at the base of the tote board, causing a tremendous explosion.

He released one last set of grenades in a final attempt to shake the drone free from Icarus.

Icarus had been continuously moving, not realizing that he was slowly driving the upside-down drone in the direction of the turf. Now completely exhausted, the large bird reluctantly let go of the drone and he was now free of its weight. The bald eagle sped away from the tote board.

Glen finally had his clear shot and immediately took it.

From the roof of the grandstand came a cascading stream of bullets, complementing a huge burst of laser energy. Both began slamming into the drone. The falling drone and its final release of grenades tore a gaping hole in the far side of the tote board.

The Chinook paused just long enough to allow a crew member to get some photos before it quickly lifted higher, turned, and sped away. The sniper's guns were silent, and a large segment of the crowd stopped and quickly turned to look at the carnage.

The equine ambulance drove across the dirt oval and through an opening in the rail. It stopped next to Donnie and the horse. Donnie stood, uninjured, and stepped aside to allow the workers to put up a screen and block the view of what was happening on the track.

About half of the crowd stood quietly while the other half wept for what they perceived was the death of Towers Above. It was a cruel hoax, but it had to be done that way.

The screen was removed about fifteen minutes later as the ambulance drove off the turf and headed for the exit.

The track announcer spoke into the microphone, asking

everyone to say a prayer for Towers Above.

The Commonwealth of Kentucky is not only a Red state, but a Christian state as well.

At long last, Towers Above might get to live life peacefully. Rob, Donnie, and Mike would make that decision sometime in the future.

CHAPTER 25

Mike was in the passenger seat of the ambulance. When a thoroughbred is injured on the track, generally the animal is taken first to a nearby stable where there's radiography equipment, to determine the extent of its injury. If the diagnosis is determined to be hopeless, then the horse is mercifully put down.

This was not a hopeless diagnosis. The equine twin of Towers Above was simply sleeping from the sedative Donnie had injected.

The ambulance arrived at the stable where another trailer was waiting with its engine running. Several of Donnie's farmhands were already at the stable awaiting their orders.

"Men, please help transfer this horse to the other trailer, and then if need be, someone help take the ambulance back to the track. I've already talked with the track's assistant veterinarian—he's now in charge. Thanks for your help," Mike said.

After the ambulance pulled away, Mike, who was now in back with the horse, administered naloxone to reverse the effects of the etorphine.

"Wake up, c'mon—wake up," Mike said repeatedly over what seemed an eternity. Finally, after five minutes, the sound of a deep whinny and heavy breathing echoed throughout the trailer. The horse's head jerked up, then quickly fell back down onto the floor.

"C'mon, buddy ... get up! I've got some carrots and peppermints for you." Mike passed a piece of candy in front of the thoroughbred's nose—it was a struggle, but the horse finally stood up.

He was woozy, but the candy seemed to stimulate him enough so that the carrots soon also became appetizing. Mike waited another half hour before tethering the horse securely for the ride back to the farm.

Donnie was there waiting when the ambulance pulled into the entrance of the farm. He punched in the code to open the electric fence and once the look alike horse was safely back in his stall, Donnie said to Mike, "By God, I think we pulled it off!"

Donnie and Mike couldn't stop smiling as they left the stable.

Mike suddenly stopped walking and said, "Oh my God. Did you call Tommy and tell him what happened? If Rob sees a special bulletin on TV that Towers Above is dead, Lord knows what his reaction might be!"

"I messaged Tommy as soon as I got into my truck. I did try calling, but he didn't answer his phone," Donnie replied.

"Let's hope he checks his text messages ... it could be ugly if he doesn't," Mike stated.

∩ ∩ ∩

Charles' security officers were having a hard time hauling Alia away from the rail. She brought one of them down with an unexpected ninja-type move, but another officer took her to the ground with a sleeper hold. Her body went limp and the now recovered first agent happily placed the handcuffs on her. She remained pinned on the ground until two additional track security officials arrived on the scene. Her feet were zip-tied before the four officers carried her to the track's holding room.

Charles met Ted outside the holding room and they went through the contents of Alia's purse. There wasn't much—a wallet with an obviously fake ID, lipstick, her throw away cell phone and a knife. It was more like a switchblade, but not of a style that Charles or Ted had ever seen in America.

It was a cad-cam ceramic knife!

Both men immediately realized how the knife went through the magnetometer without detection.

"The CIA will want to have a look at this knife. They'll check for DNA matches connected to a series of murders down in Mexico and at the border," Ted said.

"We can't hold her here indefinitely!" Charles replied.

Ted responded, "Let me give Steven a call. He'll be able to tell us what our next move is."

Ted stepped out of the room and made the call. He explained to Steven what had happened at the track and asked for guidance regarding Alia.

"I'll have a couple of agents at the track within two hours. Put all of her possessions in a bag and avoid touching them with your fingertips. I won't be there, but if anything more is discovered, immediately let me know. Thanks, Ted—and good work!"

Steven's next call was to Stan in Langley, Virginia.

∩ ∩ ∩

Fahim was already well on his way to St. Louis. He was heading west and hoped to get through Missouri by day's end.

Before he started off on his journey, Fahim had gone downstairs to where Len was sleeping. He unlocked the cage and told his captive that if he turned around, he'd be dead. Fahim next told Len to place his hands behind his back and they were zip-tied together. Lastly, Fahim placed a cloth bag over Len's head, cinching it tight. For good measure, he used duct tape to secure it even tighter. With hands bound and head covered, Len was dressed only in his underwear and was barefoot.

"Today is your lucky day. We're going for a ride and then I'm going to turn you loose," Fahim said.

Len said nothing. He didn't have any illusions of being set free—the pain of being tortured trumped any hopes he had of being allowed to live.

Fahim led him to the stairs and verbally guided him up the steps. They slowly walked through the kitchen to a side entrance. Once outside, Fahim led his hostage to his car and maneuvered him onto the front passenger seat.

Fahim drove about twenty miles to Mountain Side Links, an eighteen-hole public golf course. He pulled onto a service road where golf carts were stored at night. Fahim got out to first see if anyone was around, and seeing nobody, returned to the car. In one swift motion, he pulled Len out of the passenger seat and dumped him on the ground. Thirty seconds later, Fahim was gone and Len was lying on the dirt road. Fahim knew someone would find Len before dusk— and as he drove away, he knew the one thing he'd sorely miss were the cheeseburgers served at the clubhouse restaurant.

Mountain Side Links was Fahim's home course. He had a regular foursome that he played golf with at least once a week when possible. Golf was just one American pastime he'd grown to enjoy. There were several other things in America that Fahim found enjoyable. At the top of the list was freedom. He had his own business and could come and go as he pleased. He still believed Allah was his God, but the people he had friended, as well as his employees, were no longer considered infidels to him. "Live and let live" had become Fahim's mantra.

Fahim had become Westernized and he knew it—in fact, he was no longer an Islamic zealot. Black and white had morphed into different shades of grey. Yes, he wished the entire world would adopt Allah as their God—but if that wasn't to be, then so be it. Those who worshipped a different God weren't infidels, and they didn't need to be enslaved or ultimately killed.

If only it were that easy to change an Islamist's mindset. Every religion has its zealots. As long as some Islamic imams continued to preach that Allah is the only God and non-believers needed to become slaves or be murdered, then the world would continue to be in turmoil.

In two days, Fahim would be in Arizona, starting work with the new landscape company he'd bought from proceeds he'd made when selling his Kentucky business.

At first, the crowd that remained after the drone attack just sat or stood in hushed silence. By the time the gates of the sixth race opened, most of the crowd was leaving the track through the exits. Some patrons were sobbing, and the words frequently heard among the people talking were "I can't believe what I just saw!"

Thoroughbred racing had taken a huge blow to the gut.

By the tenth and final race, only diehard fans remained at Woodlands Park. Reporters and television crews waited for permission to cross the dirt oval and get closer to the spot where the beloved horse had fallen and the worst structural damage to the track's tote board had been inflicted.

Within minutes, the reporters went live nationwide, with words and pictures telling the tragic story of the death of Towers Above. The news was beamed across the world!

When the connection to Muhammad's cell phone went dead, he knew Alia had been captured. He ran to his car and in less than a minute he was safely away on the main road.

It was just five minutes later that a police car pulled into the parking lot of the church. The cop was responding to a call from the secretary's husband, who reported that his wife was missing. He wanted someone to investigate if she was still at the church, along with her car.

The officer found both.

He spotted the car immediately and then headed to the entrance of the church, expecting the door to be locked. Instead, it opened. The officer immediately spotted the woman face-down on the floor. He wanted to try to revive her. Rolling her onto her back, he saw the slit throat.

Within minutes, the parking lot and church were teeming with state and local law enforcement, along with FBI agents.

ᑎ ᑎ ᑎ

Muhammad returned to Fahim's house, fully intending to take out his wrath on Len. He called for Fahim, but there was no reply. He headed downstairs where he spied the open, now-empty cage.

The rage began to build, and Muhammad promised Allah that Fahim would pay for his traitorous actions.

Muhammad turned on the television to watch a news report about what had happened at the track. A smile crept across his face as the reporter stated that Towers Above had been killed.

That's just partial payback, you son of a bitch, Muhammad silently raged. That thought quickly vanished upon hearing the reporter also state that one terrorist—a female—had been captured.

An angry scream exploded in the room. Muhammad grabbed his prayer rug and knelt, begging Allah for the strength to find Rob Becker and complete his jihad.

∩ ∩ ∩

A golf cart attendant discovered Len with his head still covered, stumbling around and running into things.

∩ ∩ ∩

I was sitting in Tika's family room, watching TV. I was scrolling through the channels with the remote when I came across TVG—horse racing's cable television channel.

Scrolling across the bottom of the screen was a banner news bulletin that read TOWERS ABOVE KILLED IN TERRORIST ATTACK AT WOODLANDS PARK RACETRACK.

Not unlike Muhammad, my scream of anguish filled the entire house. Tommy was on the front porch and had just finished reading Donnie's text message. He rushed into the house and found me sobbing uncontrollably.

Marty and Tika were outside in the garden and also came running after hearing my scream.

"Rob, stop! Let me explain what happened," Tommy shouted. I pulled away from him in anger.

"Rob, it's not true! He's alive!"

Marty and Tika burst through the screen door, watching as Tommy restrained me with a bear hug, trying to calm me down. Marty began holding me also. Her arms had the long-time feel of someone who knew how to comfort me in a way that Tommy couldn't provide.

"Rob, please listen to me. Look at this text from Donnie!"

I read the text and looked back at the television, trying to determine which news was fake. "What the hell am I supposed to believe?"

Tommy answered, "Against my better instincts, I'm going to place a call to Donnie. Don't expect me to do this every time you have a breakdown. Okay?"

I nodded my agreement.

"Donnie … this is Tommy. Would you please tell Rob what happened at the track today ... and would you make it quick? I don't know who might be listening!"

It took Donnie less than five minutes to bring me up to speed.

"Oh God, thank you, Donnie. I owe you big time," I said before handing the cell phone back to Tommy.

# HAPTER 26

Will was reviewing the day's security digital videos once again. He watched as Muhammad dropped Alia off at the side entrance, with the video showing her as she was admitted onto track property.

Something made him watch that segment of the video over and over again. Suddenly, he realized what was bothering him. After Alia got out of the car, a male patron ran up behind her, and he followed her through the turnstile. Will continued to watch Alia on the video—and everywhere she went, the stranger was right behind her. When she finally situated herself on a bench near the rail, the man was slightly to her right, ten feet away. Will reviewed the video several more times.

What are the odds of a total stranger literally following Alia everywhere she went? Will thought to himself.

Grabbing the cellphone, he called both Ted and Charles and told them about what he'd seen on the video. He was convinced there was a third suspect involved in the day's activities.

Within an hour, Charles and Ted arrived back at the track.

The three men watched the video several times, with Charles and Ted coming to the same conclusion as Will.

Will looked through other videos, searching for one that could provide a frontal view of their mystery suspect. After about fifteen minutes, he settled on one segment of video, stopping to enlarge the face on the video as much as possible. He made photocopies of the mystery man in the video.

Meanwhile, Charles was on the phone with Steven.

"I hate to tell you this, but we believe there was another person of interest at the track today. I'll be sending you the video along with a good frontal photo of the guy," Charles stated.

"Thank your security team, please," Steven replied.

Within half an hour, Steven received the information by email, which he immediately encrypted and sent to Stan at Langley.

When Stan arrived at his office the next morning, he opened this latest email, adding it to a collection of information he'd already compiled from Saturday's events at Woodlands Park. He called his assistant into the office, asking her to forward the information and photo on to the Facial Recognition Department to run through the forensic identification program and determine if there was a match.

As Stan waited for the results of the forensic identification search, he reviewed the NSA's Stingray conversations from Saturday, because he had previously alerted the NSA to have all three Stingray towers surrounding Woodlands Park operational on that Saturday.

The conversations between Muhammad and Alia were crystal clear. Their cellphones were not encrypted—and it was confirmed that Alia was a spotter for Muhammad. That information alone would be enough to incarcerate her for the rest of her life.

With the new information from Will, Stan now had new questions about a collateral conversation that took place at the same time as Alia was talking with Muhammad. While this particular conversation was encrypted, the communication unscrambling software program that NSA was using, in this instance, was very sophisticated.

Stan made a call to the specialized department within the agency, asking that they turn up the heat on breaking down the code and deciphering the encrypted conversation.

He'd been down this road many times in his role as head of the CIA—and knew it was now time for patience. Kicking back in his chair, Stan admitted to himself how much he missed his good friend Tommy, and the experience Tommy brought to the intelligence field.

By the end of the day, Stan had an answer to the mystery man's identification—he was either Wayne or Todd Gail.

"Are you shitting me? What are the odds of having to deal with identical twins for a second time in six years?" Stan asked himself.

The profile folders of the brothers included an informational summary on each man. Wayne was a retired Army Ranger. His brother Todd, also a Ranger, was currently a subcontractor working at the Bluegrass Station in Avon, Kentucky. The Bluegrass Station was a depot for some of America's most secret military and special ops equipment. Lockheed Martin and Raytheon were just two examples of the military-industrial complex once referenced by former President Eisenhower, with each having active facilities on-site. Bluegrass Station was also home for the National Guard—and not just National Guard soldiers from Kentucky.

Only one other facility in the US—Area 51 in Nevada—has as many secrets and levels of security. There's not one intelligence agency that doesn't know that Bluegrass Station is a special ops haven, Stan thought to himself.

The Gail brothers had normal profiles. There were no unusual financial transactions in their histories, and their lifestyles fit the average statistics of other Americans their age, with similar levels of education.

Stan normally wouldn't have been concerned about the brothers after reading their profiles, but something was nagging at his mind. He needed more history about Wayne, and wanted details about Todd's specific duties at the station.

Calling his assistant again into his office, Stan gave her notes that he jotted down with tasks that needed to be done. They included assigning his two best operators to dig further into the backgrounds of the two brothers. But first he'd have to make it legal—and do it by the book.

That meant he'd have to get FISA court approval in order to proceed any further. Unlike the FBI and their illegal use of the Foreign Intelligence Surveillance Act court against President Trump and his friends, Stan was determined to follow the letter of the law!

His notes indicated a few of the things he wanted to investigate about the brothers, including:

1. Any social media activities
2. Parents' history
3. Detailed military histories
4. Political affiliations
5. Friends' histories
6. Criminal histories

Stan made another call to the department responsible for decoding and deciphering the encrypted conversation to see if they had any information for him yet—but the answer he got was not encouraging.

His mind gravitated again to Tommy. In the past, Tommy

would kidnap a suspect and break them down with enhanced interrogation. But after the Antifa Revolution, the ground rules totally changed. Stan couldn't take the same chances as he did in the past.

"This is going to take some time," Stan mumbled as he closed his office door and headed for home.

CHAPTER 27

It was late in the evening when Steven finally arrived at the track. He was accompanied by three other men, whom Charles and Ted assumed were CIA operatives.

"Charles, Ted … please give your security detail my thanks for bringing Alia down. I need all of her belongings and then we'll be off to the Bluegrass Airport up in Lexington. I wish I could tell you where she'll be going, but I don't even know," Steven told them.

"I'd be very careful with her—and would make sure she's well restrained during the short trip to DC," Ted told the other men. "She's had some excellent martial arts training."

In five minutes, Steven, the three unidentified agents, and Alia were gone, leaving just Ted and Charles together with their individual thoughts.

"I think she's going to New Mexico for trial. The families of those dead border agents need to see her receive some American justice," Ted said.

Charles quickly answered with his own thoughts. "I think she's taking an overseas trip."

"Huh?" Ted asked, giving Charles a questioning look.

"She has to be interrogated, and any enhanced questioning can't happen here in America, or in Guantanamo, for that matter! Mexico is out because of the drug cartels. Their government couldn't hold on to a goldfish if it was necessary! I think she'll be turned over to the Kurds, and you can count on having some CIA operatives present during her questioning."

Charles' guess was correct.

∩ ∩ ∩

Stan needed to confirm how much Len had told Muhammad about the whereabouts of Rob Becker. He knew Alia would be dealt with a degree of finality after she was broken down—and he really didn't care how they obtained the information from her.

He also knew that Len would have to be debriefed. The only problem with that would be that Len was already a victim of Muhammad's enhanced interrogation and he couldn't tolerate another dose of the same tactics from the hands of CIA agents.

My safety was at stake, and if necessary, they'd move me to an alternative site. After all, the CIA never limits its options.

There was a dual purpose in choosing to hide me in Oral, South Dakota. Stan knew that Tommy had long wanted to get back together with Tika—and he knew that I couldn't resist practicing dentistry. He had arranged with Tika to have something set up where I could do dental work on native Americans—and the Agency spared no cost in setting up a clinic on the reservation near Oral.

Stan had no idea, though, that it would take a couple months before the enhanced interrogation of Alia would finally get her talking and produce results.

Once she talked, all the information gathered through her interrogation was forwarded to the CIA's IT department. In turn, the IT techs entered the data into a software program that also encompassed the Estes Park/Allenspark region of Colorado. It took just one day for Stan to get the computer-driven results indicating that the odds of finding Rob Becker were one in fifty thousand! The Western mountain states were not that populated and the amount of square miles that Muhammad would have to cover were staggering. Besides that, South Dakota was just barely included in what is considered part of the West. Stan liked having higher odds, but sentimentality got the best of him, and he finally agreed that Rob and his wife Marty could stay in Oral, South Dakota.

The CIA operatives that were with the Kurds ended their report of Alia's interrogation with a two-word summation: Alia terminated.

So much for her future.

In the meantime, Stan had no choice but to flood law enforcement agencies throughout the western states with Muhammad's photo—with and without a typical ISIS beard—and he would continue to do so until the terrorist was either captured or killed. Stan had no clue where other ISIS terrorists might be located. Right now, it was Stan's job to figure out what Muhammad's next move would be.

He prayed that he hadn't and wouldn't screw up!

# CHAPTER 28

For the most part, Tommy was able to share with me what was happening at my Kentucky home. However, I would have been naive to not expect that some intelligence information was being withheld from me. One question utmost in my mind was why Steven was still living in my home, now that Marty and I were gone. It made no sense to me.

For Tommy, his son being at the Becker home in Kentucky was a possible game-changer. While Marty and I were in Indianapolis, Bates Security was busy installing a sophisticated network of cameras, motion sensors, and infrared equipment in our house. If a field mouse came within four hundred yards of the house, an alarm would sound. Shrubs were also strategically planted that provided cover and allowed Steven to sneak out of the basement undetected. He would then position himself in a perfect hiding place to scope out the woods two hundred yards in front of our home.

In Tommy's mind, with Muhammad now the only known ISIS zealot remaining in southern Kentucky, it made sense for the man to break into our home, looking for additional information that might narrow the scope of his search for Marty and me.

There were at least a half dozen times before the day of the drone attack that Steven locked onto someone who seemed to be staked out in the woods and observing my home. During one evening, two individuals, separated by no more than three hundred yards, were spotted surveilling the house.

On the evening when Steven and his fellow agents picked up Alia and were driving to the airport, Tommy called his son.

Can you talk right now?" Tommy asked.

"Yes. Go ahead," Steven replied.

"Now that Muhammad has lost his companion and also his hostage, I would expect him to come knocking within the next couple of days. In fact, I'm guessing it will be tomorrow night. I've alerted Greg, Rusty, John, Ralph, and Casey to show up in the van tomorrow morning. Make sure Greg backs into the driveway. Open the garage door, have him back the van in and then close the garage door.

"Then tomorrow evening, have Greg open the garage door and drive the van out of the garage. Ralph will walk out, get in the passenger side, and then both of them will leave. Make sure the house looks like it's empty before they're gone. And if nothing happens tomorrow night, do the same thing again the next night.

"Once Muhammad breaks into the house—kill him instantly."

"Dad ..."

"Look, son, this guy has killed more innocent people in his lifetime than you can even imagine. He's a callous assassin! Don't try to capture him, because one of your teammates—or you—will most certainly die. Do you understand me?

"Answer me!"

The mobile connection was broken abruptly.

"Damn that boy!" Tommy shouted. "He's too far away this time for me to make a difference." Tommy glanced toward the sky and said a silent prayer—asking the Lord to guide his son in making the right decision. He also knew that asking the Lord to help his son kill someone was perhaps the ultimate oxymoron.

Tommy hadn't talked with Stan in a while. When Stan's assistant told him that Tommy was calling, he knew it had to be important.

"Hey, Tommy … what's up?"

"I need a huge favor, Stan!"

Tommy then told Stan about the trap designed to take down Muhammad. Knowing his son's personality and his aversion to violence, he asked Stan to get in touch with Steven's fellow agent, John, and order him to take the kill shot if and when Muhammad tried to enter the Becker home.

"Stan, you know Muhammad won't break into the Beckers' house with just a knife! The slightest bit of hesitation could result in one of our agents being killed. When we were in the wilderness around Mt. Hood, Steven admitted to me that he hesitated before taking out one of Antifa's leaders who had his rifle pointed at my head!"

The subsequent silence indicated that Tommy had made a strong argument.

"Okay, Tommy, against my better instincts, I'll talk with John and tell him to bring Muhammad down. I'm telling you right now—your son is not stupid. He'll know what's going down. If I lose him as an agent, then that's it, Tommy. There will be no more favors from me and no more contact with Langley."

For the second time in just fifteen minutes, Tommy had someone hang up on him.

Tommy was itching to be back in the hunt, but doing so would mean he'd probably lose Tika for the final time.

As he walked back toward the house, every foul expletive in Tommy's vocabulary filled the air around Oral, South Dakota.

# CHAPTER 29

A s Stan was driving home, he couldn't help laughing to himself. "I have absolutely no idea which twin was at the track. At least if I flip a coin, I'd have a fifty-fifty chance of being right."

As quickly as his laughter started, it was cut short. Stan couldn't stop thinking about his last meeting with Bud, the head of the DIA. Stan had mentally buried the specific part of their conversation that concerned the activities of a possible secret global organization.

On this night, the thread of that earlier conversation wouldn't go away and just kept gnawing at Stan. During all his years in intelligence work, Stan had dealt with verifiable issues. Waiting for something or someone unknown to act in an evil fashion against America or one of its citizens was foreign and disconcerting for Stan.

He was determined to unravel the mystery of this supposed globalist entity.

"Perhaps Wayne and Todd are agents connected with a global cartel," Stan uttered out loud, before shaking his head and saying, "Nah!"

⋒ ⋒ ⋒

Muhammad checked his watch as he left Fahim's home. It was now sunset, and it would be totally dark by the time he arrived at the wooded area fronting Rob Becker's home.

There was a dirt road off to the right that was most likely used for ATVs—and Muhammad exited the main road and drove into the woods from that trail. He stopped the car, popped the trunk latch, and got out. He headed to the rear of the car and grabbed his AK-47 from the trunk. He strapped it on and loaded up a satchel with several bullet filled magazines. Walking about fifty yards, Muhammad quickly dropped to the ground and began holding a night vision scope up to his right eye. He scanned the Becker house and grounds for fifteen minutes. He observed nothing.

He paused and prayed to Allah that the action he was about to undertake would be successful, and if not, then he would martyr himself just as Nadal Hasan wanted to do during the 2009 Fort Hood shootings.

He headed back, walking to the main road before proceeding toward Rob's house.

Steven was camouflaged in his usual position and had picked up Muhammad's infrared signature when the terrorist first arrived on the property across from Rob Becker's home. Speaking quietly through his airbuds, Steven gave a heads-up signal to the rest of his unit who were positioned inside the home—warning them that an unidentified stranger was on the move.

Muhammad was now standing in front of the Beckers' home. He paused and again surveyed the area.

Muhammad started up the driveway, eventually veering left toward the front door.

Reaching the front door, he pushed the doorbell.

Steven slowly wiped the perspiration from his brow and whispered another warning to his men.

"On your mark!"

Muhammad rang the doorbell again and slowly swung the AK-47 in a forward position. He switched off the AK's safety and checked the front door to see if it was unlocked. It wasn't. Stepping back several feet, he unleashed a barrage of bullets into the front door's locking mechanism. Stepping forward, he tried once more to open the door, but it was still locked. He threw the left side of his body forcefully into the door, with no success.

He reloaded with a new magazine and stepped back a second time, preparing to unleash another barrage of bullets into the door when Steven stood up and took aim.

"Can I help you?" Steven shouted.

Muhammad immediately turned and realized he had no choice.

The unmistakable shout of "Allahu Akbar ..." began filling the night air.

…and Steven had already pulled the trigger of his bolt-action MK 21 rifle.

Muhammad never got the chance to finish saying Akbar. The bullet slammed into Muhammad's forehead just below the lower part of his right eye socket. The bullet deflected slightly to the left before exiting the back of the terrorist's skull, accompanied by several pieces of skull bone and brain tissue.

Tommy was wrong.

Steven lowered his weapon. There was no sign of any emotion on his face.

He silently said to himself, "Thank God that's over."

∩ ∩ ∩

Stan's cellphone began to blare. It was 2:00 in the morning. Stan answered and immediately realized that John was calling from Kentucky.

"Muhammad is dead, sir," before Stan could even say hello.

"What! Good God, man … tell me what happened!"

"Sir … Tommy's son took him out! Muhammad was trying to shoot his way into the house and Steven took the shot! Sir … I'd like to ask a favor."

"Go ahead, young man," Stan replied.

"That conversation we had about me taking the kill shot … it never occurred. If there's a recording of our conversation, I'd like it to be destroyed. If there are notes about our discussion, I'd like them scrubbed."

"Soldier, I guarantee your request will be honored—and this conversation never happened. Thank you for calling. Good night."

"I'll be damned," Stan said to himself.

He sent a text to Tommy that said:

Muhammad is dead!
For once, you were wrong!
Steven took him out!
No fatalities for our team!
I'll talk with you when I get details from Steven.
There will be a total information blackout. Muhammad and Alia never existed!
Please acknowledge that you received this information!

Stan mumbled to himself, "That was unexpectedly easy! I wonder who the next assassin will be?" He crawled back into bed and was asleep almost immediately.

It took just an instant for Tommy to hear his cell phone

notification sound of Stan's message coming to him in Oral, South Dakota.

He read the message, slamming his fist into the arm of the recliner. Tika, who was streaming the television show *Naked and Afraid*, was startled.

"What ... what just happened? Tell me!"

Tommy turned toward Tika with a huge smile on his face.

"Your son—no, our son—just became a man," Tommy stated.

Even though Tika would never like what Tommy and now Steven were involved with, she listened to Tommy explain the entire situation that Steven had been a part of and its final outcome. Tommy watched silently as a slight smile crept across her face. He wasn't about to ask if the smile was because their son was safe, or because she was proud of Steven. He just assumed it was both.

 **HAPTER 30**

The next morning everyone was awake and already having breakfast.

"What's the occasion—why is everyone up?"

"Tika has some work to do over at the health clinic, so we decided to take you and Marty there to get a peek at the facility," Tommy replied.

"Okay," I responded. It sounded harmless to me.

We were there in about an hour. The clinic appeared to be newly constructed. We entered into a reception room, and several administrative workers waved at Tika. After passing through the patient entrance doorway, we walked down a hallway with several examining rooms branching off of it.

We all paused by a door with a brass nameplate that read: Dr. Gary Tucker, D.D.S., firmly affixed to the wood. I didn't even recognize the name, but I should have, because it was my new identity.

That name was on my Social Security card, our bank account, my retirement funds ... everything!

Tommy opened the door, and we all entered my office.

"Have a seat in your office chair, Dr. Gary," Tika said with a broad smile on her face.

Then it hit me. *This is really my office*, I silently told myself. I sat down behind the desk still slightly dumbfounded. I opened the center desk drawer and saw that somehow, many of the knickknacks from my old practice had made their way to South Dakota. I could feel the onset of some tears of joy. "How did Tommy know? He and I were together in Oregon when I said that I'd never practice dentistry again! Obviously, he does know me like a brother. And to think ... I thought I was great at deception."

"Let's go meet your staff," Tika said.

My new receptionist was Sharon. Next, I met two of three hygienists, Michelle and Mary. Barbara, who worked part-time, was not present on this day. I was then introduced to my chair-side assistants, Sarah and Evelyn. All told, the staff was a mix of youth and maturity but most importantly, experience. It was a humbling moment.

From there, we went to the operatories where dental care services would be crafted. On the countertop were my glasses—complete with magnification and my LED headlamp battery. Obviously, Tommy and Marty had been conspiring for weeks.

The old cowboy adage "When you fall off the horse ... the best thing to do is get right back on" apparently also applies to dentistry!

I would soon be back in my dental saddle.

Everyone proceeded to a conference room where we enjoyed a late-morning brunch. Each member of the staff talked about their family and work experiences. Afterwards, I thanked everyone and asked when my start date would occur. Sharon lifted a shopping bag up on the table and removed a dental gown, which she handed to me.

"There's a six-year-old in operatory Number One. He has a toothache that needs treatment."

"And the rest of the afternoon?" I asked.

"You're booked until 5:00 p.m.," Sharon told me.

I looked at Marty and said, "Pick me up around 6:00 tonight, please!"

∩ ∩ ∩

Marty was prompt and before I left, I thanked the staff for their warm welcome. I was tired, but it was a good tired. Dentistry is a rewarding profession—and as dentists, we're all aware that our patients for the most part would rather be anywhere else than in a dental chair, submitting to our poking and prodding in their mouths.

As Marty drove home, I reminisced about Dr. Robert Tootle. Single-handedly, he was responsible for my successful dental career. As a part-time, one day a week educator with a separate private practice, he taught me the most important patient technique ... the painless injection of anesthetic. A painless shot in the mouth always sets the table for a pleasant dental experience.

Now, here I was far away from the Midwest, introducing the same technique to native Americans.

Towers Above was a dream come true, but dentistry would always be my number one true love!

As we drove into Tika's driveway, Tommy was standing on the porch awaiting my arrival.

I climbed the three steps to the porch and Tommy invited me to sit with him for a few moments. I took a seat in a Cracker Barrel-type rocker.

"Rob, I'm going to show you a text I got from Stan last night."

I read the message and literally felt my heart skip a couple beats.

"For real, this is verified?"

"I talked with Steven today. Rob, I didn't think he could do it. I expected that if there was a direct confrontation with Muhammad, Steven would let him take the first shot. Mt. Hood was his first live fire experience and I was not convinced he'd have the gumption to take a 'make my day' type of decision."

"So where does that leave me, Tommy? How many others want a piece of me?"

"Rob, I wish I had the answer to that. Stan has no concrete evidence of another group backing an assassination attempt against you. However, he does respect Bud, head of the DIA. Stan is perhaps being overly cautious, but right now he's working on another potential threat—not only directed at you, but possibly to others in the future.

"We have to let Stan do his investigation, Rob. Marty seems to have settled in here in South Dakota. You've got a clinic to run, and I know the community is happy you're here."

I lowered my head, closed my eyes, and rocked back and forth for a few minutes. The cool prairie breeze was comforting on this evening. I stopped rocking and turned toward Tommy.

"If and when Marty and I return to Kentucky, promise me you'll explain why you ever left this region of America. Okay?"

Tommy reached toward me and extended his right hand.

"Deal," he said ... and we both shook on it.

CHAPTER 31

Five months had passed since I returned to the practice of dentistry.

Marty and I had become solidly established in Oral, South Dakota, but we still struggled with our name changes. When someone would shout out, "How ya doing, Dr. Tucker?" it took more than a couple seconds to register in my mind that they were calling out to me. By now, folks had become used to my pause—and a rumor soon spread that I was slightly hard of hearing. It wasn't as much an issue with Marty, because most everyone simply called her Marty.

It was now late September and time for the annual buffalo roundup at Custer State Park—home to a herd of about fourteen hundred buffalo that graze, breed and live in the park year-round. However, the more than seventy-thousand-acre park in western South Dakota does have limitations—and if the herd grows too large, the land can't support the annual grazing of the buffalo population. The roundup helps ensure that doesn't happen.

The roundup is held annually to adjust the population count and to brand the calves born during that year. The branding, on the calves' haunches, shows the year each calf was born. An auction held in November reduces the herd count down to a thousand. That number stays consistent until new calves are born the following year. As a matter of course, older bulls are excluded from the roundup, basically because they are ornery and can be dangerous.

This would be the first roundup for Marty and me, the clinic was closed for the weekend celebration. Visitors come from across the US and many other countries to watch an actual Western roundup of these majestic American Bison. Visitors enjoy a vantage point from any number of viewing areas in the park.

These past five months had given me a new and calming sense of purpose. I'd almost forgotten that I was still probably someone's target.

∩ ∩ ∩

During these months, Stan had grown increasingly impatient and frustrated. Wayne and Todd Gail had done nothing that even hinted they were individuals to be concerned about. The agents following them were bored out of their minds.

After Muhammad was killed—and the ISIS threat apparently eliminated for the moment—Stan arranged to talk again with Bud. Stan hated to grovel for a second time, but he desperately needed another favor—he wanted to get an operative inside Bluegrass Station to spy on Todd Gail. He knew that as acting Director of the DIA, Bud had the Pentagon connections to get one of Stan's men placed on the inside and working alongside Todd.

During his conversation with Bud, Stan learned more than he expected.

"You know that both of those men are special ops and they are excellent snipers! If Chris Kyle was still alive, I'd put them up against him every time on a gun range."

"Yes, I knew that," Stan responded, lying through his teeth.

Within a week, Stan had an agent named Dennis in place.

After a month, Todd seemed to accept Dennis' presence. The area Todd was working in at the time didn't have the highest security level. While he still perceived Dennis as a possible spy, there was nothing in the building that was considered top secret. Besides, Todd had other business that needed immediate attention.

"Dennis, I'm taking a couple weeks of vacation starting on Monday. Hold down the fort while I'm gone."

Ⴖ Ⴖ Ⴖ

Dennis told Stan that evening that Todd Gail would soon be traveling.

"Where were you when Todd brought this up?"

"Boss, we've been inventorying a bunch of heavily armored GMC Yukons and Toyota Land Cruisers. The building has hoists used to stack and rack dozens of these vehicles. The glass on these vehicles is at least three-plus inches thick, and some of them had obviously been in areas involved with special operations. Hell, one had to have been hit by an RPG.

"So, we're about to break for lunch and he drops the vacation announcement on me—and he was nonchalant about it. After lunch, Todd takes me to another building that is packed to the hilt with 'Bug Out' backpacks and tells me that I'll be working there while he's gone. Bluegrass Station is the Disney World of special operations!"

"Do yourself a favor, Dennis. Don't go sniffing into other areas unless someone orders you to do so. I suspect he's still testing you."

When the conversation ended, Stan called the agent watching Wayne Gail's home to let him know that Todd would be on the move and that he should continue to be on his toes with Wayne.

Sure enough, on Sunday when Todd left for the Louisville airport, Wayne left his home at the same time and was also headed toward Louisville. Stan was quickly alerted to the twin's activities—and once each man arrived at the airport, copies of their itineraries were retrieved, courtesy of the NSA. Todd was headed to Costa Rica, while Wayne's destination was Grand Cayman. Agents shadowing both men watched as they checked in separately and retrieved their boarding passes. Each man then headed for the same terminal ... about five minutes apart.

The men entered the same restroom separately, but both emerged together ten minutes later—and one of the twins had changed clothes. They also had exchanged their driver's licenses and boarding passes while in the men's room. Now both were similarly dressed and pulling the same style of carry-on luggage. The two proceeded to their respective departure gates, boarded their planes, and were on their way.

The CIA agents watching the twins were now unsure if Wayne was now acting as Todd or vice versa! Stan and his agents had been gamed and were embarrassed.

Stan messaged the CIA bureau chiefs in both countries—and pictures of the twins were attached to the message, along with a description of the clothing each was wearing. When their planes landed, Todd was on Grand Cayman Island and Wayne was in Costa Rica. Each man had also been tagged for continued surveillance by the CIA. At their respective airports, the brothers stopped at the first available restroom. When each man came out, their clothing and facial appearance had totally changed.

At the same time in both locations, the now-clueless CIA agents continued to wait for their respective twin to emerge before finally deciding to go into the restroom. Each restroom was now empty—and the trash container was filled with clothing and decals that had been removed from each twin's luggage.

Mission Impossible was no longer just a Hollywood production—it was happening in real time!

Back at Langley, Stan was furious—but at least he now had confirmation that the twins should definitely be considered as threats. They obviously had known they were being shadowed.

Stan placed another call to the two bureau chiefs—giving strong orders that they find both men. Stan knew that if nothing else, the brothers would eventually have to leave and return to the US—and the Agency would then connect with each man. Only this time, there would also be incognito agents on both planes.

What Stan didn't know was this type of shell game was a ploy regularly used by the twins—and they had it down to a fine art. The bulk of their joint wealth was hidden in a specific Grand Cayman bank, but the bank account was in Todd's name. Even though he and Wayne were identical twins, facial recognition technology employed by the bank would immediately detect any difference between Todd and his brother. Knowing this, Todd visited the bank at least once a year to make a substantial cash withdrawal.

Todd left the bank with the down payment on a contract hit that had yet to be fulfilled.

The remainder of his vacation on the island would be spent in the million-dollar oceanside condominium the brothers owned. The next day, Todd would take his first dive.

The sport of diving in the Cayman Islands was superb.

# CHAPTER 32

Stan contacted Steven and asked him to have Tommy call. He hated the Agency's new protocols but could live with them … up to a point. And that point hadn't been reached quite yet.

It took just slightly more than an hour until Tommy called Stan. Both phones were highly encrypted.

"What's happening, Stan?"

"Remember that intense conversation we had a while back, about a possible global connection? Thanks to Ted and Charles' security detail at Woodlands Park, I think we've discovered some folks who might fit our profile for globalist allegiances."

"Shit!"

"Well, Tommy, you better double up on that word because you're not going to believe what I'm about to tell you next!" Stan replied.

"Go ahead—spit it out!" Tommy retorted.

"The assassins are identical twins, and I'm not messing with you!"

"Fuck!"

Tommy very seldom used those type of expletives. The memories of past turmoil and strife were immediately front and center in his mind.

"I'm listening, Stan. Go ahead and give me the details."

Stan spent the next few minutes going over what he'd learned about Todd and Wayne Gail.

"Honestly, Tommy, I think you and Dr. Becker are safe where you are. The twins certainly don't seem to be in a hurry to find you."

Tommy mulled that over. "If these assassins are as connected to billionaires as you think they are, I wouldn't be so sure. Right now, I'm certain their connections are combing through every detail about Dr. Becker's family and looking for any clues that might prove to be a weakness and could easily be exploited. Then bingo … we'll be flushed out of hiding." Suddenly, he could go no further with his concerns.

"You still there, Tommy?" Stan asked.

"Yeah, Stan, I was deep in thought. Please promise to keep me in the loop—I'm begging you. No bit of intelligence should be considered trivial! Promise me, Stan!"

"Do me a favor, Tommy. Sit down with Rob Becker and dig deep into the history of each member of his family—search for any flaws or cracks that exist now or in the past. The best defense is a good offense. If we're proactive, we may just shut down these global elitists and prevent them from accomplishing their goal."

"I will, Stan. Take care." The call was disconnected.

Tommy slumped into the recliner and realized just how little he knew about my family members. Other than my middle daughter that he'd met earlier and listened to as she described her son's vaping issues; that was it.

It was late in the day. Tommy decided to wait until the next morning to sit down with me and begin probing through my family's history.

∩ ∩ ∩

I was surprised to see Tommy up and about early on this Saturday morning. He had grown comfortable living a life of bliss with Tika, over the past several months. Seeing his contentment was a side of the man I'd never before witnessed.

This morning was different, though. I was staring at the old Tommy … he was all business, and that meant something serious had happened in the last few hours. I braced myself for a worrisome conversation.

"Go ahead, Tommy … start talking. You're about to explode!" I stated.

Tommy's eyes widened as if they were speaking aloud to me and asking, "Am I that obvious?"

"Stan and I spoke last night—there's a possibility that the Agency has identified some people who are showing an interest in your whereabouts." Tommy slid his cellphone toward me—its screen displayed a picture of the two people of interest. The identical faces were Todd and Wayne, and both were dressed differently.

"Are one or both of these guys assassins?" I asked.

"Most probably, yes and yes—think 'Double Mint Gum,'" Tommy replied.

"You're shitting me!" I exclaimed.

"That's my sentiment, too! Let's cut to the chase. I know you have three daughters, but other than the one I met whose son has a vaping problem, I want you to think of any weaknesses or vulnerabilities one of your other family members might have and could be exploited."

I closed my eyes and thought about the lives of each of my daughters. None had done jail time and none had any DUI charges. They all were successful career women. My oldest had run a small business for years. I was certain that each daughter had probably experimented with marijuana, but I had no idea if any of the three had experimented with more potent drugs.

Except for Harry, to the best of my knowledge, the other four grandchildren weren't addicted to any drugs.

"Tommy, the only member of my immediate family that might have a problem is my grandson Harry. Hell, Tommy, I tried marijuana after finishing dental school. I was on active duty at Newport Naval Station. I guess Harry would be the most vulnerable to anything evil."

"You alerted Stan about Harry's problem and your field agent supposedly is tuned in and paying special attention to his welfare."

Tommy spoke again. "Okay then, I'll reinforce with Stan that your grandson, Harry, is the most likely person in your family who could end up compromised. The rest of today, though, I want you to think intently about each and every member of your family and try to remember anything you might have forgotten. Remember—no person is infallible. These bad guys thrive on human weakness. Thanks, Rob."

"With Thanksgiving and Christmas just a couple months away, do Marty and I at least get the chance to talk with everyone in our family—and what about our sending them gifts or some money?"

"Rob, I knew this question would come up, and I understand your emotions. What you've got to understand, though, is that you and Marty are off the grid. I'll talk with Steven, who in turn will talk with the agents we've embedded with each family. The gift lists will be approved by you and Marty and sent on to Langley. A withdrawal from your retirement account will cover the expense, and the gifts will be bought and shipped from DC!"

"But ..."

"No buts, Rob! If packages were to arrive at your family's homes from Custer, South Dakota, and a porch bandit happened to strike—well, he or she could be an operative working for a globalist group that's looking for you! Now do you understand?"

Tommy was tapped out. He got up and left the house. No doubt he was either texting or calling Stan.

That was fine with me, but for the first time in quite a while, I wanted to be back home and closer to my family.

CHAPTER 33

Usually the month of December flies by in the blink of an eye. For Marty and me, the month seemed to last an eternity. The only positive for me was the twelve inches of snow that fell quietly on Christmas Day. As Marty and I took a walk, it felt like the Lord was covering up all the sins that had occurred on Earth during the past year.

Little did we know a far greater disruption in our lives had already been unleashed in mainland China.

Rather than warn the rest of the world that a virus other than Influenza A or B was ravaging one of their provinces, China's leaders chose to be silent. If Chinese citizens were going to die and their economy was going to take its lumps, their government officials decided it was best to "see no evil, hear no evil, or speak no evil." Finally, when the outbreak of this illness had become severe and had spread worldwide, the Chinese Communist Party was forced to reveal the existence of this new virus. It was as if the CCP was saying, "If we have to suffer, then the rest of world is going to suffer with us."

Marty and I so wanted to be close to our children and grand-kids and help soothe the crisis for them in our true home of Kentucky.

The Governor of South Dakota was almost alone nationwide in her governance stance to not institute a statewide quarantine. Two South Dakota counties were hit hard with the COVID-19 virus, and the elderly in those counties were advised by her to isolate themselves because the disease was most life-threatening for senior citizens.

I was also forced to quarantine, as dentists were deemed to be non-essential health professionals, with the one exception being a true dental emergency requiring attention. The American Dental Association also asked its members to close down in order to save masks, gowns, and gloves for hospitals and their attendant staffs.

Statewide, the native American reservations were allowed to blockade access roads to their reservations.

Suddenly, I became someone I swore I'd never be. I found myself sitting with Marty, Monday through Friday, watching *The Price Is Right* and *Let's Make a Deal.*

I wondered if the same type of mental torture was occurring throughout the other forty-nine states.

The well-known adage "Idle hands become the Devil's workshop" seemed to be the appropriate nationwide mantra, as news reports indicated that our society was unfortunately in the perfect storm for people with present or past addiction issues.

That included my grandson, Harry.

I sat down with Tommy in mid-March, expressing my concerns about Harry's welfare. What I didn't know was that Tommy had come to the same conclusion as I and that the Agency had already assigned an additional agent to shadow Harry.

Neither Tommy or I realized that the additional agent would be too late—virus or no virus—and probably would never have been timely. The deck had been stacked against Harry months earlier.

∩ ∩ ∩

Jeb Johnson was probably the only substitute teacher in the country with a net worth of five million dollars. If anyone met him or was invited to his townhouse, they would have come away thinking that he was a regular middle-class guy. That's why he was paid so well.

As a substitute teacher, he'd established himself as a superb educator. In late November, he received a call that he was needed at Man O' War High School in Fayette County—and he knew he'd get the job two days earlier. After all, his was the only name in bold letters within the Board of Education's list of substitute educators—and that meant he was highly regarded.

It's amazing how easy it was to hack into the district's computer database.

Man O' War High School was the school Harry attended.

Because the substitute position was going to be long-term, Jeb arrived early for his indoctrination. Part of the information he received that first day was the Vape List, so named because every student who had been caught vaping or was suspected of doing such was on the list. Harry's name was on the list, but there was an asterisk by his name. Jeb asked for an explanation.

"That student used to vape, but we've been working with his parents on his addiction, and we believe he's been clean for several months," the counselor replied.

"So, if I could ask, who on this list would be considered his friends...you know, the ones that he hangs with?" Jeb asked.

The counselor didn't hesitate in answering. In fact, she was quite impressed that Jeb was that intuitive. She put a check mark by the name of each student that Harry had been or still was close friends with.

After Jeb wrapped up his training and got into his car, he sent a text to Wayne Gail which read, "I've obtained the necessary information."

It would take a few days before the bait and trap would be set.

Harry and his parents had no clue of the danger Harry was about to be subjected to.

Time was on Jeb's side.

 **HAPTER 34**

It was the official first day of spring. One positive about treating only emergencies was that the downtime allowed me to reflect on the world's turmoil. I was sitting on Tika's porch, sipping my coffee in the cloudless weather, when Tommy suddenly appeared and quietly joined me. We exchanged good-morning pleasantries, but I continued to sit in silence while absorbing God's beautiful start to a new day.

Out of the corner of my eye, I could see that Tommy was busy on his cellphone. No doubt he was reviewing text messages from Steven and Stan.

Tommy had changed. I didn't mean physically, but certainly mentally. I could only speculate, but I assumed his love for Tika had never waned, nor had her love for him. Each of them had matured and with more than just a tincture of time, their youthful attraction for each other made their recent reunion one that would now be an inseparable bond.

For me, the downside of this renewed union was a lessening of Tommy's sense of urgency for the situation that was developing miles away.

The old saying that "for every action, there's an equal and opposite reaction" was fully on display.

In my mind, Tommy had lost some of his edge.

The Tommy I had come to know over the past several years was a man who was always a step ahead of the bad guys. Now he was no different than Towers Above had been in his most famous race—one which ended in a tie for first place, known in thoroughbred racing as a dead heat finish.

Tommy completed his morning business, and I couldn't resist poking the bear.

"I sure wish you were back in Kentucky overseeing the situation! Don't get me wrong … I'm not saying you don't care, but I've got to ask … do you?"

I watched Tommy's jaw muscles start to twitch and flex. I'd obviously gotten his attention, as his face flushed red.

"Okay, Rob, you've made your point. You have no idea how painful and unfulfilled my life had become, and how much I longed to be back in Tika's arms. Are you really begrudging me for how I feel now? You and Marty are safe here. I did what had to be done, and I'm not about to apologize for your being here in Podunk, South Dakota where no one can find you. Jesus, Rob, I can't be everywhere. I have to trust my fellow agents!

"You have no idea how frustrating it is to be up against a foe that might as well be invisible. Stan has bought into the idea of a globalist group or whatever you choose to call them.

"I don't think I need to remind you about the multi-millionaires and even billionaires that make a living from thoroughbreds—just as you have with Towers Above. They're up in Central Kentucky and are America's bluebloods of horse racing. That also includes all of the Middle Eastern-owned farms. They all despise you. I'd be willing to bet they all have a globalist mentality.

"I agree that there's an amorphous entity that has as much financial clout as any of our seventeen intelligence agencies. They also have access to the latest and best technology. This has resulted in conspiracy theorists rallying around a group known as

QAnon and their believers are right of center, politically.

"On the other side of the spectrum, there are individuals like George Soros, Tom Steyer, and other progressive billionaires who are very generous with donations to groups that tend to support progressive socialistic ideas and these folks would love to see capitalism curbed, at a minimum.

"Hell, the conservative Koch brothers have a problem with Trump. I can't stop liberals from donating to 501C3s that have satisfied the necessary federal paperwork. What the non-profits do with their money gives me the right to philosophically disagree, but again, it's their choice. Antifa is probably currently getting funding from several 501C3s. Black Lives Matter is being funded by almost all of the big Fortune 500 companies.

"Antifa is now nationwide, even though we believed we had defeated them. A Marxist-Socialist society is their answer to the problems they believe exist in America.

"Sure, we can have a strong belief as to who might be a participant in this globalist lovefest. However, their playbook is legal— and the actions of those who protest have been deemed legal. When they start destroying property that they don't own, then they're breaking the law.

"If the community refuses to arrest the lawbreakers, there is nothing I can do, legally. Our constitution allows us the option of voting those politicians who turn a blind eye to these lawbreakers out of office. Likewise, if the community wants to elect anarchists and communists to positions of power, that is their right to do so.

"The great thing about capitalism is that the businesses affected by radicals can leave their current community. California is losing businesses to Texas, Utah, Idaho, and Colorado by the hundreds. The same goes for individuals. If a person doesn't like the political direction their city or state is adopting, then they can move to a community that matches their philosophy.

"The frightening thing is, our society has become polarized. The 'us' and the 'them' are equally split. The last time that happened, our country went to war—a civil war. And there is nothing in our country's constitution that says we can't do that again!"

"I need to get home to Kentucky, Tommy!"

"Rob, you can't. That's exactly what your enemies want you to do. They don't have the foggiest idea where you and Marty are. You must have faith in the agents back home."

I stood and started to go inside. My frustration was beyond control, and I didn't want to say anything else that would escalate the situation.

"Where ya going, Rob?"

I stopped in my tracks. "Why do you care?" I said, and immediately wanted to take those words back.

Tommy didn't skip a beat. "I just thought you'd want to know Chevytothelevee's ultrasound results. One thing is certain, she's not carrying twins. The ultrasound that was done at sixty days shows she's carrying a healthy thoroughbred."

"C'mon, Tommy … you're not telling me the sex of the foal."

"Oh, that … sorry about that! She's carrying a stallion."

"Yes!" I thrust my closed right fist up into the air.

"I'm not done. Mike says the delivery day will be here before we know it, and he'll be moving in with her when delivery is imminent."

In the blink of an eye, my attitude changed. "Thanks for sharing, Tommy. I really appreciate it."

Podunk, South Dakota wasn't that bad after all, I thought to myself.

 **HAPTER 35**

Man O' War High School's Vape List was quite extensive and included students of both genders. The private detective agencies that Wayne contracted with had one directive—to find out who the drug dealers were at Harry's high school. The half dozen investigators believed they were on a mission for some parent or group of parents who wondered if their child was into vaping or even more potent drugs.

A tactic I'd used as a teenager to mislead my parents—by saying I was going to the library to study with so and so—was apparently a faux tactic still used in the 21st century.

However, with the COVID-19 viral pandemic complicating lives, it was really difficult, if not impossible, for teens to sneak around after school hours.

…and then the schools were closed to in person teaching and students were now schooled online and at home.

For those students having both parents working in essential businesses, it was open season for obtaining and doing drugs. It was like the Avon lady dropping off an order.

On the other hand, for students who had parents that were also confined to their homes, the dealer's delivery became more difficult. Each addict would get his or her delivery on a specific day, and that individual determined the drop site.

For some deliveries, the drop could be as simple as depositing the product in a mailbox. The teen would just have to be the one who got the mail. Most other drops would be in a designated outdoor location—usually a shrub in front of the home.

It took more than a month to determine who was dealing.

Once that was accomplished, the private detectives confined their time to staking out the homes of Harry's addicted friends. Eventually it was determined that a single dealer was serving all of Harry's friends and was probably the source of his Juul pods.

The detective agencies compiled their reports and as directed, shipped the reports by UPS to a fictitious individual with a mailbox at the UPS store. Within 48 hours, all the reports were in Wayne's hands. It was now time to initiate the second phase of his deceitful plan.

Jerry Jameson was Todd and Wayne Gail's go-to man. Both twins always assumed they were being shadowed, which is why Jerry often did a lot of their heavy lifting. Jerry also had a mailbox at the UPS store. He picked up his marching orders, and within three days, had assembled all the information he needed.

Being a Kentucky State Police trooper had its benefits. It now became a matter of what evening Jerry would harass Harry's supplier.

∩ ∩ ∩

Every profession has its weak performers. Whether it's from a lack of morals or simply believing he was above acceptable norms and society's laws, Jerry was corrupt.

Being a trooper for Kentucky's State Police served as a means of making money ... lots of money, especially since his salary was a pittance compared to what Todd and Wayne paid him. As an officer of the law, Jerry had power over people that others don't generally have—and thus the means of accumulating wealth by circumventing the very laws he had sworn to uphold.

His grey sedan had been following Anthony for several minutes, but Anthony had no idea a trooper was following his vehicle—until he saw the blue lights flashing in his rear-view mirror. He immediately pulled over.

Jerry called in a "10-46" and the radio crackled back a confirmation.

He approached Anthony's car slowly, eventually positioning himself slightly behind the window on the driver's side. Anthony lowered the window, waiting for the usual license and registration request.

"Anthony—do not turn around! Put your license and registration away. I know you're carrying a smorgasbord of drugs in the car, and you have so many prior offenses that one more will send you away for quite a long time.

"I could call for backup, but I'm not going to do that. Instead, I am going to ask a favor of you. All I want you to do is give this Juul and a week's supply of pods to Harry. And don't tell me you don't know what I'm talking about. Nod if you understand."

Anthony nodded in the affirmative.

"Next Monday night at 10:00, I'll be waiting for you in the parking lot of the dinner theater in Nicholasville. It's in Brannon Crossing. Again, nod if you understand."

Anthony bobbed his head up and down once more.

"Okay, get your ass out of here!"

Jerry had baited the line and was more than willing to be patient. The COVID-19 quarantine, especially for teens willing to cross the line, was the perfect storm for the devil's work. He figured the nicotine pods would last a week.

The next supply of delivered pods could possibly reward Jerry quite handsomely.

# CHAPTER 36

Harry was nicotine free—almost. He was now in the second month of wearing the lowest dose nicotine patch—his last patch. In just a couple of weeks, Harry would complete the six-month cycle he'd been on, to wean himself from his addiction.

Like so many others, my grandson was also COVID-19 bored and felt isolated. He hadn't seen his friends in weeks. Yes, he understood why the CIA agents were always nearby, but he was angry—and that anger was directed at me. Harry held me responsible for being kept on a short leash.

The only endorphin-releasing pleasures he had were the hidden *Playboy* magazines he thought his parents were unaware of, and his electronics.

His primary tech toys were a cell phone and laptop computer. Attached to those devices, like leeches, were popular apps that also stimulated the same endorphin releasing centers of the brain: Facebook, Instagram, Snapchat, and TikTok.

When Anthony texted Harry that he had some vaping pods and a brand-new Juul, it was no different from the biblical story of Adam and Eve. Harry was being offered the temptation to take a drag from a modern-day forbidden technology-laced fruit known as the Juul.

Vaping is a fire that burns white hot in so many of today's teens, including Harry—and this fire just had gasoline thrown on top of it!

For the next three hours, Harry tossed and turned as his mind wrestled with the temptation now offered to him.

I recalled from my teen years a Saturday morning cartoon show with an animated character that was depicted as an angel, perched on the left shoulder. The angel was debating a diminutive devil seated on the right shoulder. The two polar opposite characters argued back and forth, with the angel saying "Don't do it," while the devil espoused "Go ahead—try it—just one time!"

Harry finally fell asleep. Fatigue had given him a temporary reprieve from further emotional turmoil.

The next morning, the mental tug-of-war resumed. Harry wanted to talk about what was stressing him out, but he couldn't bring himself to admit to anyone that he was in turmoil. He needed to do something that could clear his mind.

Hoping for a distraction, Harry and his chaperone of the day, agent Lawson, went to the high school where he took shot after shot, on goal, on the soccer field…until he felt both legs begin to cramp.

After a brief rest, Harry tried to resume the workout, but he was tapped out.

Agent Lawson understood Harry's mental state and tried to help.

"Harry, we can stay here all day if you want. When I was your age, my passion was basketball. There were times when something would be eating at me, and I'd shoot hoops until sundown. Do you want to talk about what's bugging you?"

Harry's next two shots came nowhere close to being corralled by the goal's net.

"I know why you're protecting my family, and my grandpa is

responsible. I hate him! You can't do this forever! At some point, all of this has to come to an end!"

Harry didn't know how clairvoyant that statement would prove to be!

"When this epidemic finally ends and things return to normal, are you still going to shadow me? When I go on a date with some chick, are you going to be right there with us? C'mon, man … give me something positive to believe in!"

"Harry, I'd love to be able to answer your questions—but I'm not part of the chain of command. Unfortunately, I'm also not privy to any set timeframe or information about your family's current situation.

"I think you're wrong about your grandfather. There are millions of Americans who believe he's a true hero and patriot. I'm willing to bet that when you're older, your thoughts will flip and do a total one-eighty, and you will feel totally different about him!

"Son, I know something's eating at you—and I fully understand if you don't want to share anything with me. I do know that your parents love you and would be willing to give up their lives for you!

"When you finally decide what you're going to do with the situation you're in, make sure that decision won't hurt or embarrass your folks or yourself!"

Well, that doesn't help me much, Harry said to himself.

He continued with that train of thought. *Oh, what the hell; one Juul pod can't hurt me! If nothing else, I'll just go back on the patch again or chew some nicotine gum!*

The drive back was silent. Upon arriving home, Harry immediately went to his bedroom and slammed the door. Kathy looked at Agent Lawson with questioning eyes.

"I wish I could help, but I have no idea what he's thinking. This quarantine is not healthy … and especially not for hormone-ravaged teens. I'll stay up late tonight to make sure there are no shenanigans. If you don't mind though, I could use a good nap right now," the agent told Kathy.

It was at times like this when Kathy would rely on advice from Marty and me, but that was not an option today.

Meanwhile, Harry texted Anthony. He only wanted one pod and the Juul—giving Anthony specific instructions on delivery. It was arranged for 3:00 that next morning, when Harry would drop a sock attached to a fishing line from his bedroom window. Payment was promised when the quarantine was over.

Anthony was always prompt—after all, a drug dealer never misses a sales appointment. And of course, Anthony didn't just put one pod in the sock—he gave Harry five—enough for nearly a week, along with the brand-new Juul.

The devil had won on this particular day!

 **HAPTER 37**

It was Monday night and Jerry arrived early at the parking lot of the dinner theater. Anthony showed up five minutes later, pulling alongside the trooper's car. Both men lowered their windows.

"Give me an update, Anthony," Jerry exclaimed.

"Harry only wanted one pod, but I gave him a week's worth, plus a new Juul. I haven't heard anything from him since the delivery."

"You will ... Harry probably vaped sparingly at first and undoubtedly increased his nicotine consumption each day after. I suspect that he'll text you no later than mid-week.

"I've got three new pods I want you to give him, along with five more regular tobacco pods. If he asks what's in these new pods, tell him they contain nicotine derived from Cuban tobacco leaves that were harvested in the last year. These pods also contain some THC. The marijuana was cultivated right here in the Commonwealth!

"I tried one of the blended pods last weekend and it really mellowed me out. If he asks how much they cost ... tell him there's no charge and that you're giving them to a select few customers to get some feedback. If everyone likes them, then my supplier will start producing more of them."

Anthony grabbed the three pods and stared at them for a few seconds, silently thinking to himself, *I'll be damned if I give Harry all three of these! I need to sample at least one of them myself.*

Jerry was staring intently at Anthony's expression and when a smile crossed the drug dealer's face, Jerry knew exactly what he was thinking.

"Now don't you go trying one of those yourself; they're for Harry!"

Jerry knew there was nothing better than trying a bit of reverse psychology on a teen.

He passed an envelope through the open window to Anthony, who quickly took it.

"There's a little something for yourself. Don't go spending it all in one place!"

Anthony opened the envelope and pulled out a wad of Benjamins. He began counting, stopping finally when his tally reached five thousand dollars.

"See you next week—same day and time?" Anthony asked.

Jerry answered "Sure," before starting his car and waving goodbye … but thinking, *No, you won't be seeing me … ever again!*

Jerry didn't feel one bit of remorse that he'd neglected to tell Anthony about another ingredient in the special Cuban Juul pods.

ᴖ ᴖ ᴖ

Kathy recognized that something had changed.

The first five months with Harry wearing the nicotine patches had been stressful, especially the first month when the patch was delivering the highest dose of nicotine. Compared to then, this last month was paradise.

Kathy and Mike dropped the hammer on Harry at the start, giving him an ultimatum—either deal with the problem here at home in Lexington or be enrolled in Culver or a similar school out of state. The choice, with treatment at home, was to undergo a six-month regimen of patch therapy, and Harry knew his parents had researched Culver and had information about the facility's program. The decision was partially his.

Harry admitted he had a problem and begged his parents not to send him away.

It was mental torture at first for him to give up Juuling. One day at a time soon became his mantra. He was Juul-free for a month and slowly his confidence and self-esteem began to rise. At first, Kathy continued to remind Harry that he was still addicted to nicotine. After the second month of wearing the twenty-one-milligram patch, Harry's family held a party celebrating the successful completion of his first two months of nicotine freedom.

At the end of four months, the family held another celebration—Harry had finished the last of his fourteen-milligram patches.

Now, with the final month of patch therapy looming on the horizon, Harry's personality seemed to be going nowhere—and in fact, the teenager was in reverse gear.

Kathy thought back a few months and made the connection. She realized that Harry's personality began reverting to that of an angry teen whose life had become ruled by an addiction—just a couple of weeks into the nationwide COVID-19 quarantine and home schooling. She also remembered a conversation she and Agent Lawson had one week earlier, after he and Harry returned from the soccer field.

"Agent Lawson, do you mind sitting and talking with me about what you believe is happening to my son?"

"Certainly, ma'am, I'd be happy to share."

Agent Lawson began to speak.

"I'm not big on long dissertations, so this will be brief. When

I was first assigned here, I wondered if everyone realized how big a deal this was going to be for Harry. Kicking a nicotine habit is harder to do than someone weaning off heroin. I don't have personal knowledge of that, but it's a statistic presented in every smoking secession class. The same goes for any tobacco product, including dipping.

"I've been around quite a lot of smokers who tried to quit and for the majority, it usually takes more than one attempt to end the habit! I suspect that he is once again vaping or chewing a tobacco product. If he was doing combustible tobacco, we'd smell it in the house or on his clothing.

"I hope this has helped. Oh … and one last thing, he's got to have the nicotine products hidden somewhere in this house!"

Kathy nodded in agreement and decided to wait for Mike to get home from work before confronting Harry. Ironically, Harry had just texted Anthony asking for more Juul pods.

Anthony texted back.

Will make the drop tonight!
Same time as before?
New tobacco product with some THC.
Enjoy.

Harry didn't text back—and he had no idea it was going to be the longest night of his life!

 **HAPTER 38**

At the same moment that Kathy was waiting for her husband to get home from work in Lexington, Kentucky, I had just gotten home from a schedule full of emergencies. Marty was waiting for me on the porch of Tika's home.

Whether it was in Kentucky or South Dakota, whenever Marty was outside waiting for me to get home from work, it meant something serious was on her mind.

"Hey Marty, did you have a good day?" I asked as I climbed the porch steps.

"Please sit with me!" she answered.

I sat down next to her on an antique glider from the 1950s that had obviously been restored.

"Okay, Marty, spit it out. What's bothering you?"

"You're going to think I'm foolish, but I've been thinking all day about our grandson, Harry. I keep having a vision of him lying on grass somewhere, with his eyes closed. He was not in his bed. I know you're going to say there's nothing wrong about that, but this premonition is frightening me."

I didn't doubt Marty for a second. Over our lifetime together, she had other revelations which usually became reality, but not necessarily in the same manner she had described. Throughout my life, I also had interactions with individuals who were in another ethereal dimension. Mine were after death experiences with my mother and father-in-law.

"Is Tommy here?" I asked Marty.

"He's inside helping Tika with dinner," she told me.

I went inside and asked Tommy if he could give me a few minutes of his time. Five minutes later, the two of us were alone in the family room.

"I know you think you know all about me, but there are certain circumstances not only in my life, but Marty's also, that only our immediate family knows about. What I'm about to tell you has only been shared with our children until now." I went on to elaborate about Marty's lifetime premonitions as well as my own crossing over experiences I had with my mother and father-in-law.

"Tommy, I know there's no way you'll let us travel back to Kentucky—but please, I'm asking you to talk with the CIA agents who are protecting our daughter's family. There's something going on with our grandson. Hell, there's no way you've forgotten what Kathy told both of us about Harry's vaping!"

Tommy had not forgotten. In fact, he was surprised it had taken so long for something bad to happen.

"Tell Marty I'm on it. Thanks for sharing with me," Tommy said. He had no idea which agents were at Kathy's home and called Steven to find out.

"Hello Dad, how's it going out there?"

"Steven, your mom says hello and we—yes, you heard me say that word—are doing fine. But that's not the reason for my call. Dr. Becker's middle daughter Kathy, living north of you in Lexington, has a teenager who's going through what you did when you were a teen. Only now, his nicotine is delivered by vaping. I warned his mother that drug dealers were becoming chemists and introducing hard drugs into used Juul pods and recycling them. I know you've got names and cell phone numbers of the men guarding the family. Would you give them a call and see how Kathy's son, Harry, is doing?

"If he's still vaping, then tell the agents to get their hands on some Narcan. Tell them that a doctor's prescription is not necessary—they can go to CVS or Walgreens and ask the pharmacist for a two-pack of Narcan nasal spray containers. If the pharmacist hassles your agents, then have them show their Homeland Security badges.

"I'm going to hang up, but call me back after you've talked with your team up in Lexington."

∩ ∩ ∩

Steven didn't have the detailed information, so he called Stan. Five minutes later, he had both agents' cell phone numbers and decided to call Agent Lawson before calling Agent O'Brien.

"Agent Lawson, this is Steven. Do you have a moment to talk?"

"Yes, sir, I do."

"I know you've been tasked to watch over Dr. Becker's daughter and the rest of the family."

"Yes, sir!"

"I'm going to cut to the chase and ask you if you believe the son, Harry, is vaping or doing any other drugs."

"Yes, sir ... I do. However, I've only been here the past four months. I understand he's been wearing nicotine patches for nearly six months and is on his final seven-milligram patch. I've got to tell you that up until this past week, I felt sure that he was almost free of his addiction. But during this last week, he's demonstrated too many tells that he's back using some product with a higher level of nicotine. The mood swings, outbursts and frenetic actions all point to what I'd call a bipolar individual. Then, after he feeds the addiction, he's fine. But later when he needs an endorphin boost, his actions are almost manic in nature. He becomes a very angry teen.

"This evening, his parents turned their house upside down looking for his hidden stash of pods and a Juul. He's denied having anything. They just finished searching and found nothing. There's been screaming and yelling, as well as name-calling. Tears have been shed and nerves are frazzled."

"That's not good! Here's what I need you to do. Let O'Brien know you're going to CVS or Walgreens, whichever store is open all night. I want you to pick up two packages of Narcan nasal spray. Each package has two units of nasal spray—you'll have four doses. The cost is around eighty-three dollars per box of two units. Put it on your charge card and Langley will reimburse you.

"If Harry gets hold of any pods that have been enhanced with other drugs and he has an adverse reaction, I need you to administer the Narcan nasal spray immediately. Do you have any questions?"

"No, sir!" Agent Lawson replied.

"I hate to do this, but I want both you and Agent O'Brien to stand watch tonight. You guys can decide who takes the first watch after midnight. Continue each night until hopefully you see a return to normalcy in Harry ... and thank you!"

Steven wanted to drive to Lexington and do his own search, but he still needed to watch over my house. He agonized over what the teenager was going through. Steven had basically gone through the same turmoil when he was younger, but technology had changed the game and made taking endorphin-releasing drugs far more dangerous than when he was a teen.

 **HAPTER 39**

gent O'Brien took the first watch. During this time, he
logged five miles just circling the house.

He checked his watch, noting that it was time to switch with
his fellow agent. It was at that moment he realized they hadn't
discussed how to handle the changing of the guard.

Entering the home through the patio door, Agent O'Brien
went directly to the family room where he expected to meet agent
Lawson.

It was the same moment Harry dropped the sock out of his
bedroom window and Anthony sprinted toward it to make a
hasty delivery. In fifteen seconds, Anthony loaded the Juul pods
into the sock, gave a tug on the fishing line, and briefly glanced
up as the sock was hoisted to Harry's bedroom window.

From start to finish, the entire drug transfer took less than
two minutes, while the agent switch was still ongoing, validating
the saying, "Communication is key."

Early on this morning, the devil had sheer luck on his side!

∩ ∩ ∩

All wasn't so smooth before the delivery, though. Anthony
had no previous idea that what appeared to be a security team
would be patrolling the house, but he'd arrived early and seen
a man encircling the home with regularity. Anthony timed the
agent's route and realized that an exchange would be impossible.

He truly had no idea how long it would take to sprint to the house, wait for Harry to drop the fishing line baited with a sock, load the Juul pods, and then run away without being seen.

A now nervous Anthony started to text Harry but quickly stopped, as he suddenly realized the security guard was heading for the patio door. He erased the first text message and wrote instead, "Drop NOW!" He ran as fast as he could toward the house, amazed that the timing between himself and Harry was perfect. It was almost like being a part of an Olympic relay race.

It was now 5:00 in the morning and Harry was exhausted. He looked at the refurbished Juul pods and decided the best thing to do was place them in his hiding spot. If his parents heard him stirring, they'd realize he was just going to the bathroom and would quickly fall back to sleep.

Shutting the bathroom door, Harry went directly to the toilet—not to stand or sit—but to remove the cover of the toilet tank. Attached to the underside of the tank top with Velcro was a baggie containing empty pods and his Juul. He removed the Juul and the used pods, then placed his new pods in the baggie and secured it back in place.

He flushed the toilet a couple of times in case his parents were listening, washed his hands, and quietly returned to his bedroom.

He placed the Juul in the waistband of his underwear, along with the empty pods. In a few minutes, Harry was fast asleep.

∩ ∩ ∩

Anthony finally reached his home. Maybe his mom would hear him getting home late—and maybe not. She really didn't care what he did. There was no dad to back up any discipline, so there was none.

He was also tired, but not so sleepy as to stop himself from loading one of the doctored pods into his Juul. The used pod with its unknown ingredients snapped right into place on the stem of the Juul. In the stem was a recharged battery. That piece of the apparatus had been plugged into a USB port on his computer.

Anthony wasn't into hard drugs. He had never dealt heroin or opioid pills. Marijuana, however, was okay and couldn't hurt anyone, as far as he was concerned. In terms of it being a gateway drug, he believed that information was bunk.

It was time for Anthony to get high!

Not knowing the contents of the pod made him initially hesitate when he drew the first vapor into his mouth and subsequently into his lungs. He'd expected it to be like a Juul tobacco pod and was pleasantly surprised that it wasn't harsh. He thought he detected a bit of mango flavor.

The next two hits were stronger pulls of air that transformed into vapor. The endorphin centers of Anthony's brain were now fully turned on. He looked outside and the first glimpses of daybreak were gradually appearing. Sunrise quickly became a vivid display of unbelievable bright colors on the horizon. He inhaled deeply a couple more times and the THC took control of his brain's pleasure center.

He continued drawing vapor deeper and deeper into his lungs, hoping to enhance his high.

Then just when it seemed the sky was going to climax into the best sunrise he'd ever seen, the bright light began to lessen. He drew in more and more vapor and finally after multiple deep hits, daylight disappeared.

In a panic, Anthony turned his head from side to side and then realized he was blind.

His optic nerves had shut down fully, but instead of taking in deep breaths of air from the room, Anthony decided that a couple of more deep pulls on the Juul would bring him back to a normal high—if there ever is such a thing.

In a few more seconds, his central nervous system decided to call it quits!

At a quarter till seven in the morning – just a few hours after he dropped off the Juul pods at Harry's house, Anthony's soul left his body.

Satan's work was half complete—the second half had temporarily been postponed.

∩ ∩ ∩

Jerry had a rough idea how his plan would unfold. For him, Anthony was a means to an end.

Jerry was the only person that Anthony could identify, so it was imperative that he had to die. After Jerry gave the tainted pods to Anthony, he began to monitor the police radio. He knew he couldn't stay awake 24/7, so he enlisted Wayne and Todd's help in the monitoring.

He was back on duty and in his patrol car the morning of Anthony's demise when the code words indicating a "212" came across his radio. Jerry decided to respond to the call, even though the address given was within another police officer's geographical jurisdiction.

When Jerry arrived at Anthony's home, he had no clue who was inside. As he entered the home, he came across Anthony's mother, who was being comforted by a neighbor. He made his way to Anthony's bedroom, where the medics and metro officers were gathered. Jerry went into the bedroom where the body was already on a gurney and covered with a sheet. The coroner was also there, ready to take the body to the morgue and begin the necessary autopsy.

"What have we got here, Doc?" Jerry asked the coroner while lifting the sheet to look at the body of the deceased.

"If I were to guess, I'd say he probably died from a drug over-dose," the coroner said before elaborating further. "The deceased had a Juul tightly grasped in his hand. The e-cigarette was prob-ably compromised with some fentanyl. It won't be the first time I've seen this!"

Jerry released the sheet, letting it flutter back down on Anthony's face. He said goodbye to the metro officers and left the home.

"One down, one left," Jerry said while fastening his seat belt and placing the cruiser into drive.

# CHAPTER 40

"I can't sleep," Kathy said, nudging her husband.

"What time is it?" Mike replied.

"It's 4:00 in the morning! I've been tossing and turning all night. He's got to have those damn Juul pods hidden somewhere in this house. All I can think about is what Tommy, my dad's friend, said before Dad went into hiding!"

"Refresh my memory," Mike told Kathy.

"Maybe I didn't tell you then ... but anyway, Tommy said drug dealers are now refilling used Juul pods with fluids that contain some very potent drugs."

"Like what?" Mike asked.

"THC, heroin, some drug called fentanyl, and methamphetamine derivatives—I think that's all of them." Kathy answered.

"What's fentanyl?"

"I don't know what it is," Kathy answered, starting to cry.

Mike pulled his wife closer, trying his best to comfort her. Silence filled the bedroom for the next few minutes before Mike spoke again.

"Let's ask both agents to help. They probably have a lot more experience searching for something hidden—and in places that you and I would never think of. We'll ask them for help come morning, after they've had breakfast. Now let's try to get some sleep, okay?"

Although still shedding some tears, Kathy managed to

mumble "okay" as Mike rolled over to his side of the bed to get back to sleep. With her mind still running rampant and still unable to sleep, Kathy began to think of the places in each room of the house that could harbor the Juul pods.

∩ ∩ ∩

Harry had set the wake-up time on his iPhone alarm for 6:00 a.m.—and it went off right on time. Getting up, he headed to the same bathroom he'd used to hide his stash a few hours earlier and after entering the shower, the morning's plan began to crystallize in his mind.

He knew it was just a matter of time before one of his parents found his stash—and figured it would be his dad who would lift the lid off the toilet tank and turn it over, revealing the hidden treasure.

After toweling himself dry, Harry removed the baggie from its hiding place attached with Velcro to the underside of the tank lid. He removed the used pods from his sweat pants, wrapped them in toilet paper, and with just one flush, they disappeared. He then tossed the baggie and Velcro into the toilet bowl, and with another flush, disposed of that evidence in the same way.

Harry's early arrival at the breakfast table took Kathy by surprise—and he was prepared for another volley of accusations and contentious exchanges.

"You're up early. I take it that you're going somewhere—who are you meeting?" Kathy asked with disdain in her voice.

"I'm going for a run. I'm on the soccer team, remember? Did you forget that I have a conditioning regimen to keep up with? I'm sure you'll have one of our guards follow me, right?"

"I'm going to ask one more time. Where are you hiding the

Juul pods?" Kathy pleaded with her son.

"I don't have time for this! Tell your bodyguards I'll be running on the Legacy Bike Trail, starting near the Horse Park." Harry pushed his bowl of Cheerios away, stood, and gave his mother a parting scowl.

After hearing the slamming of the garage door, Agent Lawson entered the kitchen, taking a seat in his usual spot at the table. He was dressed for the day in his running gear.

"Was that how Harry typically interacts with you when he's angry?" Lawson asked.

"Unfortunately, yes. Surely you remember how you were as a teen," Kathy answered.

"I was eavesdropping when he lashed out at you, and I think he was gaming you. All of that was just BS. He's daring you to have me follow him. The kid's good—and yes, I used to pull that negative psychology routine on my parents when I was a teen. When you see Agent O'Brien, tell him where I'm going, okay?"

He grabbed his sneakers and was outside and headed to his car. Finding directions to the bike trail with his phone's Waze app, he quickly took off to follow Harry.

∩ ∩ ∩

Harry had a good ten-minute lead on the agent. As he ran on the trail with regularity, today's trip would be the same, except for the special "dessert" he was carrying.

He had no idea that this run would turn into a race—for his life.

Agent Lawson dutifully followed the directions on his phone. He was maintaining an average of eighty mph on I-75, know- ing that the Kentucky State Police pretty much give a pass to residents doing ten miles over the speed limit—and the agent didn't need to be pulled over right now. He figured he'd make up time when running, since a five-minute mile was still a pace he could easily keep up with.

At the park, Harry did his usual stretching and warm up exercises before starting to run—and his lead on the agent was now only six minutes.

As the agent got off the interstate exit, KDOT workers who were cutting the grass were crossing from one side of the exit ramp to the other, causing a delay of traffic and slowing the agent down. Lawson's make-up time was now at least eight minutes. Pulling into the trail's parking lot and finding a space to park added another minute to his time—and he still had to lace up his running shoes. The agent was almost back to the ten-minute deficit.

It was a beautiful day and Harry was halfway through the three-mile run. As he rounded the next bend, Harry couldn't wait any longer. Forcing himself to a stop, he veered off the trail to a grassy knoll on his right, sat down and retrieved his contraband. After clicking the pod into the stem of the charged Juul, Harry inhaled, dragging in a deep breath of nicotine, THC and fentanyl. The lead time was now seven minutes.

Agent Lawson was digging down deep for that extra speed to catch up with Harry, while still managing to surveil both sides of the trail in case the boy made a detour.

Harry was now in his third minute of mellowing out. As it had been with Anthony a few hours before, the THC kicked in first and the Lord's colorful natural beauty of the surroundings had intensified. With each drag of the Juul, the fentanyl continued working its sedative effects, sucking Harry into the drug's deadly black hole.

It was as if Harry were on an operating table, and the anesthesiologist was instructing him to count backwards from one hundred. Rarely does anyone ever make it to number ninety-five. If Harry had been counting backwards, his optic nerves would have stopped working at ninety-nine.

What just earlier had been a stupendous array of rainbow-like colors had now turned into nothingness! Everything had become pitch black and Harry was totally blind in both eyes!

What the hell? he thought.

The devil's work was almost finished—Harry lapsed into unconsciousness.

Agent Lawson rounded the same bend, running past the grassy knoll. Suddenly out of the corner of his right eye, he thought he saw a body lying supine on the grass. "Shit—damn it!" he exclaimed.

Lawson quickly retreated a few steps and in just seconds, dropped to his knees alongside Harry. He shook Harry, but to no avail. Next, he felt for a pulse in the carotid artery. "Thank God, he's got one," Lawson said under his breath. He quickly rolled Harry over onto his stomach to prevent him from aspirating any possible vomit while at the same time, grabbing his phone.

"9-1-1 ... what's your emergency?" the dispatcher asked Lawson.

"I'm about two miles from the Horse Park entrance on the Legacy Bike Trail. I'm just off the trail, on a grassy knoll, with an unconscious young man—please send help," Lawson calmly and clearly stated. The 911 dispatcher relayed the information to the appropriate Life Squad rescue unit and the Kentucky State Police, while continuing to collect pertinent information from the agent.

After hanging up, Lawson reached in his right pocket and retrieved one of two double packs of Narcan nasal spray. He took one unit of the spray and inserted the neck of the container into Harry's nostril and administered a first dose of Narcan. Moving away slightly, he looked for signs of consciousness, glancing down at Harry's hands to see if there was any movement in the extremities. The agent spotted the Juul still clasped tightly in Harry's right hand. He took it out of Harry's hand and put the Juul in his own pants pocket. Next, he checked for any other Juul pods Harry had on him—and instantly he hit the drug jackpot. He put the rest of Harry's happy juice in the same pocket of his pants.

Lawson checked Harry's pulse again, but nothing had changed. He decided to give the unconscious teen a second dose of Narcan.

Agent Lawson didn't know, however, that because Harry's heart rate was so low and the heart's strength so weak, the boy's blood pressure was barely forcing enough blood supply into the nasal capillaries. Some of the Narcan was being absorbed, but not nearly enough to reverse the effects of the fentanyl.

The agent heard the sound of a siren in the distance, and during the next few seconds, the sound grew stronger.

A Kentucky state trooper was first to arrive on the scene, followed shortly by the Lexington Life Squad—both units being driven along the bike trail in order to reach Harry.

Trooper Kessing approached Agent Lawson, while the paramedics attended to Harry.

"Are you Mr. Lawson?" the trooper asked.

"Yes I am," he said while pulling a Homeland Security badge out of his left pocket.

"I need a moment with you," Lawson told the trooper.

The trooper and agent retreated out of earshot of the medics.

"The boy is under Executive Branch protection, Trooper Kessing," Lawson explained.

"Obviously you're not doing a very good job, and by saying the Executive Branch, am I supposed to assume you mean the POTUS?"

"Yes, I do," Lawson replied, resisting the urge to escalate the incident with a comeback insult. "The report you're going to write will never exist. In fact, this entire incident never happened, okay? If you like your job…I expect you to cooperate! I'm going over to talk with the paramedics. I trust that you'll honor my request."

Lawson turned and walked away, leaving Trooper Kessing with a dumbfounded look on his face.

"Gentlemen, I'm with Homeland Security. I administered two doses of Narcan nasal spray. As you can tell, nothing has happened yet. If you don't mind, I'll follow you to the hospital. You need to know that this patient vapes. I suspect he got hold of a doctored Juul pod, so assume the worst as far as the pod's contents. I will not give you or Officer Kessing the pod or the Juul that he used. And yes, I took it out of his hand." He repeated the same warning he'd just given to Trooper Kessing, to both paramedics—along with ten crisp new $100 dollar bills.

The paramedics finished hooking up an IV and began running fluids into Harry's body.

"Well, Mr. Lawson, you've saved this young man's life for the moment! Don't follow us too closely, but we're going to UK's emergency room," the senior paramedic stated.

Within twenty minutes, the entire group arrived at the entrance to the hospital's emergency room.

Harry was still unconscious.

For Agent Lawson, the day couldn't end soon enough. He sprinted through the emergency room doors, flashed his badge, and was guided further into the bowels of the hospital where a special team of doctors and nurses who had seen drug overdoses far too many times in their careers were triaging other overdose cases. Harry immediately became their primary concern.

Harry was alive, and yet he wasn't. Medicines were delivered to stimulate the strength and frequency of his heartbeat, along with another dose of Narcan, this time given intravenously.

Agent Lawson just stared at Harry's lifeless body.

There's not going to be a quick fix, he thought, quickly realizing how bad a pun he'd just made.

It was time to bring others up to speed.

Before calling Kathy and Mike, Lawson called Steven in Southern Kentucky.

In a few minutes, details of the day's events would speed both east and west.

This major conundrum had only just begun!

CHAPTER 41

Agent Lawson wanted to be certain that he correctly followed the chain of command, before calling Harry's parents.

Steven was the next link in the chain and technically responsible for the actions of agents O'Brien and Lawson. Needless to say, this situation was totally unexpected. After filling Steven in with all the details of the situation, followed by a half-minute pause, Steven basically answered a question with a question. He asked his agent if he was comfortable breaking the sad news to Harry's parents.

"Not a problem, sir," was his reply.

As soon as Agent Lawson hung up, Steven called Stan, giving him the update he'd just received from Lawson.

A day full of surprises just kept on giving.

"Steven, I need you to do the agency a huge favor. In fact, I need you to do me a favor. I want you to talk your father into coming out of retirement. Don't doubt for a moment that as soon as Rob Becker finds out his grandson is in a coma, he'll find a way to get back to Kentucky. I'm guessing that is exactly what some person or persons want! They want Rob to come out of hiding. It just makes sense.

"Steven, your dad has been my wild card for years. I'm not out in the field anymore—those years ended long ago. Your dad was the one I depended on to always come up with a plan. Please don't misunderstand me; you've done one hell of a job! You're going to be every bit the agent your father has been. The only thing you lack is experience.

"It won't be easy convincing your dad to come back. Tell him I'll have a contract in his hands by this evening. I guarantee the contract will spell out how this will be the last time he'll be called upon!"

After ending the conversation and promising that he'd relay the message to his dad, Steven continued to stare at the phone for a few seconds. A backhanded compliment was the last thing he'd expected from Stan. He took a few deep breaths to oxygenate his brain because the next conversation would need every bit of oxygen to coax his dad to again leave Tika.

∩ ∩ ∩

Agent Lawson texted his partner with the bad news. He wanted him to be prepared for the eruption of emotions when the call was made to Harry's parents. O'Brien replied with a thumbs-up emoji.

Agent Lawson tapped on his cellphone screen once and was immediately connected to Harry's home. Kathy answered.

"Mrs. Stevens, this is Agent Lawson—I caught up with Harry on the Legacy Trail and I'm with him right now!"

"What? Where?" Kathy replied.

"I'm at UK's emergency room. Your son had a bad drug reaction and right now he's not awake but seems to be stable." Agent Lawson was doing his best to blunt the shock of the word "now" to Kathy.

It didn't work.

There was no reply, just a lot of background noise.

"Hello ... anyone? Hello?"

"Sorry about that, brother," O'Brien's voice said suddenly.

"She fainted!"

"Is her husband, Mike, there?" Lawson shouted into the phone, hoping he'd be heard above the commotion at the other end.

"Yes, he is and as soon as we stabilize Mrs. Stevens, we'll be on our way to the emergency room," O'Brien responded.

"When she comes to and collects her wits, I'm sure there will be lots of questions. Be honest with her. Tell her that Harry's in a coma and his breathing is shallow; his heart rate is very slow. Don't tell her that in my opinion, Harry's about as close to death as a person can be," Agent Lawson said. He was truthful as well as brief, concerning Harry's condition.

"We'll be there shortly," O'Brien answered, hanging up.

$$\cap\ \cap\ \cap$$

Tommy was just finishing breakfast when his cellphone rang. He looked at the caller ID and answered.

"Hey son, what's going on?"

Steven began the briefing and finished with the latest ER update on Harry.

"Is Stan in the loop?" Tommy asked. Steven confirmed that he was, took a hard swallow and sprang Stan's request on his father. The silence lasted just long enough that Steven was forced to say, "Dad ... are you still there?"

"I'm going to pretend I didn't hear what you just said. But in case you think I did, the answer is no!"

"Well, Stan's sending you an e-mail with a contract tonight. Why don't you look at it?" Steven suggested, pressing forward with the issue still at hand.

"Son, I'll read it, but I'm telling you right now—I'm not

leaving my home. I've spent a lot of years regretting ever leaving your mother. I can't take a chance of losing her forever," was Tommy's response.

"So instead you're willing to let Dr. Rob Becker be assassinated ... because that's what's going to happen when he makes his way back to Kentucky!"

"You don't know that. Rob Becker is once again practicing dentistry out here. He's not going to walk away from a dental clinic where he's in charge."

"Dad, you truly are living in a fantasy world! You really don't believe that family doesn't trump work. For God's sake, Dad ... his grandson is in a coma and is probably going to die. As soon as the news breaks that Rob Becker, one of the owners of Towers Above, has a grandson in a hospital in Lexington, Kentucky, in a drug-induced coma, you can bet he and Marty will return home. Hopefully it's not to help bury their beloved grandson. Jesus, Dad, quit thinking with your dick!"

The phone went silent. Steven was lucky—he couldn't hear or see the rage in Tommy that he'd just caused.

# CHAPTER 42

Jerry was getting ready for the shift change when Trooper Kessing entered the Georgetown Kentucky State Police Post.

As Kessing was changing out of uniform, he glanced to his right and spotted Jerry.

"Hey Jerry, there wasn't a full moon last night but there was some crazy shit going on out there."

"Care to share?" Jerry replied.

"Had a kid OD out on the Legacy Trail early this morning. So, I immediately think it was possibly a bad Juul pod loaded with fentanyl because of the other kid that died last night. I start to search for evidence and this guy walks up to me and says he's with Homeland Security. He then proceeds to tell me he has already recovered a Juul with the attached pod—and he's not giving it up. He then basically threatens me and tells me he's working for POTUS. This Homeland guy then tells me that if I like my job, there won't be a report filed.

"I called in and talked with the captain—he told me to write down the Homeland guy's ID number and snap a photo of his badge, as well as a photo of the victim and the victim's pertinent information."

Jerry, now at complete attention, asked the only question that he was concerned about.

"Was the kid alive?"

"Barely," Kessing said.

"He's at UK's ER, right?" Jerry casually asked.

Kessing, now back in his civvies, answered "Yep" and left.

Jerry assumed his main target had successfully been eliminated, but he needed confirmation. He didn't feel comfortable sniffing around UK's emergency room, especially with all the COVID-19 patients who were probably there. Instead, he called Todd who didn't answer his phone. Next, he called Wayne.

"What's up, Jerry?" was Wayne's greeting.

"I think I have a relative in the UK emergency room. He would have arrived this morning. I'm pretty certain it's going to be next to impossible to visit him with all the COVID-19 crap going on. Do you or your brother know anyone that's working in their Emergency Room Department?" Jerry laughed to himself about how he'd just spoken in code, knowing that Wayne and Todd's conversations could possibly be monitored or picked up via any NSA cell tower. He wasn't going to chance implicating himself.

"Offhand I don't, but let me check with my brother," Wayne replied.

Jerry thanked Wayne and ended the call. It wasn't more than five minutes later when Todd called Jerry.

"I have a friend who works in the ER. Let me see if they can help get the information you're looking for, Jerry. I'll get back to you."

Jerry thanked him, shaking his head in amazement. "Is there any place where these two guys don't have someone that's already on their payroll?"

The next thing Jerry did was to stir the pot. He called a local nationally affiliated television station and asked to speak with Vicky Clarkson in their news department. He didn't use his personal cellphone but instead called from a throw away phone he kept handy.

"Newsroom—what's on your mind?" a voice answered.

"Vicky it's me, Jerry! I was cruising near the Legacy Trail this morning and I swear I saw Dr. Rob Becker's grandson being attended to by the paramedics. Another trooper told me that he was taken to UK's emergency room. I called there, but they wouldn't divulge any patient information. Have you guys heard anything?"

"Jerry, thanks for the tip! If I find out anything, I'll call you back!"

Within minutes, a news van was on its way to UK's emergency room, while another van proceeded to Kathy and Mike's home. The vans would remain at both locations, waiting for undeniable confirmation that Rob Becker's grandson was hospitalized.

When a celebrity in any state, let alone the country, has a family member that does something newsworthy, that family can quickly expect sensationalism-type reporting. During the next twenty-four hours, reporters camped out at the hospital and at the home of Harry's parents, and it didn't take long to confirm that Dr. Becker's grandson was in the hospital. What had been a story worthy of being local news now became one of national interest.

∩ ∩ ∩

Tommy was irate!

He walked outside, down the porch steps, and out to the road. It wasn't a moment for throwing a tantrum, and deep down, Tommy knew that. However, if Steven had been physically present when relaying Stan's request, Tommy would have decked him.

The farther Tommy walked, the more his mood softened.

Finally, he came to a dead stop on the side of the road.

In those ten minutes, Tommy had finally come to grips with what he had mentally buried months earlier. Oral, South Dakota wasn't the agency's first choice of refuge for Marty and Rob. The only other person who knew that was Stan.

Tommy had lobbied Stan for the South Dakota location and Stan had granted his wish.

Now he had to convince Tika that his leaving her now would be for the absolute last time. He turned and jogged home, praying she would forgive him once again.

As he approached the house, Tommy spied Tika sitting alone on the porch. He climbed the steps and slowly walked over to sit beside her on the glider. Tommy gave the glider a push with his feet to get it started rhythmically moving back and forth.

"Tika, I hope you can …"

"Yes Tommy, I will forgive you!" Tika said softly in answer to Tommy's unfinished question.

"How …?" Tommy stammered.

"Tommy, when you fall asleep, make sure someone's not in earshot of you!" Tika replied. "You forget that you talk in your sleep. It's not every night, but when you repeatedly have the same dream, it's not hard to figure out what's on your mind. Look, I didn't go into this blindly! I never stopped loving you, but I knew that I couldn't compete with your first love—America. It's a shame our country will never get a chance to know just how much you love her.

"I'll not make you promise that once everything is over, you'll come back. I do ask one favor though—make Dr. Becker promise that he'll find someone to run the reservation's dental clinic. If there is one blessing that has come from your return to Oral, it has been the clinic."

Tommy buried his head in Tika's chest, feeling the tears now forming in the corner of his right eye. She held him tightly against her breasts while continuing to push the glider back and forth ... back and forth.

# CHAPTER 43

The sun was just setting when Tommy checked his e-mails—sure enough, there was a message from Stan—but it was in his junk folder.

The contract read like a construction bid with points listed.

- Demolition of existing edifice … $250,000.
- Environmental clean-up of the footprint that said edifice previously occupied … $250,000.
- Determine the cause and eliminate it from any future reoccurrence.
- Indemnification of legal costs: to be determined … with maximum being $250,000.
- Costs yet to be determined … $250,000.00.

First, Tommy would tear down Todd and Wayne's network of corrupt individuals in Kentucky. More importantly, Stan was giving Tommy permission to interrogate Todd and Wayne, using any methods necessary to determine and unravel the hierarchy that both men were partnered in and/or employed with. Finally, in the event of any legal entanglements, there would be sufficient funds to defend Tommy from any and all liabilities.

This gibberish was Stan's way of telling Tommy what he wanted done without fear that a computer hacker would decipher the message.

Tommy read the contract again and then asked Tika to read it.

"What happens if all this goes south and fails miserably?" Tika asked.

Tommy stared at her for a few seconds. *Where did that come from?* Tommy thought to himself. *Obviously she believes this contract includes her. She has bought in! I guess it's time to make our relationship official.*

A smile slowly crossed Tommy's face.

"Well, it's not going to fail—and that answers your first question. And secondly, I've got a question for you! Will you marry me, Tika?"

Tika realized she was trapped. After all the years of being despondent and filled with past regrets, she could end the remorse with a simple affirmative answer.

"Damn you, Tommy!" Tika answered while jumping into his arms and wrapping both legs around his waist. "Yes, Tommy, I will marry you!"

Just that quickly, both contracts were sealed with a long embrace.

Stan would just have to wait a few minutes before he received Tommy's electronic signature on the contract.

The next morning, Tommy was up well before sunrise. It was time to sit down with Marty and Rob, explain what had happened just a few hours earlier, and what their response would entail.

∩ ∩ ∩

Marty and I entered the kitchen filled with the aroma of coffee brewing, mingled with the smell of bacon and eggs.

"Well, to what do we owe this occasion?"

Tommy didn't bat an eye. "Rob, it's your grandson, Harry," Tommy bluntly said.

Before I could speak, Marty screamed.

"What's happened to our grandson, Tommy?"

"Marty, I'm sure Rob told you about the conversation I had a while back with your daughter Kathy. It was about doctored Juul pods. This morning Steven texted me the results of Harry's blood test and it was fentanyl that caused him to almost die. If Agent Lawson hadn't administered Narcan nasal spray, he most certainly would have died!"

The force of the terrifying news left both me and Marty speechless for several seconds. Then Marty buried her head in my chest and sobbed uncontrollably.

"Who ... what?" I managed to utter.

"Steven was with investigators from Lexington's narcotics division most of last night. They are ninety percent certain that a young man named Anthony, a young man who died a few hours before Harry collapsed—also from a tampered Juul pod—was Harry's drug dealer!

"Rob, the folks who want you dead are the ones ultimately responsible for Harry's condition. They really didn't care if he died. What they wanted is for you to show yourself. They know you've disappeared, and Harry's foiled murder attempt was designed to flush you out and into the open.

"Steven talked with the attending physician, and he has been advised that Harry could possibly be in a coma for months! He's stabilized, but is also in the same condition as a purposely drug-induced head trauma patient would be put in.

"We can't afford to let this situation go on for months. So yes, Rob, we're going back to Kentucky. If Harry's attempted murder was designed to flush you out, then your return will be on our terms. We'll be the ones doing any flushing.

"Over the next several days, we'll set up plans for our ruse. Meanwhile, you and Marty are going to need to get some black clothes. We're going to have your grandson's fake wake and a celebration of his crossing over!"

Marty had slowly stopped sobbing, but Tommy's last words produced sounds I'd never heard during all of our years of marriage.

"Marty ... Marty ...! Please listen to Tommy for a second, I'm begging you." Marty turned toward me, trying to choke off her tears.

"Tika is all in on this. In fact, before we leave Oral, she and I are getting married. Rob, I'd like you to be my best man, and Marty, Tika would be honored if you were her matron of honor. Tika did ask one favor of me, Rob. She wants the clinic to be fully staffed. She needs you to guarantee that before we leave for Kentucky, someone will be here to fill your shoes."

"I'll have the name of an individual for you as soon as possible, Tommy. But I need Stan to personally do the interview with the individual. Just know that if that person says yes, then he or she will know where I've been living and working. My cover will pretty much be blown because that individual knows me as the old me, and not someone named Dr. Tucker! I can't even imagine any dentist taking this job without knowing that the recommendation came from me, Dr. Rob Becker."

"Point taken, Rob. It's Stan's problem now!" Tommy said, smiling.

# CHAPTER 44

Every way I analyzed the situation, if Harry didn't survive, I would be responsible for his death. If only I had died along with Mark, my grandson wouldn't have been targeted. That painful reasoning repeated over and over in my mind, giving me an excruciating headache.

Marty went to bed sobbing—literally crying herself to sleep. Sleep wasn't an option for me at this moment...or so I thought. I put on a jacket, went outside, and plopped myself down on the antique glider. With my right lower leg draped at a forty-five degree angle and my right foot planted firmly on the floor of the porch, I began pushing. The glider began rhythmically moving back and forth, giving me the same calming motion I remembered as a child.

That calming motion was what put me to sleep.

My mind slowly drifted down a path that one's mind should seldom travel. One shouldn't continuously dwell on their own death—or the death of a family member. As I slumbered, my thoughts flashed back in time to two strong memories of drug-related deaths.

One was from a few years earlier, while the second was even more recent, and both were very dark.

∩ ∩ ∩

What was striking about the drug-based deaths of two youths was their heavenly connection to earthly butterflies!

A fellow dentist had shared the first memory with me. It was as vivid in my dream as it was the time she shared her thoughts.

She had lost her son to an overdose of OxyContin, an event not uncommon in the '90s and during the early millennial years. Her son had overdosed on multiple occasions—and eventually the addiction took his life.

The dentist sat with me one night at a dental study club meeting and afterward, began telling her story. We talked late into the evening hours.

After his passing, she found a therapist who managed to help her heal and move forward somewhat. She told me the toll the loss of one's child takes never allows a parent to fully recover emotionally.

"NEVER," my sleeping mind said.

My mind was deep in the memory she had shared with me that night and the special moment she said took place during her son's graveside service. It was as if she were right there dreaming with me.

"A monarch butterfly landed on my chair, pausing long enough to make the visit more than just a coincidence. That experience was randomly reinforced several more times when the grief of my son's loss hit me hard—again and again.

"Indeed, each time remorse rears its head, no matter what the season is, a beautiful butterfly or moth appears. It's always a comfort to me," she shared.

I was remembering how she firmly believed these occurrences were not random but were meant to reveal that her son was now in a good place and at peace. As we talked, she emphasized that there was not a day when the loss of her son didn't make its way into her mind—poking at her to make certain she hadn't forgotten.

"Indeed ... butterflies are the Lord's messengers!"

Within seconds, my dreaming took me to the second event. A LPN nurse who Marty knew, had shared with me her story—again, including how butterflies eased her pain.

She was talking about how she lost her youngest daughter to drugs in 2019. The daughter was twenty-two years old when the coroner declared her drug overdose as accidental.

It also wasn't a death that could be blamed on poor parenting. During her teen years, anger issues reared their ugly head inside this young woman. Her parents recognized that counseling was in order—and it was determined that she was suffering the effects of long-term bullying when she was very young.

The diagnosis of PTSD was another example that this mental malady is not limited to just soldiers!

The social insecurities continued throughout her teen years and her life was further compromised when she became enamored of and addicted to social media outlets.

On the February evening when she overdosed, all her social and personality weaknesses were taken advantage of. She was murdered—involuntarily!

That particular evening, a friend invited her to join up with her and her boyfriend. Perhaps if she had known that the boyfriend was a drug dealer in his late thirties, she'd not have gone. The partying occurred at the residence of the boyfriend. Sometime late on that ill-fated night or during the next morning, her daughter stopped breathing.

It was 1:00 that Saturday afternoon, almost 24 hours later, when either the girlfriend or the drug dealer decided to check on her still body and discovered that she wasn't breathing.

A lethal combination of oxycodone blended with fentanyl had murdered her!

The partying that night most probably began with her mellowing out with marijuana.

She wasn't told that the hybrid oxycodone pill also contained fentanyl.

Her daughter had been undergoing drug screening every month and was "clean" for several months prior to her overdose.

In combination, each drug depresses the central nervous system to the point where nerve signals controlling the involuntary process of breathing had stopped functioning. The post mortem examination revealed that these two drugs, along with THC, were found in her body—and both of the individuals partying with her that night denied any knowledge of how the drugs got into her body.

How could that be true?

A few weeks after her death, guilt became too much for the girlfriend to bear. She confessed to the dead girl's mother that the evening of partying on that February night was a continuous roller-coaster ride of mood elevators—and she was very sorry for what happened. What she failed to emphasize during her confession was the intimidation she and her drug- dealing boyfriend used, in convincing her mentally fragile daughter to try the hybrid drugs.

Weeks later, the friend changed her mind about any further sharing of that Friday's events. She was no longer sorry enough to testify in front of law officials, when the chips were on the line!

The deceased's mother wanted me to know that her daughter loved butterflies. Not because they were a product of a not so beautiful cocoon, but because the metamorphosis produced a creature that represented a new beginning.

I could envision the butterfly tattoos her mother and two older sisters now sport in commemoration of her life.

My mental fog began to lift.

I started to wake up and realized the glider had stopped moving! My foot was more asleep than my brain, but quickly my dreaming resumed.

Harry wasn't the only one in the family to ever become addicted.

Different times result in different types of addiction. My teenage misstep was tobacco.

Harry's addiction to nicotine was the same as mine years ago, but the delivery system—a Juul—was vastly different.

While I did combustibles, by the time marijuana was added to the smorgasbord of dopamine activators, I had grown up and chose not to go that route.

Then, later in life, when I needed multiple surgeries on my left shoulder, I was introduced to opioids for pain relief. They served their purpose and allowed me to continue practicing dentistry throughout almost a decade of pain. I also was introduced to the dark side of these opioids. Besides three trips to the emergency room for an irregular heartbeat, I hated how angry I would become when the effects of the pain pill began to wear off. I promised myself to never chase the high these medications produced.

Suddenly, my dreams turned into a nightmare!

Harry had died!

His heart had stopped pumping.

My body literally spasmed as I thrashed around on the glider, which had stopped minutes earlier.

I sat up and looked around to see if anyone else was present on the porch.

Now fully conscious, I rested back on the glider, relieved beyond measure that this had all been a dream.

What was so different between my teen years and Harry's? I wondered.

When I was a teenager, finding a drug dealer wasn't a way of life, and my drug of choice—nicotine—was readily available. Then it hit me—in today's times it's all about having more choices...all bad ones! In today's world, drug dealers offer a smorgasbord of dopamine stimulators. That's the difference!

Marijuana has pretty much replaced alcohol. Whoever believes marijuana isn't a gateway drug is full of shit! Drug dealers today also have a full menu of mood modifiers—yours for the asking—and sometimes not for that much money! If THC is no longer a fulfilling experience, one can easily add cocaine to the mix.

And if that's not good enough, well, a teen can just as easily add heroin or meth to their plate of goodies.

But wait ... there's more! Don't forget to add in all the pills with names that pharmaceutically end in "pam."

Keep in mind that the majority of these drugs come across our southern border. The Communist Chinese government encourages the manufacturing of these drugs, while the Mexican drug cartels reap the financial benefit of selling them. That's just one reason why Trump wanted a border wall built.

But for those of us who have lost a child, a grandchild, or for that matter even an adult family member, it's not just the mental anguish and pain that we suffer from! We are affected by how the mental and physical toll trickles down to multiple family members.

And by God, if somehow Harry does die, someone has to pay. There will be consequences! I've had my time in this world. It won't matter if I cross over—someone is going to pay the price for what they may have done to my grandson Harry!

The faint hint of a new day was showing itself on the horizon. I opened the porch door and headed inside, wanting to crawl into bed with Marty, but instead I walked into Tommy's chest.

"You're just now going to bed?" was all that Tommy said.

"Yes, I'm going to bed, if you don't mind," I replied gruffly.

"Well, sleep tight, because when you get up, we need to talk," he warned me, while proceeding to my still-warm spot on the glider.

 HAPTER 45

Stan was in his office early, anticipating an e-mail with a signed contract from Tommy, his go-to agent—and he wasn't disappointed. Stan was further rewarded by the ringing of his cell phone, showing Tommy's mobile number on the screen.

"You're up early. Already chomping at the bit, huh?" Stan said laughing.

"I haven't slept at all, you prick! If you intend to piss me off, I'll void that contract I know you're looking at right now," Tommy replied.

"Okay, so what have you come up with? And mind you, I haven't had my coffee yet," Stan warned.

It was Tommy's turn to laugh!

"It's good to be back, boss! I have to say, I'm not surprised that Rob's grandson is the one that's compromising our stay out here in the Black Hills. It's really a shame, though, that he's the weakest link and was purposely targeted!"

"I've got to ask—is there any improvement in his status?" Tommy asked.

"No, he's still in a coma. Nothing's changed, Tommy," Stan sadly replied.

"Well, here's what I intend to do. We're going to flip the script, Stan.

"If they want the kid to be the bait, then so be it! Since he's supposed to be dead, we're going to make him dead. They want

Rob Becker in the open, so we'll accommodate them that way, too. What better scenario could Rob's potential killers ask for... holding a graveside service for the kid in order to kill Rob Becker!

"That's part of the setup, being graveside, and I'm going to leave the details of that for you, Stan. If Todd and Wayne think they're better snipers than Chris Kyle was, then we're going to make them prove it."

"Do you have any details worked out for me, Tommy?" Stan asked.

"Nope, not yet—but I've got a general plan outlined in my head. Give me the rest of the day and you'll have it in your mailbox by midnight. But know that I am expecting help from our R&D department! Agent Double 007 can't be the only one with access to some secret high-tech stuff."

"Gotta go, Stan. Look for that plan tonight," Tommy said before ending the call.

Putting his phone down on the glider, Tommy picked up his iPad Pro, tapped on the Google Earth app, and typed in Lexington Cemetery. The search was on, and in just a few seconds, the computer had zeroed in on an image of one of America's iconic cemeteries.

From Mary Todd Lincoln's family to perhaps America's most historic Speaker of the House, Henry Clay, the cemetery's arboretum-like setting was going to be the final resting spot for Rob Becker's grandson, Tommy thought.

Tommy didn't know exactly where Rob's family plot was situated in the cemetery, but that wasn't his priority at the moment. He wanted to get a feel for landmarks within the grounds of the cemetery, so he could focus on them when he got back to Lexington. He also needed to determine the four relative compass points. That way he could communicate those waypoints with other agents at any moment in time on any day.

He knew that the Agency might move a satellite into the proper position at least a day before the graveside service. That eye in the sky would perhaps be one of two look-down systems that would provide the necessary intelligence needed to capture Wayne and Todd attempting murder. Perhaps the second set of eyes might be aboard a U-2 spy plane—circling above in the stratosphere and out of sight.

Tommy took a pause to write a note to himself.

"Check the long-range weather forecast for the day of the memorial service. If it's supposed to be cloudy, the service should be postponed. One can't see what can't be seen."

Tommy closed his eyes for a minute, trying to crawl into the minds of the two assassins who were now his foes.

Where would they set themselves up to take a clean shot? How do they get onto the cemetery's grounds without detection? More importantly, how would they make an easy escape? And finally, what is my end goal? How do I put this entire adventure to bed once and for all?

That last question was the most pressing one for Tommy. How could the agency continue ad infinitum to protect Dr. Rob Becker? Deep down inside, he didn't believe there was a way.

# CHAPTER 46

Donnie had been awake since daybreak, ready for the new day and thinking of projects still to be done. The drywall in the ranch home was finished, and soon it would be time for the carpet and flooring to be installed. His thoughts were interrupted by the sudden appearance of his wife.

"Hey honey, Mike just called. Chevytothelevee is starting to foal—you better get down to the barn!"

Donnie ran out of the kitchen and to his truck, yelling a thank you to Val, and headed to the foaling barn

In the barn, Chevytothelevee was lying on a bed of fresh straw, panting. She had just finished a round of pushing and was collecting herself for more. Donnie and Mike knew the newborn colt was going to be big—several ultrasounds had already revealed as much. He was ready to be born—in fact, the front legs were sticking out of the birth canal.

"How's she doing, Mike?" Donnie asked.

"So far, so good. This next push or two will determine if I need to reach inside of her and help out."

"How so?" Donnie asked.

"C'mon, Donnie ... I thought you'd read everything written about Secretariat! When Secretariat was foaling, his hips were locked in the birth canal and the vet had to step in and assist with the birth."

"Is he going to be ...?"

Donnie's question went unanswered as Chevytothelevee was in the throes of another push. The mare was giving it her all, but the foal didn't move any further and Mike knew it was time for him to help. He thrust his gloved hands and arms deep inside the birth canal, wrapping them around the foal's shoulders to help it move. Chevytothelevee let out what sounded like a huge grunt of thanks and continued pushing. Quickly, the head and shoulders appeared—and Mike couldn't believe how large they were. He would later say that he'd never seen shoulders that huge on a newborn foal.

By now, Mike was sweating as profusely as the mare. Chevytothelevee had briefly stopped the rhythm of thrusting, but her panting had become more rapid.

Mike was having trouble grabbing onto anything in the birth canal. The foal's hips were just beyond his reach and his arms weren't going to suddenly grow any longer.

Jesus—how long is this foal? Mike silently wondered.

"Donnie, get down here and help!" Mike commanded.

Donnie dropped to his knees alongside Mike, waiting for instructions. "Your arms are longer than mine, so grab some gloves and take my place. Reach in and feel for the hips. You'll know by touch. Latch on and start pulling when she starts pushing again."

Two minutes later, the colt made its entrance into the world.

The newborn foal was breathing on its own, but Donnie and Mike weren't focused on that.

"Good God, Donnie—have you ever seen a foal like this?" Mike's eyes looked like two full moons.

Donnie was stammering, but none of his words made any sense. He swallowed hard, finally stuttering out "No, No, No," while shaking his head in further astonishment.

A bit more composed, Donnie now asked, "How much do you think he weighs?"

Mike's face was flushed—but whether it was from exertion or exhilaration was unclear. Finally he replied, "Ninety pounds, easily." Mike later said he had no recollection of saying that.

Chevytothelevee struggled to her feet and interrupted the men still gazing at the foal in amazement—as she began cleaning the beautiful young chestnut colt. The foal had white stocking designs on each of its back legs and a very tiny white star-shaped blaze on his forehead. He wasn't a total replica of Secretariat, but he was very close.

Now finished cleaning her baby, Chevytothelevee began nudging the colt with her nose. The newborn struggled to stand up on untested legs, and with a rhythmic rocking motion, finally succeeded in standing upright for the first time.

Both men were in awe of what the Lord had manufactured.

"What's his name, Donnie?" Mike asked.

Donnie's eyes widened, answering the question with a question.

"I thought you knew his name, Mike. What is it?"

After both men stopped laughing at their mutual confused state, Donnie said something that perhaps could resolve the situation.

"I got a text this morning from Rob's friend, Tommy. It said that he, Rob, and Marty were coming home in a few days. Remember, it was Rob's dream that originally started this entire adventure—so how about we give Rob the honor of naming this future Triple Crown champion?"

"I totally agree, Donnie," Mike said.

Suddenly it dawned on Mike why Donnie had not been in the foaling barn.

"Jeez, Donnie, I totally forgot about the house. Is the carpeting going to be installed in time for everyone's arrival?"

"Yep, it's going down pretty soon. Steven said he'd be out later to help finish Rob and Marty's bedroom, as well as the guest bedroom for his dad. Once you're comfortable with the situation down here, come on up to the house and take a look," Donnie replied.

"Rob and Marty can't help but be surprised with what you've done, Donnie. The idea of duplicating their home here, on your farm, is truly a selfless act of kindness. You should be very proud," Mike said, giving a courtly bow in Donnie's direction.

Donnie walked over to his friend, wrapped an arm around Mike's shoulder, and pulled him close.

"Thanks for those kind words, Mike. I'm just thankful that Rob forgave me after the Nidalas and Towers Above fiasco I helped create. You know, Mike, I almost ruined something real special—something that each of us had going for a long time... something that made us not just partners, but lifelong friends.

"Ours was and still is a bond that very few ever get to experience. It's funny how people casually throw around the word friendship when they really have no clue as to what that really means. My building that house and welcoming Rob and Marty to live here on my land until the Lord finally calls them home, well...I can't begin to tell you how wonderful I feel inside. You want to talk about an endorphin release ..."

Donnie's head dropped slightly toward his chest in a useless attempt to hide the tears that were welling up.

Mike was also tearing up. He extended his right arm, duplicating Donnie's earlier embrace, and sign of friendship and love!

"Thanks, brother! Thanks for reminding me just how much our friendship means," Mike softly said.

 **HAPTER 47**

Donnie returned to the ranch house filled with optimism and joy. He could hardly wait until Chevytothelevee's foal was two years old and taking his place in the winner's circle after his first Grade One race. Donnie's mind also happened to be racing with ideas for the colt's name.

Bounding up the porch steps, he began calling out for his wife, Val. As he entered the kitchen and passed through to the great room, he saw her standing still in front of the television—in obvious anguish and with hands clasped together.

"Val ... Val—didn't you hear me calling? Hey, what's going on?" As Donnie walked closer, he spied the banner on the television screen, scrolling below the live coverage and a reporter talking.

The banner read "Rob Becker's grandson found in a drug-induced coma."

Donnie stopped dead in his tracks and listened to the reporter. She was talking about Harry and that he was found unconscious on the Legacy Bike Trail. The reporter didn't hesitate in linking Harry's coma to a recreational drug encounter—and then she shared that with her viewers.

Donnie was still processing the devastating news as Val turned to him, her eyes overflowing with tears. The yin and yang of that moment slammed into Donnie with a force he'd rarely before experienced in life.

He sat down to process and think for a moment about what he'd just heard on the news. Getting back to his feet, Donnie retraced his steps to the porch deck and called Tommy. There were three rings before Tommy finally answered.

"Tommy here ..."

"Tommy, this is Donnie in Kentucky calling. Please don't hang up!"

Donnie began talking, summarizing in one minute the bizarre day that started with the birth of a foal and ended with the information about Harry being broadcast nationally. Tommy shook his head in amazement at what he'd just heard. He thanked Donnie, assuring him that he'd relay the information to Rob. He quickly decided to get the exchange of information over with. The last thing Tommy wanted was for Rob or Marty to see their grandson's name being smeared on national television.

Rob and Marty were in the kitchen with Tika, preparing an early dinner. Tommy walked in, took a seat at the kitchen table, and immediately cut to the chase.

"Rob, Marty ... I just got off the phone with Donnie. Chevytothelevee gave birth to a handsome chestnut colt this morning. Donnie said the newborn colt is like no other he's ever seen.

"Donnie also said that he and Mike agree—and would be honored, if Rob would name the colt. In addition, with your approval, they feel that there should be no press release about the birth at this time, taking into consideration what's happening right now."

I could sense that Tommy was holding back some other news. Call it intuition, I just knew there was something he wasn't telling everyone, and it was eating at him.

"Did Donnie take any pictures of the colt?" I asked Tommy.

Tommy shook his head no.

I then asked if there was anything else—and Tommy nodded yes.

"The news about Harry and the drug situation has been picked up by the national media. The world now knows about your grandson and his current medical situation. I'm truly sorry, Rob."

I quickly answered him.

"You and I have been through a lot these past few years. I can tell there's still something else rattling around in your mind ... so why don't you spit it out."

Tommy looked down at the kitchen floor.

"Rob, I know that you've become somewhat of a celebrity, but there's no way this should even be a national story. It's a shame that the mainstream media doesn't devote more attention to the crises surrounding all the overdose deaths occurring these days among our young people. Someone had to have purposely dropped a news tip with the intent of flushing you out of hiding, Rob. It's sick. Really sick!

"Rob and Marty, I need permission from you to go ahead with a plan that ends this nonsense—and ends it now!"

Tommy stared at me, before shifting his gaze toward Marty. It took me a few seconds to realize he was waiting for some kind of signal or words from me before he'd continue.

"I don't know about Marty, but I'm all ears, Tommy!" I interjected.

Looking at both of us, Tommy began unraveling his plan.

"I was hoping and praying that with your new identity and new living environment, you could live out your new life in peace.

It's now obvious that is not going to happen! If Harry never wakes up from his coma, the bad guys will simply move on and target someone else. They'll keep up their efforts until you finally show yourself—and then they'll kill you, Rob.

"So instead, we're going to be proactive and give them what they want! Rob, you're going to die!

"You will die at Harry's mock funeral. It all will be like an illusion—just like a believable David Copperfield type of created trickery. The world will mourn your passing!

"Oh, and by the way, we will capture the bad guys during this faux memorial service and eventually learn who has been behind all of this."

I began laughing and couldn't stop.

"Rob—stop! I'm not shitting you. I don't have all the details, but that's the rough plan."

Still laughing, I managed to finally respond.

"Look, Tommy … I'm all in. If you can get this albatross that's been wrapped around my neck off of me, I'll be forever indebted to you! I only have one question—when do Marty and I get to go home?"

Tommy shot me a look of disgust before turning and walking away. The big reveal was over for the time being.

# CHAPTER 48

Marty and I went for a walk after dinner. Being a short distance from Sturgis, South Dakota with its rising COVID-19 numbers was of little concern to most of the citizens in Oral, including Marty and me. The two of us had created our own exercise loop that was about two miles from start to finish— a distance that gave us time to not only view the beauty of prairie life, but also to vent!

"The way you acted before dinner wasn't funny! You owe Tommy an apology, Rob. More importantly, who's going to break the news to Kathy that her son is going to fictitiously die, along with you? You're assuming that she and Mike will be willing to go along with Tommy's plan. I think you need to have a talk with your daughter before the idea behind this James Bond plan goes any further," Marty sarcastically stated.

As usual, I wanted to win the conversation, but before I uttered even a single word, I realized just how correct Marty was.

"You're right," I conceded.

∩ ∩ ∩

Upon our return, I looked for Tommy. After finding him, we both sat down on what had become our official meeting hangout—the front porch. I claimed the glider.

"Tommy, I'm not being accusatory, but don't you think you've got the proverbial cart before the horse? You haven't talked with

Kathy and Mike about Harry being declared dead. For that matter, where is Harry going to be stashed? The details of this esca-
pade are woefully lacking.

"I don't have a phone, and neither does Marty. I think you're
going to need our help convincing Kathy and to a lesser extent,
Mike, to go along with your plan!"

Tommy swallowed hard. One of his faults was negativity when
questioned about what he could or couldn't do.

"Well—first, you and Marty are still not getting a cell phone!
Yes, I'm going to need your help in persuading Kathy and Mike
to go along with the plan. In fact, go get Marty and we'll make
the first call right now. I figure it will take at least three or four
conversations before Kathy finally gives in and says yes. I only
have one demand. I get to offer my two cents during any of the
conversations—and I get to do this at any time."

I went inside and got Marty, explaining what was about to
happen. And damned if Tommy wasn't right.

Our first call with Kathy didn't last more than a couple of
minutes. As Tommy predicted, Kathy immediately balked at the
idea of declaring Harry dead. But that didn't stop Tommy from
slipping in the first of what I refer to as "teasers." They seemed to
be designed to reassure Kathy that what was being proposed was
the right course of action to take.

"Kathy, this is Tommy. I'm sure you remember me—and
hopefully in a positive light! I just want you to know that your
son will be safely housed in a hospital-like setting, with skilled
and competent health care workers. All of the medical treatment
tools used to care for Harry currently will also be available for
use in his new home. You won't need to worry about anyone that
might not have Harry's best interest in mind."

Brief, concise and to the point—Tommy's point!

I quickly realized what he was doing. His words were intended to keep positivity high while casting aside anything that could be perceived as a negative. He'd continue to do this until he finally convinced my daughter that the safest location for Harry was not in the hospital.

His second "teaser" was later that same day. Marty placed the call this time—and Tommy again finished the conversation.

"Kathy, I hope I didn't upset you earlier today. I just want to add that POTUS will be kept in the loop regarding your son's care. He is indebted to your father for how he helped thwart Antifa's attempt at starting a revolution in Portland! You take care now."

There were two more calls the next day. The turning point was when Kathy asked her first question, indicating that she was becoming resigned to accepting Tommy's plan.

"So, you're telling me that Harry will have round-the-clock care as well as all the necessary equipment and drugs required to resuscitate him in case he goes into cardiac arrest?"

Tommy smiled and clenched his fist, punching the air at an invisible foe and celebrating the moment.

"I'm guessing one or two more conversations will be all we need," Tommy stated.

Now Tommy had me asking a question.

"So where is my grandson's care going to be delivered?" I asked.

He smiled and replied, "It's going to be at the farm where Towers Above resides. Donnie has agreed to have Harry recover at his farm."

Tommy knew about the newly constructed home that was meant for Marty and me, but he wasn't about to give that secret away. He was also a master with words. He slipped that important word "recover" into his response to Kathy. It was subliminal and perhaps just enough to coax Kathy to give in.

"When is all this secret stuff taking place?" Kathy asked.

I had to cover my mouth, since I was laughing. My daughter hadn't yet realized that she was about to say, "We're all in."

Tommy, though, wasn't about to let the moment slip away.

"So, Kathy, are you in or not?"

There was a long pause. The three of us on the porch hundreds of miles away from Kentucky were literally holding our breaths.

"Well ... I guess I'm in!"

It was my turn to take a swipe at the air with a closed fist. It felt good.

# HAPTER 49

Tommy called Steven, letting him know that Harry's parents were on board with the plan of declaring him dead, and the subsequent move of Harry to Donnie's farm where he would continue to receive medical care.

"This is Steven."

"Hey son, how's it going?" Tommy was specifically asking about the move of the Beckers' furnishings—a project Steven had been working on for the past month.

"I've got nearly everything moved. They are really going to love their new digs!" Steven answered. "So, what's up, Dad?"

"We're going to flatline Harry! His parents have finally bought into the plan. Stan's been busy tying up some loose ends. After he's finished, I'll get Marty and Rob back to Kentucky and then we can pull the plug on Harry.

"I have no clue which local mortician we can trust and work with to pull off this ploy. We're also going to need someone to pick Harry up from the hospital and take him to the funeral home. From there, we need an EMT service to transport him to Donnie's farm.

"Obviously, we're going to need some background checks on all of these middlemen ... unless someone already knows some locals that the Agency has worked with in the past and who can keep their lips zipped.

"Hello? Steven ... you still there? Jump in anytime, son."

"Dad, I'm here. What do you want me to say? I don't know a soul here in Lexington—but let me talk with Lawson and O'Brien and I'll call you back."

∩ ∩ ∩

Steven hung up and called Agent Lawson, explaining in detail what was happening and what was needed to make it all fall into place.

Agent Lawson was a lifelong resident of Nicholasville, Kentucky, a town about ten miles due south of Lexington. His father had been an oral surgeon before dying unexpectedly from a heart attack. When Steven mentioned the need for a mortician, Lawson began laughing.

"What's so funny?" Steven asked the agent.

"I think I've got just who we need!"

"How so?"

"My dad used to collect precious metals and then cash them out when a scrap metal collector would stop by his office."

"Huh?" Steven replied.

"I'm sorry. I got ahead of myself. My dad would extract teeth and salvage the crowns that had been placed on the teeth by their regular dentist. Over time, he'd build up quite a collection of different metals. Once a year, a saleswoman would stop by his office. She would weigh all the crown and bridge metals, and visually determine which restorations had been crafted from precious metals versus those made from non-precious metals. By the way, precious metal crowns are made of gold, platinum, and palladium.

"She would tell my dad how many grams of worthy metals he'd collected and would offer him a cash payout or a payout in gold coins. Hell, my dad had quite a collection of American

Eagles, South Africa Krugerrands and Canadian Maple Leafs.

"Now here's the kicker! This woman's next stop was to a specific funeral home. The mortician who owns that funeral home was also harvesting gold crowns and other metals from the deceased.

"Best I can figure, right before they'd load a body into the hearse, to leave for the cemetery, someone from the funeral home would tell the immediate family members to go to their automobiles.

"Then, very quickly—in no more than a minute—the mortician would force open the deceased person's mouth and using pliers, he'd snap off any teeth that had crowns on them. They'd also harvest partial dentures that contained any type of metal. Bottom line … that's grave robbing, even though the deceased wasn't quite in the grave yet!"

"Wow!" Steven gasped.

"I know where that funeral home is located. O'Brien and I will go there and flash our credentials. After we explain to the owner how much jail time he's facing, I doubt we'll have any problems convincing the mortician to help us out. Who knows, he might even give us a referral for some EMTs."

"Okay, let me know what happens, Lawson—and thanks." Steven couldn't believe his good fortune. Once again, a favorite Rob Becker saying, "If you don't ask the question, you'll never get the answer," rang true.

Everything Tommy had expected to happen had pretty much been realized—but Harry's condition still put a huge kink in the plans. Harry was supposed to have died. Tommy didn't dare tell me or Marty that, but Tika was privy to Tommy's dilemma.

Once again, Tommy found himself sitting on the glider alone. Tika eased in next to him and cuddled closely.

"So how are you going to solve the conundrum now that Harry is in a coma?"

"What ... how did you?" he tried to ask. Tika put her hand gently over Tommy's lips before putting both hands together, placing them under her head and closing her eyes.

"I'll be damned! Talking in my sleep again, huh?"

Tika nodded. "As I told you earlier, you really need to correct that habit!" she said, laughing.

"I wish everything could be easy. Now we have to figure out a way to sneak Harry out of the hospital without the bad guys figuring out what we're doing! I haven't threaded the needle on this one yet. If you have any ideas, I'd love to hear them!" Tommy stated.

Tika shook her head and pressed her body even closer to Tommy.

Tommy, now thoroughly distracted, didn't hesitate. He stood, and with a smile and a come-hither movement of his index finger, motioned for Tika to follow him into the bedroom.

Their time together was growing short all too quickly.

# HAPTER 50

S tan got Tommy's text about two hours after going to bed—
and Tommy knew his boss was most likely already asleep. He
was purposely priming Stan for the discussion they would have
the next day.

Stan figured that turnabout was only fair and the next morning, called Tommy back at six in the morning, Washington, DC
time, which was four in the morning in South Dakota. He really
didn't expect Tommy to answer and was getting ready to leave an
obnoxious message when a cheerful Tommy answered.

"Thought you were going to catch me still sleeping, huh?"

Stan was dumbfounded. He and Tommy had played this time
zone game by phone far too many times.

"Okay, you win this time, but I'll even the score! What's up,
Thomas?" Stan asked.

Tommy ignored Stan's formal use of his name.

"How's the kid, Stan?"

"No change, Tommy. Lawson gives me an update every six
hours. He talks with the attending physician every day and the
prognosis hasn't changed. Harry could wake up from the coma in
an instant for no apparent reason, or he could continue to sleep
like Rip Van Winkle for God knows how long. And don't even
say what's on your mind, because I know what you're thinking.

"I've already talked with POTUS, and he's given the green
light to have Harry's identity changed ... if and when the kid

comes out of the coma. Until that time, Harry will remain incognito wherever it's believed he can be safe."

"C'mon, Stan, deep down you know I don't want the kid to die. It's just that it would've been so much easier if ... oh hell, never mind! So, what have you found out about the attending physician—or anyone else who's involved in Harry's care?" Tommy asked. You could tell by the tone in his voice that Tommy was begging to hear something positive.

"Well ..."

Tommy had been down this road before with Stan and immediately detected an opening—a hint that Stan knew something that could work in their favor.

"A certain doctor is apparently having an affair with a head scrub nurse—and she occasionally works on the ICU floor. It's amazing how often this happens among healthcare professionals. I've talked with several doctors about this, and the typical rationale for why these clandestine relationships happen is because they all work in such close quarters. I was never one to believe in pheromones ... but who knows? I must say Tommy, the older I become, the more I'm set in my ways.

"I'm going to have Lawson make them an offer they can't refuse. Incriminating photos will push both of them over the edge and make them realize they have no choice but to help us. Our men have been watching and have learned which hotel they typically rendezvous. Tomorrow is the day for their usual weekly get-together. Cameras have already been installed and a few more photos would be helpful. One of our men will be working the front desk tomorrow to handle the check-in and give them their access cards to that particular room."

"I can't check out any enemies from South Dakota, Stan. I

need to get back to the Commonwealth—Tika understands and is supporting me. But I need a flight, like yesterday!"

"Calm down, Tommy. I need you to wait until the doctor and nurse are both totally committed. The reward has to outweigh the risks, and it has to be enough to prevent any possible last-minute cold feet or outright craziness on their part. The last thing I need right now is to burn our only chance for pulling off this grand illusion. I have to believe that their upcoming tryst will provide us with the necessary incriminating evidence which convinces them both that there is only one option to keep their secret safe!"

"Okay Stan, I'll sit tight for a couple more days, but that's all. If there's no flight scheduled for me to travel by the end of the week, I'll book the trip myself!"

"Talk to you in a few days," Tommy promised before hanging up.

Stan rested back in his chair. On his desk was an engraved metal nameplate displaying his favorite mantra: *THE COMMON DENOMINATOR IS???*

Stan stared at the engraved plate intently for at least thirty seconds. *Some things never change*, Stan silently told himself. *Yeah, that's right…always follow the money!*

The Agency was busy compiling its understanding of the "common denominator" on two fronts. The first was with the Lexington Cemetery and its workers. Agents were putting together a list of employees and their individual net worth—specifically looking for any recent financial indicators that a particular individual had been compromised.

Stan had also directed agents to determine who was responsible for the leak about Harry's overdose to the press—and Lawson was the first to be interviewed. While not a suspect himself, the agent had arrived on the scene just after Harry had overdosed and had subsequently interacted with a number of different people. Stan believed that the leaker was most likely someone from that group.

 HAPTER 51

I was surprised to find Tommy already awake and ready for the day—he was usually the late riser in the house. I tried to strike up a conversation but was quickly rebuffed.

"Catch you later, Rob; things are a bit hectic today. I need to tie up some loose ends."

"Not so fast! Remember, I need your cell phone to call my friend to see if he'd be interested in working the clinic."

"Damn, Rob, I totally forgot. Here…and just keep it in case you need to place another call," Tommy said, while handing me his phone. That last statement by itself was even more surprising.

Tommy wasn't the only one with loose ends to tie up. I'd been given approval from Stan, allowing me to talk with that long-time dentist friend back in the Midwest.

Dr. Mike Frank was a few years younger than me but was every bit the skilled and compassionate dentist that I hoped the public perceived me to be. Mike was one of just a few dentists I could trust one hundred percent when it came to running the clinic in South Dakota. We were both fortunate to have practiced our trade during what many considered the golden years of dentistry.

During the 1980s and through the advent of the millennium, the dental profession was such that most folks with dental insurance were able to go to the dentist of their choice. In those days, dental HMO and PPO insurance plans had little to no effect on either of our practices. In fact, each of us started our dental careers as an employee of a group practice and were able to build our clientele without much interference from any one individual or entity. When I broke away from the group practice that I had contracted with, I asked Mike to join me. He declined.

Then came the Great Recession and with it, pretty much the end of a patient's freedom of choice—not for just dentistry, but all of the health professions. Suddenly, virtually every dentist was offering PPO services for almost every dental plan. Since Mike and I had pretty much shunned such plans, our well-established business models began to suffer. I retired and pursued my thoroughbred dreams while Mike continued practicing—each day dreading the new financial confinements that PPO dentistry brought to his practice.

∩ ∩ ∩

I was surprised that it only took an hour to make the presentation to Mike. He had sold his practice a year earlier and the bitter taste of health care—provided by Federal and State governments as well as insurance companies—had finally faded away.

My biggest challenge was convincing Mike that he didn't need to worry over what the government was paying to meet the dental needs of Native Americans. The history of Native Americans and their sacrifices through the decades made such issues almost non-existent now. Any conflicts with government agencies were short-lived.

Mike promised he would think about the offer and get back to me within a few days. If his tone of voice, after I told him how little time it took to travel to Breckenridge and Steamboat Springs, Colorado or Big Sky, Montana from Oral, South Dakota was any indicator, I knew I had struck a favorable chord.

For Mike and me, our quality of life had become the major overriding issue, as we were heading toward our senior-most years.

Mike wouldn't have any skin in the game and the salary he would draw would not be impacted by the typical financial concerns of a private-practice dentist.

He also wasn't a young dentist with significant dental school debt of two-hundred fifty thousand dollars or more hanging over him every day. Nor would he have to worry about setting and meeting daily production goals that could lead to the diagnosis of unnecessary dental work.

After our conversation was over, I felt certain that Mike would take the job. Marty heard me end the call. She came outside and joined me on the glider just as I let out a sigh of relief.

"You ready for tonight?" Marty asked.

"What's tonight?" I responded.

"Damn it, Rob ... you forgot, didn't you?"

I had—and there was no legitimate excuse for my forgetting.

"The wedding. Damn...I'm sorry Marty. Is there a special marriage ceremony that is typical of the Lakota tribe?"

"No, believe it or not, there isn't a ceremony. Back in the day, if a couple wanted to be considered married, they would just live together," Marty said.

"Are you kidding me, Marty? The Lakota tribe was definitely ahead of their time, weren't they?" I replied.

"Whatever you say Rob. Go shower and get ready for the Justice of the Peace and a plain vanilla type of Christian ceremony."

Giving Marty a peck on the cheek, I turned and headed for the shower, humming "American Pie." Once Tika and Tommy said "I do," there would be nothing to stop us from returning home to Kentucky.

 **HAPTER 52**

The next morning, after an evening free from any distractions, Tommy emerged from the honeymoon suite just long enough to join me on the porch. It was just slightly before noon.

"Rob, do you have a few minutes?"

I broke out laughing before trying to answer him with a straight face.

"I'm not sure when the heck I wouldn't have time for you, my friend—but let me check my schedule!"

Reaching into my pocket and pulling out an imaginary day planner, I pretended I was flipping through invisible pages.

"I believe I have at least a half hour available at this very moment, sir," I told Tommy with a straight face.

"Okay, smart ass—stuff it!"

Tommy plopped down next to me and unfolded four 8" x 11" sheets of photo paper that were taped together. Glancing at the composite picture, I quickly realized it was an enlarged look down view of the Lexington Cemetery.

"You recognize it, right?"

I nodded.

"Rob, can you point out roughly where your family gravesites are?"

I took the composite photos of the land and began tracing the roads in the cemetery with my index finger. It took me three tries to finally settle on what I thought was the location where my ashes would be spread someday in the future.

"I think this is the spot, but don't hold me to it."

"Now close your eyes and determine the compass points on the plat," Tommy asked.

I didn't have to close my eyes for very long. Tommy handed me a black marker and I started with the north compass point and rapidly finished with the other three points.

"Now Rob, I want you to close your eyes and pretend you're a sniper. Starting with the northern compass point, mentally scan three hundred sixty degrees. When you're ready, open your eyes and indicate if there's a clear shot from points A, B, C and so on, until you've covered all of the compass points."

It took only thirty seconds to think about what Tommy had asked. The only points that presented a clear opening for at least two to three hundred yards would be those originating from the east and due south direction, and then finally from the southwest. All other compass points would present potential problems if I were the shooter—or so I thought.

After I pointed at those areas on Tommy's plat, he abruptly stood, thanked me, and left the porch.

I didn't realize it would be dinner time before I saw him again.

What I also didn't know was that Tommy was on the phone with Stan for most of the afternoon talking strategy.

∩ ∩ ∩

Tommy gave a rough outline of what would go down at the cemetery. He also included the addition of a possible new employee—an agent—who would be part of the cemetery's landscaping crew.

For his part, Stan had new information concerning the leaks.

Once it became clear to Stan that the person who leaked Harry's situation to the media had been positively identified, then there might be a need for some enhanced interrogation. Stan knew that would be the time for Tommy to head back to Kentucky.

"Are you about done, Tommy?" Stan asked.

"Yeah, that's pretty much all I've got," was his response.

"Okay ... one more thing. Pack up what you need and get on back to the Commonwealth. Your flight is at six tomorrow morning. You're going to need back-up—and Steven is going to be otherwise occupied."

"Let me think on that, Stan. I'll try to have a name for you when I arrive," Tommy replied.

After the call ended, Tommy went looking for Tika.

"I need a few minutes with you Tika," Tommy said with a voice indicating that this would be a difficult conversation.

"Okay dear," Tika replied haltingly.

They went into the bedroom where Tommy seated himself on the corner of their bed, looking up at his bride while gently holding her hands close to his chest. Tika moved closer and gazed down at Tommy.

"It's about to start. I ... I leave early tomorrow. I want you to know that I'm the happiest I've ever been in my life. But these things I do for our country, well ... I know you'll never be able to wrap your arms around what it is that I do!

"I want you to know, this is my last time. This particular assignment has become personal for me. I never expected to become a close friend with Rob Becker.

"Sometimes—no, most of the time—I feel like our friendship is a one-way street. I don't think Rob knows how much he means to me. I've stepped back and analyzed the relationship, and realize the reason that I love the guy is because he's a dinosaur. He's a throwback to a time when the people who formed our nation—the founding fathers—knew that what they were doing would never be perfect! But they were nonetheless convinced that they were creating the best path to a true, lasting democracy on earth."

Tika took her hands from her husband and placed her right index finger on Tommy's lips to silence him.

"I understand. Just promise you will come back to me! We were too full of ourselves years ago, and we weren't totally committed to one another. I also know that our marriage wouldn't have lasted back then!

"But now...we are!" she said while removing her finger from his lips and sitting on the bed next to Tommy.

Neither one spoke.

# CHAPTER 53

It was three in the morning—Tommy was already up and on his way to Ellsworth Air Force Base. He said no goodbyes to Marty or me, and that hurt.

We had expected to return to Kentucky when Tommy did. Now, having breakfast with only Tika present made it even more uncomfortable.

"You going to tell us what happened yesterday?" I asked.

"What do you mean, Rob?" Tika replied.

"C'mon Tika. Someone, most likely Stan, was responsible for Tommy leaving so early this morning—without us, no less. How come?" I fired back at her.

"Rob, you think you know Tommy. Well, you don't! Years ago, when Tommy and I first hooked up, he'd just started with the Agency. The job fit his personality perfectly at that time. He was done serving in the Army as a Ranger and was anxious to get on with his life. He wanted a big family and so did I. But he wouldn't commit to marriage. In fact, he considered marriage as a liability. He truly believed the bad guys could leverage our marriage and that I would be in constant jeopardy!"

"Tika, you don't need to explain any ..." Marty tried to interject, but to no avail.

"Marty, please. I need to finish!

"Back then, I should have bit my tongue and accepted our relationship as it was...but I couldn't—and ultimately I didn't.

I was nearly to term with Steven when Tommy left me. If only I had stopped him. Call it being too proud or stubborn. Hell, I don't know!

"Then Steven was born, and every year Tommy came and spent his vacation time here in South Dakota. I didn't worry financially because Tommy took care of my house payment. Initially, I thought it was Tommy paying the monthly mortgage, but later found out that it was the Agency.

"I always talked to Steven about his dad, but never about what Tommy did for a living. Tommy wanted it that way. What I didn't realize was Steven wanted to be just like his dad—and more! He enlisted in the Army after graduating high school and was determined to be a Ranger, just like his dad.

"You know the rest of the story. The failed revolution in Portland was a godsend for Steven and me. You know that Tommy was an only child. Just last night, he told me that he loved you, Rob, and he considers you the older brother that he never had. I know that sounds hokey, but I believe him! Maybe someday he'll open up with you, but until he does, you're just going to have to believe me."

"Tika, I ..."

"Rob, I'm not finished!

"Tommy has this bad habit. He talks and acts out in his sleep. At first, he was fine. Then, when Muhammad entered the picture, the nightmares kicked in and Tommy started yelling and actually fighting back in his sleep. I don't know if you've witnessed someone with virtual goggles on their head and how they strike out at some imaginary foe—well, it's exactly like that! I've literally had to give him space, otherwise I would've been clocked.

"In hindsight, it is funny. The problem is, in this particular recurring nightmare, he's losing the battle. The nightmare always ends with him on top of the mattress, kneeling. His hands are behind his back and his head is bowed—he's in the same position that an ISIS mercenary normally would have their infidel prisoner assume!

"He yells out the same thing every time he has this nightmare …'Come on, damn it. You worthless piece of pig shit. Get on with this. Finish it already!'

"Then and only then does Tommy finally stop screaming—and that's when I grab him from behind, cradling him until he stops thrashing.

"Every time afterwards, I asked Tommy if he could describe where he is during the nightmare, but he can't identify the location. The reason I'm telling you this is because he always said that the nightmare is in the future.

"Since I won't be going back to Kentucky with you, I needed you to know about this recurring dream. I'm not trying to burden you or make you feel obligated in any fashion, but I do want you to keep your antennae up whenever and wherever you can. And Rob, thank you!"

I was at a loss for words at this moment.

Marty answered for me!

"He will, Tika. I promise you he will!"

 **HAPTER 54**

Steven was definitively tasked to determine who was leaking information to the mainstream news media in Lexington, Kentucky.

He met first with Agents Lawson and O'Brien to brief them. Since Lawson was the agent on the scene when Harry overdosed, it made sense that the leaker was most likely a first responder who was present on the Legacy Bike Trail that tragic day.

More than once, Lawson shook his head at the irony of the investigation and how it was described. Higher ups were calling his work to find the leak as "contact tracing," but given that it was 2020 and the COVID-19 pandemic was ravaging the world, that context seemed to be overkill.

Lawson wasn't dealing with a virus—he was doing a simple criminal investigation. Period. End of story.

The paramedics who were on the trail that day were the first to be interviewed by Lawson. The two men were brought to the federal building in downtown Louisville, and it was apparent that each man was more than a little frightened. They immediately recognized Lawson as the federal agent on the Legacy Trail when he walked into the interrogation room.

"First, I want you to know that you've done nothing wrong! What I'm doing today is conducting a routine investigation and nothing more. If you want an attorney present during this process, we'll contact that person and then wait until they arrive. I don't know if either of you have ever taken a polygraph, but I will be testing each of you separately. Any questions?"

Neither paramedic objected to the lie detector test. A technician wheeled the polygraph equipment into the room, hooked up the first paramedic, and then left the room.

Later, after finishing the second polygraph, Lawson thanked both men, giving them a final admonition before they left.

"Each of you has the other's back, and if either one of you tells anyone what went on here today, both of you will be spending some very special time with me. I would certainly hate to stain your personal work records, but I will if necessary. Are there any questions?"

Again, there were none.

Later that same day, Lawson welcomed Trooper Kessing of the Kentucky State Police into the interrogation room. The trooper was accompanied by his lawyer, Larry Sawyer—and that in itself led Lawson to believe he was about to get to the crux of the matter and identify the leaker.

"Mr. Sawyer, Trooper Kessing, I want you both to know that our meeting here today has nothing to do with any legal issues and there will be no charges leveled as a result of any information coming out of this meeting. So, Mr. Sawyer, please turn off your recording device."

The lawyer reached into his coat pocket and turned off his digital recorder. He nodded, giving Lawson permission to proceed.

"Trooper Kessing, you recognize me, correct?"

"Yes, I do."

"Just so we're clear, I'm going to show you my credentials."

Lawson pulled out his Homeland Security badge, giving it to Kessing to examine.

"Is that what you remember seeing previously, Trooper?"

"Yes, I remember the badge," Kessing said.

"And do you remember our conversation about the victim and my relationship with him on that day?"

"Yes sir, I do."

"Our meeting here today can end with a positive answer to my next question—so please take your time in answering.

"After you and I parted ways that day, were there any instances in which you shared information about the events that occurred on the Legacy Bike Trail that day?"

Trooper Kessing leaned toward his attorney, cupping his hand to shield their discussion on how he was about to answer. The discussion between the trooper and his lawyer was indiscernible to the agent.

"I think I know what you're searching for, Agent Lawson. You want to know if I told anyone the details of what took place on the bike trail. The answer is yes. I told another trooper about what happened on Legacy Trail.

"His name is Jerry—and yes, thinking back to that day, Jerry seemed very interested in what I was telling him. His full name is Trooper Jerry Jameson," Kessing revealed without any additional coaxing.

Lawson couldn't believe his good fortune.

"Gentlemen, please excuse me for a few minutes," Lawson said. He got up, left the room, and called Steven. After telling him about the three interrogations that day, Lawson asked Steven if there was any reason to question Trooper Kessing any further. Steven responded in the negative. It was obvious to Steven, from what he'd learned from Lawson about the day's interviews, that Trooper Jameson was the leaker. A local news reporter in

Lexington was still regularly providing updated and detailed reports about Harry's condition. They had even reported earlier about Lawson's presence on the bike trail, identifying the agent as the one responsible for handling the situation with the people that were present on the trail that day.

Before ending the phone conversation, Steven directed Lawson to shut down the investigation and to resume his duties at Kathy and Mike's home, along with Agent O'Brien.

Steven called his father next—assuming correctly that Tommy was chomping at the bit for some action.

Sitting in Rob Becker's new house in southern Kentucky was boring, and he'd only been there a little over forty-eight hours.

"Hey Dad, Langley will be sending you information on Kentucky State Police Trooper Jerry Jameson. He's the leaker. I imagine he's got an inside contact with an employee at the hospital, because the network affiliate is continuously giving updates on Harry's status. He's probably feeding it to some local reporter who thinks this story is their chance for an Emmy. And Dad, be discreet," was Steven's caution to Tommy.

Tommy waited patiently for the information from Langley, wondering who his new partner would be. It was times like this that Tommy always choked up slightly, missing his former partner, Danny, who had been killed during the "Portland Insurrection."

# HAPTER 55

It was mid-evening when Tommy finally received Jerry Jameson's résumé.

He initially looked it over quickly, then taking his time, slowly re-read the résumé twice more.

"That's about what I expected," Tommy said to himself.

By all appearances, Jerry was a model citizen—an ex-marine who'd served multiple tours in Afghanistan. He had been awarded the Purple Heart, the Defense Distinguished Service medals, and had been honorably discharged. He was the perfect personification of the type of individual that the director of the Kentucky State Police liked to hire as a state trooper.

Stan checked his watch for the third time before his cellphone finally began to vibrate.

"You're slipping, my friend. I'm thinking you've had far too much time in the sack, huh?" Stan blurted out, trying to hold back a hearty laugh.

"Stuff it, and quit snickering, asswipe!" Tommy barked.

"Wow, aren't we touchy tonight?" Stan retorted. "Have you looked at Jameson's profile? You know he's skilled in more than just basic Survival, Evasion, Resistance and Escape military training. Well, he won't escape, but you're right … he will resist, evade and most of all survive. You don't have a lot of time. I think I know what you're thinking, but spit it out anyhow, Tommy."

"I hate wasting taxpayers' money. What's our budget, Stan?"

Stan hesitated just briefly before making an executive decision. "I'm betting Jameson is a total mercenary. You bring him in from the cold and we'll see what his demands are. I do ask, though, that you make it real clear that he does have a voice, but there are limits to what we'll allow. I would also stress that if he declines our offer, we'll put the word out. He'll understand that we won't have to take him down—his own guys will clean everything up. Get cracking, Tommy. I'll get the word out to the housekeeping crew to get the safe house ready for company.

"Oh, and by the way, your new partner is O'Brien. Take it easy on him—he's not Danny. There's no one that could be another Danny! You know if I had the power to bring him back, I would, Tommy."

"Thanks, Stan, I appreciate your kind words. I'll break in O'Brien, and it will be the right way!"

Tommy kicked back for a few seconds, reflecting. "It always comes down to just one thing—money!" he mumbled.

Stan called Agent Lawson next, telling him to let O'Brien know that he was to join Tommy immediately at Rob Becker's new house. Stan asked the agent to also advise O'Brien that he would be Tommy's partner until the assignment was completed.

His last call was to Steven.

∩ ∩ ∩

Steven understood Stan's decision—and was actually grateful that he wasn't going to be his dad's partner. For one thing, he wasn't exactly a fan of his dad's tendencies to go rogue. Steven represented a new breed of CIA agent, compared to the nonconformist agents of an older generation who he felt were more antiquated in their techniques. As far as Steven was concerned, his dad was more the Harry Callahan type of character portrayed by Clint Eastwood in the Dirty Harry movies some four decades previous.

What Steven didn't realize was that his father had thought the same of older agents when he first started his career with the agency. The only difference between then and now was all of the technological advancements in weaponry and techniques that had evolved over the past quarter century.

Steven also knew that O'Brien straddled the two generations between himself and Tommy. If there was anyone who could get along with his dad, it would be O'Brien.

Stan was counting on O'Brien being the yin to Tommy's yang, while Steven knew that O'Brien was the one agent who would balance his dad's impetuous nature and hopefully keep his father alive.

That's all that Steven could ask for, considering this would most probably be his dad's last CIA-sanctioned caper.

# CHAPTER 56

The first thing Tommy had to do was figure out Jerry Jameson's routine and habits. Everyone has them. Some are based on superstitions, while others can be traced to old wives' tales. Some habits can be fleeting and may appear baseless, while others might revolve around a physical issue.

What Tommy was hoping for was Jameson having a habit that he and O'Brien could easily exploit.

Tommy needed to set up a meeting with O'Brien. It was important to him that they have a one-on-one so he could size up his new partner.

∩ ∩ ∩

O'Brien was getting bored just sitting around Kathy and Mike's house. Their son Harry was still in a coma, so there was really nothing for him to do.

It was nearly sundown when Lawson pulled in the driveway and entered the house. He immediately asked Kathy if there was any change in Harry's condition, and she shook her head. He asked where O'Brien was, and Kathy directed him to the living room, where he found his fellow agent pacing back and forth, wearing a path in the carpet.

"What the hell are you doing? Okay, let me guess … you're tired of feeling invisible and useless, aren't you?"

"You bet your ass I am. I'm doing nothing here. I need to do something, just anything!"

"Well, you will soon. Steven called this afternoon and told me that you are now his dad's new partner. I've got Tommy's cell phone number and address here for you and he already has your phone number. He's about ninety minutes south of here, not too far from I-75. You better get going ... you don't want to get off on the wrong foot. I'll see you soon, but keep in touch."

O'Brien's face broke out in a broad smile as Lawson gave him Tommy's information. The agents said their goodbyes, and O'Brien went to pack his overnight bag. Checking his phone, O'Brien read a text from Tommy. He responded that he would be on the road in thirty minutes.

There was a lot to think about during his drive south—and O'Brien had no firm idea what to expect from this assignment. The likelihood was high that he needed to size up Tommy, despite already sensing that he'd be perfect working with an older agent.

He'd heard countless stories about Tommy's supposed escapades and wondered what it would take to confirm that Tommy indeed wore a symbolic "S" on his chest!

Tommy felt like a teenager getting ready to go on a first date but would never have admitted that to anyone else.

Danny had been Tommy's partner for most of his years as a field agent—and Tommy had assumed after so many years together that he and Danny were invincible. He had been certain that the Lord would never allow anything to break their bond— until a fluke bullet fired from a pansy-assed Antifa puke's AK-47 weapon proved him wrong. He loved reminiscing about past assignments he and Danny had conducted over the years.

"Well, it's time to get on with it! One final assignment …

"Lord, I'm begging you, please protect me from death while I continue to do good for you and your Kingdom. Amen," Tommy whispered to the heavens, knowing that he was asking the Lord to choose one side over another!

The doorbell rang and Tommy beckoned O'Brien to come inside.

O'Brien was the first to break the ice.

"It's a pleasure to finally meet the man who has such a rich history with the Agency! I am looking forward to working with you."

Tommy took the compliment in like a sponge, before spitting out his response.

"O'Brien, what a crock of shit. You've been working on your bullshit remarks all the way from Lexington to here. Tell me what you really want to say before I try to kick your ass right now!"

"Okay … here's the truth. I'm honored to work with the agent who just might be the biggest wild card and fuck-up to ever walk the corridors at Langley."

O'Brien stared at Tommy, waiting for his response. At least thirty seconds passed before Tommy finally blinked.

"O'Brien—welcome to my world. That statement was awesome, and I'm the one who's honored! Now … I have to ask a few questions. Have you ever conducted any enhanced interrogations?"

Nothing like cutting to the chase—this guy really is a wild card, O'Brien thought to himself.

"No. I haven't. But I'm guessing your next question is twofold. Would I have a problem participating in this type of activity, and secondly—do I have a problem with it? You should know that I'm really a pragmatic person and I also know that there are times when non-physical interrogation is not going to cut it! The situation we're going to be dealing with probably won't work with a long-term interrogation—there just isn't enough time. With that said, I'm going to tell you that if you ask me to do something I don't have the stomach for, please don't force me to cross that line."

Tommy wasn't going to say so to O'Brien's face, but he was impressed.

"O'Brien, you and I are going to be fine, just fine! Let me show you where you'll be bunking. Get to sleep, because we'll start the day before daybreak. Trooper Jameson goes on duty early tomorrow morning, and we need to shadow him to see if he has any weaknesses we can exploit.

"Good night, partner!"

# HAPTER 57

The next day at five in the morning, Tommy and O'Brien separately began the drive along I-75 to their destination.

They were headed toward a specific Kentucky State Police Post. The FBI had given Stan details on when Trooper Jameson clocked in and out and had also provided his home address and phone number. Stan passed the information on to Tommy.

This particular week, Jerry was working the day shift. The plan was for both men to follow Jerry once he left the post to begin his shift.

O'Brien would be positioned the closest to Jerry's cruiser, with Tommy about a quarter mile behind him. Each agent would do a vehicle version of leapfrog and reverse positions about every five miles.

The younger agent knew that initially Jerry had no way of knowing that he was being followed, but that didn't keep him from wondering why Tommy seemed so blasé about following Jameson—until Tommy's voice boomed loudly over the speakers in O'Brien's vehicle.

"In case you're wondering, another Kentucky trooper by the name of Kessing placed a tracking device on Jameson's cruiser. I can see you ahead of me. I'll tell you when to speed up or slow down. I'll also let you know when it's time to flip positions. We don't want him to notice that he's being followed."

∩ ∩ ∩

Jameson hopped onto I-64, heading east toward Lexington. If no other officers were cruising the expressways around Lexington, then he would roll on all of them until lunch time.

Tommy and O'Brien watched from afar as Jameson issued speeding tickets throughout the morning. Around noon, the trooper shut down his K-band radar and headed to the city for a lunch break.

At this particular moment, Tommy and O'Brien were about to learn one of Jameson's regular habits—but were unaware that his particular habit would meet their needs.

Jameson drove a short distance to the Hyatt Hotel—a structure connected to the Lexington Convention Center. He left his car in valet parking before disappearing into the hotel.

O'Brien also pulled into valet parking, tipped the parking attendant, and entered the hotel. He took a seat on a plush chair near the entrance, right next to the lobby, waiting to hear from Tommy. His earpiece came alive.

"Where is he?" Tommy asked.

"I have no idea," O'Brien replied.

"This is just a hunch, but check the men's room," Tommy told his partner. Just as O'Brien was about to pull open the men's room door, Jerry pushed on the other side and quickly brushed past O'Brien.

O'Brien checked the stalls and then the trash can, but saw nothing. He hurried back to his car.

The chase was on again—and O'Brien reconnected with Tommy by phone.

"I think he took a dump in the hotel's bathroom! He's

obviously just a common guy, I guess!" O'Brien said, laughing.

"Maybe that's a clue he dropped for us—not taking into account the deposit he just made in the men's room," was Tommy's spirited reply.

The rest of the afternoon was uneventful.

At the end of his shift, Jerry returned to the Highway Patrol Post, changed back into civilian clothes, got into his own car and headed home.

It was nearly time for their shift to end too. Tommy and O'Brien followed Jerry to his home before handing the observation of Jameson over to a couple different agents for the evening watch.

Tommy was determined to sniff around a bit, and he bunked at the Hyatt that evening.

O'Brien returned to Kathy and Mike's home, showered, and went to bed. He was mentally tapped out.

∩ ∩ ∩

The next morning, Tommy and O'Brien parked their cars a half mile away from the KSP Post.

"Good morning, O'Brien. I have to ask—do you have a first name? I mean everyone seems comfortable calling you by your last name."

"My first name is Jay. Some of my friends call me J.O. Whatever you're comfortable with is fine. So, what did you find out at the Hyatt last night?"

"Well, I'm sitting at the bar and it's just me and the bartender. We strike up a conversation and I casually mention that there must have been some excitement at the hotel during lunchtime.

"He then says, 'How so?'

"I mention the KSP cruiser parked out front. O'Brien, most of the time I don't do a lot of talking. I'm not like most bartenders who have the gift of gab. They make it their business to know what's going on—that's how they earn those big tips!

"So, the bartender starts laughing and I ask him, 'What's so funny?'

"He says to me, 'I wish I had a Benjamin for every time I've been asked that question.'

"I say, 'Well'?" - and wait for him to answer!

"He finally says, 'That's Trooper Jameson. He thinks the Hyatt has the cleanest toilet stalls in the Commonwealth.

"The bartender then elaborated, telling me that on four out of five working days, like clockwork, he comes into the Hyatt and takes a crap.

"Now at this point, I'm nearly doubled over with laughter when he adds, 'the staff has a daily lottery!' Each staff member picks the time when they think he'll come into the hotel and go into the men's room. The precise winning time is determined by when his hand first touches the bathroom door.

"It must have been five minutes before I stopped laughing.

"So, if Jameson follows that same routine again today, then we have that unique habit that I talked about.

"Okay, here we go—Jameson's on the move. We've got to get cracking."

O'Brien and Tommy began to follow Trooper Jameson once again. On this day, Jameson focused on the roads of western Fayette County. And sure enough, just after noon, he headed toward downtown Lexington and ultimately the Hyatt Hotel.

It was time for his daily constitutional.

After lunch, Jameson varied from his routine of patrolling the roads, instead heading to Masterson Park. Once in the park, he headed for the farthest soccer field where he parked the cruiser and waited. Tommy and O'Brien parked their cars further away, but were still in a position to observe the trooper. Ten minutes later, the agents watched as an SUV, with a local television network's logo on the side, entered the park and proceeded to where Jameson was parked. Tommy lifted the Canon camera to his face and began snapping pictures.

Tommy could now say with certainty that he had concrete evidence of who was responsible for the leaks about Harry. It wouldn't take much work to also determine which hospital insider was working with Jameson.

# HAPTER 58

Tommy intended to run his final plan by Stan and then patiently await approval. He figured there would be one more day of chasing Jameson around—just in case the trooper had another habit that could work to their advantage.

Tommy sent two texts—one to Stan and one to his son.

"Stan, it's time to bring Rob and Marty back to the Commonwealth. What say you?"

"Steven, I need a van to transport some valuables to our vacation home."

With that second message, Tommy was putting his son on notice that the agency's safe house was about to welcome its first captive "guest," in quite a while.

The biggest surprise of the day was that Dr. Mike Frank was arriving in Oral, South Dakota sometime around mid-morning.

ᑎ ᑎ ᑎ

I met Mike at our home away from home. As I stepped down from the porch to greet him, Mike seemed hesitant to grasp my welcoming hand, saying, "I'm here to see Dr. Rob Becker. Can you tell me where he is, please?"

Chuckling, I said, "Mike, it's me. Rob. They did a bit of work on me! Do you like it?"

"Damn, Rob! Oh my God ..."

After Mike regained his composure, I introduced him to Tika

and then drove him to the clinic for further introductions.

After getting a bite to eat, Mike and I sat down to go over the clinic details when unexpectedly, Mike interrupted me with a sentence that basically blew me away.

"Since we last talked, my wife and I had a heart-to-heart discussion—life is far too short."

My mind went blank! *He's going to back out! Now what do I do? I've got to get back home!* These were just some of the first thoughts that overwhelmed me.

"You okay, Rob? You look like you're about to pass out. Sit down, please!" Mike stammered.

"Mike, I'm sorry. If you want to back out ..."

Mike held up a hand to silence me.

"Rob, don't misunderstand me! What I was going to say is that my wife and I have always had our hearts set on living out here in the West. This job opening here in South Dakota gives us an opportunity that we never thought could happen. It's only a hop and a skip from here to Steamboat and Big Sky for skiing. That sure beats hauling skis and winter apparel on a plane... and I can hire a young dentist to help out and fill in when I'm gone. It's an ideal situation for us here in South Dakota."

I reached down into my portfolio bag and pulled out the contract documents. In an instant, the contract was signed.

Mike wanted to hang around the clinic for a while longer, so I headed home.

When I got there, Tika was sitting on Tommy's porch seat, and Marty was on the glider. I slipped into a seat next to her. It was obvious that Marty had been crying and I knew it wouldn't be too long before I might be in the same condition.

I started to speak but Tika stopped me.

"Rob, please don't say anything! No matter how hard you try, I know your true home is back in the foothills of Appalachia. If you and Tommy hadn't met, there never would have been the clinic. The entire tribe is eternally grateful for your good deeds.

"Please ... I want you to come here every now and then to see us—and don't wait for Marty to suggest it!

"I only ask one favor of you. Whenever you can, please reinforce with my husband that he needs to come home after this last adventure is completed."

Tika stood and walked over to the glider and hugged Marty before hugging me. There was no virus-related social distancing during this moment. It was a moment of love. And sure enough, I began to tear up.

I entered the house with my sobbing wife, as we walked toward our bedroom for what might have been one of the last times.

At that moment, I sincerely doubted I'd ever see Tika again.

# CHAPTER 59

Agent Lawson wasn't much of an actor. The assignment he'd been given was rather disgusting, he initially thought. He'd never cheated on his wife—and wasn't about to do so, but he wasn't going to be judgmental about the doctor and nurse and their illicit relationship, either.

It was mid-afternoon when Dr. Jim Saylor checked into the "No-tell Hotel." That wasn't really the name of the hotel, but given its reputation, it might as well have been.

The elevator climbed to the sixth floor and stopped. The doctor got off, turned right and walked about thirty paces to the room, unlocked the door, entered the room—and immediately became aroused. This was the place where he could cast aside all the stresses that a Type A surgeon carried on a daily basis. He also believed himself to be a great lover and thoroughly enjoyed demonstrating that skill with Karen Haven, the scrub nurse who had worked alongside him for more than two years.

He pulled out his cell phone and punched the numbers on the glass. Karen answered and listened but said nothing.

"The room is open for romance and I'm more than ready!" was all Jim needed to say.

In less than five minutes, Karen passed through the hotel's lobby and was inside the elevator heading up to the sixth floor. She sniffed the air in the elevator, easily detecting Jim's cologne. She too was now fully aroused as the elevator doors opened.

Once in the room, it didn't take but a few seconds for their two bodies to become entwined in passion. Karen's clothes were flying everywhere—Jim's were already on the floor.

She pushed Jim down on the king-sized bed and began administering her sexual magic.

The video cameras started to record their actions the minute Jim walked in the room. Lawson wondered if the agents watching the recording might be as excited as the room's occupants were.

He stared at his watch, waiting for the signal to make his entry into the hotel.

Almost immediately, his phone pinged, indicating that he had a message.

"Round one just ended. Hurry up—and finish your business for the day. We need to get back to our videotaping!"

Lawson wasn't amused.

After his elevator ride, he knocked loudly on the door. He waited about ten seconds and this time pounded on the door. He heard "What the hell," and a voice on the other side of the door shouting, "What is it?"

"Room service! I have some libations for you, sir!"

The door was cracked open about three inches and Jim's face partially filled the open space that was created.

"Go away. I didn't order any liquor. Get lost!"

Lawson backed up a bit and then did a full-force body slam into the hotel door. Jim scampered toward his clothes, but Lawson, who was now in the room, wasn't taking any chances. He quickly drew his weapon and a red laser point of light appeared on Jim's naked anatomy.

Jim was also packing a weapon, but obviously he wasn't wearing a holster for it at that moment. Raising both hands and protesting, he shut up when Lawson placed his left index finger to his lips while the right hand held the gun. Lawson gestured Jim back to the king bed and Jim obeyed the silent order. Lawson wanted to laugh, but it was at that moment when he first glimpsed Karen…and for a brief second, found himself envying Jim…a bit.

"Folks ... I'm Agent Lawson and here's my badge," he said, pulling out his Homeland Security badge.

CIA agents never showed any real identification. Being active inside America's borders is forbidden.

The doctor was going to do the talking, even if it meant staring down the barrel of an automatic pistol… buck naked.

"What the hell do you want?"

Lawson reached into his rear waistband and pulled out an envelope full of pictures. Flipping it in Karen's direction, the sheet dropped, thus revealing her not so abundant but nevertheless perky breasts. His brain registered a "wow," which thankfully did not escape his lips.

She quickly pulled the sheet back up as the two lovers began looking at the photographs.

"Okay, you've got the goods on us! How much money do you want?"

"Your country doesn't want any money. The hospital that you are credentialed with has a patient who is presently in a coma. You undoubtedly know who I mean. Now listen up!

"The young man is going to die—but not for real—it will be a pretense. The two of you are going to be present when he 'dies.' Doctor, you are going to declare him dead. If any other staff comes into the room, you're going to dismiss them and usher them out of the room. After things quiet down, both of you will accompany the body down to the hospital's morgue. Some men from a Lexington mortuary will be waiting at the morgue's exit doors. They will help you load the body into their hearse. At that point, you both are on your own.

"Here's a certified check. The agency I work for believes this is more than enough compensation for both of your efforts. Don't just stare—take a look at the amount!"

Both Jim's and Karen's eyes widened.

Lawson couldn't resist staring at Karen.

"Well ... is that amount doable?"

Karen and Jim looked at each other, as the sound of their voices tripped over the words coming out of their mouths. They both seemed to believe that the amount was quite generous.

Jim blurted out, "If we do what you ask, is that all you'll ever want from us?"

"I wish it was that cut and dried. So, I'm going to say yes, but there will always be a chance the country will need your help again sometime in the future. If so, you'll always be well compensated for your assistance. I have to tell you, I'm pretty sure this beats the alternative where you both lose your jobs, as well as your spouses—if that's applicable...and that should mean something!"

Jim raised his hands, signaling for Lawson to stop.

But Lawson had one last thing to say.

"I'm going to assume you're giving me an indication that both of you are all in with this. I will be your contact for the foreseeable future—and I already have your contact information.

"I'll leave it up to the two of you to develop and implement the technicalities and procedures for transporting someone to the morgue—including, in particular, a supposed dead person who is still alive. I am thanking you now for your help ahead of time ...

and have a good rest of the day!"

Stealing one last peek at Karen, Lawson turned to leave the room, while picking up some drywall that had fallen to the floor—a result of the door that he'd slammed into earlier. He closed the door quietly.

Tommy's plan was slowly coming together.

∩ ∩ ∩

About 1:00 a.m., Tommy messaged O'Brien, telling him they should meet in the lobby of the Hyatt lobby at 11:00 a.m.

But first, he needed to do a preliminary test in preparation for what was going to happen. Going to the refrigerator, Tommy grabbed a vial containing a tranquilizing medication. He sat down, carefully loaded the syringe with a tiny amount of etorphine, and injected it into his leg. Instantly memories of a not-too-distant past came flooding back.

His eyes now closed, Tommy let his mind travel back a few months to the Miami Airport and that day when he and his then partner Danny were running down a concourse looking for two people. Advancing quickly in the direction of the agents were their targets, Mark and his girlfriend, who were in an airport courtesy cart that was heading to baggage claim. Tommy and Danny quickly jumped aboard the cart—with each agent simultaneously injecting etorphine into the cart's two occupants, instantly immobilizing both of them.

Instead of continuing to the baggage claim area, Tommy took control of the cart, driving it outside to a waiting EMS vehicle.

Several minutes later, Tommy forced his eyes to reopen, blinking several times as his mind returned to reality and back to the present moment. He discarded the syringe and grabbed a new syringe, loaded it and returned it to the mini-refrigerator. He placed the "no housekeeping" sign on the outside door handle. Another to-do item was crossed off his list.

Next on the list was conducting practice runs with his Apple watch timing function until he felt certain he could do it perfectly. Then it would be time for sleep.

The next morning, Tommy grabbed his car keys and headed downstairs to the hotel restaurant for breakfast. After breakfast, Tommy went to the lobby, found a comfortable chair, and settled in to wait. It only took five minutes for him to fall fast asleep.

O'Brien was on time and upon entering the lobby, spied Tommy sleeping soundly in the chair. Taking an empty chair next to him, O'Brien closed his eyes and pretended that he was also asleep.

A sudden half snore indicative of sleep apnea exploded from O'Brien's mouth and woke Tommy up quickly. He spotted O'Brien seemingly asleep next to him and panicked, thinking they'd both slept past Jameson's daily visit to the men's room.

"Hey, man ... wake up! What ... what time is it?"

O'Brien slowly opened his eyes, grinning widely at Tommy.

"You son of a ... damn it, O'Brien!"

A still-laughing O'Brien pointed at his watch. Tommy realized he'd been had, and the twitch that started at the corners of his mouth slowly broke into a broad smile.

Ten minutes later, Jameson walked into the Hyatt Hotel. Tommy started the timer function on his watch. O'Brien didn't need prompting—he got up and headed to the restroom. Once inside, he saw that Jameson was holed up in the handicapped stall. O'Brien finished his business and as he headed to the door, removed the miniature camera he'd placed on the opposite wall from the stall's door earlier. The camera inside the stall was still broadcasting. When Jameson finally emerged, Tommy stopped the timer.

He shook his head in disbelief. Jameson had been camped out in the stall for seventeen minutes and forty-two seconds.

Both men watched as Jameson exited the Hyatt.

Tommy spoke first. "We can't let him settle into his favorite stall. I hate to tell you this, but you're going to have to crawl under the stall's opening after locking the handicapped stall door, and then lock yourself in the other stall. I'll get some fake legs for you to place against the base of the toilet in the handicapped stall in case Jameson decides to bend down and check things out.

"I'll enter the men's room and engage him in some chit-chat. In fact, I'll chat him up so much that he'll turn his back on me. When he does, that's when I'll inject him with the juice!

I'll leave the wheelchair outside the bathroom. Once he collapses, I'll fetch it. You'll place him in the wheelchair, and I'll cover him up with the blanket. You put that funky hat that you've been wearing on Jameson—nobody will know the difference. Let's head up to my room and go over the plan a few more times. It's on for tomorrow!"

 **HAPTER 60**

Tommy was wound up and he knew it. He couldn't get to sleep but knew that taking any sleep aids the night before snatching someone could be counter-productive. His angst came from a conversation he and Stan had earlier in the evening. The words spoken by Stan were disconcerting.

He understood that the Agency is supposed to be apolitical, but at the same time knew that those who worked for the CIA were pragmatic—at all times. That was why Stan's words seemed so ominous to Tommy.

"I need to tell you, it's imperative that you wrap up this Rob Becker assassination plot and do it soon!"

Stan's admonition stemmed from the presidential polling recently completed by the research wonks at the CIA. While generally the numbers were never one hundred percent cut and dried, there were indications that the current 2020 presidential election was going to be a nail- biter, and that was worrisome.

"The Agency's conclusion is that the 2020 presidential election is going to be too close to call," Stan blurted out.

"Are you telling me that POTUS could actually lose against the 2020 Democratic ticket?" Tommy asked.

"Yes, I am! Look, Tommy, you can doubt the polls all you want. Hell, in my spare time. I love checking out the polls online with MSN! Their home page has these polls embedded among the news stories. I'm the mainstream media's nightmare and definition of a 'shy' voter. I get on polling sites and.lie.

"I give them a wrong age or a wrong ethnicity. Hell, I'll even throw in a lie about my gender ... and I've got to tell you, I'm not alone. Our in-house polling indicates that thousands of folks are doing the same thing!

"The bottom line is, if POTUS goes down to defeat, at the very least you and I will get our pink slips. Any ongoing questionable activities involving Rob Becker will be immediately shut down."

....and Stan fell silent.

"Damn, Stan! I'm not certain I want to process everything you just laid on me! I can honestly tell you right now, that it all starts going down tomorrow ... so stay tuned. Gotta go. I'll be talking to you!" Tommy said.

Tommy once again tried to relax and fall asleep but was unsuccessful. Knowing the solution to his insomnia, Tommy called his wife—and thirty minutes later, he was sound asleep.

ᐱ ᐱ ᐱ

Tommy was up at six in the morning and down in the Hyatt's lobby forty-five minutes later to meet up with O'Brien for a quick breakfast and the start of their day.

"If you're finished, let's head back to the lobby and sit somewhere closer to the men's room. Today's wild card just might be that Jameson decides to stop by earlier to check out his personal bathroom," Tommy told his partner. Both men laughed at their shared imagery of Jameson having a gastrointestinal emergency on this particular day.

After they were positioned close enough to the restroom, Tommy got up and headed back to his hotel room to get his gun, the wheelchair, and two carefully loaded syringes of etorphine. He also placed the two artificial lower legs on the seat of the wheelchair, covered them, and headed back down to the lobby, where he had a surprise for O'Brien.

"I forgot to tell you that yesterday, I elicited the assistance of the hotel's bell captain! Right now, he's standing over there by the entrance's automatic door. It's amazing just how much a Benjamin can influence behavior, especially during these pandemic days. One person's Grover Cleveland is another person's Benjamin," Tommy said, laughing.

O'Brien's reply was instant.

"What the hell is a Grover Cleveland, and what exactly is the bell captain going to do for us?"

"The thousand-dollar bill has President Grover Cleveland's picture on it, hence the name. And our bell captain will remove his cap and put it back on twice in a row when he sees Jameson's cruiser pull into valet parking."

It was nearly eleven o'clock, and Tommy was getting antsy.

"Let's go set up!"

Tommy got up and started pushing the wheelchair toward the restroom, leaving O'Brien with no choice but to follow. Once at the door to the men's room, O'Brien turned toward the entrance of the Hyatt just as the bell captain took off his cap and put it back on...two times.

"Uh, don't look now, but your bell captain friend just gave us the signal. Damn, Tommy, you're psychic!"

Tommy quickly gave O'Brien one of the syringes. O'Brien stared at it with a questioning look.

"It's a spare—you may need to use it!" Tommy told him.

Grabbing the fake legs from the wheelchair, O'Brien opened

the bathroom door and headed to the handicapped stall as Tommy stood watch through the open doorway. Entering the stall, he placed the legs in a realistic position, locked the door, and shimmied his body under the stall's opening. He waited for Tommy to give him the go-ahead to take a position in the other vacant stall.

Tommy nodded. O'Brien disappeared into the other stall and Tommy closed the outside door to the restroom. He took a position behind a partition, and within seconds he was watching Jameson as he went into the men's room.

Tommy counted to five, and then he entered the men's restroom.

He passed through the door and was greeted by the open end of a nine-millimeter Glock in Jameson's right hand, pointed directly at him. So much for the bell captain's help! Jameson waved the gun at Tommy in a silent commanding fashion, to advance all the way inside the restroom.

"Officer, I have no idea what I've done wrong, but I won't argue or resist. If you want me to cuff myself, just say the word. But please, sir, I'm begging ... lower your weapon."

O'Brien was listening to the one-sided discussion and immediately uncapped the syringe.

"I'm coming out ... don't shoot," he said from inside the stall.

O'Brien calmly emerged from his stall as Tommy started to convulse. The seizure seemed real and even O'Brien hesitated, not realizing Tommy was giving his partner an opening to jab Jameson with the syringe.

The younger agent recovered quickly and lunged at Jameson, depositing the needle and its drug contents into the trooper's arm. The drug, aided by Jameson's heightened blood pressure, was quickly coursing through his bloodstream. Before he could act, Jameson's legs began to buckle, and his eyes started to roll upwards in their sockets.

Down went Jameson.

Tommy placed both hands on his knees and took a deep breath. "Thanks, partner. I owe you big time."

In less than five minutes, the two agents meticulously cleaned up all the evidence of their caper and loaded Jameson into the wheelchair. The three men then exited the Hyatt.

Tommy unlocked the vehicle doors remotely, allowing O'Brien to single-handedly lift the blanketed Jameson from the wheelchair. He carefully placed their unconscious captive into the van's cargo hold. O'Brien went to his car, climbed in, and waited for Tommy to lead the way.

As both vehicles passed by Jameson's cruiser, a police dispatcher's voice could be heard over the radio, calling for Trooper Jameson.

 **HAPTER 61**

O'Brien hadn't paid any attention to the beauty and geology of Kentucky's Appalachian Mountains. He was on the interstate heading south from Lexington, traveling along the fringe of a mountain chain.

Still following Tommy's vehicle, O'Brien couldn't take his eyes off the glorious sights of the rolling hills. He couldn't believe that he had just seen an actual coal vein in a geologic cutout along I-75. He didn't realize that millions of years earlier, these very mounds were once much higher than the current foothills. In fact, there was a mountain range that easily rivaled the modern-day Rocky Mountain National Park. He marveled at the stark beauty of this particular section of a mountain range that runs along a route from Georgia to Maine.

Now, off the interstate, O'Brien and Tommy continued along more rural country roads. After another hour, Tommy turned onto a gravel road, and headed toward a grove of trees in which a deceptively modest-looking cabin was nestled.

O'Brien parked next to Tommy's van, got out and yelled, "Where the hell are we?"

In a low voice, Tommy answered, "Believe it or not, we're just outside of Irvine, Kentucky—and I don't want Jameson to know this!"

Tommy returned to his vehicle and opened the rear door to find Jameson stirring, but still well tranquilized.

"Give me a hand, O'Brien."

After removing their hostage, they propped him up, supporting his body against the side of the rear bumper. Tommy pulled out a twin pack of Narcan from his pocket and administered the first dose of the tranquilizer-reversing drug. The effects were immediate—Jameson's eyelids popped open, and he began breathing deeply and quickly.

Tommy realized Jameson was hyperventilating and slapped the trooper with the palm of his right hand. The last thing he needed was their hostage passing out.

O'Brien propped him up further. Tommy stepped forward and cinched up the hood that was over Jameson's head.

"Okay, Trooper, I'm going to lead you toward a building that's your new home. Nod if you understand."

Jameson, who had not yet uttered a word, nodded. O'Brien led the hostage in a back-and-forth manner meant to confuse Jameson. He figured Jameson was counting each step taken and once inside the door, would memorize that number.

The agent was correct. Jameson figured he'd never travel the same path again, but you never know, he told himself.

O'Brien assisted Jameson as they climbed the steps and entered the cabin. Tommy took over and led Jameson about thirty paces before stopping and turning toward a wall with an opening where a dumbwaiter had been. Tommy removed Jameson's shoes and slacks. Then, using a pocket knife, Tommy vertically sliced through the front of Jameson's shirt from the neck to the bottom of the shirt tails.

Standing only in his briefs, socks, and cut shirt, Jameson felt the hood lifted from his head, and he was guided head first into the dumbwaiter opening.

Tommy removed the handcuffs.

The only thing Jameson could see was what appeared to be a slide that went all the way into the basement. It wasn't the typical seven-to-ten-foot drop. He guessed it might be twenty- plus feet to the bottom.

Tommy began chatting Jameson up.

"This slide ride is the coolest thing in this cabin, but the last part is brutal! You're going to end up in a foam-filled pit."

Just like that, Tommy released his grasp on Jameson's ankles.

Jameson picked up speed and for a fleeting moment took flight, only to slam into several foam cubes in the pit. He looked up and saw the slide retracting.

Tommy closed the door, beckoning O'Brien to step back with him.

"Doc Becker has a saying. It's 'Let it bench cool.' I asked him once what that meant and his answer was that in dental school, when for whatever reason someone wanted a time out, the phrase 'let it bench cool' was spoken. He said it directly referred to any dental laboratory procedure that required some aging of whatever dental product was being fabricated. That product would some-times sit for hours on a bench table ...cooling its jets!

"So, we're going to let Jameson bench cool for a bit. His mind is spinning and he's wondering who we're working for and what we want. That will be followed with wondering what his top downside risk is. In my experience, an effective captive bench cool takes about two hours. There's usually some frozen pizza in the fridge, so let's have an early dinner. It's going to be a late night."

Jameson crawled out of the foam pit, spitting out dust, dirt, and mold for about a minute. There was no drinking water in the quarters—just a toilet and a half roll of toilet paper.

The mind games had begun, and it was pretty much as Tommy had described. Jerry mentally jacked himself up for enhanced interrogation by hypnotizing himself. Memories of his SERE training came flooding back, including an interrogation timeline which reminded him that he'd be the most vulnerable after a couple of hours of incarceration.

Jameson and Tommy were working from the same playbook!

# CHAPTER 62

It was somewhere around one in the morning when Trooper Jameson finally fell asleep.

He had about an hour of pre-REM sleep before Tommy and O'Brien roused him from his slumber.

An enhanced interrogation room was adjacent to the room with the foam pit. The connecting door between the two rooms was opened, and five minutes after his rude awakening, Jameson poked his head through the doorway.

Tommy was seated at a table in a darkened room, and his partner was nowhere in sight. Tommy knew he was nearby. After all, O'Brien was Tommy's insurance policy in case Jameson somehow got the drop on him.

"Don't be shy, Mr. Jameson ... come on in," Tommy called out.

Jameson was skittish, behaving like a caged animal being released back into the wild. He entered the room, squinting in the direction of where he thought the voice came from. Advancing further into the room, he still couldn't see Tommy. Now within just twenty feet of his captor, Jameson halted as the room was suddenly flooded with blinding light.

O'Brien was standing in the corner of the room, his eyes covered temporarily with night vision goggles. When the lights flipped on, Tommy, who had control of the tableside light switch, simply closed his eyes. The Agency had taken care of all contingencies when it constructed the cabin.

"Have a seat, Trooper....please!"

Jameson sat on a metal folding chair and surveyed the various items in front of him on the table. At the same time, O'Brien stepped forward, holding his automatic against the back of Jameson's head.

"Trooper, put your hands behind your back."

Jameson paused briefly while considering if a dive toward the revolver and bullets on the table would be a wise move and finally deciding that now was not the right time to make a move. He extended both arms backwards instead, immediately regretting that move as he was once again handcuffed.

It was Tommy's turn. "Now that we've got your attention, let me go through my treasure trove of torture tools and techniques that are set up in front of you."

With a laser pointer, Tommy began his presentation.

"This antique tool is perhaps the most creative! It's an old crank telephone from the early twentieth century. When it's cranked, a wonderful jolt of electricity is generated. It speeds through the wire and wherever that exposed wire touches your skin ... Yowser!"

Tommy was in his element, loving every moment of his theatric performance. It was time for a live demonstration!

He walked around the table, stopped, and stood next to Jameson. O'Brien took Tommy's now empty seat at the table, waiting for his cue to start cranking.

Tommy pulled the wire as far as it would go, then nodded to O'Brien. Electricity began coursing as Tommy slowly placed the end of the naked copper wire against Jameson's right temple, completing the circuit for the surging electricity.

Jameson's head recoiled and Tommy shifted the wire's position while still maintaining contact with Jameson's skin.

Tommy started to laugh.

Jameson—and even O'Brien—were taken aback. The obvious joy Tommy was deriving from this torture was way over the top!

"Funny, asshole, real funny," Jameson uttered.

"Oh, wow, you can speak! Well, let me demonstrate another tool."

Grabbing the pulp tester from the table, Tommy glanced at Jameson's face to see if he recognized the diagnostic dental tool. Seeing no response, Tommy put on a pair of latex surgical gloves and dipped the tip of the pulp tester into the open end of a tube of toothpaste.

"So, Mr. Jameson, this is also an electrifying tool. It's used in dentistry to determine if a tooth is alive or dead. The dentist places the tip—and you can see it's already covered with a tiny bit of toothpaste—on the crown portion of tooth structure and I slowly spin this dial which is numbered from one to ten. When a patient flinches, that number on the dial is recorded.

"If the tester reaches ten and there has been no flinching by the patient, that's an indicator that the nerve of the tooth is dead! Most of the time, a patient raises their hand or flinches at the number 3-5 range on the dial. To keep this quick, we're just going to skip those lower numbers and set the dial at the maximum and that's number 10!"

O'Brien stepped forward and put Jameson into a headlock. Tommy forced Jameson's lips open while placing the tip of the pulp tester on three different incisors, pausing in between each placement for effect.

Jameson literally thrashed around in his chair each time Tommy placed the tip of the tool on another tooth.

Again, Tommy began laughing.

"Rather shocking, huh?" he stated while laughing at his own joke.

Tommy could see it in Jameson's eyes—the man was looking for an opening to punish him.

"Isn't that something, Jameson? Dentists always say they want to be trusted and they aren't going to hurt anyone, but then they use these kind of tools. What the hell's up with that?

"Okay, now I'm going to show you my smallest tool! Look at this tiny needle! My good friend Dr. Rob Becker showed me this. Maybe you've seen him on television—he's the owner of a famous thoroughbred. He also has a teenage grandson named Harry." Tommy let his last remark sink in for a few seconds.

Jameson shook his head without any comment.

Tommy then dropped the hammer.

"Don't tell me you don't recognize that name! You've got a lot of skin in this game…all of it connected to whether that kid lives or dies!

Tommy stared at Jameson and didn't blink. Jameson stared right back, not twitching one iota either.

Tommy turned, ready to resume the torture. He held up a drawing that anatomically showed specific nerve pathways within the oral cavity, for Jameson to see. Using his index finger, Tommy pointed at the nasopalatine nerve emerging from a tiny bump located behind the back of the two upper central incisors in his mouth. Tommy ungloved and re-gloved in case Jameson was confused, he also pointed in Jameson's mouth, exactly where the nerve was located. Finally, pulling out a larger needle, Tommy moved directly in front of Jameson—holding the needle at eye level so Jameson could easily see the size of the needle—and now it wasn't so tiny.

"Look at the size of this mother fucker, Jameson! Can you imagine just how much pain there'd be if I stuck this needle into that tissue on the roof of your mouth?"

Tommy didn't wait for Jameson's answer. He went back to his seat at the table and turned off the lights. It was time for O'Brien to act. Within seconds, he was all over Jameson with a choke hold that immobilized him. Tommy came out of the darkness, still gloved but now wearing a face shield. In his hand was the smaller needle, still in its sheath.

Tommy knew Jameson would refuse to open his mouth. Sliding his index finger past Jameson's lips, Tommy poked further back in the mouth where the jawbone juts up to the skull. After one final hard push, Jameson's lower jaw was forced open, enabling Tommy to shove a couple of mouth props between the man's upper and lower molars.

Jameson twitched...a lot!

Assisting with their captive, O'Brien tilted Jameson's head back as Tommy stabbed the needle into soft tissue directly behind Jameson's top two front teeth. Anywhere on the roof would have hurt, but Tommy had learned the mouth's anatomy well—and he was dead on the target.

The moment Tommy punctured the gum tissue was the moment he owned Jerry Jameson.

The room filled with the sounds of screams the likes of which Tommy had heard only once before: in the forest around Mt. Hood when Rob Becker unleashed the same horror on an Antifa revolutionary.

"I'm going to kill you and your friend, you sons of bitches!" Jameson screamed, struggling wildly.

"Not tonight, asshole, not ever!" was Tommy's retort.

Five minutes later, Jameson was back in his room, deeply craving a pain pill—the sort derived from a poppy plant. The irony of the situation was crippling.

CHAPTER 63

The Air Force plane was due to land at noon. Marty couldn't wait to get back home, and me...not so much! I was apprehensive about seeing my daughter. If I had any answers about Harry's condition, I'd share them with her in a heartbeat. If that meant that I would have to die doing so—I would! What pissed me off most was the fact that Communist China would get off scot-free if Harry died. There was no doubt in my mind that the CCP took great pride and joy in seeing the death and destruction of America's youngest generation. My heart ached for the thousands of young people hooked on their smuggled opioids and other illegal drug-based derivatives.

We were picked up in Louisville by Donnie and Val. Val immediately spied Marty standing there waiting. I stood a few feet away, acting like a total stranger.

"Marty, where's Rob?"

"He was with me just a second ago," my wife answered Val while not giving me away.

I couldn't control my laughter any longer. Both Val and Donnie had no clue that I'd been right there within ten feet of them for the last ten minutes. To all appearances, I was just another traveler waiting for their ride.

Marty could tell I was about to lose it and turned in my direction.

"Rob ...there you are! Get over here!"

"Jesus Marty—I'm not your pet!"

Both Donnie and Val looked like statues frozen in place with their mouths wide open—and suddenly, they realized it was me.

"Damn, Rob, they sure did some great cosmetic work on you!" Donnie said.

We proceeded to the car and continued laughing for another twenty minutes or so during the drive home in Kentucky. Thoughts of our home had pretty much filled my mind over the past few days—knowing that my home was the one calming constant that would always be the same no matter what was happening in my life.

During the drive, we chatted about Towers Above and his foal, especially how he was developing. I told them the foal's name would be Towers Destiny. Donnie and Val voiced their immediate approval.

As was my usual habit when I wasn't the driver, I managed to nod off for a few minutes.

In my sleepy haze, I saw the foothills looming closer and suddenly realized that instead of taking the usual route to our home, Donnie was headed toward his farm.

"Uh … Donnie, I know I've been away for a while, but I think you missed the turnoff to my house."

"Geez, Rob, I'm sorry. We were talking about Towers Destiny and I was thinking you'd want to see the foal that I believe is going to fulfill that dream of yours."

"Dream—what dream?"

"Rob, you're slipping a bit! I'm talking about that day you handed each of us that contract—and a portfolio of papers outlining your path for creating another Secretariat."

"No problem, Donnie. We're halfway between both locations

now—so drive on, my friend!" I told him, eager to see the colt.

We arrived at the farm, went through the electronic gate, and drove up a slight hill to the farmhouse. As we rounded the bend in the road, I spotted a new structure that looked remarkably just like my home, down to the same Hardie Board siding.

"Well Donnie, go ahead and cancel that drive back to my house. I'll just bunk in this house. It looks every bit the same as mine!"

"Okay!" Donnie answered, stifling a laugh.

I glanced over at Val, who had turned away from my gaze. I thought she was trembling, but later realized that she was laughing.

Getting out of the car, I climbed the steps to the porch and immediately spied a glider that looked just like the one on Tommy's porch in Oral, South Dakota. My head was spinning, and I had to sit down. I literally felt like I had become part of a *Twilight Zone* adventure. I looked at Marty, and she also had a pained look on her face.

Donnie knew me well and could tell I was agitated and very confused. "Rob, calm down and breathe slowly," he told me.

"This is a replica of your house! The glider arrived just a few minutes ago—in fact, it was on the plane you just flew in on! It was transported here on a Ryder truck that passed us shortly after we got on the road. My farmhands unloaded it and put it quickly together as soon as it was delivered here. Tika wanted you to have the glider!

"The same goes for the house. Val and I, along with Steven, have been moving your possessions here over the past three weeks. Rob, if it hadn't been for you and your dream, I'd never be as blessed as I am now.

"Welcome home, Rob and Marty! Val and I hope you don't mind that we're your immediate neighbors … hopefully for many years to come."

I lowered my head, trying hard to tamp down my emotions, but failing miserably. Marty wasn't concerned about crying, as she rushed to Donnie and wrapped him in a loving hug, while tears streamed from her eyes.

"And our old house?"

"It sold a couple months ago. We finished moving everything just last week. I told our neighbors that we were building a single-family home on our property for a cousin of mine."

"I have a hunch that someone by the name of Tommy was involved in this surprise!" I responded.

Donnie nodded.

I didn't want to spoil the euphoric moment, but nonetheless said softly to myself, "If you both only knew that I'm supposed to die in the next few days, maybe you wouldn't have gone to so much …"

I couldn't finish the thought.

 HAPTER 64

The mental tango Tommy was engaged in with Jerry Jameson was exhausting. Tommy was no longer a young man, and the give and take took more of a toll than it would have just five years earlier.

He stopped the interrogation at four in the morning. O'Brien wanted to pick Tommy's mind but could tell it wasn't the time to do that.

Retreating to the main floor, Tommy pulled his mobile phone from his rear pocket. There was a text from Stan.

As he read the message, Tommy's expressionless face became very animated. There was a smile, quickly followed by a furrowed brow. The pen in his hand had found its way into Tommy's mouth—tightly clenched between his teeth. Tommy realized his teeth were also grinding against the pen and he forced his jaw to relax.

Stan's message was certainly a game-changer. Tommy looked at his watch, wondering if he should call.

"Hell, he's called me at worse hours of the night," Tommy rationalized to himself while placing the call. Stan's phone rang five times before going to voicemail. Tommy hung up and called again. In fact, he called nine more times. On the eleventh call, Tommy's phone sprang to life!

"What the hell do you want at this ungodly time of morning?"

"You confiscated Jameson's cruiser. Why?"

There was dead silence on the other end for at least thirty seconds. Tommy waited until Stan finally realized that if he hung up, Tommy would only continue to call.

"Sometimes it pays to be honest and straightforward. I called the director of the KSP and explained our situation. Anyhow, I just had a hunch there might be something of interest in that cruiser—and there was!

"Underneath the driver's seat was a refurbished Juul pod. I sent the pod to our lab for analysis and damned if it didn't have the exact amount of fentanyl – ratio wise - that was in the Juul pod that Agent Lawson retrieved from Harry on the bike trail.

"Jerry Jameson was dealing drugs, thus abusing his position with the KSP. If Harry dies, then Jameson could be charged with first-degree murder. And it gets even better! That same night, another teenager died from a similar fentanyl overdose. The kid's name was Anthony, and he went to the same school as Harry. The chemical analysis of Anthony's Juul pod also tested positive for the same amount of fentanyl.

"Jerry Jameson is one screwed-up dude. And now he's an island unto himself. The Kentucky State Police have no use for him anymore. If he's sent to prison, he'll be murdered in short order. Both Lawson and Trooper Kessing believe that if we let him go free, either the folks that hired him will let him dangle in the wind and ultimately kill him, or a fellow trooper will exact final punishment. Either way, he's a dead man walking right now.

"I'm not telling you what to do, but any offer we make him right now would most probably be accepted."

"Damn, Stan, thanks! I need you to confirm that I can still offer the amount that we discussed."

"Yes, Tommy, offer away. We always have room for a throwaway agent. We're not going to jump through any hoops to save him if he should ever get in a bind. If Jameson's smart—and I believe he is—he'll accept our offer."

"Is there anything else I should know?" Tommy asked.

"Rob Becker and his wife are back in the Commonwealth. Anytime you want to initiate your plan is fine with me. I'll be flying to Lexington tomorrow. I need to be at the upcoming faux funeral service. DC is a hot mess right now. We've got Antifa and Black Lives Matter protestors running rampant on the streets without any consequences, and COVID-19 numbers are off the charts. The 2020 Presidential election is next week, and I really need a break!"

∩ ∩ ∩

Jerry was nearly asleep. He'd spent far too much time mentally plotting his escape, despite knowing that sleep was his much-needed ally if he was going to continue to resist the next two or three rounds of interrogation.

It wasn't more than fifteen minutes later when the lights in the pit room were glaring brightly again.

Jerry knew that was the signal indicating it was time for round two. The door to the pit room opened as Tommy and O'Brien entered. Tommy had his weapon drawn and pointed squarely at the trooper.

"Turn around, Mr. Jameson."

O'Brien advanced, ordering Jerry to extend his arms backwards. Jerry did as he was told, while purposely keeping his wrists further apart. When he sensed O'Brien was getting ready to cuff him, he whirled around, leaned in, and reached for any part of O'Brien's body he could grab hold of. The next thing Jerry knew, he was on the floor attempting to sit up, and letting out a guttural "oh shit." He touched his face to wipe the blood from the side of his split lip, and felt a welt beginning to swell beneath his right eye.

Jerry quickly realized that O'Brien wasn't to be trifled with.

"Okay, Jerry, let's try this again," Tommy said.

This time, Jerry complied. O'Brien led him back to the interrogation table where all the props were still in place.

Tommy took his seat at the table.

"I'm going to address you as Jerry. Jerry, you and I need to start being honest with each other. No more bullshit and no more posturing!"

Jerry remained stone-faced even as the layers of swollen facial tissue threatened to cut off sight in his right eye.

"At first, my partner and I were trying to figure out why you were so interested in a kid named Harry who'd overdosed on fentanyl on the Legacy Bike Trail. But in just the last few hours, it has come to my attention that a used Juul pod refilled with a liquid concoction of nicotine and fentanyl was retrieved from under the driver's seat of your police cruiser. My guess is you accidentally dropped it.

"A chemical analysis conducted on that tampered Juul pod directly ties you to another Juul pod that was retrieved from a young man named Harry, on the Legacy Bike Trail. And damned if there wasn't an additional vaping pod found in the house of a teen who died from a similar fentanyl overdose during that same period of time. That teen's name was Anthony. Both boys go to the same high school and in fact, were classmates!"

Tommy paused a few seconds while mentally gauging changes in Jerry's body language. The biggest tell was Jerry's skin color.

When Tommy first started talking, Jerry's face was more on the red side—most likely a result of lingering anger over the thrashing he'd received from O'Brien.

Now, Jerry's skin was a flushed-out pale white, so much so that Tommy wondered if the man was going to faint.

"The way I see it, if Harry dies, you'll be facing two charges of first-degree premeditated murder. Damn, Jerry, that should earn you the death penalty. If you somehow manage to get off, I expect the folks that you've contracted with will want to eliminate you before you spill your guts!

"And the brotherhood of the Kentucky State Police will be standing in the wings—right behind the folks who hired you for 'specific contracted service.'"

Tommy paused, just sitting and staring at Jerry. One minute turned into two minutes and Jerry still didn't react. Tommy looked at the second hand on his watch as it circled the numbers a total of four times before reluctantly deciding to move forward with another round of enhanced interrogation.

"These next items on the table that I am going to show you, are the tools I use for what I call Tommy Roulette. The last time I performed this routine, my prisoner ended up with half of his ear shot off."

Tommy laughed, remembering that moment, and at first, didn't hear Jerry speak in a barely audible voice.

"Excuse me, I missed that. Did you just say something?"

"Make me an offer," Jerry said in a low whisper.

Tommy didn't hesitate. When Stan gave him the financial green light, Tommy came up with a monetary package that he personally would be comfortable with. It was an amount that when invested conservatively, would generate a reasonable annual income derived from stock dividends and interest, no matter how the stock market was performing.

"Five million—to be renegotiated every other year, with any increase being limited to five percent," Tommy replied.

"Your name is?"

"Oh … no, Jerry, not until I have a signed contract! Look Jerry, I came up with the numbers myself. I'm really no different than you are. Five million dollars is a decent chunk of money. Furthermore, you're not being sidelined. You'll be working for the federal government. Initially, you'll take a somewhat lengthy vacation of our choosing. When you re-emerge, you'll have a new identity, which means your name goes bye-bye!"

This time Jerry responded more vociferously!

"How about ten million with no renegotiation until after five years?" Jerry asked emphatically.

Tommy knew the deal was almost complete—and wasn't willing to negotiate further. Any additional contract modifications suggested by Jerry had now become a personal issue for himself.

"Look, Jerry, you just pissed me off. Keep in mind that my initial plan was to show the anatomical structure of your oral cavity to O'Brien—so he could practice sticking you with a needle over and over again. We can always return to that plan if necessary!

"Look, I take pride in what I do for this country. How about you just saying yes to the five million? You show the agency what you can do, and then two years from now, maybe you can negotiate a new contract. At that point, I'll be long gone from the scene. Take the deal, Trooper Jameson!"

Jerry had been keeping his good left eye on Tommy, but now looked over at O'Brien. He wanted to hold out for more money, but the thought of more tortuous stabbing inside his mouth gnawed at his psyche.

"Okay, I'll sign, but not until I know your and your partner's names."

"Alright. My name is Tommy and his name is Jay—and there will be no last names—ever!"

Taking the official CIA contract from the lap drawer, Tommy pushed it and a pen toward Jerry. O'Brien removed the handcuffs, and in just a few seconds, the contract was signed by Jerry and pushed back across the table.

The cuffs never went back on.

The hope was high in Tommy's mind that Harry wouldn't die. If Harry crossed over, well ... he didn't think he could ever face Harry's soul.

 **HAPTER 65**

After the Q&A session that lasted over an hour, Jerry was led back to the pit room by O'Brien. The only difference between this particular interrogation and the previous one was that Jerry was no longer handcuffed and his mouth wasn't hemorrhaging. It was mid-morning, and he was finally going to be able to sleep.

Jerry was in fact quite happy to switch employers and allegiances. He'd been working with Todd and Wayne for just over six years—and a fair amount of his time and effort was still pretty much only investigative in nature. He'd always wondered why they didn't just hire detectives. The only thing he could figure out was that they didn't want, as the saying goes, "too many cooks in the kitchen."

In reality, Wayne and Todd were micromanagers—doling out their investigative needs in a manner that ensured no one person could leverage their knowledge base—and of course, to save on expenses.

Whenever Jerry received an assignment from the two, his first step was to do a Google search in hopes of finding useful links and information about the target. Jerry always adhered to one mantra that was a constant in all his investigations: FOLLOW THE MONEY!

While Harry's Google footprint was small, Jerry looked for the shortest path—just like in the game Five Degrees of Kevin

Bacon—and soon discovered that Harry's grandfather was Dr. Rob Becker. He strongly sensed that Dr. Becker might somehow be involved in his current assignment.

Jerry also thought that Anthony and Harry had been somehow involved in the drug-related death of another fellow student—and in his mind, their deaths might be perceived as justifiable retribution!

∩ ∩ ∩

After grabbing a beer from the minifridge, Tommy sat down in front of the laptop to write his report for Stan. Even though the assumption was that the twins were taking orders from some person or entity that had global connections, the Agency still had to try and connect all the dots. Jerry had already shared that he'd been with Todd and Wayne numerous times at a shooting club—and his experiences led him to believe that the twins were not planning to contract out any future assassinations. Further compounding this belief was the fact that both twins were excellent marksmen and on numerous occasions visitors at the shooting range. They practiced using the only weapon they felt comfortable with—a Remington 700 with a Nightforce scope and an SR-25 suppressor. The twins seemed to believe if this particular weapon was good enough for Chris Kyle, it was certainly good enough for them.

Another issue Jerry thought was odd—Wayne and Todd were never anywhere visible during their time spent shooting at the club. They selected targets for their session, but then disappeared out of sight. Jerry could see the targets and at times would watch as a bullet hit the target. He would continue to watch as minute by minute, more bullets hit the mark and the target began to shred. Then suddenly out of nowhere, the twins would reappear. After asking where they were shooting from, Jerry always got the same eerily frightening response!

"We're far enough away, but always close enough to be effective!"

With the conclusion of Jerry's second and final interrogation, Tommy needed approval from Stan to let Jerry stay in Lexington for the time being. The trooper's disappearance had become a non-issue—no one was asking questions about his disappearance. The KSP never reported he was missing, and the staff at the Hyatt assumed his cruiser had broken down when a tow truck arrived and removed it from the valet parking lot.

Tommy figured as long as Jameson wasn't publicly declared as AWOL, Wayne and Todd might still call on him with an emergency request for additional services.

At the end of his report to Stan, Tommy asked how the future graveside "theater production" was shaping up. He was anticipating the upcoming scenario of a murder during a funeral that would take place within the next ten days.

The report was done and sent to Stan in an encrypted e-mail. Tommy kicked back and stared at his watch—it was time to get on with it, and he began timing how long it would be before Stan called him.

O'Brien took a seat across from Tommy and realized his partner's mind was occupied elsewhere. Jay took strong issue with the fact that Jameson would be allowed to walk—without being charged for one murder and possibly a second!

Tommy, however, failed to detect that his partner was bothered.

After being ignored for a couple more minutes, O'Brien

finally lost it. He slammed his fist down on Tommy's desk, effectively ending the timer on Tommy's stopwatch.

For the next thirty minutes, the two agents went back and forth, arguing the pros and cons of Jameson's reprieve from any punishment.

This new breed of thinking that was a part of O'Brien's professional persona only confirmed to Tommy that it was time for him to retire.

# CHAPTER 66

Dr. Jim Saylor walked into Harry's hospital room, unannounced and unnoticed, all the while hoping that Harry would miraculously open his eyes and greet him. He gazed around the private room and visually took in everything that was happening with the patient.

A group of EKG leads were trailing from Harry's chest, forming one main body of wires which were connected to a computer and a monitor screen at his bedside. From the computer monitor, he could see each "lub-dub" beat of Harry's heart instantly transform into an electronic upward spike, followed by an almost equal-sized downward spike—the dub.

The pattern on the monitor was mesmerizing and repeated itself over and over again. As long as it continued, there was life—but maybe not so much in Harry's situation right now.

Harry was also wearing what looked like a swimming cap with multiple wires flowing backwards, carrying an electronic signal that measured neural activity from different areas of the brain. In Harry's case, there was mostly zero activity present. The fact that there was the slightest bit of activity, though, meant Harry wasn't dead.

The monitoring of Harry's heart as well as his respirations were updated thousands of times on a daily basis.

Dr. Saylor moved closer to the IV bag and examined the contents coursing through plastic tubing into one of Harry's veins. At that moment, the half-filled bag hanging on the metal pole held a mix of electrolytes that Harry's body needed in order to survive.

He examined the feeding tube that was inserted down Harry's esophagus and into his stomach, and immediately paused to write himself a note. He never had to deal with a feeding tube previously, but knew there were a couple ways of delivering food to someone in a coma. One was via an esophageal tube, and the other was through a surgically placed tube passed through an opening in the abdomen and connected to the digestive tract. Jim recognized this was something he had to bone up on, and quickly! He had an enlightened moment and went over to the room's waste container, saw that there was a used plastic container of liquified prunes and oats that Harry had been fed for breakfast. It was probably the most expensive cereal and fruit breakfast Harry had ever consumed, the doctor thought to himself.

Before ending his examination, the doctor lifted the sheet. He spied a catheter inserted into Harry's penis, with fluids ending up in a collection bag. He noticed that the amount of fluid flowing into Harry's body pretty much matched the level of fluid leaving it.

Jim next went to the counter where extra medical supplies being used in Harry's care were stored. He took a picture of the product number and manufacturer of the catheter with his mobile phone, and he took one of the unused catheters and hid it under his shirt. Next, he photographed each piece of equipment being used for Harry's care, as well as all the other supplies.

Every single item and procedure now being used to keep Harry alive in the hospital would have to be on hand when Harry continued treatment in another medical setting outside of the hospital. It took a few minutes more for Jim to enter notes on the rest of the medical inventory into his cell phone. Factoring in the liberal numbers of supplies, Jim felt sure he'd be ordering a month's worth of supplies at a minimum.

The doctor had what he'd come for and as he was leaving the room, Agent Lawson and Kathy, Harry's mother, were about to enter.

"Excuse me, Doctor ... Dr. Saylor, right?" Kathy asked, trying to catch a glimpse of the doctor's name tag.

At that same moment, Agent Lawson and the doctor locked eyes. Both men, now with crimson colored faces, had recognized each other. Only this time, Dr. Saylor had his clothes on.

"Yes ... that's correct. I'm Dr. Jim Saylor, and you are?"

Kathy introduced both herself and Agent Lawson. She asked Dr. Saylor how Harry was, assuming he was involved in Harry's care.

"There's no change, ma'am. I'm sorry I don't have better news," was Jim's reply.

Kathy smiled before entering the room to be with her son.

"What the hell are you doing?" the agent questioned emphatically.

"I'm doing what you want me to do, dammit! I have to familiarize myself with the patient and his needs. You don't know jack shit about what's going on in there," Jim retorted, nodding toward Harry's room.

"Stay right here—don't move!" Lawson replied as he disappeared into the room. Lawson re-emerged within just a few minutes and grabbed Saylor by the elbow, leading him to the elevators.

Five minutes later, both men were seated in the hospital's cafeteria.

"Okay, tell me what you were doing upstairs," Lawson stated curtly.

"I was taking inventory of everything the hospital is using to keep the young man alive! I'm sorry, I didn't mean to be abrupt. Look, I need to order at least a month's worth of medical supplies. But there's some expensive equipment that's also needed and I don't have the finances to buy them. In fact, I have no idea how much an EKG machine costs. And I don't know the first thing about some of the wires and the computer monitor that the kid is hooked up to. I took pictures of all the equipment, plus all the supplies. I'll put a list together tonight, but I have no idea who you are or where to send an e-mail. Plus, I'll need at least a forty-eight-hour advance notice of the date and time this event will go down."

Lawson was humbled. "Listen, Doc, I'm sorry I was a prick. Seeing you in the room surprised the hell out of me. Just so you know, I'm not the one in charge of this caper. Once you send me the information, I'll send the info on to my superiors—I assume they'll be the ones to order everything. I'm also going to venture a guess that forty-eight hours won't work—our agency pretty much works within a twenty-four-hour window of time. But I'll let you know when we have all the equipment set up—and I would expect the event to take place shortly thereafter. If you don't have any more questions, I need to get back upstairs now."

Dr. Saylor had no other questions, and the men shook hands. In the palm of Lawson's right hand was his business card—complete with email address and phone number.

The doctor had all the pertinent information he needed now. A slight smile creased the corners of his mouth as he shook his head side to side in disbelief that he had a role in something this clandestine.

# CHAPTER 67

Tommy hit the road early, but O'Brien remained behind at the cabin with Jameson, just in case he changed his mind. Tommy figured O'Brien was more than capable of handling the trooper.

He'd checked the long-range weather forecast for Lexington and in ten days, the Kentucky weather was going to be perfect for Harry's funeral service and Dr. Becker's assassination.

It was now crunch time and Tommy needed to view the Lexington Cemetery, three dimensionally, and not just in look-down mode as provided by Google Earth.

Todd and Wayne Gail had become even more of a concern, even though neither man had made any false moves. In fact, other than the earlier Caribbean caper when they'd switched clothes to alter their appearances, as they traveled to separate destinations, the pair had become quite boring.

The ornate entrance to the Lexington Cemetery was like traveling back in time to the mid-nineteenth century. The iron gates were almost two stories high and looked Anglo/Euro in design. As he proceeded onto the grounds, the transition from urban to rural was immediate. Tommy slowly traveled north-northeast along a roadway marked by a single unbroken yellow line, to Section 54.

Following that yellow line farther took him to the northern limits of the cemetery's land. Rows of grave markers were not visible, and then Tommy was surrounded by unmarked gravesites, intended for future sales. He continued in an easterly direction until he could go no further. An antiquated chain-link fence blocked all access even though there were fewer grave sites on the eastern side, just beyond a rusted fence.

Tommy continued at the posted five miles per hour speed limit and after driving a bit south, he turned west and by sheer luck, knew he was finally headed to the right section. It took only five minutes more to find the Becker family plots. Marty's mother and father were interred about two feet laterally from Rob and Marty's future resting place.

Tommy got out of his vehicle, immediately doing a slow-motion, three-hundred-sixty-degree scan.

In less than a couple months it would be winter, but already most of the trees were barren. *Where would a sniper have an unhindered shot at Becker?* he silently asked himself. Tommy assumed, when looking at the terrain online back in Oral, South Dakota, that the best shot would come from the south, but now he realized how wrong he'd been. The best shot, if he were taking it, would be from the east. On the eastern horizon was a lone two-and-a-half to three-story high building and Tommy guessed it was probably about three hundred thirty yards away. He mentally tagged the building as sniper haven number one.

The second-best possible vantage point was just slightly north/northeast, where there was a trailer park on the boundary line of the cemetery grounds. Tommy envisioned an assassin setting up a sniping perch, perhaps on the roof of one of the mobile homes, taking the shot and killing his prey before making a quick escape. The trailer park seemed roughly the same distance away as the first sniper haven location.

Returning to his car, Tommy put all the info he just gathered into his mobile phone before calling a well-known funeral home in Lexington. With COVID-19 putting restrictions on social gatherings, he asked about indoor services at their facility and how it compared to a graveside event. Kentucky's current COVID-19 recommendations were: no more than fifty people at a gathering, with social distancing a minimum of six feet apart. The spokesperson at the funeral home noted that a graveside service would be less strict with social distancing rules, but the number of folks allowed to attend remained at fifty.

Tommy mentally noted that Rob Becker would be seated facing east during the graveside service. That positioning would give both sniper #1 and sniper #2 positions for perfect head shots. It really made no difference to Tommy where Rob's brain tissue would come to rest.

He started the car and made his way out of the cemetery. Heading west, he turned onto the road that would take him past the trailer park. He then turned right onto Chiles, heading slowly to Douglas Avenue. It was at Douglas and Chiles that Tommy came upon the almost three-story building he'd seen from the cemetery. He stopped to add this new information into his phone before making his way back to Leestown Road.

Tommy had one last job to complete from his to-do list—and it involved a particular television news reporter. Jameson had given Tommy the name and cell phone number of the reporter who was the contact he'd been feeding information to, concerning Harry. Earlier, he had Jameson contact the reporter, telling her to be at the usual rendezvous location in the park, at three o'clock sharp that afternoon. Vicky Clarkson was an aspiring and ruthless woman who could not have cared less about Harry.

Masterson Station Park and the soccer fields were off of

Leestown Road—and it took only minutes for Tommy to get there and position himself near the park entrance.

Sure enough, Vicky was prompt and drove into the park. Tommy remained several yards away. She headed to the farthest soccer fields in the park and backed into a parking spot to wait. Tommy pulled closer and stopped about a hundred yards from where she was—and outside of her view. He put his car in park and called the unscrupulous news reporter.

"Ms. Clarkson, Officer Jameson is not coming today, but I'm here and I am looking at you right now! I see you looking at your cell phone, right now! Don't hang up!"

"Who is …?"

Borrowing from the movie *Die Hard*, Tommy was quick to cut her off and answer. "Ms. Clarkson, "just call me a fly in the ointment." Mr. Jameson will no longer be your source for information concerning Rob Becker's grandson, Harry. If you do as I say, I promise that you'll be a celebrity and your news story may even garner you an Emmy. Do you understand what I just said to you?"

"Yes, but …"

"If you want to stay alive, here's what I expect from you! In eight to ten days from now, you are going to get an update on Harry's condition—and this communication will be by cell phone. You will report, on air, only the facts that are given to you and you'll be restricted to the time frame that's provided. Any deviation from these instructions will result in your very quick demise. Don't doubt me, and don't go seeking support or assistance from the Lexington police or the FBI—are we clear?"

"Yes, but …"

"Ms. Clarkson, it's time for you to leave, so go—now!"

Tommy ended the conversation and immediately grabbed a snack he'd packed that morning. He turned and picked up the *Lexington Herald* newspaper from the passenger front seat. To all appearances, he was just someone reading the paper and eating his lunch in the park.

The reporter started her car, driving quickly from the gravel lot to the paved main road of the park, her tires kicking up loose gravel everywhere. In just fifteen seconds, her car sped past Tommy's vehicle, without her even giving a sideways glance.

Tommy watched from his rear-view mirror as she sped out of the park. Putting the newspaper down, he put his right index finger to his lips and wet it ... as if preparing to put the winning mark on a chalkboard.

It was all coming together.

HAPTER 68

When Tommy got back to his room at the Hyatt, he called Stan and this time, the conversation was all business. When it came down to crunch time—the gamesmanship ceased!

"Hey boss, I just finished with the news reporter and the cemetery logistics business. Where do we stand right now?"

"Well, I'm just checking in at your hotel, the Hyatt. Adam and Eve accompanied me on the flight from Andrews. The tech guy who's joining our team is quite informative. Tomorrow, you're scheduled for an all-day training session—and Steven, Lawson, and O'Brien are also included."

"C'mon, Stan, throw me some crumbs. Don't treat me like a college freshman just out of high school."

"Okay, you're right. So, Tommy, here's some homework for you. The company that manufactured Adam and Eve for the agency is Boston Dynamics. They've been working on robotics for over thirty years. What's different with their products can be defined by one word: legs."

"Stan, you're messing with me!"

"Tommy, quit interrupting me! The technology everyone thinks of first when someone says "robot" is the Roomba. That vacuum cleaner has wheels and a track drive—and it works great on a flat surface. The Mars Rover is essentially the same as a Roomba, but again it operates pretty much on just a flat surface. Okay, Tommy, now give me an example of a robot that doesn't get around with wheels or a track that it rolls on?"

Tommy lowered his head and closed his eyes for a few seconds. Then it came to him.

"C-3PO," he finally responded.

"Bingo," Stan fired back.

"Wait! What do you mean? Oh, I get it ... these robots have legs? You're telling me that Adam and Eve actually have legs and no wheels or tread-track that they function on? Holy shit ... that's amazing!" Tommy exclaimed to his boss.

"So, Eve will replace Marty and Adam fills in for Rob Becker ... and that's all we're talking about today. Get some sleep and I'll see you tomorrow morning at seven o'clock. Good night, Tommy."

Tommy's brain shifted into high gear. He wasn't a big fan of the internet, so he had to wait a bit while his cell phone downloaded the YouTube app. As soon as it was complete, he began viewing movie clips from the *Star Wars movie series.*

Tommy had no clue that C-3PO was a Neanderthal when compared to what he'd see the next day. Next, he opened Boston Dynamics' company webpage. He had some homework to do.

∩ ∩ ∩

The next morning, the entire Langley crew gathered in one of the Hyatt's conference rooms, along with Stan and a tech representative from Boston Dynamics. In the corner of the room were two crates about six feet high by three feet wide. Stan introduced the tech, Wes, who was tasked with being the facilitator for the remainder of the day.

He began his presentation with a brief but thorough history about his employer.

Tommy, now armed with an advantage from researching the company the night before, wondered if Wes would talk about the military applications of their products. His eyes were beginning to glaze over, when suddenly Wes grabbed a touch screen tablet from the lectern. The tablet was complete with joysticks, and he began to tap on the touch screen.

Both crates sprang to life. The crates began to vibrate. Unknown to the other attendees in the room, the boxes had doors that opened inward. Very slowly, the two robots emerged. They both walked forward and took turns doing three-sixties before stopping. Adam was a perfect replica of Rob Becker before his Indianapolis cosmetic modifications, while the other robot was a perfect copy of the pre-enhanced Marty.

Steven, Tommy, and Stan were the ones familiar with Marty and Rob and their physical appearance before Oral, South Dakota, and all three of them were sitting in astonishment with their mouths agape. Their eyelids could not have opened any wider!

Tommy got up from his seat and slowly walked close to the Rob Becker robot. He reached out with his right arm and haltingly began moving his hand toward robot Rob's face, finally touching the robot's left cheek and following that with several more facial pokes.

Tommy was the first to speak. "Are you shitting me?"

Those words pretty much summed up how Stan and Steven also felt.

Wes touched the tablet screen and both robots came back to life. He proceeded to put the robotic pair through their paces.

Wes placed several small orange soccer cones on the floor, spaced out and in staggered positions. He tapped the tablet screen and both robots began weaving their way through and around the cones. Wes tapped the screen again, and this time the robots jogged in and out between the cones and then suddenly reversed course and went in the opposite direction. After they came to a halt, Wes toggled on the joystick, causing both robots to return to their crates and the doors closed.

"I think we'll break for some coffee and compose ourselves. We'll meet back here in fifteen minutes," Wes stated.

For the rest of the morning and into the early part of the afternoon, Wes covered the anatomical details of Adam and Eve. During the quick lunch, Stan handed each member of the group a synopsis of how Adam and Eve would be used during Harry's funeral service.

After lunch, everyone had an opportunity to operate the tablet controller and the robots. Stan strongly believed in multitasking and besides, he had no idea how Rob Becker's assassination would unravel. Everyone needed to be prepared.

If this was Tommy's last seminar as a CIA agent, it was one hell of a send-off.

 HAPTER 69

A couple of days after Tommy's distant confrontational face-off with Vicky Clarkson, Jerry Jameson called her to confirm she was on board with the instructions she'd received from Tommy.

"Vicky ... this is Jerry. Please don't hang up!"

"Jerry, you're a worthless piece of shit! What the hell do you want?"

"I'm truly sorry about what happened. You're not the only one who's been compromised!"

Jerry was walking on eggshells. He hoped Tommy hadn't figured out that his relationship with Vicky was more than that of a source.

"You've got to believe me, Vicky. This story is not just about Harry—it's way bigger than a high school soccer player who overdosed. If you're not all-in on this, these people will find someone else who gladly will be."

He was done dangling the carrot. It was time for her to take it—or not.

Vicky thought about hanging up, but emotions got the best of her.

"After all our years together, I should know you're usually right. It's just that the other day the guy in the park was really unnerving ... then afterwards, I was really pissed off at you. I want your assurance that you'll be the one dealing with me. I swear I'll end this if I have to deal with that man ever again!"

Jerry whipped his head around and stared toward a listening Tommy, who at that moment, was almost gagging on his saliva after doubling over with laughter. Tommy quickly recovered and nodded affirmatively several times.

"I'll relay your feelings—and I can almost guarantee he'll be fine with me being your contact person again. I gotta go ... but expect the action to pick up in the next few days. Bye!"

Jerry looked at Tommy once more and determined there were no further words needed. He realized that Tommy had set them both up. Vicky was now equally compromised and trapped.

∩ ∩ ∩

Marty and I still couldn't believe what Donnie and Val had done for both of us. One moment, I was mentally searching for a way to pay Donnie and Val back for their kindness—but then I would come to the conclusion that both of them would be offended if I did something like that. I had learned my lesson out in South Dakota.

Marty sensed my angst.

"Rob, come sit with me. You know Rob, when we had your 50th birthday party with all the folks that you considered close friends…you didn't run out the following day to buy them all gifts."

"Huh?" I replied.

"You never thought twice about buying gifts for all your friends who were more than happy to get you a gift because they loved you and valued your friendship. Ever since I've known you, you've always had a problem with this type of situation. Rob, friends give others gifts out of respect and love. They don't expect a thank you gift in return. They willingly give because it makes them feel good inside.

"If you feel an obligation to immediately gift back to someone, you deprive your friends of that emotional high, and that's actually a theft that hurts your friends. Rob, you and I aren't perfect and never will be. People don't make friendships based on the gifts they receive. They have friendships because relationships are built up over time—relationships that make folks feel warm and fuzzy inside. Rob, that's called love.

"Please don't go spoiling your friendship with Donnie. We're living on his farm now, and we're in a new version of our old house. If you go and piss him off, our life is going to become pretty miserable. I'm moving on, Rob—you need to do the same."

I slouched back in the couch and realized just how right she was. Marty always had her own gift of breaking through my layers of insecurity and glass-half-empty feelings.

Before she left to be with Harry, we embraced and I told her, "Tell Harry I'll be coming to see him in a couple days. Who knows, maybe he'll come out of his coma, knowing that Pop Pop is coming to visit."

∩ ∩ ∩

It had been a week since Todd had heard from Jerry. It was time to call his twin brother.

"Hey T-bro, what's happening?"

"I was wondering if you've heard from Jerry. It's been over a week since I talked with him," Todd stated.

"That's not normal for him," Wayne said.

"The reporter has also gone missing. I called the television station this morning and they said she was on vacation. I find it odd that both of them are AWOL at the same time. Maybe it's time for a drive-by of Jerry's home.

"Besides, I need to see if I've been successful in shaking the guy who's been following me. How about you and your shadow? Were you able to shake loose from the dude?" Wayne added.

"The food delivery switch was sheer genius," Todd answered. "The driver came to my door carrying a pizza. I invited him inside and we swapped clothes. I put on the sunglasses he was wearing, plus his baseball cap, walked out to his delivery car and left. The guy who'd been following me never budged from his parking spot down the street. When I got to the end of my street, I took a right turn, went a few feet and took another right, then parked on the street that backs up to my property. I parked, then walked through the back yard and in less than a minute, I'm back standing in my kitchen paying the dude off. We switch clothes again and he leaves through the back door, cutting through the back yard to his car—with a Benjamin to the good in his wallet.

"So, when the time comes for us to visit the cemetery and knock off Rob Becker, I'll have a rental car delivered to the address directly behind my house. The rental car driver will call and ask where I am. I'll tell him, 'Stay put, man, you're at my parents' address.' Then, I'll cut through the back yard to where he's parked, sign the papers, and come back home. Later, I'll call my food delivery guy and we'll practice the ruse at least once before we do it for real! I'm stoked—it's too damn easy! I have to go, Wayne. I have a feeling that it's all going down within a couple of weeks."

Todd wasn't clairvoyant, nor was he a psychic—but he could feel that all hell was going to break loose soon.

# CHAPTER 70

A few days before my visit to see Harry, Donnie and I were standing by the fence line—admiring Towers Destiny in his paddock alongside his mama, Chevytothelevee.

"Rob, what's going to happen with Harry? What I mean is, how long is he going to be ..."

"Donnie, I totally understand. Harry's in purgatory and he doesn't even know it. He's basically being used as bait right now—and when he supposedly dies, they'll kidnap him and bring him here to my home. He'll eventually come out of his coma ... I just feel it."

"You know, Rob, that isn't going to be easy. It's going to be damned near impossible to sneak him out of the hospital."

"Donnie, when Tommy came up with this scheme out in South Dakota, I thought the exact thing you're saying right now. It's going to take a miracle to sneak the boy out."

"You need to talk with Mike...Rob. He's close friends with the hospital's CEO! Maybe Mike could coax an IOU out of the guy."

"Damn, Donnie, I didn't know that," I said in surprise.

"Tell you what, Rob. I invited Mike out here today and you can talk to him in person...he should be here in about an hour. Maybe he can set up a meeting for both of you. I can hardly wait to see if he recognizes you!"

Sure enough, Mike had no clue as to who I was when he arrived. The three of us laughed for a good ten minutes after I described what I went through to become the new me. Donnie brought up the situation with Harry and I followed with details surrounding the planned fake death as it had been told to me by Tommy.

Mike was a quick read.

"Damn, Rob, does Kathy have a Do Not Resuscitate on Harry's hospital medical record?

"Now that you mention it, I'm inclined to think not!"

"Rob, that type of declaration would make everything so much easier. The plan you described overly complicates the entire shebang. Let me talk with my friend, Hal Gentner—he's CEO of the hospital. I'll have him call you ... what's your cell number?"

"Mike, I don't have a cell phone. It's for my own good. You know, it's as Marty always says; I'm the worst person ever when it comes to keeping secrets. This entire MIA scenario is probably God's plan for keeping me alive for a while. Have him call Donnie, though, and then he can bring me up to speed."

As expected, Mike followed through.

The next day, Hal Gentner called Donnie, telling him the DNR designation needed both Kathy and her husband's approval, along with their written signatures, in order to make the DNR tag valid.

Using Donnie's cell phone, I called Kathy and explained why a DNR designation was needed on Harry's chart. She then brought up my upcoming visit to see Harry, reminding me that only one family visitor was allowed to be in the room with Harry because of COVID-19.

"Dad, when you get to the lobby, they'll have you sign in first and they'll take your temperature. I strongly suggest that before you head to the hospital you take your temperature a couple of times," she advised.

I thanked my daughter and handed the mobile phone back to Donnie.

To me, it seemed like everything was now in place—it was time for my grandson to die in order to live!

What saddened me was the recent lack of any communication between Tommy and myself. It had been weeks since I'd last seen my friend, let alone talked with him. However, there was no way anyone was going to deny me the opportunity to see my grandson for possibly the last time!

I was unaware of the actions already taken by the hospital CEO. He'd placed the highest security marker on Harry's name and room number at the visitor check-in desk. Hal wasn't taking any chances with the care of a high-profile patient.

Not only did that heighten the security and tighten up the check-in process, it also required the staff to immediately notify the CEO if anything or anyone showed an interest in Harry.

Harry's hospitalization now meant that Hal's working hours were no longer normal. He was now on call twenty-four/seven.

 **HAPTER 71**

The 2020 election was over, but not completely. The civil tension across America was still stifling.

Unlike after the 2016 election, ISIS—even though still a very real entity—had been mostly forgotten by the world's population in the aftermath of 2020. This Middle Eastern terrorist organization had, for the most part, been minimized.

POTUS had safely navigated the international scene without having to commit American troops to any new theaters of war.

…and then the Communist Chinese regime decided they'd had enough of the American president and his "Populist/America First" brand of politics … it had to end!

The president's anti-China policies had become quite irritating to this Asian country and accidentally or not, China unleashed a worldwide pandemic—a viral disease known as COVID-19. Virologists predicted there'd be over a million American lives lost before the virus would run its course. Despite POTUS' constant referral to COVID-19 as the "China virus," other than Australia, most countries throughout the world gave Communist China a pass.

Backed by the American mainstream media, someone had to be at fault for the overall viral discomfort and loss of life during 2020, and the blame fell squarely on POTUS' shoulders.

Casting aside his brutish behavior, I believed anyone that was as willing as President Trump was to close our borders and shut down the flow of illegal drugs into America…well, that individual had earned my vote! The origin of the COVID-19 pandemic just reinforced the resolve of my personal election choice!

∩ ∩ ∩

The day was unseasonably mild, with nary a cloud in sight—it was time for me to visit my grandson. It was ironic that Harry was in a coma and wouldn't have to come to grips with me not looking like the Pop Pop he knew. I hit the road early and arrived at the hospital a little after eight in the morning.

After registering at the visitor's desk, I had my temperature taken and was told to take a seat in the lobby. No other directions were given. The nursing station on the fifth floor was notified of my presence, as was CEO Gentner.

I waited for ten minutes before going back to the registration desk, asking if there was a problem. I was told that the staff on Harry's floor was busy gathering up the breakfast trays, and that I'd be allowed to go upstairs in just a few more minutes.

Meanwhile, Dr. Jim Saylor and his accomplice, nurse Karen, had entered Harry's room.

Karen began disconnecting equipment that was attached to Harry. The leads and adhesive pads connected to Harry's ECG were carefully peeled off his body and skin. Dr. Saylor watched as each pad was removed. With half of the leads still remaining, he told Karen to rip the remaining ones off with a quick jerk, hoping that type of uncomfortable stimulus might rouse Harry out of his coma. Sadly, it was not to be. I walked into the room and watched as Karen ripped off the last pad. Realizing immediately what was happening, I challenged the nurse.

"What the hell are you doing? Is Harry conscious?"

"Excuse me, Mister ... whoever you are, we must ask you to leave, please!" Dr. Jim stated.

"Well, excuse me back ... I'm the young man's grandfather and the nurse just removed his ECG leads! So how the hell are you going to tell if he's alive or not?"

It quickly became obvious to me that I could continue hurling insults until I was blue in the face. My presence was now an inconvenience, and both of them were unwilling to call for help.

"What are you planning to do with my grandson? You obviously don't care if he lives!"

The nurse turned away from Harry, brushed past me, and exited the room. I turned my eyes to the doctor and just stared. As soon as she left, Karen broke into a run. I'd failed to see the red light blinking on and off on the monitor above Harry's head.

Karen arrived at the nurse's desk just as the floor nurse in charge was about to call a Code Blue on the hospital's intercom system. Karen knew that the Las Vegas type "Eye in the Sky" had been videoing her and Dr. Saylor's actions. She also knew that Harry's status had been updated to DNR.

"Don't do it—the patient's dead! Dr. Saylor is in the room right now—and we both watched the young man code. The doctor was trying some different physical stimulations on the patient in hopes that he'd respond. Then the patient's grandfather walked in the room and we had no idea he was coming to visit. He was yelling at us when the patient died. We had no choice but to respect the DNR!"

Karen's breathless and emotional explanation hung in the air for what seemed to be an eternity.

"Okay. Let me call for a gurney to take him down to the morgue," the chief floor nurse stated.

They'd done it. Dr. Saylor and Karen had pulled it off!

Meanwhile back in Harry's room, Dr. Saylor had no choice but to tell me the truth.

"I have no intention of harming your grandson. We're supposed to take him downstairs to the morgue. He'll be picked up and transported to a funeral home, where he'll be officially declared dead. From there, he'll be moved by ambulance to a horse farm in southern Kentucky. The nurse and I have been tasked with accompanying Harry on his journey and to keep monitoring his vitals. In short, we are his lifeline."

I could feel my face becoming flushed and I bowed my head.

"Hey, Doc … no problem. Shake a leg—time's a-wasting." I turned and quickly left the room.

Three minutes later as I waited for the elevator, I began to laugh. "What were the odds of me picking this particular day to visit?" I mumbled to myself.

Back downstairs at the registration desk waiting to sign out, I was approached by a suited stranger wearing the requisite protective mask. He introduced himself as the hospital CEO and asked how my grandson was doing.

"Honestly, I don't think he's going to make it. He certainly doesn't look like my grandson. But thank you for your concern."

A half hour later, I was driving along the same road that Harry would soon be traveling. This was a time when I really missed having a cell phone. Marty was right, though—if I had one, I'd be calling everyone I could, telling them about my morning.

∩ ∩ ∩

Once the doctor and nurse were successfully away from the hospital, Dr. Saylor made a call to Agent Lawson, letting him know that Harry was now on his way to the funeral home. When the conversation was ended, Lawson called Tommy and gave him the update. In turn, Tommy called Jameson, advising him to call his reporter girlfriend.

It took only thirty minutes for the people of Kentucky to receive the breaking news that the grandson of Kentucky horseman, Dr. Rob Becker, had died.

It was time to get ready for a funeral service.

CHAPTER 72

Stan was working in a room off of the Lexington Cemetery business office. The room overlooked the entrance to the cemetery and its massive entrance gates.

Spread out on his desk was a plat map of the entire cemetery and the surrounding neighborhood residences. The only details not on the map were the natural breaks in the fence from aging, along with any recent openings in the chain-link fence that could have occurred in the last few days.

Stan had less than three days until the graveside services for Harry—which meant that marking and recording the fence breaks was his first priority.

The difference between neutralizing bad guys in the wilderness around Mt. Hood compared to doing such on the grounds of the Lexington Cemetery was quite obvious. The number of innocents who could unknowingly get ensnared during the assassination of Rob Becker was too much for Stan to process at that moment.

Stan had already argued with the cemetery CFO about restricting access to the cemetery entrance to just those individuals coming for Harry's service. What he really wanted was to prohibit those folks that on any given day could visit the grounds to exercise, meditate, or just enjoy the cemetery's diverse animal and plant ecosystems. In short, hundreds of folks routinely roamed Lexington Cemetery's property—and their reason for doing so had nothing to do with death or visiting a grave.

While he'd lost that first debate, Stan was determined to argue his position again and again until Harry's memorial service was over.

⌒ ⌒ ⌒

The Army was on board with providing a hover drone that would operate at a stationary two-mile altitude. The drone's function was to provide a live infrared video feed of the cemetery and the adjacent neighborhoods. Stan knew that any uninvited individuals could pose a threat. Their detection and location would immediately appear on a computer monitor in his field office. It would then be Stan's job to determine if someone was a hostile intruder or not.

The physical shape of the drone was similar to a quadcopter, but fifty times larger in size—nearly as big as a pool table. It easily weighed a half ton and was equipped with batteries that enabled the drone to hover for three hours. The drone's propellers were a third-generation advancement from those employed on the stealth helicopters during the takedown of Osama Bin Laden. The Army was kind enough to also lend the agency some techs who were familiar with the drone's operations.

After his check of the fence was complete, Stan supervised the erection of Harry's memorial shelter tent. Thankfully, the five-day weather forecast was promising.

There would be seating inside the tent for family relatives, but those who were delivering eulogies would be seated outside.

Also located inside the tent, would be a section reserved for Wes from Boston Dynamics—along with Adam and Eve.

The two robots, Dr. Rob Becker (Adam) and Marty Becker

(Eve), were close to the heights and weights of their human counterparts.

Every impression of my face, head, and shoulders that had been done months previously in Indianapolis had served their purpose after all.

Stan conjured up images of the "Old" Rob Becker emerging from the tent with his wife Marty. They'd take their seats outside with the robotic Marty seated a row behind Rob. When it was time for the robotic Dr. Becker to eulogize his grandson, the mechanical legs would stride to the podium and then Dr. Becker would give a heartfelt send-off for Harry. At some point during the speech, Rob's robotic self would be murdered, and his grieving robotic wife would cradle him in her arms as fellow mourners scattered from the horrific scene. The robots' actions would drive home the terrible tragedy that had just occurred.

∩ ∩ ∩

A few minutes away, east of the cemetery, Tommy was holding a meeting with Steven, Lawson, and O'Brien at the Hyatt Hotel.

"Men, the weather looks good this entire week. Jameson has leaked the details of Harry's memorial service to Vicky Clarkson … so the trap is now set. So far, Todd and Wayne continue to be nonentities and pretty much off the grid. However, there had been increased food delivery action at each man's home.

"So, okay, our goal is the capture of the snipers. Having said that, I need to be realistic. When cornered, the snipers could easily turn their weapon on themselves and we'll gain nothing. Also, assume the assassins will be wearing protective gear, which doesn't leave us much anatomy to shoot at.

"My opinion is that we're going to need a fair amount of luck to capture our bad guys without injuring them. Every one of you will be on a com-link with Stan—he'll be your eyes in locating the assassins.

"Once they're captured, they'll be transported to the cabin. One of you will accompany me and the hostages—and I want you to know I doubt there will be any prisoner survivors once this is over. This will be my last service for our Republic. What happens will be on my shoulders alone!

"Do each of you understand? Let me hear you ..."

In slow succession, there were three clear "yep(s)."

"We'll meet again tomorrow and head to the cemetery for a mock take-down. Any questions? Okay, I'll see you all in the hotel lobby at eight in the morning. Dress casual tomorrow. When we get to the cemetery, we'll change into groundskeeper-type work clothes."

# HAPTER 73

Vicky Clarkson performed her media role perfectly. She broke the sad news of Harry's death while standing in front of the hospital entrance.

The next day, she reported on the particulars of the memorial service. Included in those details was a planned drive-by tribute from Harry's soccer teammates and other classmates because COVID-19 had changed all things normal!

Not to be outdone by television news, the Lexington daily paper published the exact timing of events in their print and digital newspapers.

Steven and Lawson were assigned to work the trailer park quadrant while Tommy and O'Brien had the subdivision of houses to the east of Harry's grave site.

…and all four men were already too late.

The night before Harry's service, Todd and Wayne pulled off their food delivery ruse. Not only that, they took one of the nation's top food delivery company's "COVID-19 business model" to a totally new level.

The twins made their food deliveries under the cover of darkness.

Todd went first. His targeted mobile home at the trailer park had only one resident. As a matter of fact, the guy was a groundskeeper at the Lexington Cemetery. Todd knocked on the door and the elderly resident cracked the door open slightly. Todd thrust the food delivery bags toward the man, forcing him to open the door even further.

Todd pounced. The old man fell to the floor and soon his limbs were zip-tied and his mouth duct-taped shut.

Todd searched the house for a cell phone but found none. There was a land line, though, and Todd lifted the receiver off its cradle, disabling it. The small kitchen window would serve as a good perch from which to scope in on Rob Becker—and take a shot.

Wayne had selected a house that was nearly three stories high. He followed his brother's script to gain entry. Once inside, he knocked out the man who had answered the doorbell. He then headed to the kitchen where he wrestled the wife to the ground and then he knocked her unconscious. He quickly zip-tied her hands and feet, and duct-taped her mouth before heading back to the husband to give him the same treatment.

Wayne then proceeded to inventory each room in the house, searching for additional occupants. There were none.

Both brothers settled in with their hostages and soon, each twin was fast asleep.

Meanwhile, three hundred yards away, Adam and Eve were in a state of electronic sleep. They were in the back of the memorial tent, in silent mode, conserving their power for the next day.

Adam was dressed in a black suit and camel-colored outer coat while Eve was elegantly attired in a very conservative black dress with a black cape, suitable for someone mourning a loved one.

… and Harry was still, for the most part, dead.

Inside the tent, Wes took the first watch while Tommy grabbed some sleep. He was pumped and it took longer for him to fall asleep.

At about two in the morning, Wes and Tommy switched positions. Now, when he needed to stay awake, Tommy found himself easily nodding off. He even called Tika, who was two time zones to the west of Kentucky. They talked for forty-five minutes.

After the call ended, Tommy put on his night vision googles and slipped out through the back of the tent. He trained his gaze toward the trailer park's mobile homes, searching each one for anything suspicious. He remembered his original instincts, which were that the assassins would probably be on the roof of a trailer or the house.

Now, though, his thoughts were changing. *There's more than enough trailer elevation to take the shot from inside,* Tommy determined silently. Then it hit him … if both assassins were inside their respective buildings and not outside in nature's elements where infrared scanning would easily detect their presence, then the drone flying high above wouldn't be of much assistance.

"I'm fucked," Tommy told himself.

Now in a panic, Tommy pulled his cell phone out and called Stan at the Hyatt Hotel.

"I knew it, the one night that I need my sleep … and sure enough, you interrupt it! What the hell do you want?" Stan ranted.

"Tell me that the drone that's two miles high has the ability to do thermography through a building as well as spotting individual snipers who are outside all by their lonesome. If you say no… well then, we're screwed as far as determining sniper locations!"

"Well, Thomas, I wondered when you'd realize that there

might be a problem!"

Stan let Tommy stew on his statement for a few seconds.

"Relax, Tommy, that drone is equipped with the latest and best FLIR technology. You know that company clearly has a sparkling history of innovation in temperature gradient technology.

"I've been running diagnostic tests with the drone for the past two days. I've got thermography images that show where even the slightest crack or open window might be. I also have photos of all the individuals out and about at all times of the day and night. So, you can go to sleep now," Stan gruffly said before hanging up.

What he didn't tell Tommy was that before the sun even rose the next morning, the memorial tent would be brimming with Army techs, arriving at dawn, and seated at tables covered with computer monitors displaying the surrounding trailer park housing and homes adjacent to the cemetery. The thermal profiles would continuously be analyzed and updated every sixty seconds.

Any window unexpectedly opened would create a new thermal image which would then flash on the monitor. Once the breach was confirmed, Stan would make the call as to what specific trailer or house was possibly harboring a shooter.

Tommy didn't have the heart to tell Stan he was actually on watch. At least Stan had given him the stimulus he needed to stay awake. For the next few hours until the Army techs arrived, Tommy continued to scan the trailers to the north and the houses to his east, while wondering where an assassin might be hiding— perhaps even spying on him—with a night vision scope, through a slightly cracked-open window.

# CHAPTER 74

It was almost six o'clock in the morning when the gates to the Lexington Cemetery opened. Two black vans filled with Army techs proceeded toward Harry's final resting ground.

Once there, the techs quietly started up the gas generators outside, while inside the tent, another group of Army personnel powered up their computers and video screens.

Wes was already awake and going through the start-up protocols for Adam and Eve.

Tommy had finally crashed and was fast asleep.

∩ ∩ ∩

A small satellite dish was assembled and mounted on the back of the tent. It was aimed in the correct direction and established communication with a geosynchronous satellite that linked everything within range of the drone, positioned two miles up above the cemetery. By sunrise, the monitors had come to life, with images of trailers and houses appearing on the screens.

Images showed any surface that was poorly insulated and more porous to the environment as one specific color, while anything well insulated would trend toward tame colors on the spectrum.

The army techs were constantly refreshing their images. If an area that had been consistently one certain color suddenly became more brilliant in colors, the change could be an indication that perhaps a window or door had been cracked open, with heat escaping. People out in the open air would show up as bright figures on the computer screen. Stan had trained with these army techs for several weeks and he would be the one making the call if anything abruptly changed or became suspicious.

The service for Harry started at ten, with the drive-by procession of Harry's soccer teammates and classmates occurring first. As the cars streamed by the tent, some students got out and knelt down to say a prayer before placing flowers at the grave site. Others paused and remained in their cars while tossing flowers toward the grave or gently dropping them in the grass just off the road. A number of stuffed teddy bears were also placed at or near the grave site.

By eleven, the stream of cars had slowed to a trickle—it was now time for Rob and Marty's robotic counterparts, Adam and Eve, to take their seats.

Stan placed one final call to Jeff, the cemetery CFO.

"Jeff, this is Stan. Have all your workers showed up today?"

"Everyone but Ken is here."

"Is that unusual, Jeff?"

"If you count zero absences over the past year, then my answer would be yes!"

"Okay—where does he live and what's his phone number?"

Stan could hear papers being shuffled for a few seconds in the background as he waited for an answer. When Jeff returned to the phone, his response nearly floored Stan—Ken lived in a trailer overlooking the back side of the cemetery.

"Are you shitting me?" Stan shouted into the phone. He took down Ken's phone number and made the call. The message he heard was as expected. "The number you're calling is not in service," the auto recording stated.

Stan began looking for Steven and Lawson and found them in five minutes.

"I think I may have found one of our assassins—and I would hate like hell to have an innocent civilian killed during this ruse. Here's the address. Neutralize the SOB and throw him in a van. Good hunting, men!" Stan advised.

∩ ∩ ∩

The pastor was the first person to leave the tent and walk out toward the podium. He took a seat while the rest of the memorial entourage emerged from the tent.

Donna, Marty's sister, was going to sing two beautiful hymns and close the funeral service with the singing the Lord's Prayer. She sat down next to the pastor.

Emerging next were Kathy and Mike. They took seats in the first row closest to the trailer park but facing east.

Wes activated Adam and Eve, and each robot walked out and took its seat. Adam would be the first to eulogize his grandson and was seated one row in front of Eve.

I was surprised at how many of our relatives came to the service. Marty and I had tried our best to discourage them from attending because of COVID-19. A bevy of aunts, uncles, and cousins were all seated inside the tent. A canvas divider separated the army techs and Stan from the family members. Of course, everyone was masked.

I knew I would be blamed for what was about to happen, but Marty and I just couldn't trust telling anyone that the memorial service was a hoax. None of the family recognized me, which I found amazing. What wouldn't be so amazing was the horror they were about to witness.

Vicky and her television crew were stationed a bit northeast from where the pastor was seated. Her camera man had already shot some cemetery scenes and waited patiently for the eulogy.

The pastor stepped up and introduced himself and the soloist, Donna. After an opening prayer, Donna stepped forward to sing an a cappella rendition of "Amazing Grace."

Following the reciting of the Lord's Prayer, it was time for Dr. Rob Becker to honor the life of his grandson Harry.

Adam rose and approached the podium.

It was showtime.

# HAPTER 75

I was standing inside the tent's entrance watching Adam, my robotic twin, as he began to deliver his eulogy for Harry. I had written the words myself and recorded it twenty-four hours earlier. I couldn't help but admire how good my duplicate looked, and I suddenly remembered why Adam was so perfect! "So that's what all those impressions were about, back at Indianapolis—damn!"

Even though Adam would be mouthing my words, there was no doubt whose voice was coming out of the robot's mouth. I felt safe but wanted to turn away and not watch my identical, artificial replica take an assassin's bullet.

Steven was standing on a slope below the side of the trailer, facing the cemetery. He and Lawson had no intention of busting in and trying to rescue Ken, the missing cemetery employee. They prayed that the shooter—after taking his shot—would beat a hasty retreat out the front door and toward the road. Lawson had already visually scoped out all the cars parked in front of the trailer, but he had no time to run their license plates.

He ducked down behind some bushes and waited.

Like Steven and Lawson, Tommy and O'Brien had moved into position—and were watching the three-story house. The house had one exit at the lower level, adjacent to the back yard. There was also an entrance that opened to the first floor of the house from the front, along with a third entrance into the garage from the side of the house.

Tommy silently hoped that all the action would be at the trailer park home.

∩ ∩ ∩

Stan was looking at video as the eulogy began. The army techs were rolling through color-enhanced pictures when one of the men suddenly yelled out, "Bingo!"

"Blue trailer at twelve o'clock—a window just opened!"

Stan confirmed the change in the heat signature, quickly communicating the information to Steven and Lawson, who heard it clearly through their ear buds.

It wasn't more than thirty seconds later when another shout of "Bingo" was heard.

"Three-story home, due east! A second-story window is now half open!"

Again, Stan confirmed the thermal image change and this time, notified Tommy and O'Brien.

Adam continued the eulogy.

The programmed robot rambled on, reading and speaking, while I was getting antsier by the minute. I watched in horror as suddenly, Adam's skull literally exploded—he had been shot! Pieces of fake bone, along with shards of fake skin and artificial bloody brain tissue, looking somewhat like cauliflower, sprayed forth. It couldn't have been more than two seconds later when what was left of the robot's skull rocketed toward the tent's entrance as a second bullet hit the back of Adam's head. The entire incident seemed surreal, in a manner very similar to watching the Abraham Zapruder film of JFK's assassination.

Wes tapped on the tablet's controller screen and Adam's robotic body crumpled to the ground. Eve, the robotic version of my wife Marty, quickly sprang to life, rushing to her husband's side as anguished sounds of grief emanated from her robotic lips. She gently raised Adam's body into her arms and began rocking back and forth, wailing at her loss.

I literally lost my composure and couldn't believe tears were actually forming in my eyes. The stark appearance of just being assassinated sent a horrific message to all the world—Dr. Rob Becker, part-time dentist, thoroughbred horseman, and co-owner of Towers Above and the young stallion, Towers Destiny, had been shot and killed by two assassins on this morning.

The video taken by Vicky Clarkson's news crew only served to hammer home the viciousness of my death. The gruesome video would now be replayed thousands of times worldwide.

Finally forever, I was now just Dr. Tucker ... period!

My frenzied relatives tried to escape anywhere they could and hopefully to safety.

∩ ∩ ∩

The front door of the trailer was forcefully thrown open. Todd emerged, immediately taking a hard right, and running as if his life depended on it. Lawson hadn't expected that maneuver, but quickly recovered and took aim.

Todd had no idea what brought him down. Lawson's bullet caused him to stumble and lose stride before he fell to the ground. By the time Lawson reached the shooter's side, Todd was unconscious and bleeding profusely.

The femoral artery was barely nicked, but it would prove to be enough of a tear to end Todd's life. Using his belt as a tourniquet, Lawson tried to stop the bleeding but quickly realized the assassin was dead.

Lawson texted Stan, telling him that his lone shot had brought down the trailer park assassin and was sorry that his aim had been too perfect—and fatal!

∩ ∩ ∩

At the house, Tommy was in a prone position halfway between the garage and the front door.

Wayne slowly opened the door. He had removed the plastic zip ties from his hostage's ankles, pushing the woman forward toward the garage for about ten feet—effectively blocking any clean shot from Tommy's Glock.

"Mr. Gail, release your hostage now!" Tommy shouted.

"No way! Clear a path or she dies!" Wayne yelled back.

O'Brien had just emerged from behind some bushes and was some fifty yards behind Wayne and his hostage. He was pantomiming frantically and gesturing for Tommy to string out the hostage negotiation.

As Wayne started to again move forward with his hostage, Tommy took a shot, bouncing a bullet off the sidewalk in front of Wayne and the woman. It ricocheted into the siding, causing minimal damage. The woman's knees buckled, and she went limp.

O'Brien was now in a full-out sprint, as Tommy's mouth fell open in awe. He'd seen Olympians run the 100-meter dash before, but now was mesmerized as his fellow agent covered the fifty-yard distance in mere seconds.

Tommy managed to bounce another bullet just as O'Brien dropped down and rolled his body against the back of Wayne Gail's legs, flipping the assassin upside down.

Wayne's first reaction was pure reflex as his grip on the hostage loosened. Tommy was now on his feet, sprinting toward Wayne, but O'Brien was already back on his feet and had quickly knocked Wayne out with one blow. The agent was standing over Wayne, willing him to resume consciousness so he could flatten him one more time.

Tommy helped the woman to her feet and made sure she was okay, as O'Brien placed the handcuffs on Wayne. Tommy turned and went inside to find the rescued woman's husband, and quickly returned outside with the male hostage who was brimming with gratitude.

The two freed hostages wrapped their arms around each other.

Tommy turned toward O'Brien.

"Oh my God! Where the hell did that take-down move come from?

"Wait, don't tell me! You played football, didn't you! That chop, or should I say roll block, was so damn smooth. You played a whole lot of football, didn't you?"

O'Brien just smiled.

"Well from now on, it's no more O'Brien. You're now 'Jay O,' as far as I'm concerned."

Tommy walked a few feet and placed his right arm over his fellow agent's shoulder in an act of gratitude.

Rob Becker's fake demise was complete, and Tommy was relieved that only one assassin would receive enhanced interrogation.

 HAPTER 76

O'Brien brought the van to the front of the three-story house, and together he and Tommy loaded a cuffed Wayne into it for a ride to the cabin near Irvine, Kentucky, where he would be interrogated.

Normally a haven from frantic life, the Lexington Cemetery had become a madhouse. The grounds were teeming with officers from the Lexington Police Department and Kentucky State Police, while reporters and video crews from every local mainstream network news station had arrived on the scene.

The county coroner was huddled with Stan. I could only imagine how Stan was going to convince the doctor that a death certificate for a robot named Rob Becker was imperative—and that there would be no autopsy.

Stan even went as far as to FaceTime with the president, stressing the urgent reality that Rob Becker— or at least the robotic version of him—had to be officially declared dead!

That the reality of my existence on earth would officially be over didn't bother me. I carried no life insurance, so there would never be any issue of fraud, and the thought of another assassin coming for me was now over. *The end*, I told myself.

Tommy knew what it would take for the coroner to buy in— and how to help Stan with his predicament.

As I was wondering about the death certificate and how that would be handled, I saw Wes enter the tent carrying a small duffel bag. He handed the bag to Stan, who in turn placed it under the table, sliding it along the ground with his foot toward the coroner while gesturing for him to look down.

The county coroner opened the bag, noting it was filled with stacks of neatly packaged one hundred-dollar bills. The doctor took the bag and headed out of the tent in the direction of the parking lot, quickly returning with a signed blank death certificate in his hand.

∩ ∩ ∩

With their surveillance duties over, the army techs were now acting as gatekeepers—deciding who could or could not have access inside the tent.

Media types were probing along the exterior of the tent, looking for any weak areas or openings that would allow camera crews to see inside the tent and film anything going down inside.

Stan excused himself and called Tommy.

"How's your prisoner?"

"Well, his back and head are bruised and concussed in that order—a result of O'Brien flipping him backwards and landing him on his head. We're about to head to Irvine, unless you'd rather we not go."

"No, get going! I need answers! Dr. Becker needs answers—and Agent O'Brien needs to learn how to get answers! Good luck … and Tommy, I have no clue which of the Gail twins died. I'll try to have that information for you shortly! Later …"

Driving down I-75 toward Irvine, Tommy wondered how much had really been accomplished over the past several months.

He ticked off what had actually taken place:

Dr. Becker was now a victim, as was his grandson—each now supposedly dead.

Two ISIS terrorists had created havoc from south of the border all the way to Kentucky … resulting in the death of four people.

Tommy slowly shook his head to clear his thoughts, as O'Brien decided it was time for some answers.

"I need clarification Tommy, and I don't want to be confrontational or accusatory. How many agents have carte blanche when it comes to enhanced interrogation?"

Tommy mentally digested the question for half a minute or so before answering.

"The only thing I can tell you is … I'm not the only agent. There are others, but I'm not privy as to who they are and how many there are. What you need to understand is that there are situations when there's not enough time! Such instances are rare, but they all demand quick and decisive action!

"If I had to give a number, I'd say that I have been involved in a couple dozen sorties in my career—even some overseas and some during a war. Now that I look back, I can't help but shake my head and sometimes ask 'why?' There has to be a better method.

"I'd love to justify what I've done as being righteous. I'd love to say with certainty that my actions saved innumerable lives. I'd love to state that I made a difference in everything … but I can't. My actions will probably be judged by historians—and I'll be long gone when they do.

"I've kept written journals and I've documented it all. My wife Tika has them. I gave her the name of an obscure writer who has agreed to look at the information and possibly ghostwrite a tell-all book, if it's deemed worthy. Perhaps it'll be like the movie character John Wick, and my history will be preserved forever!"

Tommy took a deep breath and paused for a few minutes.

O'Brien was blown away by Tommy's complex answers.

"So ... why me?

"What I mean ... am I in training to take your place?" O'Brien asked.

Tommy again took several seconds to craft his reply.

"The answer to your question is—maybe. You've already seen a fraction of what's in my bag of enhanced interrogation tricks that we used with Jameson! So, yeah—when we start on the twin, I'll be showing you what works and what doesn't.

"A lot of what I do is theater. The interrogation is probably fifty percent psychological and the rest physiological! Once we're finished breaking him down, it will be decision time for you.

"…so yes, Jay O. I did pick you as my replacement!"

# CHAPTER 77

Stan did a field identity test of Lawson's kill, and it was determined that Todd was the unfortunate twin. He messaged Tommy with the information.

Tommy had just a short window of time in which to operate. In reality, Stan could have ended the search for the people who had initially contracted with Todd and Wayne Gail to kill Dr. Rob Becker—after all, Rob was, for all intents and purposes, now dead.

Based on that, it was tempting to walk away—but that wasn't how Tommy operated. Even if Stan had said, "That's all, it's a wrap," Tommy was still willing to go rogue.

The hunt would end when Tommy said it was over, and not until then!

The November election was now a thing of the past—and Trump had lost. The inauguration of the new president would take place on January 20, 2021—which meant Tommy had about sixty days to wrap everything up.

Tommy and Agent O'Brien were about to again implement the same interrogation techniques they'd used with Jameson. After shoveling Wayne into the dumbwaiter chute, Tommy continued his enhanced interrogation training seminar with O'Brien.

"The key to success in breaking down this twin will be a fifty-fifty combination of psychology and sleep deprivation. Unfortunately, that means our sleep patterns will also be affected.

Both twins undoubtedly are skilled in martial arts and have had SERE training, so both of us need to be awake when we bring him to the smorgasbord table."

"Can I have first dibs?" O'Brien asked.

"Well, I was going to start our hostage with some simple water boarding. He's undoubtedly had some experience with the procedure—I want to build his confidence up and then have it come crashing down!

"Boarding is a two-man job. Let's do it for a half hour or so and see where we are ... okay?" Tommy responded.

"What's after the boarding?" O'Brien asked.

"We'll do the antique crank phone/naked wire interrogation. I'll crank and you can place the end with the exposed copper wire wherever you want," Tommy told his partner.

∩ ∩ ∩

Stan's message was opened. Tommy's hostage was now officially identified.

The interrogations that night went as expected. Wayne breezed through the water boarding and the hot wire stimulation—and O'Brien was a quick read when it came to torture.

Tommy was a good teacher. He explained to his young agent what he would have done differently—while never suggesting any change in a condescending manner. Every suggestion began with "next time, you might want to give this a try."

"Let's get some sleep. I'm setting the alarm for two hours from now.

"Wayne won't be sleeping. He gets to hear a little Van Halen and some ZZ Top. I'll crank up the bass enough to cause the foam cubes in the pit to start vibrating."

∩ ∩ ∩

Both agents had been able to sleep during those two hours, but Wayne didn't. He definitely looked strung out as O'Brien led him toward a chair across from Tommy at the interrogation table.

On the table were shooter muffs, a pair of glasses, a five-shot revolver, and several bullets. The Tommy Russian Roulette routine was about to begin.

"Okay Wayne, I really love this particular interrogation technique. I'm going to load this gun with bullets—some are blank cartridges and some are live. I'll spin the barrel and pull the trigger. Behind you is a target. I can take aim or not ... so no name-calling.

"When I ask a question, I expect an honest and reasonable answer! And by the way, I don't think either of us told you that your brother died a few hours ago in an exchange of gunfire in the trailer park, across from the cemetery. My first question is: How long has Trooper Jameson been employed by you?"

For three minutes, Tommy waited patiently for an answer.

"Okay, time's up ... and that's a non-answer."

Tommy loaded the revolver before putting on the special glasses that enabled him to see whether the next bullet was a live or blank round.

After placing the shooter earmuffs on, Tommy took aim.

The sound was deafening. The bullet sailed over Wayne's head and hit the drywall. Wayne flinched a tad.

"Damn ... I need more practice!" Tommy uttered out loud.

"Okay, let's try again. You and Officer Jameson have known each other—for how long?"

One minute passed and then another—with still no response

from Wayne. Tommy moved up the sequence of the shots. He loaded the next bullet and gave the barrel a spin. Once more, a live round was in place.

Taking aim, Tommy wondered how good his "ear" shot would be.

Again, a loud boom filled the room.

"Aww shit, Jay O.! I just shot off half of Wayne's right ear!"

O'Brien grabbed several two-inch gauze pads and began applying pressure to stop the blood that was oozing out of the arterioles and veins in their captive's ear. Wayne's face and neck were beet red, a sign of just how pissed off he was—and how much he wanted to deck Tommy.

"Fucking ass-wipe!" Wayne blurted.

"Well, thank you, Wayne. Coming from you, I'll take that as a compliment. Tell you what ... let's even up your ears," Tommy said, while reloading the gun.

He gave the cylinder another spin—this time a blank cartridge was loaded and ready to be fired. Tommy got up, walked around the table, and now standing next to Wayne, pressed the weapon into Wayne's temple and pulled the trigger.

Wayne strained to cover his ears, but his cuffed hands prevented that, and now he could hear only from the hemorrhaging ear. Tommy knew Wayne had been analyzing his pattern of shots.

After reloading once more, Tommy checked the cylinders, noting that all five bullets were live. He didn't want to damage any more body parts, but stopping now would give an indication of weakness.

Tommy sat down and took aim at Wayne's left ear. In a split second, the bullet tore through ear cartilage before slamming into more drywall.

"Dammit, Wayne, I'm sorry. I screwed up your other ear," Tommy apologized as he burst into a laugh.

"I'm going to kill you … you son of a bitch!" Wayne shouted in a primeval guttural voice.

Tommy walked back toward Wayne and sat down on the edge of the table.

"I tell you what. You answer all my questions and I'll unshackle you and give you the opportunity to have at me. Deal, huh?"

Wayne nearly answered yes, but stopped himself, knowing that the globalist contractor who hired him would annihilate his entire family.

Tommy watched Wayne's face intensely! He could almost hear the tug-of-war going on in Wayne's brain.

This guy's one tough dude, Tommy thought.

# CHAPTER 78

After getting Wayne safely secured in the pit for the remainder of the evening, Tommy sat down with O'Brien to analyze their situation.

"This guy is probably going to be among the top five toughest individuals I've ever tried to break down. He's resolute in not telling me anything. In my experience, a detainee eventually hints at giving something up. With Wayne, the more enhanced my interrogation is, the more he hates me. I don't mind that fact, but I don't want to be the only reason he continues to resist. We'll let him listen to more heavy metal while we get some much-needed sleep. I'll wake you in about five hours," Tommy told his partner.

Before closing his eyes, Tommy checked for any messages on his phone. There were none, but Stan's cell number appeared three times as a missed call earlier that night. Stan had left no message, which was unusual and curious to Tommy. He placed the call.

The cell phone rang four times before Stan answered.

"Three calls and no message isn't like you. What's going on?" Tommy asked.

"I've been checking overseas contacts, and I may have found something. I just can't let loose of the idea that some globalist entity might have a connection within the thoroughbred community. That's the only thread that Rob Becker and his partners have, and it's all due to Mark's finagling with the genetic makeup of Nidalas.

"So ... I shared what's been happening to Mark Shaw and Rob Becker with our Saudi agent, Halim. I asked him to sniff around with his Arab connections in the thoroughbred world and try to determine if there's something there ... anywhere!

"Halim suddenly interrupts me, saying that he personally had been interrogated three times about a missing journal or diary that Mark Shaw had kept. This diary apparently originated immediately after Mark arrived in Saudi Arabia with the very ill Nidalas.

"Halim then told me that he discreetly investigated whether these interrogations were isolated or widespread incidents and learned a few days later that every farm employee was also asked about the diary.

"The person who owns Nidalas is a Saudi Royal with satellite farms across the globe. That's a huge corporate operation, Tommy—and it represents a ton of money. Incidentally, just a few miles from where you are right now is one of his satellite farms, and it has been operating for many years.

"We certainly don't have the time to launch a full-blown operation to determine if there's a Middle Eastern connection to the Mark Shaw/Rob Becker assassinations, but feel free to use this information, which by the way is still speculation, during your interrogation of Wayne."

"Jesus, Stan, you're a bit late in dropping this shit on me. If, and that's a huge if, this information pans out, don't you dare try and stop me from traveling overseas!"

Tommy's statement was met with silence for a few seconds.

"Tommy, I can't stop you from striking out on your own. I'll support you as much as possible, but officially, you'll be on your lonesome."

"Thanks, Stan, that's pretty damn magnanimous of you. Bye!"

∩ ∩ ∩

Marty was on a mission, and she would not be denied. She sat by Harry's bedside during her every waking moment. She read the daily sports news, especially the soccer news, out loud to Harry.

She gleaned any and all information about people in a coma and shared that out loud with him too.

She also physically attempted to stimulate Harry by testing his reflexes. Every hour on the hour she began the cycle—starting with the plantar reflex and then the pupillary accommodation reflex.

That was followed by testing the ankle jerk reflex and the patellar reflex. The rubber-tipped tendon hammer was always by her side and at the ready.

It was a Saturday morning, and I was down at the stable spoiling Towers Destiny and pissing off Towers Above. The more carrots and apple bits I fed the young colt, the more TA pawed at the ground and snorted.

When the peppermint candy came out of my pocket and the cellophane wrapper was peeled away, TA verbalized his wants. The whinnies continued until he was satisfied with the sweet treat.

Initially, Marty's ear-piercing screams blended with the sounds of some wind gusts. I broke into my best feeble run and reached the porch totally out of breath.

"Is he dead?" was my first question.

"No ... not even close!" Marty told me. "I was doing his reflex tests and I swore his knee bounced a little. Come inside and watch. Hurry!"

We rounded the hallway and entered Harry's room. He slowly turned his head and faced us.

"Nana, where am I and why do I have these wires and pads attached to my chest and head. And where's my mom?" Harry asked in a soft voice. Marty's knees buckled and she dropped to the floor.

All the grief and sadness that for weeks had cast an invisible shroud over Harry miraculously vanished from the room for good.

Marty composed herself and hurried to Harry's bedside, cradling our grandson's head while I fumbled with my phone, trying to call Kathy and Mike.

I heard Kathy answer the phone and I shouted, "Harry's awake!"

The cell phone dropped from Kathy's hands onto her hardwood floor. The emotions of the moment overwhelmed me with joyful tears of relief.

"Hurry down here, Kathy—it's a miracle!"

# CHAPTER 79

Tommy lay silently staring at the ceiling of the cabin for four straight hours.

A casual observer would have had trouble figuring out which person was being interrogated.

Knowing there would be no sleep, Tommy finally got up and headed to the kitchen for coffee and to check the video feed from the hidden camera in the pit. He saw Wayne pacing the floor like a caged animal. Tommy said a silent "good" and took a big gulp of black coffee. O'Brien entered the kitchen. He grabbed a seat and immediately began yawning.

"O'Brien, I'm going to let you play the mad dentist this morning. Do you have any questions?"

Jay O. gloved up and asked Tommy if he would help him with a review of the mental foramen puncture. Tommy nodded yes, took a seat and opened wide. Jay checked the picture in the oral anatomy textbook and using his index finger as a poker, began searching for the nerve opening between the first and second bicuspid roots on the right and left sides of the lower jaw. Each time he found the opening, he gave a little extra push and laughed.

"Don't think I won't remember those pushes," Tommy warned Jay O. as he headed to the pit door.

Tommy cracked open the door to the pit while simultaneously stepping back a few yards.

"Okay, Wayne, you can stop hiding. Neither one of us is coming in. Come out with your hands behind your back!"

Wayne grudgingly lowered his head as he emerged from the darkness. Jay O. handcuffed him, before leading him back to the table where Tommy secured both of Wayne's legs with restraints and covered his chest with a dental bib.

Both men wrestled with Wayne's head while placing the mouth props to keep his mouth open. Once the props were in position, the interrogation process became simple. Jay O. showed Wayne the thickest and longest needle from the table, before turning around and exchanging the large needle for a smaller, less traumatizing one.

The procedure began. The agent punctured Wayne's naso-palatine nerve papilla with the needle while Tommy held Wayne's head in a steady grip. The scream emanating from Wayne was ear-splitting! O'Brien used gauze pads to blot the bleeding, and he quickly shifted the stabbing needle to the mental foramen. Again, agonizing guttural screams emanated from Wayne's mouth.

Sweat was streaming from Wayne's forehead. His eyes were closed, and a pathetic moaning sound now filled the air. His blood pressure was high, at 200+/140.

Tommy quickly realized he was approaching a dead end with this particular torture technique. There was no through street and no U-turn back. He knew that if the dental torture continued, Wayne would probably have a coronary event and die. Any information would be better than none at all.

Tommy clapped his hands together, and then made a throat slashing gesture for Jay O. to see.

Just like that, Tommy flipped the script.

Tommy looked Wayne square in the eyes, staring intently for

a good minute. Wayne simply turned away from Tommy's steely look.

"You know, maybe what I'm about to do is crazy! What comes next is generally pretty much scripted. I'm supposed to introduce you to Dentistry 2.0 now that you've graduated from Dentistry 1.0. Trust me, these needles are brutal."

Tommy unsheathed an even larger gauge needle and held it in front of Wayne's face. The purpose for this was subtle, but effective. He was counting on Wayne being among the fifty percent of the general population that hates going to the dentist…because everyone hates needle sticks inside their mouth!

Judging from the fear evident in Wayne's eyes, Tommy had guessed correctly.

Wayne had experienced almost everything in Tommy's enhanced interrogation cookbook. Wayne's SERE training was rock solid, and Tommy respected that.

"Wayne, I'm impressed. Thank you for your service to our Republic. I want you to forget about the Rob Becker assassination. I'm guessing there's got to be more going on than just an assassination. I don't have your dossier in front of me, but I'll bet there's a family member or two whose lives would be on the line if you were to snitch and give up the name of the person or group that hired you. I'm correct aren't I?" Tommy asked, holding up the big needle for effect—and hopefully for the final time.

Tommy once again stared into Wayne's eyes, and again, Wayne refused to stare back.

I've got you now, you son of a bitch, Tommy silently said to himself.

Wayne remained stoic as Jay O. rose, walking to the table where he plucked a couple of vinyl gloves from the glove box and put them on.

It was time for round two.

"Damn it! I totally forgot to ask you, Wayne! You're not allergic to vinyl, are you?" O'Brien asked. His timing was perfect.

"I'll need some protection!"

"Wait. What did you just say, Wayne?" Tommy retorted.

O'Brien reached into his pants pocket and pushed a button on the remote control which turned on a pinhole camera. All three men were now being recorded.

"I have a wife and two children who will need witness protection in addition to myself. I don't have a name for you. But I do have a country. The contract originated in the Middle East, Saudi Arabia in fact. If you have any pictures maybe I could identify some of the individuals. I also have some phone numbers to track down. Hopefully that information will lead to the identity of the person you're looking for."

"Hold that thought. I'll be back in a few moments," Tommy responded.

Tommy retreated to the kitchen, poured himself another cup of coffee, and called Stan.

"Tommy, what's up?"

"Stan, my current cabin guest says his employer is based in Saudi Arabia. He says he doesn't have a specific name, but he's given me a few phone numbers. Even better is that I have his and his dead brother's cell phones in my pocket right now.

"I'm guessing the person we're looking for is a billionaire thoroughbred owner—and he's probably connected to the royal family. You've got to remember … the Saudi royal family was deemed responsible for the recent brazen death, in Istanbul, Turkey, of a Saudi ex-pat journalist named Khashoggi."

"And again, just like the 9/11 attack, expect that no royal will ever pay for the travesty," Stan stated.

"How about I have Steven bring Wayne to Langley? He'll also bring the cell phones. Eventually you'll give me your best guess as to who's my next target," Tommy said.

"Sounds reasonable, Tommy. Have your son give me a call when he's in transit." Stan hung up.

Tommy returned to the interrogation room and again took a seat opposite Wayne.

"Wayne, did you or your brother murder Mark Shaw at Woodlands Park?"

Wayne, who had pretty much avoided any eye contact with Tommy, looked up and directed his gaze at Tommy.

"If I say yes, will it make a difference? Is my answer a deal breaker? Look, there's probably no Kentuckian that doesn't know about Mark Shaw's demise. It wasn't suicide ... I can tell you that!

"Look, your superiors will be analyzing the phone numbers I just gave you. Do me a favor and put me back in my prison room," Wayne said pointing to the pit. "I've answered your questions, so if you'll do me the courtesy of a few hours of sleep, I'd be grateful."

Tommy and Jay O. led Wayne back to the pit, then returned to the kitchen. This time, it wasn't coffee that they wanted.

"Nice work today, partner. I have a question for you—do you use a blade or an electric razor when you shave?" Tommy asked.

Jay O. gave Tommy a quizzical look but answered "Blade."

"Well, put that razor away ... you're coming with me in a few weeks. Where we're going, you won't need to shave."

# CHAPTER 80

Nearly a month had passed since the capture of Wayne when Tommy and Jay O. were called to Stan's office early one morning. As they sat waiting for him to show up, each felt as if he was back in high school sitting in the principal's office, expecting to hear the consequences of an offense not yet committed!

Stan finally walked in, holding what looked like official papers that most likely detailed what the two men could or could not do in Saudi Arabia. He greeted the agents with a somber tone of voice.

"Men, I have no intention of recording this meeting. In fact, I was just informed that I will not continue to serve as the Agency's director, so there won't be any minutes taken either. You can feel free to speak openly."

Tommy laughed under his breath. "Sure, boss ... you're still in charge of the most secret organization in the world and you want me to speak openly. Yep—most definitely, speak openly is exactly what I'll do!"

Stan pretended not to see Tommy's smirk, before speaking again.

"Our Middle East special agents have determined that a Saudi royal and thoroughbred kingpin was responsible for the hit on Mark Shaw and Dr. Rob Becker."

While Stan continued to ramble on about phone numbers and evidence-gathering, Tommy wondered why his boss was so formal in his presentation, quickly coming to the conclusion that everything said in the room that morning was indeed being re-corded. He wondered if O'Brien thought the same.

Stan was still talking. "Conclusions are that even though the evidence indicts the Saudi prince, we cannot condone any equiv-alent and retaliatory action. There will be no assassination of any other individuals on our part! I want to personally say, though, that over the past five-plus years, what started out as one fantas-tic thoroughbred race has slowly morphed into a microcosm of world terrorism.

"On paper, Saudi Arabia is America's ally in the Middle East. Because of that, any American response has to be measured and considered carefully. So, what do you gentlemen have in mind?"

Tommy spoke first. "Somehow, Stan, I knew you would say just that. Just how many times will an American leader have to continue to turn their cheek and once again take this Saudi abuse, however random it may be? After the destruction and loss of life from 9/11, I truly thought that by now, our country's response would be stronger.

"Jay O. and I are traveling to Saudi Arabia. If everything goes as expected, we'll embarrass the hell out of the Saudi royal who also just happens to own multiple thoroughbred farms all over the world."

"The last I remember, I didn't give O'Brien permission to ac-company you to the Middle East," a clearly agitated Stan replied.

"C'mon, Stan, you and I just became part of the cancel cul-ture. Do I have to get on my knees and beg? O'Brien has an out—he can always say he was following orders. The only other person I need on my team is our agent who's embedded in Saudi Arabia."

Stan buried his head in both hands before finally looking

at Tommy.

"Whatever it is you've planned, if you get caught, you're on your own. There'll be no rescue from the Agency... or POTUS! By then Trump will be retired to Florida. Do you understand?"

Tommy nodded, while saying a verbal "yes" to Stan.

"Jay O. and I will be leaving tomorrow. Thanks for your help—we won't get caught!"

∩ ∩ ∩

After more than twenty-one grueling hours of layovers, changeovers, and flight time, Tommy and O'Brien finally arrived in Riyadh, Saudi Arabia. They could have taken a US military hop, but Stan felt it was better for the two to travel on an Israeli transport plane that was carrying COVID-19 vaccine.

The two agents were picked up at the airport by Halim, driving a Ford transit van which would take them to his house. Halim spent the first hour on the road making sure he wasn't followed by any Mabahith, the Saudi equivalent to the FBI.

After finally arriving at the driver's home, both men crashed and recharged after the long and tedious flight.

∩ ∩ ∩

The end of February was in four days—and it would be time for the Saudi Cup races. The two Americans intended to be present at the race where the Saudi prince's thoroughbred was expected to run and win the lion's share of the twenty-million-dollar purse for the second straight year.

The three men sat down for dinner to familiarize themselves with the tasks at hand.

"First things first," Tommy said. "Halim, were you able to get the Glock and suppressor that Stan requested?"

"Yes sir, I did," he said, placing the gun on the dinner table.

"How certain are you that the prince's thoroughbred will be accessible the day before and the day of the Saudi Cup race?" Jay O. asked.

"I've been on the veterinary team for years. I'm the one who worked hand-in-hand with Mark and the injured Nidalas."

"You know this will be your last hurrah here in Saudi Arabia, right?" Tommy asked.

"Yes sir! I'm certain Langley will have a spot for me in the future," Halim said without any remorse or hesitation.

"Okay, then. My thoughts are that you'll be the one to give the horse Lasix the day before and then again on the day of the Saudi Cup race. I'm thinking ten cc's the day before, but I'm not yet certain how much you'll give him on race day.

"It's absolutely imperative that my partner and I are both present when you administer the drug—the security cameras will catch us on their video both days. The video will show me with my Glock pressed against your back and then pointed at your head while you're injecting the drugs. That should be enough evidence to convince the prince that you were coerced into giving the drugs, so that you and your family members won't be murdered in the future.

"I can't think of any other way to impress upon the sheikh that it was a big mistake to kill Mark and Dr. Becker. If my plan doesn't work, I guess the next Agency director will have to deal with this tit for tat violence. Who knows how long it will continue!" Tommy stated emphatically.

"So be it," Halim answered back with finality.

Epilogue

Donnie, Mike, and Joey, along with myself and my facially reconstructed grandson, stood side by side on the grounds of the farm along the horse fencing, all of us staring intently at Towers Destiny.

"Today, TD officially becomes a two-year-old—and what a two-year-old he is," Donnie said in excitement, blowing a kiss in Towers Destiny's direction.

"Has he been broken yet?" Joey asked.

"Not yet," Donnie replied.

"Joey, the reason I invited you here was to let you see TD first hand and let you familiarize yourself with him. Why don't you climb over the fence and see how he takes to you?" Donnie suggested to the jockey.

She nodded emphatically, bounded over the fence, and began striding toward Towers Destiny. The two-year-old stood his ground with ears pricked up. Joey reached into her jeans pocket to retrieve some peppermint candies before extending her right hand toward the horse.

It took only a couple of seconds for both peppermints to disappear. Wanting more, TD lowered his head, sniffing and poking his snout at the pocket of Joey's jeans. Joey knew it would be useless to deny the stallion any of the remaining peppermints.

In that instant, a bond was created between jockey and horse that would last for the next two-plus years.

Joey ran her callused hands through the stallion's coat and at the same time, she leaned in against his body. Another minute passed and suddenly with one jump, the jockey was draped over the horse's back. TD was startled briefly before turning his head to the back to gaze at the first-ever person to be on his back.

Not wanting to spook the horse, Joey didn't make the slightest move. Donnie, Mike, me and my grandson - who now went by the name of Barry - could see, but not hear, Joey talking softly to her new four-legged friend. After a couple more minutes, she slid down from TD's back.

"You're smitten, aren't you?" Donnie asked.

"How much is it going to cost our group of owners to make you TD's exclusive jockey?" Donnie blurted out, quickly realizing how close he came to unmasking me in my new identity.

"Geez. I'm really sorry, Donnie. I totally forgot about the murders of Mark Shaw and Dr. Becker. Since there's only you two partners left, I'll give you a break. Until I actually begin racing Towers Destiny, I'll want a quarter million dollars ... in cash. If exclusive means I'm at your beck and call twenty-four/seven, then it will be half a million. My lodging and meals are also on your tab. Once Towers Destiny begins racing, we'll renegotiate the package. I'm thinking at that time, I'd be happy with the traditional percentage split of earnings following any race where I finish in the money."

Mike and Donnie shot each other a glance. Each man knew they could quibble about the contract's terms, but they also realized there was no other jockey they trusted or wanted on Towers Destiny's back.

"Okay, Joey. You're hired. The only deal breaker would be if Towers Destiny is physically unable to perform. Why don't we walk up to the house and have a look at your quarters?" Donnie asked Joey.

I was exhilarated. Towers Above was a great thoroughbred—but Towers Destiny was everything I'd envisioned when our group first set out to breed another Secretariat.

"Everything," I said aloud over and over again.

∩ ∩ ∩

It was five months later—and Donnie and Mike had been deferring decisions about the racing plans for Towers Destiny to me.

In my mind, if Towers Destiny was truly going to be judged as Secretariat's equal, then he should race, whenever possible, the same races that Secretariat ran almost fifty years previously during his two- and three-year-old campaigns. Only then could thoroughbred aficionados fairly evaluate Towers Destiny.

A few of the 1973 races no longer existed. I selected other races that had the same distance, prize purse, and most importantly, a high level of competition, for our horse to run.

Unlike during Secretariat's maiden race, Towers Destiny was not bumped hard coming out of the starting gate in his first event. TD trailed the field for the first two-thirds of the race—then as Secretariat had done years earlier, our horse closed the race with a burst of speed, for the win.

Last to first for the win … this couldn't be a genetic trait, could it? I wondered to myself, while smiling broadly.

By the end of October, Towers Destiny was ready for a huge test. Heading into the Breeders' Cup races, he was undefeated. The venue was at Churchill Downs, and Kentuckians would be able to see Towers Destiny compete live for the first time.

Then disaster hit.

The Jockey Club announced that they were launching an investigation surrounding Towers Destiny's "creation."

As owners, we had been upfront about the conception of both Towers Above and Towers Destiny. In fact, Mark had insisted on videotaping TA's mother and father as they mated in the breeding barn. Even after Mark's death, we were fully transparent and followed the same process in the conception of Towers Destiny.

What irritated Donnie, Mike and me was that the rumor and impetus behind this investigation originated in Saudi Arabia—from a Saudi Royal, no less—with an unsubstantiated claim that Towers Destiny was artificially created.

�’ ʘ ʘ ʘ

It was time for answers—and I was certain that they would come from Tommy in Oral, South Dakota.

Since that fateful day at the cemetery, I had decided to let sleeping dogs lie. I'd never even asked Tommy if he'd solved the mystery of who wanted Mark and me dead.

Scrolling through my phone contact list, I came to Tommy's name and cell phone number.

Seeing my area code on his phone's display, Tommy answered. "I wondered when you'd finally call!"

"I'm almost afraid to ask how so," I replied.

"I'm not going to bullshit you, Rob. After I saw the news report about Towers Destiny's creation controversy, I called Stan. Now get this … Stan had already talked with his counterpart Bud, who's still in charge at the DIA. Bud told Stan about a certain Saudi royal who is the genesis for the investigation and the source of the rumor."

"Forget that for a minute! I want to know if you found out who put up the money for the contracts on Mark and me."

My question was met with extended silence. I was about to

once again scream into the phone when Tommy realized he had no out.

"Okay, okay. O'Brien and I, along with another agent embedded in the Middle East, set up and embarrassed the hell out of that Saudi Royal. We drugged his champion thoroughbred before the running of the twenty-million-dollar Saudi Cup race. The horse won the race, but the post-race urine test revealed the stallion was drugged. In the end, the royal had to forfeit the win and give back the winnings! It's my understanding that the disgrace of being called a cheater still weighs heavily on him. What's even better is that the horse's stud fee has plummeted. This guy could actually make more money operating a glue business versus breeding thoroughbreds.

"As for me, the cherry on the sundae was letting the royal know that any further assassination contracts on American thoroughbred owners wouldn't just be embarrassing—they could prove to be a fatal decision."

I was at loss for words. I knew that without Tommy's help, I'd most likely already be dead. But now, any chance of Towers Destiny competing in a Breeders Cup race as a two-year-old was finished. It galled me even more to think that there were some American horseracing bluebloods in the Commonwealth who were celebrating our problems at that very moment.

I couldn't help but remember I'd been down this road six years earlier with Towers Above and Nidalas.

"Déjà vu certainly does suck," I mumbled to myself. A few seconds later I said goodbye to Tommy.

∩ ∩ ∩

The years that passed since Secretariat last competed were generally positive for the sport of horse racing. In addition, the advent of the new century brought about different qualifying criteria for a horse's entry into the Run for the Roses.

Across the country there were a number of designated stakes races—each having specific points for a win, place, show, and fourth place—that generated qualifying points. After accumulating a certain predetermined number of points, a thoroughbred could earn a slot in the one national race that always (except for the COVID-19 year) is held the first Saturday in May in Louisville, Kentucky.

The fact that Towers Destiny had missed running in the Breeders' Cup Juvenile Race the previous November effectively robbed our stallion of thirty qualifying points for the Kentucky Derby.

Towers Destiny had earned more than enough points as a result of his wins as a three-year-old.

The first victory was the Gotham Stakes in early March, followed by the Bay Shore Stakes on April 3rd. I should point out that the Wood Memorial Stakes, in which Secretariat finished out of the money in 1973, didn't fit Towers Destiny's qualifying path for the Kentucky Derby.

I went back and reviewed Secretariat's videos for those two stakes races in 1973 and discovered that both were eerily similar to the races that Towers Destiny would run in 2022.

Donnie focused his pre-Derby training on making sure Towers Destiny would break out of the gate quicker. This change in training was prompted because of the review of old videos from those earlier Kentucky Derby races. All the videos showed there were too many thoroughbreds vying for the rail once the gates opened.

The videos showed jockeys on their steeds, veering from the far end of the auxiliary starting gate toward the rail, in a hurried and disorderly fashion. All were determined to not be left behind, while knowing the Kentucky Derby's starts were worse than a NASCAR start!

These starts, with horses jostling and colliding with each other, reminded me of the Roller Derby. Donnie definitely didn't want our horse to be jammed in this way and never have a chance to fairly compete.

We all knew that Towers Destiny was the best but also knew that the Derby could be counted on for intangibles during race week…with the post/position drawing being just one of them. Learning that gate thirteen was TD's draw for the Derby, our hearts collectively skipped a few beats. After this draw, Donnie and Joey met for an hour—and the strategy they came up with was golden.

As planned on Derby Day, Joey had Towers Destiny break fast out of the gate, but there was no thought given to immediately heading for the rail. Instead, Joey held the reins tightly as TD ran fast and straight, while sliding slightly toward the left before the first turn.

He settled in on the outside of four other thoroughbreds and as they came out of the first turn and onto the straightaway, our horse was in ninth place. Joey coaxed him into another gear and Towers Destiny began his drive for the lead before reaching the final turn. The rest of the race was downhill for our horse as he easily flashed across the same finish line that Secretariat had crossed in 1973.

The only difference was that our horse lopped three-fifths of a second off the record time of the Kentucky Derby set by Secretariat in 1973. Prior to the running of this particular Kentucky Derby, any reference to Towers Destiny being Secretariat's equal were few and far between.

Sports coverage across the country on Sunday morning indicated that perhaps it was now time to pay serious attention to Towers Destiny.

∩ ∩ ∩

On the eve of the second leg of the Triple Crown, Joey again watched the video replay of Secretariat's record time and win in the 1973 Preakness.

Joey was fully on board and eager to see TD set new records. For many horse-racing enthusiasts, the mystique of Secretariat is everlasting, but Joey came to realize that perhaps the Preakness record time of this legendary racehorse would no longer stand. She had always loved watching Secretariat's Triple Crown victories, but now they had become a personal quest.

Records are meant to fall. They're one of the reasons people, and in this instance, an animal and its rider, compete. While it was almost sacrilegious to think about TD duplicating—or beating—Secretariat's record runs from 1973, Joey also knew that if the shoe was on the other foot, Secretariat's jockey, Ron Turcotte, would not have hesitated to try and break a competitor's record.

In the Derby, Lords Rainbow finished second to Towers Destiny. Joey figured he would be the competition once again in the Preakness.

The number of entrants in the Preakness was one half of those that ran in the Derby. Towers Destiny drew the farthest from the rail post position ... at number seven.

Lords Rainbow had drawn the number one position.

A little before post time, as if perfectly on cue, another intangible of horse racing, which was weather-related, occurred.

A storm front that earlier kicked off some light morning

showers could have helped the thoroughbreds as light rain can tamp down the dirt on the race track. However, now the sky above the track was looking ominous, and a heavy downpour would help no one!

Donnie, Mike, and I were praying. I'd shared my dream of TD's record-breaking run with my partners. We all knew that a heavy rain would not stop the race but would most likely kill the dream.

…..but then the weather gods turned kind, after all. As the first thoroughbred in the Preakness stepped onto the track, the sun broke out and a double rainbow appeared. A large segment of the crowd interpreted this colorful happening as an omen for Lords Rainbow. The betting windows were swamped with wagers being placed.

As the horses entered their respective gates, the rain stopped totally.

"And they're off," the track announcer said.

Towers Destiny had temporarily settled into last place after the start, seemingly analyzing his game plan.

As with the Kentucky Derby run, the Preakness appeared to also be the place for a repeat of 1973. TD took off, rounding the first turn and never trailed again. His sudden burst of speed surpassed Secretariat's dash to the front of the pack so many years ago.

In less than two minutes, Towers Destiny was two-thirds of the way home in capturing the Triple Crown. Lords Rainbow tried in vain to catch Towers Destiny, but his efforts on this day came up short.

Joey glanced at the time on the tote board. It wasn't official yet, but another one of Secretariat's records had fallen by the wayside.

The Preakness post-race press conference was surreal.

One reporter asked if Donnie or Mike had visited a psychic prior to the Triple Crown races and if so, had that soothsayer predicted a thirty-one-length victory in the Belmont which was coming up in three weeks?

Reporters tried unsuccessfully to get the two owners to publicly state that Towers Destiny was better than Secretariat. Finally, Donnie put an end to that line of questioning. "Secretariat's Triple Crown record times are like waving a bunch of carrots in front of Towers Destiny, daring him to do better."

The myriad of questions continued on and on until there was a show-stopper.

"Donnie, a source tells me that the owner of a Saudi thoroughbred by the name of Saladin intends to challenge Towers Destiny in the Belmont Stakes. Have you heard this rumor, and do you know anything about that horse?"

Donnie's eyes met mine, and if our roles could have magically been reversed, my "oh shit" reaction would have been far more emphatic than his. Instead, Donnie simply responded with a "No," before he and Mike got up and left the press room.

The next day was a travel day, but I was still awake well past midnight making calls to Stan, with requests I knew would be passed along to Tommy.

Throughout the night and into the next morning, déjà vu had become very real.

∩ ∩ ∩

Information available online about the Saudi thoroughbred named Saladin was sparse. Of the articles I was able to find, none made the connection to Nidalas. Whether the reporters were unaware, just plain stupid or not "woke," none of the pundits recognized the anagram. When Nidalas is spelled backwards the word created is Saladin—the name of an ancient Muslim warrior leader.

What also bothered me was the fact that Saladin was now stabled in Kentucky and had probably been in the Commonwealth for several months. I'd recently learned that Tommy was on his way to Kentucky—and I hoped he had the answers I was looking for.

It was clear to me that the Saudi royal didn't have to race his horse in the Belmont. After all, he knew his horse had no chance of finishing in the money. I'd studied Saladin's race times and yes, he was a quality stallion, but he lacked record-breaking speed. The only logical answer I could come up with was that Saladin's entrance was "payback"—and we needed to be ready.

Donnie and I sat down and made a list of ways the Saudi royal could ruin Towers Destiny's quest to win the Belmont.

"Doc, he can order his jockey to slow the race down. It's damn hard to prove, but at the request of trainers or even owners, some jocks can block or impede a specific horse. The royal knows that every second in a race this important is a precious commodity.

"Or how about a stray strike of the whip in close quarters? You already know how much Towers Destiny detests the whip! Don't think the other trainers haven't noticed that fact.

"Knowing what happened at the Saudi Cup means we have to triple our security entourage the moment we step foot on the property at Belmont Park," Donnie stated with anger in his voice.

"Well, I didn't want to tell you this, Donnie, but Towers Destiny is going to have to break instantly—he can't be leaning backwards in the starting gate. Once those gates open, Joey can't let him settle into his usual last place. That's a sure recipe for getting blocked. This time … in this race … Towers Destiny needs to be out front from the get-go," I said. Donnie nodded in agreement.

Over the next three days, Donnie and Joey practiced starts with Towers Destiny and by the end of the week, we were ready for travel to New York state.

Towers Destiny was ready to win the Triple Crown.

ᴖ ᴖ ᴖ

Tommy stopped in Lexington to pick up some documents before he too headed to New York and Belmont Park.

Once in New York, Tommy would concentrate on Saladin and the barn that Saladin was housed in, knowing that Donnie would handle security on Towers Destiny's end.

"If you were planning an attack on Towers Destiny, where would you be at the start of the Belmont?" Tommy asked himself. His immediate thought was, "If someone is going to do something to the horse physically, they'd take the high ground."

Tommy knew he had to do something to ward off any attack. He wrote a note, placed it in an envelope, and had it delivered to Saladin's barn.

The note read:

I'm here … you're here.
I warned you during the Saudi Cup … and now you're on my turf!
Saladin is a ruse!
You fuck with Towers Destiny—you die!

Tommy had no idea he had just played into the royal's hands and had done everything the Saudi wanted. It wasn't Towers Destiny he wanted to harm. The Saudi royal wanted to cancel Tommy—permanently!

∩ ∩ ∩

Our group, along with Towers Destiny, arrived at Belmont Park late on Sunday—it was now just six days before the race. We successfully settled TD into his quarters.

Four Kentucky State Police troopers were now on guard duty for TD. The officers had been granted leave from the state and were amply paid for their time by us owners.

It was soon learned by our security team how many folks were typically allowed access to the barns—and we quickly made it known there'd be no visitors, period.

It was sundown, and Donnie and Mike were ready to go out for dinner. The lead security trooper stopped us, advising that a man by the name of Tommy was on site and insistent on seeing all of us.

Sure enough, it was Tommy.

I hadn't seen him since he'd grown facial hair. My mind quickly flashed back to the one-year anniversary dinner after the fateful race of Towers Above years earlier. It was almost like Tommy had again visited Indianapolis for another identity makeover.

For the next few minutes, Tommy briefed us on what he knew—and it wasn't much. The bottom line was that he had no clue as to what the Saudi Royal was planning. Without a background in the world of horse racing, Tommy had no real clue about on-the-track racing shenanigans, and readily admitted that the greatest vulnerability for Towers Destiny would be during the actual race.

Donnie assured Tommy that Towers Destiny would take care of business on the track, before throwing a challenge back at Tommy to do his part, which was handling the off-track issues with Saladin and its owner. I could only assume that the give and take of negativity between the two stemmed from Donnie's hard feelings from his kidnapping by Tommy and subsequent forced stay at the cabin in Irvine, Kentucky.

Tommy called it a night and disappeared into the darkness. I did the same after going to my rental car and retrieving my gun.

∩ ∩ ∩

The sunrise on Saturday morning was beautiful, with no hint of storm clouds anywhere.

Towers Destiny had his traditional race day breakfast followed by a light gallop workout. Joey, as usual, had no other rides during the day's regular race card. Belmont's pre-race parade of horses was scheduled to begin at six that evening.

I was standing in the barn on the Belmont Stakes' grounds, loitering at TD's stall when a Kentucky Trooper walked toward me, accompanied by Steven, Agent Lawson, and another man I assumed was Agent O'Brien.

"Well, this is a welcome surprise! Are y'all on duty?"

Steven replied with an emphatic "No."

"We're technically off duty and drove all night to get here. Have you seen my father?" Steven asked.

It was my turn to say no, not once but several times, because I hadn't seen Tommy since the previous evening. Frankly I couldn't even remember anything that might help Steven locate his dad. I did enter all three of the men's cell numbers in my mobile phone and set up a group texting thread.

I told Donnie I was going to grab some lunch and decided to also do some sightseeing. I figured the closer it was to post-time, the tighter the track security would be. I took my time and lazily headed toward the Saudi barn. By now, Saladin was already tucked away, just like TD, in the same barn with the other "Belmont" race entrants.

With a Belmont Coney Island Water Dog in one hand and liquid refreshment—the "Belmont Jewel"—in the other, I tried to look like a typical first-time tourist wandering around lost, on the grounds of the Belmont Stakes.

Counting from the front, I peered through the fourth window, from the barn's entrance, and into a Saudi stall. A shudder climbed my spine as I spied what appeared to be a captive kneeling on the straw.. The captive's head was bowed, with hands tied behind his back—and a machete was pushed against the back of his neck!

It was Tommy!

I dropped to the ground and reached for my gun, as familiar cautionary thoughts raced through my mind.

Text the professionals, Rob!
The last thing your friend needs is Marshal Dillon busting in!
Jesus, is he about to be beheaded?
Rob, you can't wait for Steven to arrive—your friend needs your help—right now!"

In that order, these thoughts allowed me to slightly compose myself. I texted Steven an urgent message that read:

"Help now!!!!"

I kept that message thread active while muting the sound on

my phone so it wouldn't be heard by whoever was holding Tommy. Every few seconds, I'd type the word "Now" and send the message again. Hopefully Steven would have the folks at Langley trace my phone connection and pinpoint my position on Belmont Park's grounds. I told myself there had to be a Stingray tower nearby.

I needed to buy some time and decided to do my best drunk Foster Brooks imitation. Saying a silent prayer, I walked into the barn, but there was no one present to see me "stagger" in. Ducking behind anything bigger and taller than myself, I slowly made my way to the fourth window. With my drink in my left hand and my Glock with a suppressor in my right hand, I was still one stall away. I slowly opened the lower stall door and went inside to hide.

At that moment, my mind was the perfect storm of raging thoughts. What I saw just a few minutes ago through the window seemed more like it had occurred hours ago. A machete is a silent killer, and I couldn't shake the vision of Tommy's body tilted forward with his shoulders T-boned in the straw, his head off to the side—on the ground with its eyes still open.

Now, here I was replaying in my mind a child's game known as "kick the can"—in the stall of a horse barn, no less. I refused to move. I just knew that the person holding that machete would soon show himself.

Sure enough, after about five minutes of holding perfectly still, I heard a door creak and a horse whinny. Tommy's would-be assassin was on the move, but I continued to stay down.

….and damned if there wasn't another assassin following the first one. They must have decided I was gone and began conversing in what I assumed was Arabic.

I continued to stay hidden and soon realized there was no

more talking in the barn.

After counting to thirty, I slowly rose to a standing position and peered out into the barn.

There was no one there. I realized it was go time and sprinted to the stall where I'd seen Tommy. Looking inside, I realized that thankfully, his head was still attached to his body.

I must have paused too long, just staring in shock, because I soon heard, "Get your ass over here and untie me!"

Tommy was the "can" that I didn't dare kick. I didn't dare shout out, "Ollie, Ollie … in Come Free!'"

I couldn't untie Tommy fast enough! I gladly handed over my Glock, and the first thing he did was flip the safety to the off position.

A minute later, Tommy began his hunt and I remained hidden. Five minutes later both of his would-be assassins were dead.

Tommy came back to the barn, looked at me, and took a deep breath.

"I owe you, Doc. That's as close to death as I've ever been." As we walked away, Steven, Lawson, and O'Brien literally ran into both of us. Finally. Tommy began his narrative about what just took place while I was wondering what would have happened to me if Tommy had been killed.

I came to one conclusion … I would have died!

∩ ∩ ∩

It was time for the 2021 Belmont Stakes.

There was one more thoroughbred entered in the 2021 Belmont Stakes than in the 1973 race. Lords Rainbow had to prove himself as the best of the rest when it came to giving Towers Destiny a true test, just as Sham had, when he raced against

Secretariat in 1973.

Prior to the race, Joey was in the barn looking Towers Destiny over from head to tail just in case something was not quite right.

Joey found nothing visibly wrong with Towers Destiny and before leaving the barn, paused to give her horse a hug and some pre-race words.

Now most people would say, "That's just nonsense ... a horse isn't going to understand what you're saying." Joey would counter that statement with, "I've been on this horse's back his entire racing life; how do you know he doesn't?"

Joey left for the jockey's quarters to don her silks and do the weigh-in.

It was just Donnie, Mike, and myself left standing with our version of Secretariat.

"Joey is totally on board with the race plan, right, Donnie?" I asked.

"She is. The only change would be if somehow Lords Rainbow runs the race of his life and is still closely stalking Towers Destiny. In that instance, I told her to make certain that TD wins, regardless of any record time.

"So, Doc ... I've got to ask. Did Tommy tell you we're out of the woods, threat-wise?"

"No, he didn't, Donnie. As soon as we reached our barn, he and the other agents split off and went in different directions. That essentially leaves us in a situation similar to when Towers Above raced some five-plus years ago!"

∩ ∩ ∩

Approximately a mile outside Belmont Park was a young man wearing what looked like VR goggles, preparing to launch

an experimental drone. The drone was totally stealth, with op-
tics that were the latest in miniaturization. A human's naked eye
would be unable to see the drone once it climbed to a thousand
feet.

Slade had received a call at work from Tommy a couple of
weeks prior to this day. After the call, his superiors approved
Slade's travel and the use of this particular drone. It would be the
drone's first real-time deployment, and everyone wanted to see
how it performed.

The launch was flawless, and the drone reached hovering altitude in just seconds. Slade initiated live broadcasting to Tommy
and his associates thirty minutes before post time. Thanks to its
light weight, Slade calculated that the drone would easily stay
aloft for an hour and hopefully by then, Towers Destiny would
be in the "pee" barn giving a post-race urine sample, and totally
out of sight of any enemy.

"Time to get to work, men. There are some unknowns on the
roof above the grandstand, and they have long rifles!"

"Tommy here. Tell me how many?"

"I spot four bodies at this moment. They're spread out from
end to end, across the entire surface of the grandstand roof," Slade
answered.

It was now five minutes after six—the thoroughbreds were
ready to step onto the track. Frank Sinatra's "New York, New
York" began playing throughout the park venue.

Steven and Lawson made their way to the roof, and they verbally engaged the unknowns. It turned out the men on the roof
were friendly agents ... and Tommy breathed a sigh of relief.

"Slade, it doesn't look like there'll be anything bad from up
high. Is it possible for you to do a scan around the oval to see if

there might be anything at track level?"

Slade responded. "Now dropping the drone down for a look-see!"

Slade soon discovered that an individual was on the backside turn, preparing his rifle for an assassination—and his target didn't appear to be a thoroughbred.

The Saudi royal couldn't count on a clean shot at Towers Destiny. He also worried that even if shot, somehow TD would make it across the finish line for the win, before collapsing.

It was far easier to bring down a jockey. Joey was the assassin's target.

Once she was shot and dislodged from the saddle, Towers Destiny would cross the finish line riderless and would therefore be disqualified.

The communications link crackled, and an agitated Slade screamed into his phone! The drone's camera had spotted someone crouched at the beginning of the backside turn.

Tommy, standing at the rail near the finish line, held up a huge white placard with a large "D" painted on it.

O'Brien hopped the rail and began sprinting toward the backside.

Tommy immediately told Steven that Jay O. was on the track and that no one should take a shot at him.

Turning backwards for a final look-see, Joey gazed at the stands one last time before entering TD's assigned gate. She spotted Tommy's sign. Turning to the horse, she slouched down, telling Towers Destiny what was about to take place.

∩ ∩ ∩

"They're at the post ... and they're off!" the announcer's voice blared across the loudspeakers.

"Saladin takes the early lead on the rail and next to him is Towers Destiny, followed closely by Lords Rainbow on the outside. Towers Destiny and Saladin continue to battle for the lead as they finish the first quarter mile in record-breaking time. As the three thoroughbreds enter the first turn, Lords Rainbow pulls in front by a length! All three horses are now on the backside, continuing to vie for the lead!

"The same three stallions are in a pack by themselves now, side by side. Towers Destiny is beginning to pull away. He's in the lead by three ... check that, five ... and now seven lengths! We're beginning to see a Secretariat type of Belmont Stakes race—just as we did forty-eight years ago. Towers Destiny is now in front by at least eleven lengths!

"Saladin is giving way and dropping back. Lords Rainbow continues to compete, and Towers Destiny is almost to the backstretch turn! AND...OH MY GOD! it looks like Towers Destiny's jockey has almost fallen off!"

♘ ♘ ♘

Positioned on the backstretch turn, Steven hears a voice over his radio asking, "Do you have the target in sight?"

"I'm trying" Steven responded. "Yes, I see him now!"

"Take the shot, son!"

"Dad, I can't. There's another person there—along with the target! Both of them are on the ground wrestling with each other! I don't have a clean shot!"

"That has to be O'Brien. Son ... look again, dammit! Do you have a shot?"

"No!"

"Steven—concentrate, son. Pick your target and shoot, goddammit!"

∩ ∩ ∩

At the same time that TD rounded the turn, before the home-stretch, the track announcer called out in amazement:

"It looks like Joey is desperately hanging on and has rolled over on her saddle! Her head is almost banging against the rail! Towers Destiny just clocked an amazing one minute, eight and four/fifths seconds for the three-quarter mile and that's with his jockey—Joey—sideways in the saddle!

"They're coming out of the turn and Towers Destiny is in front now by at least twenty or more lengths... and NOW JOEY IS UPRIGHT AGAIN! Lords Rainbow is gallantly fighting on, even though Towers Destiny is again too much for him."

∩ ∩ ∩

Tommy made a final plea to his son.

"Steven ... good God, son ... please take the shot!"

"I don't have to, Dad! O'Brien has neutralized the assassin!"

∩ ∩ ∩

"There's slightly less than a sixteenth of a mile to go and ... NOW JOEY HAS STOOD UP IN THE IRONS! I can't be-lieve what I'm seeing. Towers Destiny is slowing! The crowd is screaming at Towers Destiny to keep running hard! I have no idea what this jockey is thinking or perhaps Towers Destiny is injured!

"Lords Rainbow is closing somewhat, but Towers Destiny

is still going to win this year's Belmont Stakes! JUST NOT IN RECORD TIME! This is just unbelievable ... WOW!

"Towers Destiny has crossed the finish line, but OH WHAT COULD HAVE BEEN!"

♆ ♆ ♆

Joey leaned forward and began talking into Towers Destiny's right ear.

"It was all of them, TD! Donnie, Mike, Doc Becker, and Tommy all agreed to the plan. There was no way we were going to topple or tarnish Secretariat's record time and his greatest victory of all—here at Belmont Park! No way!"

Towers Destiny tossed his head back and forth, as if to ask a question and Joey answered.

"You're wanting to know how I knew? Tommy's placard had a huge D painted on it! During the pre-race, Tommy told me the "D" meant only one thing ...DUCK—and that's what you felt me do! Listen up, TD—Secretariat may not be your great-great-grandfather on paper, but somewhere along the trail – you ended up with his perfect genetic sequence! You're every bit the stallion that he was – and more! I don't know how long your Derby and Preakness record times will stand up – but until Secretariat's Belmont time is bested, racing fans will always question and speculate! They'll say, 'What if Towers Destiny hadn't...

"There's no doubt in my mind about that! I love you, Towers Destiny ... to the moon and back!"

The End

Acknowledgments

I wish to again acknowledge Kathy L. Woodward, my editor for all three novels of the TOWERS trilogy. She has an uncanny ability to edit my writing when necessary. Both of us have matured as I transitioned from TOWERS ABOVE to TOWERS' PROGENY and now TOWERS DESTINY.

I also would like to thank Dr. James Crager for his medical insight in this book.

My 'beta testers' once again for TOWERS DESTINY were Donna Long and Barbara Taylor. Also, Jim O'Brien (#80) graciously joined both ladies in the proofreading of this trilogy finale. All three were indispensable in the production of this novel.

Finally, my wife Nancy was instrumental in tying everything together. She and Outskirts Press have again produced a phenomenal thriller.